Carola Dunn is the author of several mysteries featuring Daisy Dalrymple, as well as numerous historical novels. Born and raised in England, she lives in Eugene, Oregon.

The Daisy Dalrymple Series

Death at Wentwater Court
The Winter Garden Mystery
Requiem for a Mezzo
Murder on the Flying Scotsman
Damsel in Distress
Dead in the Water
Styx and Stones
Rattle His Bones
To Davy Jones Below
The Case of the Murdered Muckraker
Mistletoe and Murder
Die Laughing
A Mourning Wedding
Fall of a Philanderer
Gunpowder Plot
The Bloody Tower
The Black Ship
Sheer Folly
Anthem for Doomed Youth
Gone West

GONE WEST

A Daisy Dalrymple Mystery

CAROLA DUNN

Constable & Robinson Ltd
55–56 Russell Square
London WC1B 4HP
www.constablerobinson.com

First published in the US by Minatour Books,
an imprint of St Martin's Press, 2012

First published in the UK by Robinson,
an imprint of Constable & Robinson Ltd, 2012

This is a work of fiction. Names, characters, places and incidents are either the product of the author's imagination or are used fictitiously, and any resemblance to actual persons, living or dead, or to actual events or locales is entirely coincidental.

A copy of the British Library Cataloguing in Publication data is available from the British Library

ISBN: 978-1-78033-139-3 (paperback)
ISBN: 978-1-78033-140-9 (ebook)

Printed and bound in the UK

1 3 5 7 9 10 8 6 4 2

To all my fellow authors, and to the readers whose appreciation keeps us going.

ACKNOWLEDGEMENTS

The following people have kindly helped me in the creation of this book: Robert Bruce Thompson – science; John Barach – old cars; Stella Rondo – PhraseFinder.co.uk; Angela Carey – Irish speech; Peter Homan – dispensing chemists; Doug Lyle MD, Larry Karp MD – medical; Sue Williams, *Derby Telegraph* – local info; Nathan Williams, Reading University – tractors; Rachel Harris, FIDM – fashion; Anne Birds – Matlock Markets Administration; Neil Barratt – Matlock; Ian Walker – Daisy's car; Steve Kaye – Western fiction; Phil, CarAndClassic.co.uk – Daisy's car; Luci Hansson, aka The Poison Lady; Jon North – Matlock; Judith Harrison, British Library – Western fiction.

My sincere thanks to all of you, and my apologies if I have misunderstood, misapplied, or altered for artistic purposes anything you told me. This is, after all, a work of fiction.

CHAPTER 1

The approach was not inviting. In spite of her spiffy new – well, not a 1926 model, but *almost* new – motor car, Daisy felt discouraged.

First she had to navigate the grim, smoke-belching Potteries towns, one of those lists of names beloved of geography teachers: Stoke, Hanley, Burslem, Longton, Tunstall, Fenton. Amalgamating them into the city of Stoke-on-Trent hadn't made them any prettier.

Beyond Derby came an endless series of equally grim, grimy mining villages; rows of tiny, grey cottages lining the steep-cobbled streets. Small shops, pubs and chapels merged into the general dinginess. Here and there she saw the surface excrescences of mines – large, squat buildings of blackened brick, loomed over by tall chimneys and mysterious iron wheels.

In between, glimpses of green, precipitous slopes would have offered moments of relief had they not been wreathed in veils of autumnal mist. Daisy clenched the steering wheel with fingers crossed, praying she'd reach her goal before the mists turned to fog.

'I must have been mad to come,' she muttered to herself.

It had all started with a perfectly innocent letter.

Sybil Sutherby, *née* Richland, had been at school with Daisy. They hadn't met for many years – in fact, not since Sybil left school in 1915, a year ahead of Daisy. An occasional Christmas card in the early years had reported her marriage followed by the birth of a daughter.

Daisy hadn't been invited to either wedding or christening, but there was nothing to cavil at in that. Not only was Sybil a year older and little more than an acquaintance, the War had put paid to lavish celebrations of such events. As far as Daisy could recall, she hadn't heard so much as a whisper from or about Sybil in ten years.

Nor had she wondered what had become of her schoolfellow. They had never been close enough for that.

So she was surprised when the letter arrived. It was just a note, really. Sybil, living in the country, was coming up to London for a couple of days. She would love to see Daisy. Could they meet for coffee, perhaps, or lunch or afternoon tea?

On the day specified, Daisy had arranged to meet her best friend, Lucy, alias Lady Gerald Bincombe, for lunch at Maxim's, in Wardour Street. Though Lucy would have preferred Monico's or the Café Royal, Maxim's was conveniently near the publisher of their book on the Follies of England. In ecstasies over the success of that venture, he was eager to discuss with them another book of photographs by Lucy with commentary by Daisy.

Succumbing to her besetting sin, curiosity, Daisy had written to Sybil asking her to join them – and posted the letter before mentioning it to Lucy.

'Sybil Richland?' Lucy's outrage came clearly along the telephone wires. 'Sybil the Swot?'

'Come on, darling, she wasn't that bad. Some of the girls thought I was a swot.'

'You did have your nose in a book a lot of—'

'Lucy! You were no keener on games than I was, as I recall, though you never opened a book until forced to. In fact, I can't imagine what you did with your time at school.'

After a moment for reflection, Lucy said candidly, 'Neither can I, I'm thankful to say. I wonder what Sybil wants.'

'Why should she want anything, other than to look up old acquaintances?'

'If you'd thought that, you could have pretended to be out of town. I'm sure you, too, suspect an ulterior motive.'

'Not exactly, but I do think it's a bit odd. Surely she must have plenty of closer friends in London.'

Lucy laughed. 'Very fishy!'

'Besides, we haven't been in touch for years. Even if she happened to notice in a newspaper when I was married, how did she know where to address a letter?'

'Daisy, you're famous. She probably reads your magazine articles avidly and says to herself, "To think I was at school with her!" She wants to be seen with a celebrity.'

'What rot!'

'Your editor at *Town and Country* might have given her your Hampstead address, or your cousin, if she wrote first to Fairacres.'

'Geraldine *would* do that, without asking me first.' Daisy's second cousin, Edgar, had become Viscount Dalrymple on the death of her father and brother. His wife, Geraldine, liked to have a finger in every pie. 'Bother, do you really think that's it?'

'Who knows? Never mind, it's only lunch,' said Lucy, 'and we have an appointment directly afterwards.'

Daisy didn't like driving in central London, so she took

the tube from Hampstead and walked from Tottenham Court Road station to Maxim's. The uniformed commissionaire ushered her in with as much deference as if a taxi had dropped her off outside the dazzlingly white façade with its gilded wreaths, silvered turret and mauresque windows.

The maître d'hôtel greeted her inside.

'I'm meeting Lady Gerald Bincombe,' Daisy told him.

'*Mais oui, madame*, Lady Gerald arrived but a moment since. She requested a table on the balcony.' He crooked a finger at an underling, who relieved Daisy of her coat and escorted her upstairs.

Lucy had chosen a table next to the ornamental brass rail, banked with flowers, that separated the green-and-gold balcony from the oval opening to the main dining room below. Though a professional photographer, Lucy was also a member of fashionable society, from sleek, dark Eton crop to scarlet-painted fingertips to barely knee-length hemline. It was typical of her to want a good view of the other patrons of the establishment.

That was not the reason she gave for her choice. 'Darling, I thought we'd better hide up here. I have a frightful feeling that Sybil has probably turned into the sort of dowd one doesn't care to be seen with.'

'How unkind! Why?'

'You said she wrote from a farm, in Derbyshire of all places.'

'What's wrong with Derbyshire? Ever heard of Chatsworth?'

'Of course, but the country seat of the Duke of Devonshire can hardly be compared to a farmhouse!'

'Hush, I think this must be Sybil coming up the stairs now. She looks vaguely familiar. And quite smart enough to associate with me, if not at your exalted level. You're always telling me I have no notion of fashion.'

The young woman ascending the staircase wore a heather-mixture tweed costume. Daisy was no expert, but the skirt and jacket looked to her to be quite nicely cut, though well-worn, making the best of a figure somewhat on the sturdy side. The lavender cloche hat, adorned with a small spray of speckled feathers, matched the silk blouse. A string of pearls, silk stockings and good leather shoes – low-heeled – completed the picture of a well-to-do if not fashion-conscious country dweller visiting the capital.

Sybil Sutherby certainly didn't look like a typical farmer's wife. Though, like Daisy, her only make-up was a dab of powder on her nose and a touch of lipstick, her face was not noticeably weathered. In fact, she was rather pale, accentuating a dismayed expression that Daisy put down to Lucy's unexpected presence.

'Hello, Sybil. How nice to see you after all these years,' said Daisy, stretching the truth somewhat.

'Daisy, you haven't changed a bit.' They shook hands.

The waiter seated Sybil, handed menus all round, and departed.

'You remember Lucy? Fotheringay as was.'

'Lucy. Of course.' She hesitated. 'It's Lady Gerald, isn't it?'

'So you keep up with the news, Mrs Sutherby,' Lucy drawled. 'How do you do?'

'For pity's sake,' Daisy said, annoyed, 'we were all spotty schoolgirls together. Let's not stand on our dignities. I'm going to decide what I want for lunch, and then I'd like to hear what you're up to these days, Sybil.'

Discussing the choices on the à la carte menu thawed the ice between Lucy and Sybil a bit, to Daisy's relief. Lucy, as usual, chose a salad for the sake of her figure. Daisy, who cared less for her figure and ate in superior restaurants far less frequently, picked the *poulet rôti au citron et aux courgettes*. She'd make up for it by having the clear consommé first. Sybil opted to follow suit. Daisy had the impression that she was preoccupied, her thoughts far from the delectable selection offered.

The waiter returned and took their order.

After a moment of slightly uncomfortable silence, Sybil said abruptly, 'I've read some of your articles, Daisy. You write very well.'

Lucy gave Daisy a knowing look. 'What about you, Sybil?' she asked with a hint of a sarcastic inflection. 'Have you settled into a life of cosy domesticity?'

Sybil flushed. 'Far from it. My husband was killed in the War. I was lucky enough to find a job quite quickly, as . . . as secretary to an author. A live-in job, where I can have my little girl with me.' Her hand went to her necklace. 'I didn't even have to sell Mother's pearls. And I've been there ever since.'

Daisy decided it was a bit late to start expressing condolences, which would inevitably lead to further, endless condolences. Everyone had lost someone in the War – Daisy herself had lost her own brother and her fiancé – or in the influenza pandemic, which had killed her father, the late Viscount Dalrymple. She seized on a less emotionally fraught topic. 'Is your author someone I might have read?'

'I doubt it. A rather . . . specialised field. But I did hope to have a word with you, Daisy . . .' She glanced sideways at Lucy.

'About your work? Go ahead. Lucy won't mind. Underneath the frivolous exterior, she's a working woman, too.'

'I don't think . . .'

'You haven't got yourself involved in the production of

"blue" books, have you?' Lucy's question was blunt, but for once her tone was discreetly lowered.

'Certainly not!'

'Sorry. It's just that the way you said "a rather specialised field" tends to leave one to jump to conclusions.'

Daisy laughed. 'I'm prepared to swear that's not the conclusion I jumped to. What's the matter, Sybil?'

'I'd prefer to talk to you later.'

'No can do. Lucy and I have an appointment with our joint editor immediately after lunch. But Lucy knows all my secrets – well, almost all. She's not going to blurt out your troubles to all and sundry.'

'Silent as the grave,' said Lucy. 'Cross my heart and hope to die. My lips are sealed.'

'Be serious,' Daisy admonished her severely, 'or why should Sybil trust you?'

'It's not so much—' Sybil began, but the waiter interrupted by arriving with their soup.

By the time he went away again, she had made up her mind.

'All right, if you say so, Daisy. I wasn't sure whether . . . I know you married a detective, and I heard that you've helped him to investigate several crimes.'

'Lucy, have you been telling tales, after I've been crying up your discretion?'

'Darling, I'm not the only one aware of your criminous activities. What about your Indian friend?'

'I hardly think Sakari would have any opportunity to spill the beans to Sybil!'

'But there have been at least a couple of other old school pals you've saved from the hangman. Word gets around.'

'It's nothing like that!' Sybil exclaimed. 'Not murder, I mean. Just a mystery of sorts. There's probably nothing in it.'

'In what?' Daisy asked.

'It's an uncomfortable, troubled atmosphere, really. I feel as if something's going on, but I can't pin it down. That's why I want your help.'

'If you can't be precise,' said Lucy impatiently, 'how do you expect her to advise you?'

'I was hoping you'd come and stay for a few days, Daisy. I'm hoping you'll tell me it's all in my imagination.'

Lucy looked at her as if she was mad. Daisy was intrigued. She had indeed been caught up in the investigation of a number of unpleasant occurrences, but they had all been concrete acts of a violent nature. A mysterious atmosphere would make a change and might prove interesting. What was more, with no crime in the offing, Alec could hardly object to her going to stay with an old friend.

In someone else's house, she remembered. 'Won't your employer mind your inviting a guest?'

'Oh, no. I'm not just a stenotypist, you know, I'm Mr Birtwhistle's confidential secretary and . . . and editorial assistant.'

'Birtwhistle? I've never heard of an author by such a note-worthy name. Does he use a pen name?'

'Yes,' said Sybil, but did not elaborate, as the waiter returned to remove the soup dishes and present the entrées.

Lucy, all too obviously disapproving, turned the conversation to her and Daisy's publisher and what he might expect in the way of another photo book. Not until they parted on the pavement outside Maxim's did Daisy have a chance to tell Sybil she was game and would write as soon as she knew when she could get away for a few days.

As a result, one dreary Monday in late September Daisy found herself driving nervously up a narrow, winding lane – two stony ruts with grass growing up the middle, between dry-stone walls. Apart from the rumble of the motor of her sky-blue Gwynne Eight, the only sound was an occasional bleat from the black-faced sheep on the misty hillsides beyond the walls. Outcrops of limestone were more common than trees, and in these bleak uplands the few ashes she passed were already turning yellow.

A fingerpost on her right directed her up a still steeper, narrower, twistier lane, not much more than a cart-track. One side was open to a grassy slope, blue with harebells, with a stream at the bottom and a rising hillside beyond. On the other side, a high bank cut off the view. Overgrown with nettles and thistles, it had an abandoned air.

Eyrie Farm – the name hadn't struck her before, but now she kept thinking of it as 'Eerie Farm'. She was glad to see the line of telephone poles following the track, a reassuring connection to the world. Every fifth pole or so provided a perch to a hawk or falcon, so perhaps the name Eyrie was appropriate. What had birds used for perches before telephone poles and wires?

More pertinent questions clamoured in Daisy's mind. Sybil's reply to her letter had not informed her of Birtwhistle's pen name. Perhaps he wrote ghost stories, or wrote about and even dabbled in the occult. What had her insatiable curiosity landed her in this time?

Lucy was right: she must be crazy to have accepted Sybil's invitation.

CHAPTER 2

Daisy drove round a sharp bend and with startling suddenness found herself enveloped in fog. A bank was hazily visible on her left only because the lane was so narrow. The other side dropped into nothingness, with only an occasional boulder to mark the edge – of a precipice? Heart in mouth, she nudged upwards, tensely alert to catch the sound of an approaching engine before she met it nose to nose.

The blue Gwynne – gleaming when she left Hampstead, dust-coated now – did not like grinding uphill at two miles per hour. It stalled. A muffled *baa*-ing and the burble of running water reached Daisy's ears as she hastily set the hand brake, double declutched, and changed into neutral.

She pulled out the choke just a little, as the engine was warm – in fact, considering the hill, she was lucky the radiator wasn't boiling over. Thankful that she had insisted on buying a car with a selfstarter, she pressed it. An ineffectual whir caused a momentary alarm, then the motor coughed and started. In first gear, she inched upwards again.

Seconds later, she emerged into bright sunshine. The incline lessened. The way ran straight for a quarter mile or so. The tumbling brook was right alongside the track now, four or five feet below.

What had looked like the crest of the slope turned out to

be a minor ridge. The stream cut through it, under a stone bridge even narrower than the lane. On the bridge, Daisy stopped and gazed backwards.

Below her was a blank whiteness, as if the world had ceased to exist but for the smooth humped islands of the highest hills.

Turning to look ahead, she saw a shallow green valley opening out, protected on three sides by higher ridges. The stream tumbled down the far slope then meandered towards her. A copse stood out brilliant yellow in the late afternoon sun. A square house of grey granite, its stone roof lichened and multi-chimneyed, showed its age by its small, mullioned casement windows. Two more modern wings with larger sash windows, early Victorian perhaps, reached forwards to shelter a circular patch of colour that must be a flower garden.

Smoke trickled from the chimneys, promising warmth within. Though isolated, not *eerie* after all, Daisy was happy to note. Not really *eyrie*, either, since for that name the farm house ought to be perched on a crag, but she wasn't about to quibble.

Feeling happier about her odd errand, she drove on and parked the Gwynne on the gravel sweep, between the flower-beds and the front door. She sat for a moment in the car, tired – relieved to have arrived safely, enjoying the display of roses, chrysanthemums, asters and Michaelmas daisies in the beds and the fading hydrangeas along the south-facing wall on either side of the door. From the nearby copse of sycamores came the cawing of rooks.

Daisy shivered. The air was growing decidedly chilly.

The door had a large brass knocker in the shape of a bird of prey, appropriate, she supposed, to the eyrie. She rapped loudly.

Abruptly, before she could lower her hand, the door swung open. The woman who stood there was certainly not a maid. Short and plumpish, she wore a crimson wool frock, the hem a few inches below her knees as befitted her apparent age of somewhere just on the right side of fifty. Over it was a warm, cable-knit cardigan.

She smiled. 'Oh, hello, you must be Mrs Fletcher. I'm Ruby Birtwhistle. I was just going out to cut some asters for the dining room table.' She had a slight accent, mostly Northern English with an odd touch of American, to Daisy's surprise. She waved a hand in a stained glove, wielding a pair of secateurs. 'Excuse me, won't you? Do go on in. Lorna will have heard the knocker and be on her way.'

With that, she slipped past Daisy and headed with a brisk step for the flower-garden, followed at a more dignified pace by a stiff, elderly black-and-white sheepdog. Daisy saw her stoop to pull a weed or two.

Amused at the odd welcome, Daisy stepped into a wide, low-beamed hall. She guessed it to have been the main room of the old farm house. The beams still had iron hooks where sides of ham and strings of onions must once have hung. The floor was stone, with large, faded rugs here and there. The ambience was a trifle gloomy in spite of walls and ceilings painted white, except for the beams. Well-stuffed Victorian sofas and chairs, reupholstered in the lilac and primrose floral patterns beloved of the Edwardians, clustered about the hearth. A small coal fire in a wide iron grate in a large fireplace left the large room almost as chilly as outdoors.

Lorna – whoever she might be – did not immediately appear. Nor did anyone else, so Daisy looked about her. On either side, a staircase rose from the front to the rear of the hall. Beneath the stairs, doors to left and right must surely lead to the wings. There were two more doors in the back wall, one on each side of the fireplace, perhaps to the kitchen and what the Victorians called 'domestic offices'.

It was very quiet, could almost have been deserted, but the solid stone walls of the old building were probably responsible. Even the raucous crowing of the rooks outside was cut off by the small windows. The eerie feeling returned.

Had Sybil simply succumbed to the atmosphere of dread in the isolated house? She had apparently been quite contented to live here for seven or eight years, so it hardly seemed likely.

And dread was far too melodramatic a word for the depressing effect.

One of the back doors opened and through it came a pale, gaunt woman with grey hair scraped back from her face into a bun. She was clad in a dark-grey dress with a drooping hem, a ratty mustard-coloured cardigan and plaid carpet slippers.

At the same time, a girl appeared through the left-hand door, from the west wing. She was an elegant figure in a low-cut pink-and-black silk frock that ended quite two inches higher than Lucy would have worn in town, let alone in the country. Long, silk-clad legs ended in very high-heeled shoes that made them seem even longer.

Her head was turned to speak to someone following her, presenting to Daisy's view a long bob of chestnut hair. Daisy wondered if the colour was natural. She couldn't be sure in the dim light. It made a striking combination with the pink dress and a long string of pink glass beads. Together with the extra-short skirt, the effect could be seen as a symbol of independence – or defiance. Defiance of whom? What was her position in the household? Did she have anything to do with Sybil's mystery?

The girl turned. She looked to be eighteen or nineteen, ten years or so older than Sybil's daughter could possibly be.

Seeing the droopy woman, she said, 'Aunt Lorna, isn't it about time to light the lamps? It's like a dungeon in here.'

'I can't do everything at once, Myra.' Her Northern accent was considerably stronger than Mrs Birtwhistle's. She gestured sullenly at Daisy, who had taken her for a maid, a function she appeared to fill. 'Just coming to answer the door, I was.'

'Oh, how did you get in?' Myra asked Daisy, the words less than polite but the tone merely interested. 'You must be Sybil's friend. You've no idea what a relief it is to see a new face in this mouldy mausoleum.'

'Your . . . Mrs Birtwhistle was just going out as I arrived. She invited me to step in.'

'Aunt Ruby's always busy! This is my other aunt, Miss Birtwhistle. She's always busy, too. Do come and sit by the fire and get warm while I give her a hand with the lamps.'

'I can manage them, thank you very much! Not a thing would get done in this household if we all had to wait on your help.'

Myra ignored the censorious part of this, but blithely accepted the first part as a rejection of her offer of assistance. 'Not that it's much of a fire, I'm afraid,' she went on. 'Would you rather go to your room first? Oh, this is Walter, by the way.' She indicated with a casual wave the man who had followed her in. 'Walter Ilkton, I should say. Walter, this is Mrs Fletcher. At least, I suppose that's who you are?'

'Right, first try. How do you do, Mr Ilkton?'

Ilkton was considerably older than Myra, in his mid-thirties at a guess. Tall and fair, he, too, was dressed rather more smartly than was appropriate for a farm house in the depths of Derbyshire. He wore dark-grey 'Oxford bags' and a black blazer with an Old Harrovian tie, black with double white stripes, transfixed with a large pink pearl tie-pin.

Apart from the pearl, he would have fitted nicely into a house party at one of the more formal country houses.

The vulgarly obtrusive pearl made Daisy doubt that he was justified in sporting the tie, but when he returned her greeting, his voice confirmed his schooling. Though he spared her a glance as he spoke, his devoted – almost worshipful – attention was only momentarily diverted from Myra's manifest charms.

These were revealed more clearly as Miss Birtwhistle shuffled round lighting oil lamps. Neither gas nor electricity had yet made its way to the isolated farm. In Daisy's view, this was sufficient to account for Sybil's sense of impending doom. She could only hope modern plumbing was not likewise lacking but up here in the hills it seemed only too likely.

Be that as it might, Myra was an exceptionally pretty girl. 'Mrs Birtwhistle is your aunt?'

'By marriage. Sort of. My mother was Uncle Humphrey's favourite cousin. Aunt Lorna is his sister, so she's really more of an aunt than Aunt Ruby is. My name is Olney, though. I'm sure you'd like tea, wouldn't you? Aunt Lorna, how about a spot of tea?'

'And who's to bring in Mrs Fletcher's bags, I'd like to know? The girls have gone home already.'

Daisy was about to announce that she was quite capable of bringing in her own bags, but Myra said carelessly, 'Oh, Walter's man can fetch them, can't he, darling? Be an angel and find him. And he may as well take her car round to the stable yard, Walter, while he's about it.'

Wondering whether the 'darling' was a casual modernism or a sign of a close relationship, Daisy let herself be bustled up to her room to powder her nose while Walter Ilkton departed through one of the doors at the rear, a trifle sulkily.

'Is Mr Ilkton another relative?' Daisy asked.

'Heavens no! I made his acquaintance at a house-party last year. He's utterly dotty about me, you know. He actually wears that frightful tie-pin I gave him. I bought it in Woolworths for a shilling, as a lark. I can't decide whether it's a scream or simply too divine of him.'

'I wonder if he'd go so far as to wear it in London if you met him there.'

'Oh, I do see him in town, quite a bit.' She giggled. 'And no, he doesn't wear it there.'

'Is he staying for long?'

'As long as he's allowed, I expect. He wrote to say he was going to visit an elderly relative at Smedley's Hydro in Matlock – he has Expectations; not that he needs them, he's rich as Midas, which is why the pearl is so funny – and as he'd be nearby, he said, he'd like to pop in to say hello. Of course, Aunt Ruby invited him to stay the night. That was three days ago and he's showing no signs of leaving. Last time he visited his elderly relative, he stayed for a week.'

'Doesn't your uncle mind?'

'He's having one of his bad spells, poor dear. Aunt Ruby may have told him Walter's here, but their paths haven't crossed.'

'I'm sorry he's unwell. It's not a very good time for me to visit.'

'It's nothing serious. He gets sort of depressed and lethargic and dopy, and all he wants to do is sleep all day.'

'Rotten for him,' Daisy commiserated.

'It would cast a bit of a blight over all of us if I let it. I come down from town now and then to cheer them all up.' Myra opened a door. 'Here you are. You should have everything you need. I did your room myself. Well, with Betty. She's one of the farm girls who comes in. The other one's Etta.

Very confusing, like a tongue-twister – I get mixed up and call them Betta and Ettie. But I do help when I'm at home, whatever Aunt Lorna says! She likes to play the martyr.'

'That was my impression.'

'How right you were! Bathroom and lav opposite. Running water laid on, piped down from the spring where the stream rises. But if you'd like a bath, please mention it to an aunt in advance because the boiler takes simply ages to heat up again afterwards. Speaking of heat, I'm frozen.' She hugged herself, shivering. 'I think I'll go and put on a cardigan, however much it disappoints Walter. Perhaps even woollen stockings, if I can find any, and sensible shoes.'

'Sounds like an excellent idea,' Daisy agreed, boggling at the vision of that frock topping woollen stockings and sensible shoes. 'When you've done that, would you mind letting Sybil know I've arrived?'

Myra looked doubtful. 'Is it five o'clock? We're absolutely not allowed to disturb her before five.'

Daisy checked her wristwatch. 'By the time you've put on your woollies, it will be.'

'So that's why it's so beastly dark in the old house! The windows are bigger in the wings, so it's lighter here, but would you like a couple of candles? Unless you'd rather have a lamp? We don't usually bother with them upstairs until it's time to change for dinner . . .'

'No, no, thanks, it's quite light enough.'

'Right-oh. I'm glad you've come, after all. You're not a bit like I expected an old school friend of Sybil's to be.'

'Quite human, in fact.'

'What? Oh, I suppose I shouldn't have said that! Sorry! Come down as soon as you're ready. I happen to know Aunt Ruby's made a sponge cake for tea.'

Divesting herself of hat, gloves and coat, Daisy wondered

what on earth she had let herself in for. She hadn't expected the acme of comfort in a farm house, however well adapted for an author who could afford a secretary-cum-personal assistant. However, Sybil might at least have warned her that half a dozen people would apparently be sharing an unreliable hot-water supply and a minimal, part-time staff.

Did Mrs Birtwhistle reign in the kitchen, or merely make an occasional cake for visitors? Did she do all the gardening, too, or just pull weeds she happened to notice when cutting flowers? Was the drooping Lorna really as put-upon as she made out? Were the farm girls who came in by the day the only servants when Walter Ilkton, with his man in tow, wasn't wearing out his welcome?

Still, the bedroom looked comfortable enough.

A knock on the door presaged the arrival of Ilkton's manservant with Daisy's suitcases. A small, neat, sandy man, very correctly clad in black, he didn't look at all as if he'd be willing to lend a hand with such tasks as stoking the boiler and scrubbing the kitchen floor.

Though she was dying for a cup of tea, Daisy dawdled over making herself presentable to go down. She hoped Sybil would come and explain the situation more frankly than she had felt able to in the presence of Lucy or by letter. At least she could give Daisy more information about the inhabitants of the house.

But Sybil didn't come. Daisy was tired and thirsty. She was probably keeping the others from their tea. Besides, it might be more useful to meet them without preconceptions, without being influenced by Sybil's view of them.

Among other things she didn't know, she realised, was what sort of books the 'dopy' Mr Birtwhistle wrote, and under what name.

CHAPTER 3

With all its lamps lighted, a heavy curtain drawn across the front door to keep out draughts, and the fire built up, the hall was more cheerful and a few degrees warmer than on Daisy's arrival. Coming down the stairs, she was surprised to see, hanging over the mantelpiece, what appeared to be the skull of a Highland bull. Or did the cows also have those huge, wide-spread horns? In any case, it was an odd sight where a heavily antlered red deer buck would be unremarkable – stuffed, not skeletal.

Perhaps Mr Birtwhistle had gone shooting in the Highlands and bagged a cow by mistake. In that case, the trophy showed an ability to laugh at himself. Did he write humorous novels, ironic, droll, witty, or facetious?

Somehow funny fiction didn't chime in with Sybil's sense of foreboding. Daisy could imagine, though, how working constantly with someone else's sense of humour might destroy one's own.

Sybil came to meet her at the foot of the stairs. Behind her, three men stood up: Ilkton, impeccable but for the Woolworths pearl; a younger man, equally tall, lean, with wavy, very dark hair; and a slender youth whose crimson velvet smoking jacket, silk cravat in a red-and-blue paisley pattern, wispy moustache and rather long hair, fair and untidy, suggested artistic leanings. Water-colours or poetry, Daisy surmised. Mrs Birtwhistle and Myra were seated by the fireplace.

'Daisy,' said Sybil, 'I'm so sorry I wasn't available when you got here. When I'm in the throes of . . . typing, I get muddled if I'm interrupted, so there's a rule that no one is to disturb me. I forgot to tell people that it didn't apply when you arrived.'

'Do you have trouble reading your own shorthand, if you don't transcribe it at once? I do. But no, you couldn't keep a job like yours if you were as hopeless as I am.'

'No, it's not that. Have you met everyone?'

It struck Daisy that she was still being evasive about her employer's literary endeavours. Was it possible Lucy had been right? If Mr Birtwhistle was indeed writing obscene stories, or ribald, combining raciness with humour, Sybil might have just found out that she could be prosecuted for merely typing them.

Surely, though, she wouldn't have stayed for years in such a job, however badly she needed to earn her own living.

As these thoughts crossed Daisy's mind, she said, 'I met Mrs Birtwhistle, in passing. And Miss Olney and Mr Ilkton. Miss Birtwhistle, too, but she's not here.' Unless she was lurking in some dim recess. 'And an aged sheepdog, though we weren't introduced.'

'Scurry. Not very appropriate now he's growing old. Retired from the farm, of course.'

'He's bagged the hearth rug, I see.' The dog had raised his head and looked round at the sound of his name. Realising he wasn't being summoned, he sank back into paw-twitching dreams of rabbits, or of sheep.

Sybil smiled. 'His favourite spot at this time of year.'

They crossed the room to the group by the fireplace.

Sybil introduced the black-haired, slightly shabby Neil Carey, who turned out to have sparkling-blue Irish eyes. The artistic young man turned out to be the son of the house, Simon Birtwhistle.

'For God's sake, call me Simon,' he said. His voice had nothing of his mother's or his aunt's accents. 'I can't abide that horrible mouthful.'

'Don't blaspheme,' said his mother in fond reproach. 'Simon is writing a literary novel, Mrs Fletcher. The younger generation seems to find it necessary to use bad language, I can't think why. I'm not referring to your work, of course. I read your articles with a great deal of pleasure.'

'Thank you,' said Daisy. Bang went that theory. Surely Mrs Birtwhistle couldn't remain in ignorance of the content of her husband's books, and he could hardly produce salacious stuff without using 'bad' – if not blasphemous – language.

'So you also write, Mrs Fletcher?' asked Carey.

'Yes, mostly magazine articles about places and family history, that sort of thing. Someday I'd like to try my hand at a novel, but I never seem to find the time to settle down to it. I have toddler twins, you see, as well as an older daughter. There are too many interruptions. Do you find that a problem, Simon?'

'Certainly. One needs sustained periods of quiet thought to produce anything of literary value.'

Daisy laughed. 'I don't expect to produce anything of literary value. Something more on the lines of detective fiction.'

'Oh, that rub—' Simon caught his mother's admonishing eye and coughed. 'That kind of stuff. Carey has written a brilliant play, that was put on in Dublin.'

'For the one night, before the censor was after closing it down,' the Irishman drawled, grinning. 'Sure our government have set up what they call the Committee on Evil Literature.'

'You're all too clever for me,' said Ilkton. 'I don't pretend to be able to put together more than a bread-and-butter letter.'

'But you dance divinely, darling,' Myra assured him. 'Simon has two left feet, when he can be persuaded to take to the floor. He can't hit a ball, either, unlike Walter.'

'You play cricket, Mr Ilkton?' Daisy asked, more than willing to abandon the subject of writing, which seemed to be making Sybil uncomfortable.

'I got my Blue,' he said modestly. If he really could barely string two words together, it said a good deal about the admission standards at Oxford and Cambridge colleges, which were ruled as much by family connections as by academic brilliance. 'And I played a couple of years for Warwickshire after the War. Not professionally, of course. It's just the occasional village green match for me nowadays, though. Tennis is more my game these days.'

'Walter and I were partnered at tennis. That's how we met.'

Daisy could picture him being athletic on the cricket pitch or tennis court; impossible, though, to imagine him getting filthy and bruised playing rugby, like Lucy's husband, Lord Gerald Bincombe, let alone galloping across muddy fields after a fox, or tramping the moors with a gun on his shoulder. He was the man-about-town type, who expected urban amenities on his forays into the country. He probably had an elder brother who had inherited or would inherit the hunting and shooting. Ilkton? No, she didn't know any Ilktons.

'We can't all be intellectuals,' Simon pronounced indulgently. 'Carey has already nearly finished another play. It's historical and sure to be banned by the Lord Chamberlain.' He spoke with as much pride as if this was admirable and he'd written it himself.

'And by the Committee on Evil Literature? Dare I ask what it's about, Mr Carey?'

'Queen Anne and the Duchess of Marlborough.' His blue eyes glinted.

Daisy couldn't remember anything about Queen Anne except that she was dead, which seemed too obvious to be notable. Queen Anne's lace, she thought, but that was a type of cow parsley and hardly relevant. And there was a favourite mnemonic of her history teacher: Britain Relied On Marlborough, the initials of which were the initials of battles won by the Duke of Marlborough, but the names of the battles, what the war was about, and whom Britain was fighting escaped her. Probably the French; it usually was. Or the Irish?

'Something to do with Ireland? Oh, William of Orange was her brother-in-law, wasn't he? Orangemen!'

'William of Orange put the Irish—' Ilkton stopped as Mrs Birtwhistle held up her hand.

'Not now, if you please. Irish politics has its place, no doubt, but this is not it. Milk and sugar, Mrs Fletcher?'

The dog, in response to something apparent only to him, plodded to the door to the west wing and stood there till Simon opened it for him. 'Uncle Norman must have come in,' he said with a laugh. 'Scurry always knows.'

Tea proceeded on its customary course. After an unsatisfactory lunch in a tea-shop somewhere south of Derby, Daisy was glad to see there was plenty to eat, from bread and butter and watercress sandwiches to Mrs Birtwhistle's sponge cake, which turned out to be excellent. If she was the sole mistress of the kitchen, there was no danger of starvation.

Of Sybil's 'troubled atmosphere' Daisy detected little, apart from occasional sniping between Simon, representing the intellectual party, and his cousin Myra, whose outlook on life was frivolous. These potshots were firmly repressed by Mrs Birtwhistle before they could escalate into a squabble. She was less successful in quashing Carey and Ilkton, but they were more successful at concealing animosity with banter – Ilkton urbane, Carey volubly Irish.

Carey was Ilkton's rival for Myra's favour, Daisy suspected. Myra flirted happily with both.

Miss Birtwhistle trudged into the hall at some point and accepted a cup of tea, though she ate nothing. Mr Birtwhistle in his sickbed was not mentioned, except for a brief reference to the doctor's expected visit later that evening. Sybil was taciturn. Daisy had every intention of cornering her after tea and finding out just what she had been so hot and bothered about.

Refusing a third cup of tea and a second slice of cake, Daisy gave Sybil a Look with a capital L.

Sybil got the message. 'If you'll excuse us, Ruby,' she said, 'I'll drag Daisy away for a chat. We'll go to my office, Daisy. I have a sitting room upstairs – Monica and I occupy the old nurseries, over this hall – but the office is more convenient, and warmer, because I've had a fire all day. One can't type with frozen fingers.'

Following her towards the right-hand passage, Daisy glanced back at the group by the fire. Mrs Birtwhistle was gazing after them with a decidedly anxious expression. Odd! Perhaps, after all, there was something in Sybil's forebodings.

CHAPTER 4

Sybil's office was very like Daisy's at home in Hampstead. A couple of easy chairs stood by the fireplace, but the room's main feature was naturally a desk with a typewriter and all the expected accoutrements. Three piles of neatly aligned papers must be the original manuscript, for the editor; the first carbon for the author's files; and the second, almost unreadable carbon for emergencies.

On each side of the window were bookshelves, one side holding reference books, many of which Daisy recognised from the spines: the *Pocket Oxford Dictionary, Roget's Thesaurus*, an encyclopaedia, and so on. The other was almost filled with piles of magazines, rows of cheap paper-bound books and a set of more substantial books in colourful dustcovers. Daisy went straight to the second bookcase and started reading titles.

'*The Stranger from Dead Man's Gulch, Six-Shooter for Hire, Queen of the Prairie* ... Westerns! All by Eli Hawke. Alias Humphrey Birtwhistle, I assume.'

'Yes, of course.' Sybil added coal to the fire, poked at it, and invited Daisy to come and sit down. 'He spent ten years in the Wild West as a young man,' she continued, 'so he really knows his stuff.'

'Has this anything to do with your problem? With the

troubled atmosphere you were talking about? I've crossed the Wild West by train and seen a couple of Western films, but I wouldn't claim it's a subject I'm familiar with.'

'It's all rather complicated . . .'

'He hasn't taken to wandering round the house wielding six-shooters and threatening to shoot "them thar dad-burned rustlers," or anything like that?'

'Heavens no!'

'Myra said he's ill. Depressed.'

'Sort of. Perhaps I'd better start at the beginning.'

'It's usually a help. You've been working for "Eli Hawke" for seven or eight years?'

'Yes, we've been here since late in 1919.'

'That's right, you brought your daughter with you. She must be . . . What, nine or so? She's at school, I take it.'

'Monica just started this month as a weekly boarder at the Lady Manners School in Bakewell. The Birtwhistles offered to pay the fees. They've been very kind.'

'Then— Sorry! I won't keep interrupting, promise. You came in 1919 . . .'

'I was hired as a stenographer, mostly just to type out what Mr Birtwhistle had written in longhand, occasionally to take dictation, mostly letters. He preferred to write down the stories himself. He says he thinks on paper, not aloud. You're a writer, I expect you understand?'

'I've never dictated, but I can imagine losing my place very easily if I didn't have my own words right in front of me.'

'That's what he said. His handwriting is pretty bad, so sometimes I'd be guessing at a word, and, though he went to a good school, his spelling is atrocious.'

'So you'd correct it.'

'I couldn't let it pass, could I? His publisher was very pleased with the first manuscript I turned in. They'd been having the books typed in London, and they always had a lot of errors to contend with, either because the typist didn't correct misspellings, or because she overcorrected, making the cowhands speak the King's English.'

Daisy laughed. 'I can imagine. You must have been a real godsend to both Mr Birtwhistle and his publisher.'

'So they told me. Very gratifying. The publisher paid Humphrey more, because they didn't have the expense of the typing, and he raised my salary.'

'I should hope so!'

'After a couple of books – he was putting out three a year, believe it or not – I really started to get the hang of things. Then I started to notice inconsistencies, just odd little things like someone having blue eyes in one place and steely grey in another. At first I used to draw them to Humphrey's attention. He didn't really care. He told me to put that sort of slip right without bothering him. I began to do more and more editing. It sort of crept up on me, until I was rearranging paragraphs to make them more effective or more logical.'

'Mr Birtwhistle didn't mind?'

'He didn't even notice. By the time the galleys came, he'd be halfway through the next book. He left checking them to me.'

'Then he found out how much rewriting you were doing,' Daisy guessed, 'and your troubles started.'

Sybil shook her head. 'If he ever noticed, he didn't say a word. Everything went on smoothly in the same track until, about three years ago, he came down with bronchitis that turned into a bad case of pneumonia. He was horribly ill and took a long time to recover. He had written about two thirds of *Double Cross at the Circle C*. The date the publisher expected it was creeping up on us. In the end, Humphrey told me how he wanted the story to continue and the final scene he'd planned, and asked me to do my best with it.'

'Good heavens! Weren't you scared out of your wits? Actually writing a book is a very different kettle of fish from editing someone else's work, even if you were already doing a fair bit of rewriting.'

'I was nervous, of course, but it wasn't as if I had a choice.'

'You had your living to earn.'

'And Monica's. And I owed Ruby and Humphrey a great deal. They pretty much depend on the income from the books to make life up here tolerable.'

'I assumed he must have family money.'

'He inherited this place. The Birtwhistles were just yeoman farmers, sheep farmers, until coal was found on their land, in the early 1800s. They sold that bit of land at a good price but spent most of the money on buying and adding the wings to this house. They wanted to be far away from the mine works. They bought a couple of small-holdings up here to rent out, tenant farms, as well.'

'Adding up to a small estate.'

'Yes, raising them towards, though never quite attaining, the status of gentry. Humphrey was the eldest son of the eldest son, in spite of which he was the one to go off adventuring in America. He did a bit of silver-mining while he was there and came back with money and a wife.'

'I thought Ruby sounded American!'

'He met her in the Wild West – she was a teacher in some practically invisible town – what we'd call a village. They put in the running water here when he brought her home, but his funds didn't stretch to gas or electricity.'

'I should think it would cost a fortune to bring either up here, so far from anywhere. A generator would be more practical.'

'I suppose so,' Sybil said vaguely. 'They did bring in the telephone, just a few years ago. Anyway, until Humphrey's books started to sell, they managed on what was left plus the rent from the farms, which is shared with Norman and Lorna. I believe Norman is paid a salary out of that, for managing the place.'

'And Myra Olney? How does she fit in?'

'Myra has an income of her own, enough for her school fees at first, and now for expensive frivolities. Enough to live on in reasonable comfort, really, but not in the style she'd prefer. It's in some sort of trust, so she can't get at the capital, fortunately.'

'I presume Simon isn't pulling his own weight yet, if he ever will. I wouldn't have thought the sort of stuff he writes sells well enough to live on the proceeds.'

'If he ever finished anything and sold it! You see the situation. That's why— Well, it could have been very awkward if they weren't such nice people.'

'You mean, your finishing the book for him?'

'That was only the beginning. When I read over the entire, completed manuscript, from start to finish, it seemed ... *unbalanced* is the best word I can find. I'd tried to write in Humphrey's style. I ought to have gone back and worked harder on the part I'd written, to bring it into line with his. Instead, I edited the rest to conform to mine. I didn't rewrite the whole thing, just made a few alterations and additions.'

'Not much more than you'd already been doing,' Daisy commented.

'Exactly!' Sybil said eagerly. 'I honestly didn't think I'd changed it noticeably. And as I said, Humphrey never looked at a book again once it was sent off.'

'Even when he had never seen the completed manuscript? He didn't want to read it over before you sent it?'

'He was still debilitated, not feeling at all well.'

'So someone at the publisher's noticed the difference.'

'The editor Humphrey's been working with for years. He wasn't happy about it. He said the books had been selling well to an audience who liked them the way they were, and he didn't see why Eli Hawke wanted to go mucking about with a popular formula.'

'Oh dear!'

'You can imagine how I felt. But it was too late to do anything about it. I'd turned in the book late, as it was, and they stick to a pretty strict schedule for that sort of thing. Apparently readers had come to expect a new one three times a year. In fact, when Humphrey started writing them, they were published as serials in magazines, so he had to turn in an episode a week. Or was it monthly? It was when they started to put them out as complete books – cheap, paperbound – that he needed a secretary.'

'Who reads them? Do you know? I mean, I know my articles are mostly read by middle-class women with time on their hands.'

'Lift-boys and hotel porters, I should think.' Sybil shrugged. 'Thrills, and a little romance thrown in for good measure. No one's claiming they're aimed at intellectuals. All the same, I don't see why they shouldn't be as good as one can make them, given the limits. At any rate, I couldn't show that letter to Humphrey, could I? Not just because it revealed that I'd been "mucking about" with his work, but because, essentially, it brutally described his work as formulaic.'

'No, not the sort of thing you want to show to an invalid. So, at this point, the publisher was expecting another book in four months' time? And Humphrey was still too ill to write?'

'He was weak and lethargic. It was a really nasty bout of pneumonia, and it left him unable to exert himself. He just doesn't have any energy.'

'How miserable!'

'It is. He used to go for long walks across the hills. The Dales are quite different from Western America, but the countryside inspired him. Nowadays he doesn't leave his room for days at a time, let alone striding up hill and down dale. Sitting down and writing for hours at a time is too much for him. But while I was finishing off *Double Cross*, he'd been thinking up a plot for the next book. It took his mind off his woes and—' A knock on the door interrupted her. 'Come in!'

The man who entered was big and fair. Fortyish, ruddy-faced and dressed in comfortably worn tweeds, he could have been a farmer. He brought with him a breath of crisp, fresh air.

'I hope I'm not intruding, Sybil. I just want a quick word with you before I see Birtwhistle.'

'Yes, of course. Daisy, Dr Knox. Roger, this is Mrs Fletcher. We were at school together.'

How do you do's were exchanged. Daisy tactfully offered to leave, though dying to stay. Not by a word, a gesture, or an intimate smile did these two betray themselves, but something undefinable in their demeanour, something beyond the use of given names, suggested that they were more than a little fond of one another.

'No, stay, Daisy. I don't suppose Roger intends to go into confidential details of Humphrey's health, and you already know the history of his illness.'

Dr Knox exploded. 'If he'd only take it easy when he's feeling better! Just let him have a spark of energy after breakfast and he's up and wandering round the gardens—'

'That's unfair. He takes it slowly and doesn't go outside unless the weather is good. Ruby's terrified that he might catch cold and develop pneumonia again.'

'As he well may.'

'Come off it, Roger, not just from going outdoors, well wrapped, on a fine day. Everyone stays away from him if they have the slightest sniffle.'

'I should hope so.'

'And you're always telling me I should get more fresh air and exercise.'

'You're young and healthy. He's sixty and in ill health, though I'll be bothered if I know what's wrong with him.'

'It's as if he's gone into a decline, like a Victorian young lady when her hopes were disappointed.'

'Nonsense. He doesn't appear to be getting worse, except insofar as inactivity is taking its toll.'

'There you are then,' said Sybil. 'What he needs is more activity, not less.'

'I'd agree, if it weren't that his little outings invariably bring on a relapse. If he'd just be patient for a few days, build up his strength gradually, instead of rushing into things! He has no sense of his own limitations, that's what it amounts to, even though he knows perfectly well what the consequence will be. How can I be expected to treat him when he refuses to follow directions?'

'How many of your patients do, Dr Knox?' Daisy asked, partly with interest, partly hoping to end the diatribe.

'All too few. Sorry, Mrs Fletcher, you don't want to hear about Birtwhistle's intransigence.'

'Insofar as it affects Sybil, I'm interested. Just so long as you don't start using incomprehensible medical Latin!'

'Certainly not.' He glanced at his watch. 'I must go and check up on the old boy. How does he seem, Sybil?'

'Wishy-washy, but not as sleepy as usual. The new tonic you've started trying on him may actually be helping.'

'I hate to use nux vomica. It's really a last-resort stimulant. It's dangerous stuff, and not to be used on a long-term basis. I can only hope it will somehow break the cycle, though I've told him it's best to skip a dose if he's feeling more energetic than usual.'

'Well, for now, he's well enough to plot though not quite ready yet to insist on going out.'

The doctor sighed. 'It'll be soon enough. A pleasure to meet you, Mrs Fletcher. I'll see you shortly.' He went out through a door connecting to the room next door.

'Humphrey's study and library,' Sybil explained. 'He has a bedroom beyond that he used to use when he stayed up late writing, so as not to disturb Ruby. It comes in handy now when he's ill.'

'Very convenient. Does he have a nurse?'

'No, Ruby and Lorna cope between them. He doesn't need, or want, someone constantly in attendance.'

'I'm glad to hear he's doing better at present. I want to meet him. Dr Knox – Roger— What's going on *there*?'

'I don't know what you mean.'

'Come off it, Sybil. I wasn't born yesterday. He may not be as overtly nutty about you as Walter is about Myra, but you can't tell me he's not keen on you. And vice versa.'

'I like him.' Sybil's face was a becoming pink. 'But I have Monica to think about. And my career.'

Letting Roger Knox and Monica fall by the wayside for the present, Daisy pursued her enquiries into the career. 'You were saying, while you finished writing *Double Cross at the* something-or-other, which I take it is the name of a ranch, Humphrey was plotting a new story.'

'*Halfbreed Hero*. He really is very good at thinking up

plots. In fact, they've improved – more coherent and more intricate – since he's had plenty of time to lie thinking about them. And time to read, as well. Some of his best are based on Shakespeare's plays. *Halfbreed Hero* is based on *Othello*, for instance, though good has to triumph, of course.'

'But . . . ?'

'What do you mean, *but*?'

'There was definitely a *but* in your voice,' Daisy said firmly. 'He's good at plots, *but* . . .'

'Promise you won't repeat this.'

'I promise.'

'His characters were wooden, partly because he wrote dialogue really badly. And though his descriptions of the landscape were wonderful – after all, he's seen it for himself – they went on much too long. I always suspected the errand boys just skipped them.'

Daisy pounced. '*Were. Wrote. Went* on. Past tense. He's not writing them any longer.'

'No, actually,' Sybil admitted. 'I was just getting to that.'

'You write them.'

'It just sort of happened. He had a wonderful story and felt well enough to tackle it. Then, after a couple of days at his desk, he had a relapse. Roger absolutely forbade him to try again for a month.'

'Meanwhile, you had your editor waiting impatiently.'

'Yes, though it became more complicated than that. I don't want to sound immodest, but *Double Cross* started selling considerably better than Eli Hawke's earlier sixpenny volumes. They brought out a new edition, and then an American publisher decided to serialise it.'

'Even though the author was English?'

'They put "Eli Hawke" in quotation marks and underneath identified him as "an English gentleman widely travelled in the American West"'. Sybil giggled. 'And they paid jolly well.'

'Gosh, how awkward!'

'It was,' she agreed soberly. 'I wondered if you'd understand.'

'There's Humphrey, writing the things for aeons, then you do the writing and suddenly they start making a lot of money. Was he furious?'

'He wasn't happy. How could he be? Ruby sympathised with him, but she was too glad to get the extra money not to be pleased. The unspeakable Simon had just decided the literary life was for him, so she could see he'd have to be supported indefinitely. Not that she's blind to his faults, but she's a mother with a single chick.'

'A rooster, all crow and fine plumage, and no production.'

Sybil laughed. 'That just about sums him up. And Myra, too. Instead of marrying and settling down to have babies, off the Birtwhistles' hands, she spends all her money on clothes and gadding about, flirting with a multitude of admirers. Then she comes back here to be supported by her uncle till her next quarter's income is due. Not to mention her guests who have to be entertained. The household can really use the extra money.'

'I can see that. But after the splendid reception of your first solo work, didn't you consider setting up for yourself?'

'Naturally I considered it. *Double Cross* wasn't really a solo achievement, though. The plot was entirely Humphrey's. And, more important, so was the name on the cover – his accepted pen name, at least. I couldn't take that with me. "My" success was built on his foundation. There was Monica to think of, too. It wasn't as if the Birtwhistles withheld the proceeds. They raised my salary commensurately.'

'I'm surprised Humphrey wasn't too resentful to want to continue to employ you.'

'Oh, he soon rationalised – with the help of Ruby's persuasive powers – that by typing out so many of his works, I'd learnt to imitate his style faithfully. I continued writing *Halfbreed Hero*. Then we started to get feelers from Hodder and Stoughton. The American sale piqued their interest, and they wanted Eli Hawke's next work for their two-shilling clothbound Westerns.'

'You certainly took the Wild West by storm! But what happened when Humphrey recovered his health?' Daisy waved at the bookshelves. 'Evidently Hodder went on publishing Hawke. He didn't want to go back to writing?'

'I think he's afraid to try, after my success. Daisy, it's awful. I feel so guilty.'

'You mean— He doesn't *really* believe your writing is better than his? That the editors would take one look and say *Double Cross* must have been a fluke?'

'Something like that. Roger says he may not consciously doubt his own ability. It's just that every time he gets well enough to start work again, he has a relapse. Roger's at his wits' end, really. He's not sure whether it's actually overexertion that's the trouble, and if so whether he's doing it on purpose. Or he could be deliberately dosing himself with some sedative, only we can't see how he could get hold of anything. Or it just might be his subconscious mind causing the symptoms, which are real enough – psychosomatic illness, they call it.'

'I realise your Roger—'

'Not mine!'

'Sorry. Would-be-your Roger – deny it if you can – isn't a psychologist, but can't he get Humphrey to talk about what's going on in his head?'

'He can't force him to talk. All Humphrey will say is that he refuses to go through life lying in bed when he has the energy to get up and walk.'

'I can't say I blame him!'

'It's awfully difficult. No one else, not even Roger, can know whether or when Humphrey's really well enough to be up and about.'

'It does sound a bit as if Humphrey may be subconsciously determined not to recover fully,' Daisy pondered. 'I don't see why you should feel guilty. You saved his bacon when he was first ill.'

'I could have tried harder to mimic his style.'

'Then you wouldn't have done so well and made more money for everyone.'

'No. But . . .'

'But?'

'I have an awful feeling . . . It was something Roger said. I can't remember what, exactly. But it made me wonder if perhaps . . . No, it can't possibly be true!'

'What can't be true?' Daisy asked with all the patience she could muster.

'I think Roger may suspect that Simon or Myra is putting something in Humphrey's food.'

'Good gracious, why? Oh, more money as long as you're doing the writing, of course. Is that why you wanted me to come? To try to find out if it's true?'

'I thought you could just poke about a bit,' Sybil said defensively.

'I'm not a detective, you know. By sheer chance I've been on the spot a few times when things have happened. The only reason I've been able to help Alec once or twice is that I've already known the people involved.'

'That's all I'm asking you to do, Daisy. Get to know them.

See if you think either of them is capable of doing such a horrible thing!'

'Why don't you talk to Roger about it? Find out what made him suspect them.'

'I couldn't! He didn't actually tell me he suspects them. He didn't even hint at it deliberately. I wish I could remember what he said that put the idea into my head. But you know how it is, once it's there, it won't go away.'

'It's very likely all in your imagination. Roger might well say he never meant anything of the sort.'

'Don't you see, then *I'd* have put the horrible idea into *his* head. He couldn't help but wonder what they'd done to make me suspicious. Or he might think I'm being spiteful because I envy them for living carefree on my work.'

'You wouldn't be human if you didn't envy them.'

'A bit, yes, though I enjoy my work and I'm happy to be able to support Monica decently. You could give up your writing, couldn't you, if you wanted to? But you haven't.'

'No, and I shan't.' Daisy sighed. 'All right, so you won't discuss your suspicions with Roger. I'll talk to your suspects and give you my opinion of them, but honestly, Sybil, you mustn't expect any definitive conclusion from me.'

'At least you can be objective about it. I can't. Heavens, look at the time! We'd better go and change for dinner.'

'Aren't you going to wait and see what he has to say about Humphrey's health?'

'No, he'll go and talk to Ruby. But he's staying to dinner. He always puts Eyrie Farm last on his list.' Sybil blushed. 'Just because we're so out of the way, of course.'

'Of course,' said Daisy.

CHAPTER 5

Daisy had brought a warm woollen dress, certain it would prove to be a necessity. She dressed it up for the evening with a cashmere stole. Adding the necklace of polished petrified-wood beads Alec had bought her when they visited the American West – unexpectedly appropriate – she wondered what sort of evening concoction Myra would wear.

The girl was obviously fashion-mad, but at least she had a sense of humour about it. It was hard to imagine her deliberately making her uncle ill in order to have the money to dress in the latest modes. However, Daisy had never been particularly interested in leading a fashionable life, so she wasn't really qualified to understand how important it might seem to a pretty young girl. At Myra's age, Daisy had just emerged from her volunteer job in the office of a military hospital and was trying to find a way to earn a living. Anything had seemed preferable to residing with her ever-dissatisfied mother or taking advantage of the offered charity of Cousin Edgar, the present Lord Dalrymple, then a virtual stranger.

Simon evidently didn't feel that way about sponging on his father's hard work. Could he possibly be so wrapped up in his dream of future literary greatness that he considered it more important than Humphrey's health? From what little she had seen of him, she wouldn't put it past him.

Still, putting some sort of dope in his food would be an awfully risky business. Suppose he miscalculated and killed him? No more books. No more income.

Daisy wasn't *au fait* with the novel-publishing world, but what Sybil had said seemed logical: the Westerns sold under the Eli Hawke name were presumed to have been written by Humphrey Birtwhistle. The publisher's contracts were with Birtwhistle. If he died, they wouldn't easily accept his secretary suddenly declaring that she'd been writing them for several years and was quite capable of continuing to do so.

Besides, Sybil herself admitted that Humphrey was responsible for the plots. She might not be capable of coming up with such popular stories for herself, even with the aid of Shakespeare.

Whether Simon and Myra understood these intricacies was another matter. Perhaps they were self-absorbed enough to believe Sybil could go on writing if Humphrey died, and that she'd be willing to turn over a large part of the proceeds to the Birtwhistles. Or they might simply not have considered the possibility of an accidental overdose of whatever was turning Humphrey into an invalid.

Daisy really didn't know them well enough to indulge in what Alec would undoubtedly describe as 'wild speculation'. First things first. She applied a final dab of powder to her nose and went downstairs.

Hearing her footsteps on the stairs, Walter Ilkton – now in evening dress and without the Woolworths pearl – looked round eagerly. His face fell, because she was not Myra, Daisy supposed.

However, he said courteously enough, 'Hello, Mrs . . . er, Feather.'

'Fletcher,' Daisy corrected him with a smile. 'Not too far off.'

'Sorry! Association of both sounds and ideas, what?' He wasn't as unintelligent as he had first appeared, if he knew what a fletcher was. 'And I have a bad habit of not listening properly to introductions. the Americans are better at it, in my opinion.'

'The way they tend to repeat one's name after hearing it? Have you been in America, Mr Ilkton?'

He had, and they chatted about their experiences till Simon Birtwhistle joined them. He, too, was in evening dress, but with a cravat instead of a bow-tie.

'Oh, America!' he said dismissively when he heard what they were talking about. 'Leave it to the cowboys and Indians. The few really cultured Americans are all in Paris.'

Daisy and Ilkton exchanged a look and made a mutual decision to let this wild generalisation pass.

'What are you writing?' Daisy asked.

Simon waved a languid hand. 'Oh, just a little thing about perversion and decay in a small mining town in Derbyshire.'

'Nice and convenient for your researches.' Ilkton's bland tone failed to hide his sneer. 'Or do you write from personal experience?'

'I'm a novelist,' Simon snapped. 'And I don't mean a scribbler of popular fiction for the masses, like my father and his so-called secretary. I intend to make a serious contribution to the literature of the ages.'

'If wishes were horses,' said Ilkton, but he never completed the proverb, to Daisy's relief, because at that moment Myra appeared at the top of the staircase. Ilkton noticed her instantly.

She looked splendid in a floor-length frock of heavy silk, silvery-grey embroidered with tiny gold beads. The low neckline was filled in with gold net, more of which fell in cascades from shoulders to wrists. The effect was of almost barbaric splendour, most unsuitable for a quiet evening in a farm house. Myra descended with a superb disregard for the unsuitability.

Stifling a laugh, Daisy wondered if she had found her woollen stockings to wear underneath.

Ilkton, looking dazed, went to meet her. 'You're magnificent,' he said.

'Horrible little show-off,' said her cousin.

'I hope you know how to dance a minuet, Walter,' Myra said with a dazzling smile, batting darkened eyelashes. 'I feel nothing else will do.'

'You'll have to teach me,' he said gallantly.

'And what music do you propose to dance to?' Simon demanded. 'My Stravinsky or your tangos?'

'We don't have any suitable records for the gramophone,' Myra agreed amiably, 'but it doesn't really matter, because I haven't the slightest notion of the steps. Still, it was a nice idea, don't you think, Mrs Fletcher?'

'I'd have enjoyed watching. But it seems to me your frock would do very nicely for a captive princess in Stravinsky's *Firebird*—'

'Have you seen it, Mrs Fletcher?' Simon asked eagerly, revising his opinion of her. 'The ballet?'

'No, just heard the suite, at the Queen's Hall, years ago.' Daisy tried to remember who had taken her to the concert. She certainly hadn't had the money to buy a ticket in those days, and it had been before she met Alec.

'You're so lucky to live in London.'

'Luck had nothing to do with it. I wanted to live there so I found a job to make it possible.'

He muttered something about women taking men's jobs.

'Honestly, Simon,' said Myra, 'as if you'd ever even looked for a job! And if you did, you've already aired your opinion of Mrs Fletcher's work. You wouldn't take it if it was offered you on a gold plate.'

Simon flushed.

In an undertone, Walter Ilkton said to Daisy, 'Tact is definitely not the family's long suit. The poor dear was attempting to defend you. There's not an ounce of malice in her.' He glared at Neil Carey, who was coming down the stairs whistling an Irish tune.

'Neil,' Myra addressed him, 'the very thing: you can teach us how to dance an Irish jig.'

He grinned at her. 'With pleasure, Miss Olney. Is it this very minute you'll be wanting a lesson?'

'After dinner, silly.' She moved towards him as she spoke.

Ilkton, his lips tight, drifted after her. He was too bland, too much a man of the world to look thunderous, but Daisy was pretty sure that was how he felt. Whatever Myra's view of their relationship, his proprietary interest was obvious.

In general, Myra seemed good-natured enough, even her occasional animosity towards her cousin merely an injudicious mixture of sibling squabbling and unfortunate frankness. She just said whatever came into her head, unfiltered by what passed for her brain.

Daisy wondered whether she knew her uncle's books were actually written by Sybil. Probably not, she decided, or the whole world would know by now. Myra might well not work it out for herself, and if it were Daisy's secret, she'd try to keep it from the girl for fear of its popping out quite by accident. Yet Sybil suspected her . . .

Sybil must be too upset about the whole business to think it through. Daisy would have to remember to ask her what Myra had been told.

Simon had recollected his duty as host. He started distributing drinks, a choice of sherry, whisky, or gin with tonic or bitters. No Dubonnet or vermouth, Daisy's favourite aperitifs, she noted sadly. She accepted a small sherry.

'I wish I could offer you Irish whiskey,' Simon said to Carey.

'Sure, 'tis none so easy to find the stuff this side of the Irish Sea, excepting in the big cities. I'll make do with a Scotch, I thank you.' He pulled a wry, humorous face.

Sybil and Mrs Birtwhistle came together down the stairs from the east wing. Then Dr Knox, still in his tweeds, came in through the door below, looking worried and moving slowly. On his arm leant a tall, painfully thin gentleman in a dinner jacket of old-fashioned cut.

'Humphrey!' Mrs Birtwhistle hurried towards them, *tut-tutting*. 'Are you sure you're well enough—?'

'Quite well enough to greet my guests, Ruby. Don't fuss. Introduce me.'

'At least sit down first, dear. The ladies will excuse you.'

Once Mr Birtwhistle was ensconced in a deep armchair close to the fire, introductions proceeded. He showed no interest in Neil Carey, nor Walter Ilkton, but invited Daisy to come and sit beside him.

'Pink gin, sir?' Simon offered his father.

'Thank you, my boy.' He looked at the doctor and said half laughing, half defensively, 'No need to look like a stuffed turkey, Knox. I didn't have a drink with my lunch.'

'I'm glad to hear it.'

'You see, Mrs Fletcher, cowboys are – or were in my day – a hard-drinking bunch, and the habit is hard to abandon. The hooch we used to drink was known as whisky, but they had only the name in common. As pond water to Malvern! To this day the very word brings back the taste, and I never touch anything that goes by the name of whisky.'

Daisy didn't feel it incumbent upon her to comment on

his drinking habits. 'You actually worked as a cowboy, Mr Birtwhistle?'

'For a few years. I went looking for adventure but I started life in America as a humble tout for a travelling quack. The English accent impressed the rubes – the local yokels. I'd stand up on the seat at the front of the wagon and give the spiel, and they'd be queuing up at the side to buy "Dr Pangloss's Potent Purple Pastilles, Patent Pending."'

'Pangloss. Voltaire?' she asked cautiously.

'"All is for the best, in the best of all possible worlds." The chances of any of our marks having heard of *Candide* were extremely slim, but if they had, what could be better for their health than a little optimism?' Almost inaudibly he added, 'It's what keeps me going.'

Thinking it best to ignore this comment, Daisy said, 'I hope the Potent Pastilles didn't actually kill anyone.'

'Not in my time. They were made with "the best butter". Chicle, actually, the stuff they make chewing-gum from. Purple dye from beetroot and he wouldn't tell me what else. Useless, perhaps, but not deadly. We sold them in tins of twenty, to be taken one a day, no miracle cures to be expected till the entire course was finished.'

Daisy laughed. 'By which time you'd left town, to avoid being tarred and feathered.'

'Of course. We headed west, and by the time we reached cowboy country I'd saved enough money to buy a decent horse. As I wanted to see the country, I moved from ranch to ranch, from Montana down to Old Mexico.'

'*Old* Mexico?'

'As opposed to New Mexico, one of the United States.'

'Oh, yes. Alec – my husband – and I didn't have time to go there.'

'You've been to America, Mrs Fletcher?'

'Just a short visit, most of it spent in Washington and New York. But we flew across the country to Oregon and returned by train.'

'You flew! You had a very different view from mine, then, crawling along at horse-speed. That must have been interesting.'

'A lot of the scenery was beautiful from the air, but the aeroplane was so noisy and I was so cold, I wasn't able to appreciate it properly at the time. The view from the train was better, of course, but limited. You spent several years in the West, I gather. You must have loved the country to have stayed so long.'

'I did, and do. I have a special fondness for New Mexico, which is where I met Ruby. She misses it. We always intended to go back some day for a visit, until this wretched illness overtook me. But we won't talk of that. Ruby was a school-marm, as they called it, in a one-horse town. I was a nearly penniless cow-hand. So I took my grub-stake to Nevada, went prospecting, and struck silver.'

'Right away?' Daisy asked in surprise.

He laughed. 'Not quite. But soon enough to make some of the old-timers look green. It was a nice seam of ore.'

'What luck!'

'Yes, and if I'd worked it, I might have ended up richer, or I might have ended up dead. I didn't care to spend my time watching over my shoulder for claim-jumpers. In any case, the life of a miner didn't appeal, and Ruby was waiting – I hoped. So I sold out, went back to New Mexico, and got married. I was negotiating for some land when the news reached me, by what roundabout route I never did discover, that my father had died the previous year. Add the fact that New Mexico was suffering a serious drought, and I decided to head for home.'

Glancing at Mrs Birtwhistle, Daisy wondered whether she had had any say in the decision to leave her home and her country. She caught Daisy's eye and came over, looking anxious.

Daisy explained, 'Mr Birtwhistle's been telling me about his career, or careers, rather, in America, and how much he loved your part of the country.'

'New Mexico is very beautiful. I miss it, especially when the winter rains set in here!' She laid a hand on her husband's shoulder. 'But it just wasn't the right time to try to get a start in ranching. Even well-established people were in trouble because of the dreadful drought – not something you can imagine here in England. Also, there was Humphrey's family to be considered.'

'He'd've done better to have stayed away.' The muttered comment coming unexpectedly from behind Daisy made her jump. 'We were doing very well without.'

The dog, back in his spot on the hearth rug, creaked to his feet and moved stiffly to meet the speaker.

Birtwhistle's eyes briefly flickered towards the newcomer, then turned up to his wife. Her gaze was fixed on the intruder in an inimical stare. Birtwhistle raised his hand to cover Ruby's on his shoulder. She glanced down at him and nodded.

'Hello, Norman,' she said in a neutral voice. 'Let me introduce you. Mrs Fletcher, this is Humphrey's brother, Norman.'

Norman wore a baggy, shaggy tweed suit and an air of disgruntlement that had carved permanent lines into his face. Daisy added this to his sister Lorna's general put-upon-ness and realised that the Prodigal's return had not been welcomed by his siblings. Thirty years later, they still resented it. Did Humphrey now own Eyrie Farm, left to him by a father in a dynastic mood, or were the three forced uneasily to share?

More to the immediate point, did either alternative have any bearing on Sybil's fears?

She had no chance to contemplate the question, as Lorna came in, looked round and said sourly, 'Oh, are you eating with us, Humphrey? We'll need another place set.'

'Yes, I think I will, as long as Mrs Fletcher will excuse my leaving the table early if it seems advisable.'

'Certainly,' Daisy said promptly.

'Are you sure you're well enough, darling?' Mrs Birtwhistle fussed.

'If I weren't, I wouldn't. Simon can carve – at least, I hope Simon can carve. I spent enough time trying to teach him.'

'There are more important things in life than cutting up meat neatly,' Simon retorted. 'As a matter of fact, I'm thinking of becoming a vegetarian.'

'What?' Norman Birtwhistle burst out. 'A fine thing that'll be for a sheep farmer!'

'If you imagine I'm ever going to be a—'

'You can always keep sheep just for the wool, Si,' Myra pointed out. This soothed neither her cousin nor her uncle.

Lorna made herself heard again. 'Dr Knox, is Humphrey to eat with the rest of us?'

'Dammit, Lorna, I'm not a child!' her brother exploded. 'I'll decide for myself. I'll dine with my guests.'

His sister departed with a sniff.

'I'll set a place for you, Uncle Humphrey,' said Myra.

Walter Ilkton regarded her with an expression of doting approval. 'There's bound to be chairs that need slinging about. I'll come and lend a hand.'

'Darling, too sweet of you!' They went out together.

Neil winked at Daisy. 'Many hands make light work,' he observed lightly, and followed the pair.

'Sickening!' said Simon, scowling. 'I don't know what

they all see in her, but I wish she'd flipping well make up what passes for her mind and marry one of them.'

'I hope she won't choose your friend, Simon,' said his mother. 'I'm sure he hasn't a penny to his name. Humphrey, are you quite sure you're well enough to join us? I know Mrs Fletcher won't—'

'Yes, Ruby, I'm quite sure. Mrs Fletcher has already assured me that she won't be offended if I'm obliged to retire after the roast. I hope you're pleased, Knox. You're always urging me not to overexert myself.'

The doctor shrugged. 'It's a good sign that you're able to join the family, and I hope the company will stimulate your appetite, but one supper doesn't make a summer.'

'And one swallow doesn't make a supper,' Sybil put in.

'It's presumptuous of me to bandy words with wordsmiths,' Knox said, smiling. 'What do you think, Mrs Fletcher? I gather you're a writer, too. Do you object to being called a wordsmith?'

'Not at all. It has a nice, sensible, solid sound, like blacksmith.'

'Sensible! Solid!' Simon was outraged. 'Is that what you aspire to?'

'Your work is more like goldsmithing, no doubt,' said Daisy peaceably. 'Airy fantasies, delicate—'

'Psychological insights,' said Simon through his teeth. 'Gritty truths.'

'More like a road-mender, then,' his father remarked dryly.

'I wouldn't expect you to understand,' Simon retorted with a sulky pout.

'I'd better get your pills, Humphrey,' said Mrs Birtwhistle, 'the ones you take with meals, and put them by your place.'

'Thank you, my dear. Simon, I'll have another pink gin at

dinner. Take the bottles through, please. It doesn't seem to be doing me any harm, Knox.'

'Perhaps not. But please continue to stay away from it when you're not feeling so bright and breezy.'

'I'll settle for the short term.' Watching Simon slouch out with a bottle of gin and one of bitters, he sighed. '"How sharper than a serpent's tooth . . . !"'

'Don't you think he's just trying to find his own feet, Mr Birtwhistle?' said Daisy. 'After all, you didn't exactly follow in your father's footsteps.'

He looked at her in some surprise. 'That's very true.'

'And he's quite young yet, isn't he?'

'Barely twenty-one. At his age, though, I'd been earning my own way for a couple of years.'

'Selling patent nostrums? Don't tell me your parents approved!'

'Lord, no. I never told them. I rarely wrote after running off to America. You have children? A mixed blessing.'

'My twins aren't old enough to get into real mischief yet. My stepdaughter is in her teens, but she's a sweetheart.'

'I hope she stays that way.'

'They all go through stages, don't they? With luck, the troublesome ones don't last long.'

'Well, well, perhaps I need not give up on the boy yet. Shall we go through, Mrs Fletcher? Surely Myra's young men – though Ilkton's not as youthful as most of her catches; perhaps she won't chuck this one back? – surely they've finished moving chairs about by now.'

He levered himself to his feet with difficulty, and took Daisy's arm, but he didn't lean heavily on her for support.

As they went slowly through to the west wing, Lorna reappeared, to say sourly, 'And about time, too, or everything will be stone cold.'

CHAPTER 6

The dining room was furnished with heavy Victorian mahogany. At the vast sideboard, Norman Birtwhistle stood carving a rosemary-scented leg of lamb, having apparently taken over the task from his reluctant nephew. The aroma, together with walls painted a modern pale green somewhat relieved the gloom induced by large quantities of dark wood.

On the walls hung several Wild West paintings: a cowboy on a bucking bronco; a stern, sad-faced Indian chief; a vista of craggy mountains spreading behind a herd of cattle fording a stream—

'Oh, of course,' said Daisy, 'it's one of those American cattle you've got over the mantelpiece in the hall. I thought you must have been shooting, very badly, in the Highlands!'

Humphrey Birtwhistle laughed. 'Yes, a Texas longhorn. And I didn't shoot it.' He sobered. 'After a few years of drought, there were all too many to be found, though the longhorns did better than other stock. I hope you'll sit beside me, Mrs Fletcher, though I'm afraid I'd better not try to hold your chair for you.'

With the host a sick man, formal procedure was obviously impossible – and they were, after all, in a farm house, not a mansion.

His own chair, at the head of the table, was managed for

him by a solicitous Walter Ilkton. He subsided limply, while Dr Knox seated Daisy next to him and sat down beside her. Ruby Birtwhistle had taken her place at the far end of the table. Daisy noticed a round pill-box and a brown bottle by Birtwhistle's water and wine glasses.

He saw the direction of her gaze and shook his head sadly. 'Patent nostrums,' he said, and she laughed.

'Made from "the best butter"?'

'The very best butter. It wouldn't surprise me. The good doctor has experimented with every conceivable drug in the pharmacopoeia. But we're not going to discuss my health over dinner. Do you find time in your busy life to read as well as write, Mrs Fletcher?'

'I do, though not as much as I'd like. I'm afraid I haven't read any of Eli Hawke's books. I'd like to borrow one this evening, if I may.'

'You may, naturally, but please don't feel obliged to.'

'Not at all. Having seen a bit of Western America from above, I look forward to reading about it at ground-level, so to speak. I can't think why I never have.'

'Most readers of Wild West fiction are men, as are the writers, though B. M. Bower is a woman, I gather.'

Simon Birtwhistle interrupted. 'A glass of wine, Mrs Fletcher? It's Bordeaux, red or white. Nothing special in the way of vintage, I'm afraid.'

'Red, please.' Daisy hoped the claret would be drinkable, but the sherry had not been a good omen – not that she cared much for even the best sherry. Her palate had been somewhat refined by association with the Fletchers' next-door neighbours, a family of very superior wine-merchants. The Wild West and a sheep farm respectively were not likely places for Humphrey and Norman to have learned about wines, and Simon probably considered the subject effete.

Walter Ilkton, gravely playing wine waiter, brought her glass, along with a pink gin Simon had poured for his father. She took a sip. Not too bad. Before knowing the Jessups, she wouldn't have thought twice about it. Sometimes ignorance was bliss.

Lorna and Myra passed plates of lamb, roast potatoes, carrots sprinkled with chopped chives and cauliflower in white sauce. Gravy and mint sauce were handed up and down the table. Daisy assumed that a soup course was just too much trouble in the evenings, after the servants had left for the day.

Birtwhistle ate well. Daisy noticed Dr Knox watching with approval. In fact, his patient was too occupied with his dinner to add more to the conversation than an odd word here and there. Daisy chatted with the doctor, beside her, and Sybil, sitting opposite.

They were divided from those at the other end of the table by Norman and Lorna, both consuming their dinners in morose silence. Daisy couldn't see Simon, who was on her side of the table; not hearing his voice she assumed he was as taciturn as his uncle and aunt. From beyond them, she caught occasional gusts of laughter from Myra and her two admirers. Myra was in high spirits. The two men indulged her in persiflage, though Ilkton's voice had a slight edge that hinted at rivalry between them.

Was Myra aware that they were competing for her favour, Daisy wondered? Perhaps she found it exciting, but she was young enough to be simply enjoying the attention.

When her uncle originally fell ill, she couldn't have been more than fifteen or sixteen. The notion that she had, at that age, thought up a scheme to keep him under the weather was ridiculous. To judge by what Daisy had seen of her, she wouldn't even have realised it might be to her advantage. If someone had been systematically poisoning Birtwhistle for three years, it wasn't Myra.

What about Simon? He'd have been eighteen, and he was much brighter than his cousin, whatever one's opinion of his literary ambitions. Still, his character seemed more inclined to angry outbursts than to a long, insidious campaign to undermine his father's competence.

Daisy was about to cross them both off her mental list when she remembered that Alec always required absolute proof of innocence before eliminating a suspect. She moved them to the bottom instead. Still, she was fairly sure that either the whole business was a figment of Sybil's imagination, or someone else was responsible.

She started to consider alternative possibilities but lost the thread when Knox said, 'Don't you agree, Mrs Fletcher?' and she was forced to confess her thoughts had been wandering.

'An occupational hazard with writers,' commented Birtwhistle. He followed his last bite of lamb with the last drop of gin in his glass.

Daisy regretfully refused a second helping of lamb. She asked Norman if it were from the Birtwhistle farms. He grunted what she took for an affirmative, so she told him it was simply delicious.

The compliment cut no ice with Norman. He produced another surly grunt and gave her a look as if he suspected her of trying to turn him up sweet.

Which she was. It was going to be very difficult to do any investigating if people refused to talk to her. Not that – strictly speaking – she was investigating. She wasn't even sure that a crime was being committed. All the same, Alec would be furious if he knew what she was up to.

Comfort came in the form of apple tart with cream.

'Apples from our orchard,' Norman told her. He looked and sounded truculent. 'Cream from our Jerseys. And I grew those potatoes and cauliflower and carrots, too.' Was he trying to prove to her that he didn't live off his brother's earnings? And if so, why?

'Norman is a marvel,' said Ruby. 'He provides almost all our farm stuff, fruit, vegetables, milk, eggs, meat.'

'There's still shopping to be done,' Lorna pointed out sharply. 'I need to go into Matlock tomorrow.'

'I'll drive you,' Ruby offered. 'I need a couple of things, and we'll share the household shopping. Mrs Fletcher, Matlock is rather a beautiful little town and Tuesday is market day. I wonder whether you'd like to go with us, if it's fine.'

'I'd love to, only . . . Will you be working, Sybil, or can you spare the morning for an outing?'

'I'd better work in the morning. If I don't get going first thing, it's much harder later. If it goes well, I'll take a couple of hours off in the afternoon.'

'Then I'd love to go with you, Mrs Birtwhistle,' Daisy said quickly. Sybil wasn't much good as a conspirator. The others must be wondering why she had invited Daisy if she had no time to spend with her. And the way she had phrased her explanation made her work sound much more like a creative endeavour than mere transcribing of someone else's words. 'I don't know this part of the country at all.'

'Let's all go,' Myra suggested with enthusiasm. 'Walter, you could visit your great-uncle at the Hydro.'

'Cousin. Twice removed.'

'Much too complicated! Your elderly relative. If you drive us up that frightful hill, I can show Mrs Fletcher the view from the top. It's simply marvellous, Mrs Fletcher. Then while Walter does his duty, we'll walk down. There's a cable tram but I'm certain the cable will snap one of these days and the tram will slide down Bank Road and crash in Crown Square, or even go on down into the river.'

'How alarming!'

'So it's much better if Walter drives us up. You'll come, of course, Neil? What about you, Simon? Do come. It'll be such fun if there's lots of us!'

'Oh, all right,' said Simon.

'I'll tell you what, Myra,' said Carey, 'I'll take you pillion on my motorbike.'

'Much too dangerous!' Ruby Birtwhistle exclaimed.

Ilkton backed her up. 'Those machines cause half the accidents on the roads.'

Neil Carey wasn't having any of that. 'In the narrow lanes round about here, with walls on each side, I'd a sight rather be on my Triumph than in your great Packard, boyo. Not to mention over the bridge.'

'Until you find your legs scraping the walls.'

'Oh no, you mustn't, Myra,' her aunt insisted.

'I'll borrow a pair of Uncle Norman's dungarees. They'll protect my legs. You'll lend me a pair, won't you, Uncle?' she coaxed.

'Happen I might.'

'My dear child, you can't possibly walk round Matlock in your uncle's gardening trousers!'

'Gosh, no!' Myra's face was appalled.

Ilkton sighed. 'We could take a change of clothes for you in the car. We could meet outside one of the hotels and you could pop in round the back way.'

'Too sweet of you, Walter.' She beamed at him. 'Thanks. What a clever idea.'

Carey's motor-bicycle versus Ilkton's sweetness, cleverness and all-round obligingness: honours even, Daisy decided.

'I still don't like it,' said Ruby.

'Wasn't I after bringing an extra helmet, Mrs Birtwhistle,' Carey said. 'It'll protect her head and make her unrecognisable, both.'

'Well . . .'

'No speeding, I promise. And she can wear my leather leggings over her uncle's dungarees.'

Ruby gave in, wisely. Daisy doubted she was able to stop Myra having her own way under any circumstances.

Birtwhistle seemed amused. 'Just like Ruby when she was a girl,' he murmured to Daisy. 'Headstrong – well, she ran away with an Englishman, didn't she? You'd think they were mother and daughter.'

The last bite of apple tart eaten, Lorna got up and started to clear away the dishes. 'Myra, if you've nothing better to do . . .'

Myra jumped up. 'I was just coming.'

Ilkton hurried to help stack bowls, and Carey good-naturedly joined in.

'Can I help?' Daisy asked.

Simon, who had been saying something to Sybil, looked round. 'No, Mrs Fletcher, you stay put. I'm just going.'

'Before you disappear, Simon, I'll have another pink gin,' said Birtwhistle. 'I don't drink coffee, Mrs Fletcher. Almost worse than the abominable hooch was the so-called coffee we brewed in cans over a camp-fire. It put me off the stuff for life. As with whisky, now the very smell is enough to bring back the revolting taste. A decent cup of tea wasn't to be had for love nor money, either.'

Daisy agreed. 'It's hard to get a good cup of tea anywhere in the country. Americans don't seem to understand about the water having to be on the boil.'

'On the contrary. They associate tea with cold sea-water.' He chuckled, then seeing his brother's perplexed face, explained, 'In Boston Harbour, Norm. The American Revolution and all that.'

Norman grunted.

'We usually have coffee in here, Mrs Fletcher,' Ruby said. 'It makes things simpler. I made the coffee earlier. It just has to be carried in.'

Simon brought Birtwhistle's drink. 'Sorry, Mrs Fletcher,' he said, 'we don't run to liqueurs, and the brandy's nothing to write home about. I wouldn't recommend it.'

'Strictly for medicinal purposes?'

'That's about it. Ilkton tried it the first time he came to stay and he was horrified. He's accustomed to the finest Armagnac. He even said next time he'd come prepared. If he has, he's not sharing. I don't expect you drink whisky, but if you'd like a gin or another glass of wine—'

'No, no thank you. Just coffee.'

Myra returned from the kitchen, followed by Ilkton carrying a tray of coffee things. Daisy doubted that he was accustomed to such chores, travelling with his valet as he did. His eagerness to please was further evidence of his devotion. In fact Daisy was rather surprised that he hadn't fought harder against Myra's proposed ride on Carey's motorbike. Perhaps he realised his cause wouldn't suffer from her comparing its discomfort with the luxury of his own Packard.

Besides, if he was accustomed to seeing her in London, he must be accustomed to sharing her with any number of other admirers. Myra wasn't ready to be tied down, and she would not appreciate any attempts to spoil her fun.

Ruby poured the coffee and the cups were passed from hand to hand round the table, followed by a jug of cream and bowl of sugar.

Birtwhistle finished his drink quickly. 'You won't mind if I take myself off now, Mrs Fletcher?' he said, his articulation slightly slurred. 'I'm beginning to run out of steam. Good-night, all.' He started to push himself up out of his chair.

Simon half-rose, but Dr Knox beat him, jumping up to help his patient. Ruby Birtwhistle followed them from the dining room.

'Never could hold his drink,' Norman remarked snidely.

Sybil rounded on him. 'That's nonsense. He's ill! And he hardly ever has more than one drink, anyway – rarely any at all.'

Norman relapsed into his usual sullen silence.

Coffee was drunk with a minimum of chit-chat, even Myra subdued. No one wanted refills.

'Your turn to wash up, Myra,' said Lorna.

'It ruins my hands!' complained Myra, spreading rose-pink varnished nails for everyone to admire.

'I'll wash,' offered Ilkton. 'You dry.'

'I'll dry,' Carey declared.

'Oh, good, then I'll only have to put away. Bring the tray, one of you.'

Myra waltzed off with great good cheer. Ilkton and Carey between them loaded the tray, with somewhat less good cheer. Then they stopped and stared at each other, each apparently willing the other to pick it up.

'Oh, for pity's sake!' Simon exclaimed. 'I'll carry the damned thing. What you see in her I cannot fathom!'

Sheepishly, the others went after him.

'One thing's for sure,' grumbled Lorna, 'she won't remember to come back and put away the place-mats.'

As she went round the table gathering them up, Sybil and Daisy exchanged a guilty look and seized their chance to escape.

CHAPTER 7

Sybil took Daisy back to her office, where they could be private.

'Well, what do you think?' she demanded, poking up the fire and adding a couple of lumps of coal as Daisy sat down.

'I'm fairly certain Walter Ilkton's intentions are serious. He's completely infatuated, though how long it'll last is anyone's guess. Neil Carey seems more motivated by his enjoyment of trying to get a rise out of Ilkton. I don't believe he's any more interested in marrying than Myra is.'

'I mean, about Simon and Myra and Humphrey.'

'I'm sure they were both far too young when Humphrey first fell ill to have anything to do with prolonging his illness.'

'Oh. Yes, I suppose it is unlikely.'

'Very.'

'So I'm making an ass of myself,' Sybil said disconsolately. 'It's all in my head. I should have worked that out for myself before getting you here under false pretenses. And I can't even entertain you. I really do have to work tomorrow. But don't feel obliged to go on an outing to Matlock tomorrow if you'd rather just go home.'

'Not on your life! It's a long drive. I'm not going to do it again tomorrow.' She decided not to mention that with Simon and Myra out of the picture, other possibilities arose.

She hadn't had a chance to develop her theories. They were still far too tenuous to explain. 'Besides, I'd really like to see Matlock and the view from the Hydro.'

'It is special. You can see right over Matlock Bath to the Heights of Abraham, and down the valley to the Black Rocks and miles of country beyond.'

'Lovely. I hope it's fine. You don't work seven days a week, do you?'

'Heavens no. Ruby motors over to Bakewell every Saturday morning to fetch Monica from school. When they get back I stop writing and I have the rest of the weekend with her. It's a pity you couldn't have come at the weekend so that you could meet her and I'd be able to see more of you.'

'It was one of Alec's rare free weekends. Speaking of which, I'm amazed that no one has yet asked me what he does. You didn't tell them, I assume?'

'Of course not.'

'No, sorry. In any case, I can always tell when people know he's a copper. Even the most innocent people tend to come over all twitchy. When someone asks, I say he's a civil servant. They usually do ask, sort of as if I'm only a real person in relation to what my husband does, even though I write.'

'I know exactly what you mean. Outside this house, people think of me as a widow first, not as a competent secretary, let alone a writer. It's just as well, really, as we don't want people to know that last part.'

'I've been meaning to ask you, does Myra know you do most of the writing?'

'I don't think so. I'm pretty sure not. The rest of us agreed not to tell her, for obvious reasons.'

'In that case, I can't see why you suspected her at all. The only motive she could conceivably have for keeping

Humphrey under the weather is that you're making more money than he did. If she doesn't know, pop goes the motive.'

'Daisy, I must be blind as a bat not to have seen that. She certainly didn't know a couple of years ago, when all this began. And quite apart from her age and what she knows or doesn't know, I don't believe for a moment she has enough brains to come up with such a devious plot.'

'No, devious plots are Humphrey's business,' Daisy said, laughing.

'Perhaps I get too caught up in his to think straight about real life.'

'Then all I can say is it's a good job he doesn't write detective stories!' Daisy yawned enormously. 'Sorry! I'd better head for bed if I'm not to sleep half tomorrow away. I was up early this morning. May I take a couple of Eli Hawke's books with me? I'd like to dip into one of Humphrey's solo efforts and one of yours.'

'Help yourself. No, on second thoughts, let me give you a couple of my favourites.' She went over to the bookcase. 'Here, *Lonesome Creek* is one of his best. And *Halfbreed Hero*.'

'That's the one based on *Othello*.'

'Loosely. With a happy ending.'

'Good. I prefer happy endings, especially at bedtime. Thanks.'

'You'd better have a hot water bottle. Let's go and see what sort of mayhem those three have accomplished in the kitchen.'

As they went through the hall, Daisy noticed a telephone, in a niche under the west stairs. 'Oh bother!' she said, 'I meant to write to Alec as soon as I got here, to tell him I arrived safely. He was a bit worried about my driving so far on my own. Would it be all right if I sent a wire? I'll pay, of course.'

'Go ahead. That's the only phone in the house, I'm afraid. Not very private. And don't say anything you don't want all the operator's friends and relations to know. You know what country districts are like. I'll be in the kitchen, through that door and turn right and you can't miss it.'

Daisy sent her telegram, then went up to her room to fetch a shilling, knowing she'd forget if she didn't do it right away. The stairs and passage were dimly lit by a single oil-lamp on the landing. In the murk, it was easier to give credence to Sybil's forebodings. Daisy pondered the difference gas and electric lighting had made to the world. It was much easier to believe in 'ghoulies and ghosties and long-leggedy beasties and things that go bump in the night' when there were lots of shadowy corners for them to lurk in.

Counting doors, she found her room. Plenty of shadows here. The flickering embers in the fireplace and the last light from the hallway enabled her to see just well enough to cross to the mantelpiece and find a box of matches.

After the gloom, one lit candle seemed bright. She dug a couple of sixpences out of her purse, and was turning to leave when a tapping on the door almost made her jump out of her skin.

'Who's there?' she quavered.

'Daisy?'

'Sybil!'

'Are you all right?'

'Yes. Come in. You just startled me. "Suddenly there came a tapping . . ."'

'A raven bearing a hot water bottle. You weren't by the phone so I brought it up.'

'I came to get the money for the telegram. I didn't have a shilling and now I've gone and dropped the sixpences. Where on earth are they? They must have rolled away.'

'We'll find them in the morning.' Sybil tucked the rubber bottle with its red and blue striped, knitted cosy, under the bedclothes. 'If you're not absolutely determined to go to bed right away, do come down again.' As she spoke, she poked up the bedroom fire and put a couple of lumps of coal on it. 'Myra's given up on dancing. She's trying to get a game of Racing Demon going. But if you don't want to play, no one will mind if you just sit and read. Simon probably will, too.'

'Yes, somehow I can't imagine Simon playing Racing Demon. It seems a bit below Ilkton's dignity as well, but who knows what a man in love will stoop to. As for me, I couldn't possibly sit in a room where it was being played and not join in.'

Sybil laughed. 'If you're going to play, I will, too. I hope we have enough packs of cards. Here, I'll light your lamp so you don't have to fumble for a candle when you come back up.'

'Thanks. I haven't lit an oil-lamp in ages. I'd probably manage to make a mess of it.'

'The girls clean and fill them, so it's only a matter of adjusting the wick properly. There. Just turn it up a bit if you want more light. Look, there are your sixpences.'

They went downstairs. Daisy put the coins beside the telephone. The doctor and Mrs Birtwhistle, who was knitting, sat by the fire, talking. There was no sign of either Norman or Lorna.

In the middle of the hall, two card tables had been set up, touching each other. Ilkton, Carey and – surprisingly – Simon Birtwhistle were carrying chairs through from the dining room, while Myra directed the operation.

'Mrs Fletcher,' she cried, 'you are going to play Racing Demon with us, aren't you? The more the merrier.'

'I'd love to, if you have enough cards.'

'Simon found enough packs in the sideboard for everyone. Aunt Ruby, Dr Knox, do come and play.'

'I used to be a dab hand at Racing Demon,' Knox said nostalgically, glancing at Sybil.

'Come and play, Roger. If Ruby doesn't want to, I'll sit out with her.'

Knox looked as if that was not quite the outcome he desired. Fortunately, Ruby Birtwhistle decided to take a hand.

Eight people seated round two tables was a bit of a squeeze. Carey and Ilkton nobly offered to take the middle places on each side, where the table-legs got in the way of knees. Giggling, Myra sent Simon to one end and posted herself at the other.

'We'll have to jump up and down to reach the cards in the middle,' she pointed out. 'It'll be easier for us.'

'Are you saying I'm too old to jump up and down?' Roger Knox demanded with mock indignation.

Myra grinned at him. 'Actually, I thought it would be beneath your dignity.'

Simon snorted. 'I wouldn't describe Racing Demon as a dignified game under any circumstances.'

'Don't be pompous, Si.'

'That's enough, you two,' Ruby sat down between her son's place and Walter Ilkton's. 'Heaven help me, you sound like a pair of seven-year-olds.'

'Sorry, Aunt Ruby.' Myra sounded neither penitent, nor put out at being chastised in front of her beaux.

Simon looked sulky – if he wasn't careful, he was going to turn out very like his uncle Norman, in temperament if not in intellectual pretension, Daisy decided. He hesitated, but took his place at the tables.

The rules of the game had to be explained to Walter Ilkton, who had never played before. It wasn't complicated. Winning depended on concentration, speed, dexterity and a certain amount of luck.

'I've got it,' Ilkton said.

'Let's have a five-minute practice,' suggested the doctor.

'A couple of rounds should be enough.'

'You haven't got it, me boyo,' said Carey a trifle maliciously. 'There are no rounds. We all play at once.'

'All at once? It sounds like chaos!'

'It is,' said Myra. 'That's what makes it such fun.'

'But chaos with rules,' Ruby said firmly, 'or it's not fun. Mr Ilkton, I'll help you for a few minutes' practice. Is everyone ready? On your marks, get set, go!'

For a few minutes there was complete chaos. Half the players played as if life and death depended on the game while the other half kept an eye on what Ilkton was doing and commented freely, some helpful, some sarcastic.

'Stop!' said Ruby. Carey sneaked one last card onto one of the piles in the middle. She made him take it back, even though they were only playing for practice. 'Begin as you mean to continue,' she said severely.

'Have you got the hang of it now, Walter?' Myra asked.

'I think so,' he said, much more cautious now than he had been before.

'We're not playing for money, so it doesn't really matter,' she reassured him.

Daisy, sitting opposite Ruby, heard her say in a low voice, 'I hope you won't find it too boring, Mr Ilkton. Not playing for money, I mean.'

He glanced at the other end of the tables. 'If Miss Olney enjoys it, I shall. I normally play bridge for stakes, of course. One does. But I assure you I'm not a confirmed gambler.'

The cards were sorted and restored to their starting configuration. The game commenced. The need to concentrate precluded conversation, so for some time the only sounds were the slap of cards and occasional crows and moans from the players.

Daisy, accustomed to being beaten hollow by her stepdaughter, Belinda, or one of her friends, didn't expect to win. Her mind wandered, studying the style of the others.

Both Carey and Myra were fast and careless; if a comparatively neat pile of cards became a disorderly heap, one of the two was usually to blame. Ilkton, though handling the cards with the skill of a regular player, was hesitant and spent far too much time in deliberation for a game so unlike bridge. Sybil was quick and neat. Roger Knox was neat but slow, as if his mind, like Daisy's, was largely elsewhere. Ruby and Simon, somewhat to Daisy's surprise, both played with speed, neatness and an almost ferocious concentration. Simon even remained on his feet so as to be able to reach the central piles without bobbing up and down.

Ruby won, through sheer single-minded determination. Daisy wouldn't previously have considered those traits part of her character. Surely she couldn't be so determined to have enough money to support her son's literary ambition that she was willing to sacrifice her husband's health?

CHAPTER 8

When the game ended at last, Dr Knox departed and everyone went up to bed. Daisy was tired but wakeful. To her annoyance, she discovered she had left the borrowed books downstairs. She was sure she had been carrying them when she left Sybil's office, so she must have left them by the phone. Odd that she hadn't noticed them when she left her sixpences on the telephone table.

She almost decided not to bother with the Westerns. She had taken off her shoes when it dawned on her that leaving the books where anyone might find them was not a good idea. If either Carey or Ilkton came across them, he could hardly fail to note the contrast between the cheap paperbacked *Lonesome Creek* and the solid cloth-and-board *Halfbreed Hero*. A modicum of curiosity might lead him to investigate, and to the discovery of Eli Hawke's secret.

Daisy wouldn't give a farthing for Carey's ability to keep a secret. Though Ilkton might be persuaded to keep it under his hat, he'd quite likely mention it to Myra and then the fat would be in the fire – to mix a metaphor.

With a sigh, Daisy decided she ought to go and fetch the books.

She padded on stockinged feet to the door and peered

out. The lamp on the landing still dimly illuminated the corridor, but if everyone had come up to bed, all lights were probably extinguished downstairs. Not wanting to carry the heavy brass bedside lamp downstairs and back up again, she lit a candle.

As she stepped out into the passage, the flame wavered. When she cupped her hand round it to shelter it, huge shadows reached across the walls, clutching at her as she moved.

Udolpho, she thought, or *The Castle of Otranto*. But she was no Catherine Morland, eager to see apparitions in the flickering gloom. She was a rational twentieth-century woman. Unlike the youthful heroine of *Northanger Abbey*, she based her theories on common sense – even if Alec did usually call them wild speculations.

All the same, she hoped her candle would stay alight.

The stairs creaked eerily beneath her footsteps. Despite the draughts that sneaked through cracks and crannies, the flame survived all the way down to the hall. Coals on the hearth glowed red, to Daisy's relief. If the candle blew out now it would be easy enough to relight it.

As if in response to the thought, the light flared, winked and died. Blinded, Daisy stopped on the spot. Gradually her eyes adjusted. First she made out the dying fire's glow, then she realised the lamp on the landing shed just enough light to make the shadows blacker. The fire looked a long way away. She turned her back on it, gazed at the spot beneath the landing where she knew the telephone stood, and caught a gleam of its polished metal.

Cautiously she moved towards the phone. No unexpected rugs or furniture attempted to trip her. By the time she reached the small table, she could see well enough to be sure no books lay on it. She felt across the surface nonetheless.

She found nothing but a small note pad with attached pencil, and the phone itself. The drawer held only a directory.

Two possibilities presented themselves: either one of the household had seen the same risk as she had and removed the books, or one of the guests had already found them.

In the latter case, there was nothing she could do about it. She turned away, intending to go straight back to bed. But her nocturnal wandering had made her more wakeful than ever, and coming from the darkness under the landing, she could see quite well in the hall. She decided to go to Sybil's office, to find out whether the two books had been reshelved and if so to reborrow them.

The stone floor chilly beneath her unshod feet, Daisy walked confidently over to the fire and relit her candle. Some vagary of the wind outside lessened the number and strength of draughts on this side of the hall. The candle behaved perfectly as she turned into the east wing.

Coming to the door of the office, she reached for the handle. The door moved. It had been pushed to but not latched. She opened it.

The beam of an electric torch moved along the rows of Eli Hawke's works, silhouetting a large, male figure.

'Who . . . ?' Daisy started to enquire, before it dawned on her that the man might be a burglar and she ought to have slipped quietly away to get help.

She stepped backwards as the putative burglar swung round, dazzling her with the torch beam. 'Who . . . ?' he echoed. 'Oh, Mrs Fletcher. We sound like a couple of owls.'

'Mr Ilkton?' Daisy peered, shading her eyes.

'Sorry.' He lowered the beam to the floor. 'What are you doing here?'

'I might ask the same of you.'

'Just looking for a little reading material.'

'Funny, I wouldn't have guessed Westerns were quite your line. I'd have put you down as the Michael Arlen type, that sort of stuff.'

'You'd be quite right, of course. I was looking for our host's library, though don't you think it would be a neat compliment to him to be seen reading one of his books?'

'A bit obvious, I'd have thought. Mr Birtwhistle's library and study is through that door. But I wouldn't go in if I were you. His bedroom is just the other side and you might wake him.'

'Ah, thank you for the warning. I knew he was somewhere in this vicinity, hence my creeping about with a torch. You're right, I won't intrude next door. I'll just take a couple of these to put me to sleep.'

'That's not exactly complimentary!'

'But you won't give me away, will you, Mrs Fletcher? You'd have to explain what you—'

'What on earth are you two doing here at this time of night?' Ruby Birtwhistle appeared in the doorway to the study, lantern held high. The draught blew out Daisy's candle.

Daisy couldn't make out her expression but she sounded cross, and who could blame her? Daisy just hoped it didn't look as if she and Walter Ilkton had an assignation.

'For pity's sake, keep your voices down,' Ruby continued, 'and don't wake Humphrey. He's just dropped off.' She stepped in and closed the door behind her.

'We've been keeping our voices down,' said Daisy. 'Sybil lent me a couple of books. I left them by the telephone and someone must have tidied them away. I came to get them to read in bed.'

As she spoke, Daisy moved over to the bookshelves and Ilkton moved aside out of her way. *Lonesome Creek* and

Halfbreed Hero were in their proper places, thank goodness. She was about to retrieve them when she noticed that Ilkton was watching her closely. Did he suspect there was something fishy about Eli Hawke's authorship?

If she took both books, he might wonder why she chose one of the older, cheap volumes and one of the new. Rather than risk his following her example, making comparisons and drawing his own conclusions, she had better take just one. It would look odd if she chose one of the rather shabby, faded paper books. She reached for *Halfbreed Hero*.

'And you, Mr Ilkton?' asked Ruby.

While his attention was distracted, Daisy slipped *Lonesome Creek* from the shelf and hid it beneath the larger book. She really wanted to start with one of Humphrey's so that she could see how Sybil's style had developed from his.

'I'm merely following Mrs Fletcher's example,' Ilkton said blandly. 'I'd like to read one of Mr Birtwhistle's works.'

'I'm sure Humphrey will be flattered.' Ruby came swiftly to join them at the bookcase. 'Why don't you try his latest, *Sunset Canyon*?' She took down the last in the row and handed it to Ilkton. 'Perhaps you'd be good enough to escort Mrs Fletcher to her room, as her candle seems to have blown out.'

'Of course.' Accepting his dismissal with a good grace, he went towards the door to the passage. 'Shall we, Mrs Fletcher?'

The door opened before he reached it. In came Simon, frowning. 'What the dev ... deuce is everyone doing in here? Are we having a midnight feast?'

'Don't be sarcastic, Simon,' said his mother. 'Mrs Fletcher and Mr Ilkton are just leaving. What do you want? I take it you haven't decided in a sudden fit of filial piety to read one of your father's books?'

'I've run out of paper. I came to pinch some of Sybil's.'

'You're supposed to buy it out of your allowance.'

Ilkton hastily ushered Daisy out and shut the door behind them. 'Time we were off!' He shone his torch ahead so that she could walk without hesitation into the hall and up the stairs. 'I'm afraid you disapprove of my intrusion into your friend's office.'

'Well, it *was* an intrusion, wasn't it? You're not trying to pretend you considered it a part of the house open to everyone without invitation.'

'No. I confess I was curious. Not on my own behalf. I'm going to marry Myra, and I want to be quite sure nothing here is going to turn up unexpectedly to affect her adversely. Forewarned is forearmed. You must admit it's a rum set-up.'

'I don't know what you mean,' said Daisy untruthfully. 'You're engaged to Myra, are you?'

'Not officially.'

Daisy knew an evasion when she heard one. 'But she hasn't actually accepted you.'

'I can't see that it's actually any of your business.' He stopped at the top of the stairs and turned to her. 'Why shouldn't she? I can give her everything she wants: a comfortable home, thc latest Paris modes, pearls that don't come from Woolworths, not to mention diamonds. And a secure position in the best society.'

'It's none of my business,' Daisy said dryly, noting that he said nothing of love. Did he want her whether she loved him or not?

The best society? She wondered who he was, exactly. Walter Ilkton – she couldn't place him, but she never had taken much interest in pedigrees, nor in the high jinks of high society, as chronicled by Michael Arlen. Lucy would know. She was almost as knowledgeable as her late Great-Aunt Eva had been about the family trees of the aristocracy. Daisy decided to write to her in the morning.

Not that it was any of her business.

She proceeded to her bedroom door. Ilkton shone his torch on the door-knob. 'All right now?'

'Yes, thanks. I left the lamp burning. Next time I go visiting in the wilds of the country, I'll follow your example and bring an electric torch.'

'Can't hurt. Good-night, then.'

'Good-night. Enjoy your book.'

He glanced at the book in his hand as if he'd completely forgotten its existence. 'Oh. Yes. And you yours.'

As she got ready for bed, Daisy pondered the past half hour.

Ilkton's snooping was adequately explained by his obsession with Myra. Having convinced himself that she would marry him, he naturally wanted to know what land-mines might await her unwary feet once she became so notable a personage as his wife. He certainly had a high opinion of himself.

Daisy wondered whether he'd even open the book Ruby had thrust into his hands. Suppose he did start reading it: could it, without comparison to the earlier books, somehow give away the secret of its authorship? At the least, Ruby's intervention might give him the idea that there was a secret to be discovered.

What had Ruby been doing there? If Humphrey was having difficulty falling asleep that night, instead of his usual difficulty staying awake during the day, surely his wife's presence was more likely to hinder than help. Unless she was administering some sort of sedative – which reopened the question of whether she had been drugging him to ensure that Sybil had to write his books for him.

She had been uncharacteristically snappish, almost rude, though exactly how one was supposed to behave on finding guests wandering about late at night as if they owned the place, Daisy wasn't sure. Still, it could be a sign of a guilty conscience.

Ruby had snapped at Simon, too. She hadn't acted like a doting mother who would poison her husband for her son's sake. Did she suspect Simon of being responsible for Humphrey's persistent illness?

Simon's quest for paper, at that time of night, suggested either that his muse had suddenly struck and he intended to burn the midnight oil – literally, in this house – or that he'd needed an excuse for his presence. His age didn't really rule him out as responsible for his father's woes, Daisy realised. Who could tell how long Humphrey's genuine weakness and regular relapses were actually the debilitating after-effects of the serious bout of pneumonia he'd suffered? They must have lasted a year or more to allow time for Sybil's improvements to be noted and rewarded by increased royalties.

By then, Simon must have been at university for some time and have gained some knowledge of the world. He didn't appear to have the slightest respect for his father's writing. He could have hatched a plot to keep Humphrey from picking up his pen again.

Or Humphrey might still be suffering from permanent damage to his system from the original illness.

No nearer an answer to whether Sybil's fears were real or imaginary, Daisy gave up and went to bed. With her toes on the hot water bottle, she picked up *Lonesome Creek.* The pulp paper was already browning at the edges. She handled it with care, afraid of tearing a page.

The book started well. A mysterious wounded stranger rode up to the isolated ranch-house hidden by a bluff, on the bank of the eponymous creek, and found only the rancher's daughter at home. Intrigued, Daisy wanted to know what was going on, but as Sybil had told her, the characters were two-dimensional, hard to care about. It was a description of scenery that made her drowsy, though. It was marvellously vivid, bringing back her memories of the American West, but it went on too long.

And then she woke up, with vague memories of a dream of piloting a biplane through bitterly cold air above Lonesome Creek. She was still sitting up, the lamp was about to flicker out, the hot bottle was barely lukewarm, and the eiderdown had slipped off the bed. She rescued the book before it joined the eiderdown. Try as she might, she couldn't reach the eiderdown without getting out of bed, so her feet were icy, too, by the time she snuggled down.

No Alec to warm her feet on, she thought mournfully, wishing she had stayed at home.

CHAPTER 9

'Absolutely not,' said Ruby Birtwhistle. She stopped pouring, with the coffee-pot poised over Daisy's cup. 'Have you looked out of the window this morning, Myra? If you can see through the frost flowers on the glass, the frost is so thick on the grass it looks almost like snow. The roads are bound to be slippery and motor-bicycles are dangerous at the best of times.'

'You can't stop me. You're not my guardian.'

'Don't be childish. As long as you're under-age and you treat Eyrie Farm as your home, I'm responsible for you when you're here.'

'But— '

'Why don't you come down in the car, Myra,' said Walter Ilkton. 'It's sunny, so by the time we return the frost will have melted and you can ride back on the bike. If Carey chooses to risk his neck going down, that's his lookout.'

'No risk on me own. But 'tis true having a tyro aboard is not the best idea.' Carey grinned at Myra's reproachful look. 'Ye'll not be after knowing how to lean into a curve, Miss Olney?'

'No,' Myra conceded reluctantly.

'We'd land in the ditch at the first bend. I'll teach you, but not on icy roads.'

'Oh, all right. You win, Aunt Ruby.'

'Thank you, gentlemen,' said Mrs Birtwhistle and returned her attention to Daisy's coffee-cup.

Daisy was glad to see that Myra accepted defeat gracefully. Rather than glowering and pouting, she chatted cheerfully with Ilkton and Carey. Sybil and Simon were deep in a discussion of some knotty point of grammar. Norman Birtwhistle always breakfasted early and went off to his farms, Daisy had been told. Today he had already left to drive the farm's lorry to Derby to deliver some lambs to a wholesale butcher.

Lorna had not yet appeared, but she now came in.

As she took her place at the table, she announced in her flat voice, 'I just took Humphrey his breakfast. He says he's getting up this morning.'

'Oh no!' Ruby put her napkin on the table and started to get up, then subsided again with a sigh. 'I do wish he wouldn't. Joining us for dinner last night was almost too much for him. I'm sorry, Mrs Fletcher, you must be heartily sick of the subject, but it's always this way and it's maddening! Whenever he has a good day, he overestimates his strength and overdoes it, then has a relapse. Why are men so obstinate?'

'They see it as being resolute and determined. It's never the slightest use arguing.'

'Don't I know it! It just makes him more pig-headed.'

Ruby went on to enumerate various persuasive arguments she had tried without success. Daisy half listened, while being aware that Lorna's announcement had upset Sybil. Humphrey was certain to disturb her work-day. What if this was the day he decided to kick up a fuss about her writing his stories in her own style? Sybil must be constantly walking on eggshells when he had his good days.

Daisy refused to believe that Sybil herself was responsible for Humphrey's uncertain health. She would never have invited Daisy to come and try to find out whether some sinister plot was under way at Eyrie Farm.

Daisy was more and more inclined to think the only plots in the house were fictional. Why go to all the trouble and risk of putting Humphrey out of action only to let him surface now and then? He might blow the gaff anytime when he was feeling well, so surely his remissions were evidence that his persistent debility was natural.

With no plot to unravel, today she could enjoy the outing to Matlock without worries. To leave tomorrow would look rather rude, but the day after, without fail, she'd go home.

'You'll excuse me, Mrs Fletcher, if I go and see what Humphrey's up to. Perhaps just this once he'll listen to reason.'

'It's worth a try,' Daisy murmured.

'I'll make sure he realises I shan't be here to help if . . . I simply must run some errands. Lorna, I don't suppose you could stay at home?'

'I have errands to run, too.'

'Sybil, do you think you'll be able to manage . . . ?'

'Of course. I can get him back to bed if necessary, with the girls to help and Dr Knox is only a telephone call away.'

'True. I'll go and talk to Humphrey.'

Ruby went off, and Sybil followed a few minutes later, saying to Daisy, 'Till lunchtime. I hope you enjoy seeing Matlock.'

By the time they left for Matlock, the frost that had glittered on the leaves of the sycamores had already melted, though the grass was still white. Myra looked disconsolately after Neil Carey as he zipped off on his green motorbike, but without complaint she climbed into Ilkton's luxurious shiny black Packard, with its gleaming brass. Admittedly that was after a spat with Simon over who was to sit in the front seat beside Ilkton.

'You can sit there on the way home,' she pointed out.

'Perhaps Mrs Fletcher would like to be in front,' said Ruby.

'Not at all,' Daisy disclaimed hastily, 'I'll be very comfortable in the back.'

'And, with the hood down,' Myra said, 'the view will be just as good.'

Everyone was swathed in warm clothes and hats and scarves. The air was cold but not windy and the sun shone. Glad to get away from the tense atmosphere of Eyrie Farm, Daisy looked forward to seeing what sounded like an attractive little town. She settled on the spacious rear seat with Ruby and Lorna, the former with a wicker shopping basket, the latter with a string bag. Very characteristic of each, Daisy thought. Simon perched on a backward-facing folddown seat, one of two, on either side of the padlocked toolbox.

Walter Ilkton was an excellent driver. The heavy car showed no signs of sliding on the slippery slopes, but he drove at a moderate pace, not succumbing to the desire to impress Myra though she exhorted him to try to catch up with Carey.

Now that Daisy wasn't anxiously urging her own car upwards through mists to an unknown destination, she could appreciate the marvellous views. The sheer sweep of hills and dales rolling into the distance formed a backdrop for verges still bright with cranesbill, scabious, harebells and purple thistle.

The bare hills gave way to a narrow wooded valley, steep-sided. They came to Matlock Bath. The main street had buildings on one side and the River Derwent running along the other. On the opposite bank rose a sheer limestone cliff with a railway at its foot that disappeared at one point into a tunnel through an outcrop.

The car slowed, its engine purring softly. Myra knelt backwards on her seat to talk to Daisy. She pointed up the hill behind the buildings, where scattered houses appeared among the trees. 'That's called the Heights of Abraham, that hill. You can walk up and there are two enormous caves you can go into.'

'They used to be mines,' Ruby explained. 'You can see all the different kinds of ore they mined, back to Roman times. It's quite colourful.'

'Have we time to go there?' Daisy asked.

'Not today, I'm afraid. Unless we dropped you off . . .'

'I want to show Mrs Fletcher the view from Smedley's,' Myra objected, 'though the caverns are impressive if you go when they're not full of trippers. Matlock Bath used to be a genteel spa, Byron and Scott and people like that, but now all sorts of common people come in charabancs from Birmingham and Leeds.' She giggled. 'That sounds frightfully snobbish, but you know what I mean. They leave beer bottles and sandwich papers all over the place.'

'Oh, dear,' was the best Daisy could come up with.

'Smedley's Hydro is the place to go now, if you want to drink the water or bathe in it. They use pure spring water off the moor, not the smelly mineral stuff.' She wrinkled her nose. 'Walter's uncle is at Smedley's. Aunt Ruby, has Uncle Humphrey ever tried the water cure? Perhaps he ought to.'

'I've suggested it, but he isn't interested. He's been on the selling side of quack medicines, remember. Besides, Dr Knox is not a believer in the benefits of mineral baths, nor of Smedley's regimen, so he doesn't support the idea.'

'A lot of stuff and nonsense,' Lorna muttered.

'Dr Knox said the tonic he's prescribing now is a last

resort,' said Daisy. 'Perhaps he'll move on to less scientifically proven remedies.'

'Perhaps the stuff Uncle Humphrey's taking now is working,' Myra said buoyantly. 'He was quite chipper last night, for a while.'

'If only he doesn't try to do too much today! Mr Ilkton, is your relative benefiting from his stay at the Hydro?'

'It's keeping him alive, Mrs Birtwhistle. As he's in his nineties, that's no mean feat. He's pretty much settled there for good. I don't think he has much truck with the water cure business, but he likes the Ultra Violet Ray treatment, whatever that may be.'

'It sounds quite alarming!'

'Doesn't it? He seems to enjoy it. He's very comfortable and they take good care of him. Considering his age, he's in good shape, though wandering a bit in his mind. He does still recognise me, I'm happy to say, or did when last I visited. He tends to fall asleep in the middle of a conversation. Just a brief cat-nap, but it's a bit disconcerting.'

'It's kind of you to visit him.'

Ilkton didn't respond, concentrating on the sharp turn onto the bridge over the Derwent. On the far side, the town spread along the bank and straggled up the hill. Near the top, a massive building stretched across the hillside.

'Good gracious,' Daisy exclaimed, 'is that the Hydro up there? I didn't realise it was on such a scale.'

'It's huge. The military took it over during the War, as you might imagine. No one knows quite what they were doing up there, but they had plenty of room for whatever it was. Mr Ilkton, I won't come up with you. Would you mind letting me out in Crown Square?'

'And me,' said Lorna.

Ilkton pulled up by the clock-topped tram shelter in

front of the Crown Hotel. Approaching down the hill was a double-decker tram. As Myra had said, it looked decidedly precarious as it came clanking and grinding down the steep slope. Daisy decided walking down would definitely be the better part of valour.

Myra and her aunts made arrangements for meeting later on, then the two older women went about their business. Simon moved across to the rear seat, beside Daisy.

'I wonder where Neil is?' Myra said.

'You didn't arrange a place to meet?' Simon scoffed. 'How's he going to find us?'

'It's not a very big town,' Ilkton said soothingly. 'He'll find us. Unless he's decided to go off about his own affairs. He doesn't strike me as a particularly reliable type.'

'He wouldn't! He promised to take me home on the motorbike.'

'He knows we're going to the Hydro,' Daisy pointed out. 'He's probably waiting for us there.'

'If he didn't slide off the road and bash up his machine.' Ilkton started the Packard up the hill. The engine's purr became a rumble as it carried them smoothly up the incline. They turned left into Smedley Road, whose whole purpose appeared to be to give access to the hotel and spa.

Close to, the Hydro was even more impressive, a long, five-storey stone building topped by a balustrade on one side of the central tower and crenellations on the other. The car stopped at the main entrance. A uniformed attendant came smartly up to it.

'I'm visiting a resident.' Ilkton got out. 'My friends would like to walk on the promenade terrace.'

As the attendant opened the door for Myra, she said, 'We're expecting to meet a gentleman with a motorbike. Has he arrived?'

'I believe so, miss. A person . . . A gentleman rode up on a green machine a short time ago. I advised him to leave his . . . er . . . outer garments in the cloakroom and await his friends in the lobby.'

Myra giggled. 'Outer garments! I suppose you mean his helmet and leggings. You see, Walter, I knew Neil wouldn't let me down.'

By this time, Simon had handed Daisy down. They went into the reception area, which boasted arches, an elegant staircase up to a surrounding gallery and a palm tree on a pedestal in the middle. Myra spotted Neil at once. He was sitting on the bench that surrounded the palm tree, chatting in the friendliest manner with a middle-aged woman and her pretty daughter, presumably strangers. Myra went straight over to him.

Frowning, Ilkton said to Simon and Daisy, 'I can't very well get away in less than an hour, probably longer. You'd better not wait for me.'

'We never intended to,' Simon pointed out. 'We're going to walk down.'

'Mrs Fletcher, you won't let Myra ride down that hill on the motorbike, will you?'

'I shouldn't think she'll want to, considering what she said about the tram, but if there's any such suggestion I'll do my best to scotch it.'

'Myra will do exactly as she pleases, as usual,' her cousin said.

Seeing Ilkton's frown deepen, Daisy said lightly, 'Are you slighting my powers of persuasion, Simon?'

'Not at all, but to paraphrase that American hit song, if you knew Myra like I know Myra . . .'

'Don't worry, Mr Ilkton, we'll cope with her. I hope you'll find your cousin in good form. We'll see you down in the square.'

'All right. I'll meet you at half past noon, as arranged with Mrs Birtwhistle.'

Daisy smiled at him and he went off looking unhappy.

She thought he ought to look happier, considering Myra had found his rival on excellent terms with another young lady. But when she and Simon joined them, they found that Myra, far from being jealous, had already invited Miss Usher to walk with them on the promenade. Mrs Usher, her mother, had an appointment for a Diathermy Bath, which sounded to Daisy like some form of mediaeval torture.

They went out to the terrace. The air felt decidedly chilly after the warmth of the building. The row of chairs was untenanted as yet.

With an expansive, proprietorial gesture towards the scenery before them, Myra said, 'Look! Isn't it ripping? Some people call it Little Switzerland.'

Daisy duly admired the view. The small town spread down to the bridge and beyond rose hills and cliffs on either side of the winding river, not quite of Alpine magnificence – or Rocky Mountain, come to that – but with its own rugged appeal. Myra and Simon pointed out High Tor and the Heights of Abraham, and farther south, the Black Rocks, though they disagreed about the names of some of the less noteworthy features of the landscape.

'What's that extraordinary castle?' Daisy asked.

'It's not a real castle,' Simon said dismissively.

'Yes it is,' Myra defended the multi-towered monstrosity dominating one of the hills.

'No it's not. Real castles are mediaeval, built for defensive purposes. Riber Castle's Victorian and was never intended as anything other than a grandiose house. It was built by Smedley, the founder of the Hydro, Mrs Fletcher.'

'It looks like a castle to me,' said Carey, smiling at Myra, 'and it's called "Castle", so you're both right. Wouldn't you agree, Miss Usher?'

'Oh yes!'

It was virtually the only thing Daisy had heard her say so far. She was a pretty girl, but pale and washed-out in comparison with Myra's vibrancy.

Carey and the two girls stepped aside as a bundled-up patient was pushed along the terrace in an invalid carriage.

'Carey's trying to make her jealous,' Simon muttered to Daisy. 'Waste of time.'

'Why? You don't think she's interested in him?'

'No idea, but whatever her faults, Myra's not the jealous sort. She has a superabundance of choice, after all. We've had this situation before, what with lovelorn swains "dropping in" and staying for days. Not that I believe Carey's lovelorn.'

'No?' Daisy and Simon followed the others down the steps to the promenade gardens.

'Money's all he's interested in, if you ask me. If he knew hers is all tied up safely so no one can touch the capital . . .'

'You don't rate your cousin's charms very highly.'

'She's all right, and I'm not saying there aren't plenty who do fall for her. I dare say Neil Carey's one of 'em, but he wouldn't stick around if he knew.'

Daisy had already come to the same conclusion. 'Wouldn't it be kind to drop a hint?' she asked.

'Why should I be kind to Carey?'

'I was thinking of Myra.'

Simon cracked a laugh. 'You needn't suppose she's living in cloud-cuckoo land. She's quite shrewd, you know, underneath the fluff. I'd bet all the tea in China she's taken his measure quite accurately.'

They reached the bottom of the steps, where the couple under discussion, plus Miss Usher, were waiting for them.

Daisy saw that the chair-bound patient was halfway down a ramp a little farther along. The Hydro certainly had every amenity and no doubt charged accordingly. Carey could hardly have failed to draw the conclusion that the Ushers were well-off. His attentions to Miss Usher probably had more than one purpose.

Ilkton's aged relative must also be well-to-do, even more so than the Ushers if he could afford to live at the Hydro. On the other hand, by the time he went to his reward he might have spent most of his wealth on hotel bills, which would be hard luck for Ilkton.

Daisy was inclined to credit Ilkton's claim that he was not short of funds. However, no one ever complained of having too much money. It was quite possible that he visited the old man in hopes of inheriting whatever was left when he died, yet was entirely without mercenary motives where Myra was concerned. He loved her, Daisy was certain. Whether his love would last if they married . . . Luckily it wasn't her problem. Nor did Myra seem likely to make up her mind anytime soon.

'Miss Usher, you must be freezing,' Myra exclaimed. 'You should have fetched an outdoor coat.'

'I didn't want to keep you waiting. Perhaps we could walk in the Winter Garden?' she proposed shyly.

'Yes, do let's. It's that building at the end, Mrs Fletcher, the glass one with a dome, not the church.'

'The church is part of the Hydro, too,' Simon said. 'Old Smedley was a Primitive Methodist. They still don't allow alcohol on the premises.'

'Perhaps that's why Ilkton's great-uncle, or whatever relation he is, is still going strong in his nineties,' said Daisy.

Carey laughed. 'I'd rather die young.'

'The motorbike rather gives one that impression,' Simon drawled.

'Don't tell me you wouldn't like one, Si,' said Myra.

'Are they very dangerous?' Miss Usher asked anxiously.

As they strolled on, chattering, Daisy felt more and more chaperonish. She was glad when, after walking the length of the Winter Garden and back, Myra declared herself utterly bored with palm trees. 'Get a coat, Miss Usher,' she urged, 'and come down to the market with us.'

'Oh, I couldn't, not without asking Mother, and I can't talk to her while she's having her treatment.'

'What a shame! Neil, why don't you stay for a bit and keep Miss Usher company? On your motorbike, you'll be there as soon as we are.'

Carey obligingly agreed, claiming to be delighted though looking nonplussed. A few minutes later, Myra, Simon and Daisy set off down the hill.

'You see?' Simon said to Daisy.

'I do,' said Daisy, laughing.

'See what?' Myra demanded.

'Just that you don't particularly care for Carey,' said her cousin.

'I'm very fond of Neil!'

'You aren't exactly heartbroken by his interest in Miss Usher.'

'I didn't say I'm madly in love with him. Besides, he's not really interested in Miss Usher. He's being kind to her and trying to make me jealous.'

Simon and Daisy burst out laughing.

'What's so funny?'

'I told Mrs Fletcher you're not the jealous sort.'

'I can't see the point in it.' Myra frowned. 'Perhaps it's different if you are madly in love, but I never have been. I expect I'm not the falling-in-love sort, either.'

'Give yourself time,' Daisy advised. It looked as if Walter Ilkton was out of luck.

CHAPTER 10

Daisy hadn't visited a country market for some time. She found it interesting poking round the stalls, mostly fruit and vegetables from local farms, but a couple with bric-a-brac and one with artsy-craftsy stuff. She bought knitted caps with pompoms for the twins – blue and grey stripes for Oliver, peach and lavender for Miranda.

'I have to resist the temptation to dress them to match,' she admitted to Myra, who declared the caps perfectly sweet. 'It's easier because they're boy and girl. If they were both the same, I'd probably succumb.'

'I knew twins at school,' said Myra. 'Vanessa and Veronica, can you believe it? They always dressed exactly alike. We always knew which was which but they used to drive some of the teachers mad. I remember Mademoiselle saying in despair, "I do not understand ze English sense of 'umour."'

'It sounds as if you had a good education.'

'Some of my money was set aside for school. Mr Howarth – he's a lawyer and my guardian and trustee, and an absolute sweetie, mostly – he wouldn't let me spend a penny of it on anything else. And now, I can't spend a penny over my allowance. He'd have a fit if I ran up an overdraft! Otherwise he lets me do pretty much what I want, as long as I don't bother him.'

'Isn't it odd that your parents made a lawyer your guardian rather than your uncle?' Daisy said, wondering whether Myra's parents hadn't trusted Humphrey Birtwhistle as trustee of her money.

'Mr Howarth says it's because they were afraid he might pop off back to America.'

'That's a point. Did you dislike your school? Mine was rather a mixed bag. Parts were fun, parts were boring and parts were horrid.'

'Same here! I suppose it was worth it. I learnt deportment and elocution, though the rest of it was rather a waste. And I made lots of good friends.'

'Yes, that's the best part.'

'If it weren't for them, I'd be stuck at Eyrie Farm most of the time. As it is, people invite me to stay and to go to parties, and I meet other people.'

'Such as Walter Ilkton?'

'Yes.' Myra looked guilty. 'I know Aunt Lorna and Uncle Norman hate it when my friends come to stay, but I don't exactly invite them. If they ask for my address to write to, it would be awfully rude to refuse to give it, wouldn't it? It's not as if many come. After all, we're buried in the wilds of Derbyshire. It can be pretty boring, but you mustn't think I'm complaining. One needs some sort of background, to be able to refer to "my family in Derbyshire" and not be a single girl completely unprotected. I'd hate to be all alone in the world, and they're the only family I've got.'

'But not the family you'd choose?'

'No one chooses their family, after all. They're not such bad old sticks, especially Aunt Ruby. Even Simon has his points. Occasionally. And I like Sybil. She's become sort of part of the family. Monica, her little girl, is a darling. Oh, there you are, Simon. Where did you disappear to?'

Simon had played least-in-sight for the past twenty minutes. 'Sorry to desert you, Mrs Fletcher. I popped into the Railway Hotel for a pint, I'm afraid. There's something about going to the Hydro that always gives me a thirst.'

'Because it's teetotal,' Myra helpfully reminded him. 'I'm thirsty, too. I suppose we'd better not venture into the Railway. It's more pub than hotel. We have time for a cup of coffee in a teashop if you'd like, Mrs Fletcher.'

'If Simon will go with you, I'll look round a bit more. I'd like to find something for my stepdaughter.'

'How old is she?'

'Belinda's thirteen.'

'Something pretty,' Myra said, forgetting her thirst. 'A necklace? Look at these beads.'

'Made from local minerals, miss,' said the stall-holder.

'Or this one?' Myra mulled the selection. 'All one colour or varied?'

'I'll leave it to you,' said Daisy. 'She has red hair, so no pink, however good it looks on you.'

Just as Myra at last made a decision, Neil Carey arrived. She pressed a string of blue-and-green azurite beads into Daisy's hand, and she and Simon went to meet him. Daisy paid for the necklace. By the time the stall-holder had wrapped it in tissue-paper, the three had disappeared.

She thrust the necklace into her coat pocket and went looking for them, until she realised that she had no real desire to find them. Crown Square, where they were to meet Walter Ilkton and the car, was not far away. She wandered in that direction, looking in shop windows, until she saw Ruby Birtwhistle come out of a chemist's, tucking a small packet into her overflowing shopping basket. Crossing the street, Daisy joined her.

'Have you lost the others, Mrs Fletcher?'

'I'm not sure whether I lost them or they lost me, not that it matters. Mr Carey turned up and Simon and Myra went over to him. Next time I looked they were gone.'

'That wretched girl! Simon should know better.'

'Myra was very helpful in choosing a present for my daughter. I expect they were caught up in the excitement of Myra's bike ride and simply failed to realise I wasn't with them. No doubt they're now sneaking into one of the hotels by the back way so that Myra can put on her riding outfit.'

'I do hope she'll be safe!'

'I'm sure Carey will go carefully.' *Whether motivated by love or money*, Daisy thought, but didn't say. 'That basket looks awfully heavy. Let me carry it for you.'

'No, no, it's not so bad, and I'm used to it. Tradesmen just won't deliver to the farm.'

'Too far from town, I suppose.'

Ruby nodded resignedly. 'Luckily Norman manages to provide a large proportion of our necessities, between the home farm and the tenants. He's a very good farmer and estate manager. There's always a few things that have to be bought, though. We've had house keepers in the past who'd do the shopping, but they never stayed long. Servants don't like living in such an isolated spot with no bus service. Let's just pop in here for a cup of coffee while we wait for Mr Ilkton. Usually I can drop off stuff in the car, but I was afraid Myra would go off on the motor-bicycle on the slippery roads if we didn't come in the Packard. It's much grander than our old Jowett.'

They went into a small, rather frilly tea-shop. Daisy looked round, but either Myra had forgotten her thirst in the excitement of Carey's arrival, or they had chosen a different establishment. A frilly waitress came over.

'Morning, Mrs Birtwhistle.'

'Good morning, Maisie. Coffee for two, please. Will you have something to eat, Mrs Fletcher?'

'Not for me, thanks.' Daisy hoped Ilkton would not be late and lunch would be ready when they got back to the farm. 'Myra must be quite a responsibility,' she went on when the waitress left. 'I gather she pretty much goes her own way.'

'She's a handful,' Ruby admitted, 'a flibbertigibbet. Self-willed. But she's never out of temper and she's not completely devoid of common sense. She's surprisingly good about letting us know where she is. Her friends seem to be respectable people, thank goodness.'

'That must be a relief.'

'Very much so. One hears such dreadful tales of what goes on in some circles of society. I'm very fond of Myra. It would be wonderful if she decided to settle down with Walter Ilkton. He seems to be a steady character, who would take care of her and not be too upset by her whims. I think he's truly smitten with her, as we used to say in my young days.'

'So do I.'

Their coffee arrived, and the subject was dropped. They talked, inevitably, about the Hydro, and Daisy showed the presents she had bought for the children.

When they reached Crown Square, Ilkton was just arriving. Lorna Birtwhistle was waiting on a bench, and Simon stood some distance from his aunt. Myra and Carey had already gone off together.

'She wanted to show him Riber Castle, and he said he'd take her on a scenic tour,' said Simon, shrugging. 'They promised to be home for lunch.'

Ilkton's lips tightened, but there was nothing he could do about it. He and Simon stowed the two shopping baskets and helped the ladies in, and they drove back to Eyrie Farm.

Myra and Carey had not yet returned. Daisy went up to her room to wash off the inevitable road-dust and tidy her hair.

When she went down to the hall, the missing pair had arrived. Myra, nonchalant in dungarees and leathers, was telling Ilkton about her adventures. Simon, meanwhile, had decided riding a motorcycle was an essential part of the experience necessary to a serious novelist and was trying to persuade Carey to take him out that afternoon.

Ruby came in and sent Myra to change. Carey, whose trousers showed the effects of riding without leathers, apologised and hurried off to clean up. Next to appear was Sybil. Ruby pounced on her. 'Humphrey isn't in his room. Has he been up all morning?'

'He got up quite late and he won't join us for lunch.' Sybil noticed Ilkton's presence and lowered her voice as she continued to report on Humphrey's health and activities.

Daisy helped by asking Ilkton how he had found his aged relative. As a diversionary tactic it worked, though, after saying briefly that his cousin was unchanged since his last visit, Ilkton moved on to ask Daisy's opinion of ladies wearing trousers and riding motorbikes.

'I don't know about motorbikes. I've never ridden one. From watching, I should think they're too heavy for most women to cope with alone. But I don't see why women shouldn't wear trousers.'

'Hear hear,' Simon put in. 'Some women have better things to think about than clothes, so why shouldn't they wear whatever's most convenient?'

'Oh, intellectuals!' said Ilkton dismissively. 'I'm talking about ladies of fashion.'

'My friend Lucy, Lady Gerald Bincombe, was a Land Girl during the War. She couldn't have managed the work in a skirt.' No need to mention that Lucy had loathed both the work and the trousers! 'I've heard they wear beach pyjamas on the Riviera, and I have friends in Chelsea who wear evening pyjamas to parties. Then there's jodhpurs for riding, of course.'

Uninterested after putting in his two-pennyworth, Simon had mooched off to join his mother and Sybil. Daisy managed to keep Ilkton occupied with talk of the horrors of hoops, crinolines, bustles and the 'S-Bend' beloved of the Edwardians. Luckily Myra came down quite quickly, so Daisy no longer felt responsible for entertaining him.

After lunch, Sybil told Daisy that Humphrey was taking a nap. '"Forty winks," he said. I do hope that's all it is – I mean, that he's still feeling well when he wakes up.' She was outwardly calm, but Daisy could see she was suppressing strong emotions. 'He said, since the weather's lovely and may not last, and I have a friend staying, I should take a couple of hours off and go for a walk. Do you feel like it? There are some beautiful footpaths round here, but perhaps you've already had your fill of views for the day.'

'I'm dying for a chance to talk to you. Let's go.'

CHAPTER 11

A footpath led through the copse and up the hill. A stone wall ran along the ridge, with slabs sticking out where it crossed the path, to form a stile. Climbing it, with Sybil's hand to steady her, Daisy said acerbically, 'Here's something else that would be so much easier in trousers!'

Scattered sheep grazed the downward slope of a narrow valley. Away to their right, halfway up the opposite slope, crouched a small farm house with a few outbuildings. The song of an invisible skylark poured down, reminding Daisy of Vaughan Williams's *The Lark Ascending*, one of her favourite pieces. That made her think of Alec, whose irregular hours made it impossible to attend as many concerts as they would have liked. She wished he were at her side, striding down the slanting path, instead of Sybil.

Not that she hadn't come to like Sybil, and admire her talent, but she didn't like at all the situation she'd been landed in. She had to admit, though, that her own insatiable curiosity was equally to blame.

She looked up, trying to spot the lark, but all she saw was a buzzard turning lazy circles across the sky.

'I feel so beastly!' Sybil burst out. 'Whenever he's feeling better, half of me wants him to recover completely, but the other half worries about what on earth we'll all do if he does!'

Daisy patted her shoulder. 'It's only natural. What happened this morning? Did he want to see what you'd been writing?'

'No, he was too busy explaining a couple of ideas he'd come up with for twists in the plot, and the scenes needed to carry them out, as well. They're terrific.'

'Did he used to discuss ideas with you when he was doing all the writing and you were just typing it up?'

'Never. He'd just hand me the pages and I'd get on with it. Now everything's such a mess,' Sybil said wretchedly, 'I don't see any way out.'

'I don't believe it's as bad as that. Suppose he makes a complete recovery. Why can't you just go on working in partnership? Why should it matter if the publisher finds out? Surely all they're interested in is sales figures. You'd just have to make sure it didn't leak out to the reading public.'

'Perhaps. It's the uncertainty that's so hard to bear.'

'Isn't it always.'

'You must be bored to tears with my troubles. Tell me about your outing. Were Ilkton and Carey at each other's throats?'

'Not at all. Carey goes his merry way without much concern for what anyone thinks.'

'Just like Myra.'

'But I wouldn't call Myra mischievous, whereas Carey has more than a touch of the mischief-maker in him, if you ask me.'

'That's obvious from his writing plays shut down by the censors. He can't possibly make any money from them.'

'I imagine he lives a fairly hand-to-mouth existence. Ruby's convinced he's after Myra's money, which I dare say is true.'

'A fruitless pursuit!'

Daisy laughed. 'So I hear. If you ask me, he's just flirting for the sake of baiting Ilkton.'

'And Ilkton?'

'I'm pretty sure she's caught him if she wants him.'

'*If*. "Ay, there's the rub."'

'I'm fairly certain she doesn't. But he acts as if he's very confident of winning her.'

'Could they have a secret understanding?'

'Why? I mean, why secret? All I've heard is approval, no opposition.'

'Because Myra would consider it romantic? Playing the starcrossed lover. I can just imagine her fabricating some romantic fiction for his benefit. That the family want to keep her income in their hands, or something like of the kind.'

Daisy shook her head. 'I'd be surprised. You know her better than I do, of course, but I don't see her as either being a secret romantic or fabricating lies about the family.'

'You're right. She's really rather pragmatic and practical.' Sybil sighed. 'I'm the romantic.'

'Imaginative, rather. Besides, she's attached to the family in her way. Her practical way. They're her "background", she told me.'

'Background?' Sybil sounded surprised. 'What did she mean by that?'

'Without them, she'd be a floating single young woman without roots, and as such, not quite respectable. At her age, not at all respectable in many eyes. The family are her roots, her anchor, her ballast, whatever you want to call it. Her respectable background.'

'Is that all they are to her, after all they've done for her!'

'Heavens no. She's fond of Ruby and Humphrey, and even Simon "at times".'

'At times?' said Sybil with a smile. 'There is the odd moment when they aren't quarrelling.'

'And she likes you and Monica.'

'She does? I didn't know. I've never paid her much attention.'

'As much as anyone, I expect. She can't be described as a poor relation, but she's rather the odd man out.'

'Yes. Poor girl! I must make a point of being kinder to her. Though, I must say, she seems to have talked to you a lot more than she's ever talked to me.'

'People do. Don't ask me why.'

They walked on for a while in silence, then Sybil said, 'You know, the family may be useful to Myra, but the reverse is true, too. Her visits liven the place up no end, and Monica adores her.'

They started talking about their children.

By the time they returned towards Eyrie Farm, by a different path, Daisy was warm with exertion. The sun still shone, though a knee-high mist was rising from the grass. From this direction, the home farm buildings behind the house were visible – an empty sheep-pen, stables, sheds, a low barn and a walled kitchen-garden. A couple of Clydesdales grazed in a paddock. They paused at the top of the hill to watch a small, new-looking lorry with wood-slat sides buzz over the bridge towards the house.

'Norman's home,' said Sybil.

'Nice new lorry.'

'Second hand, but his pride and joy.'

'Bought with money from your books?'

'Partly. Luckily there's not much in the way of field crops so he doesn't need a tractor. But it's not really fair to look at it that way. The household expenses would shoot up without his contributions in kind, and he runs the estate.'

'I'd hate to be in charge of the household accounts,' said Daisy, who hated being in charge of her own household accounts.

'He does the farm accounts and Ruby does the rest. I used to keep the books straight on royalties and so on, but Ruby's taken them over since . . . my duties expanded. I've no idea how she and Norman work things out together—'

'With difficulty, I'm sure.'

'Let alone how Lorna's share in the farm comes into it all. Not my business, thank heaven.'

'As long as you're being paid your proper share of the royalties.'

Sybil shrugged. 'Who's to say what's proper? I'm satisfied. Lorna's the one who's never satisfied. How can she still – after thirty years – resent Humphrey coming home to claim his share!'

'Norman doesn't?'

'Who knows? I'd guess he'd be silent and morose under any circumstances. That's just the way he is. He and Lorna are really the flies in the ointment, as far as the dismal atmosphere in the house is concerned. Simon can be tiresome but at least he's rarely sulky.'

At that moment came a loud hail from behind. They both swung round to see Simon and Carey panting up the hill towards them.

'Bejabers, you ladies are fast walkers!'

'We thought we'd join you and we've been trying to catch up. Didn't you see us waving?'

'We were talking,' said Sybil.

'About our children,' Daisy added hurriedly, to forestall enquiries. 'Oh dear, I've even forgotten to admire the scenery!'

'Sure and you fulfilled that obligation this morning at the Hydro, Mrs Fletcher,' Carey consoled her.

'Was Myra too worn out from the motorbike ride to come with you?' Sybil asked.

'We didn't invite her.' Simon grinned. 'I persuaded Carey it was Ilkton's turn to enjoy her undivided attention for a while. Neil has the unfair advantage of the motorbike.'

'Unfair! Wasn't I after choosing the bike to give the colleens a thrill.'

'No. You bought it because it's cheaper than a car.'

'Alack, I am unmasked!' Carey said mock-mournfully. ''Tis true. 'Tis also true that after one ride most young ladies walk bowlegged for three days and choose the Packard next time!'

They all laughed as they walked down the hill.

Norman was in the yard behind the house, sweeping out the back of the lorry. Though he must have heard them, he didn't look round.

'Need any help, Uncle Norman?'

'That'll be the day! You might dirty your hands.'

Simon pulled a rueful face. They went on towards the house, Carey and Sybil ahead.

Simon said to Daisy, 'You must think we're a strange family, Mrs Fletcher.'

'All families are strange in their own ways, though different would be a better word.'

'You disagree with Tolstoy, then?'

Daisy racked her brains, without result. 'Is that *War and Peace*? I'm afraid I've always been daunted by the sheer size of it.'

'*Anna Karenina*. "Happy families are all alike; every unhappy family is unhappy in its own way."'

'I'd have to think about it. Do you consider your own family happy or unhappy?'

'Well, we can't be called happy, with my father ill and my

uncle and aunt always grumpy. But we rub on together all right, on the whole.'

'Not unhappy enough to provide material for a novel?'

'Insufficient *angst*.' He gave her an expectant look.

'If you're trying to depress my intellectual pretensions,' Daisy said tartly, 'you might as well give up. I haven't any. But I do happen to know what angst means, only because a friend of mine is an eternal student. She goes to lectures constantly. Psychology is one of her favourite subjects, and she passes on vast quantities of what she learns. Not all of it sails unheeded by my ears.'

He grinned. 'Sorry. You must admit, it's a very frustrating situation. You don't happen to know any angst-ridden families you could introduce me to, do you?'

'If I did, I wouldn't. The last thing an unhappy family needs is a stranger dropping in to take notes.'

'Isn't that what you're doing?'

Daisy sternly quelled a blush. 'Certainly not. As you've pointed out, yours is not an unhappy family.'

'Touché! You don't mind coming in through the kitchen, do you?'

'Perfect. I'm dying of thirst and that sounds like the place to get a glass of water!'

'I'll make tea. I could do with a cup. Can't wait till tea-time.'

'Lovely,' said Daisy. Simon had his points. He wasn't such a complete pill after all. 'Sybil and Mr Carey would probably like some, too.'

Bearing tea, they went through to the hall, chilly after the warm kitchen with its huge coal-fired range.

Myra greeted them with a cry of, 'Angels! I can't possibly sew and drink tea at the same time. Aunt Lorna gave me this positive mound of mending to do.' She gestured with needle and thread at the clothes hamper beside her chair. 'Walter has been reading the social news to me, but it just makes me wish I were there.'

Ilkton, standing up, waved the copy of the *Morning Post* he'd acquired at the Hydro. 'My throat's dry from reading,' he said. 'We started out with the Hydro's handbook. You simply would not believe how many different water and electrical treatments they offer, not to mention the various types of massage.'

'I'd love a quick cup before I go back to work,' said Sybil.

'I'll go and get more cups,' Carey offered. 'And hot water.'

When Sybil left, Daisy slipped out with her, feeling she'd like a little peace and quiet. 'I'm going to go and read *Halfbreed Hero* in my room.'

'Why don't you use my sitting room? You'll be more comfortable. There's a patchwork quilt you can wrap up in if you feel chilly.'

'All right, thanks. Sybil, I'm thinking of going home the day after tomorrow. Humphrey's doing well, you're busy, and I really don't think I'm doing anything to help you.'

Sybil's face fell. 'I'm sorry. You're having a very dull time.'

'It's not that. I've enjoyed myself – the card game last night, the outing this morning, our walk and getting to know you better. But I hate being away from the twins for long, and, as I said, I don't feel I'll be helping you by staying longer.'

'You have helped me. It's obvious I was imagining things. As Roger says, Humphrey's just never quite recovered from his debility after the pneumonia. We can only hope the improvement will continue this time, and if it does, face the consequences.'

'I'm sure you'll go on being a good partnership. He's getting older, after all. He'll be glad to leave most of the work to you.'

'And I'd better be getting on with it. Deadlines wait for no man – nor woman, either. I'll see you later.'

Daisy collected the book from her room and retired to a comfortable chaise longue in Sybil's sitting room. Within a few pages, she understood what Sybil had tried to explain. The descriptions of scenery were just as vivid as those in *Lonesome Creek*, but much less wordy. More important as far as Daisy was concerned – because one could always skim wordy passages – was that the characters were not stick figures, going through the motions for the sake of the plot. They came to life on the page and engaged her interest. She cared what happened to them. She could see why it would appeal to a wider audience than Humphrey Birtwhistle's straightforward adventure yarns.

She tried to work out what Sybil had done to make the difference, then gave up and lost herself in the story.

When Sybil came to ask if she was coming down to tea, she said, 'I'm very much enjoying your book, but I'm ready for another cup of tea. Did Humphrey reappear?'

'Oh yes. He's in fine fettle and full of ideas. He'll be joining everyone for tea.'

Daisy was torn between saying, 'Marvellous!' and 'I'm so sorry.' It must be very wearing for those in the know about the situation always to have mixed emotions about Humphrey's health.

Myra appeared to be unfeignedly pleased. She was stiff from riding the motorbike, and her uncle teased her about cowgirls in the Wild West who spent all day in the saddle. She played up to him charmingly.

Daisy watched Ilkton becoming ever more besotted. Carey, sitting on the hearth rug playing with the dog's ears and slipping him the odd tidbit, seemed thoroughly amused.

The evening passed much the same as the previous day, except that Roger Knox didn't arrive until after dinner.

While Ruby was greeting him, Daisy whispered to Sybil, 'Does he call on all his patients daily?'

Sybil blushed. 'He doesn't usually come so often, but when there's any change, for better or worse, he likes to keep a close eye on things.'

Humphrey was still up, sipping a second or third pink gin. 'Later,' he said to the doctor.

He and Ruby stayed by the fire, talking quietly, Ruby knitting as usual. Myra inveigled the others – Lorna and Norman having retired already – into playing Happy Families. Daisy didn't notice that Humphrey had retired until Ruby came over and quietly told Roger Knox his patient was ready to see him.

The doctor randomly distributed his hand among the other players. As he and Ruby left, Daisy heard Ruby say, 'He suddenly got very sleepy, and a bit dizzy.'

Knox said something reassuring that Daisy couldn't hear, and they went out.

They weren't gone long. When they returned, a hand had just finished, and by mutual consent, they stopped playing. Simon gathered up the pack of cards and shuffled them.

'Cocoa anyone?' asked Simon. 'It's a chilly night.'

Several people accepted, including Daisy.

'Not for me, thanks,' said Knox. 'I'd better be on my way. It was beginning to get foggy when I came up.'

'You always burn the milk, Si,' Myra grumbled. 'I'd better come and keep an eye on things.'

Ilkton and Carey went off to the kitchen with them. The doctor donned coat and hat and said good-night. Sybil accompanied him to the front door, where they stood talking in low voices for a few minutes.

Ruby picked up her knitting and counted stitches. Daisy waited till she launched the next row, then asked, 'What was it like being a schoolmistress in the Wild West? Was it a one-room school?'

'Oh yes,' Ruby answered absently, her mind elsewhere. Not on her knitting, Daisy guessed, as the needles clicked on automatically and what appeared to be a navy blue sleeve grew before her eyes. 'I had children of all ages crammed onto benches,' Ruby went on, speaking as if she had been asked the question so often she knew the answer by heart, 'some of them bored to tears and others who had ridden miles for the chance to learn.'

Daisy was about to ask what subjects Ruby had taught when an influx of cold, damp air drew her attention towards the front door. A main sitting room that was also the entrance hall had major disadvantages.

'You can't drive in that fog!' Sybil exclaimed, closing the door with a determined thud.

'I'm on call tonight,' said Roger Knox. 'I expect it's clear lower down.'

'There are plenty of other doctors in Matlock. Ring up and get someone to cover for you.'

'Plenty of doctors, but most are busy enough with patients at the hydros and won't answer calls beyond the town. My usual stand-by man is away for a couple of days. In fact, I'm supposed to take his emergencies tonight.'

'I'm sure you can find someone.'

'Make as many telephone calls as you need to, Roger,' said Ruby, putting down the knitting. 'Of course you must stay. I'll go and make up a bed.'

'Can I help?' Daisy offered.

'Thank you, but I'll get Myra from the kitchen. Simon's perfectly capable of making cocoa without assistance.'

Roger went to the telephone. Sybil came over to the fire and held out her hands to it.

'It's like a wall of cotton-wool out there. You could barely see the porch posts, all of four feet away. I couldn't let him drive in it! Did I sound like a nagging wife?'

'Hardly at all,' Daisy said with a smile.

'Oh dear!'

The doctor was still on the phone when Simon bore in a large jug of cocoa. Ilkton followed with a tray of mugs, and Carey with a plate of home-made shortbread. They looked like a parade of servants in a mediaeval tapestry of a banquet. Ilkton's usual smooth façade seemed a bit ruffled. Perhaps he saw himself part of some similar faintly ridiculous image. Or perhaps he had quarrelled with Carey, or Myra had said something that shook his certainty that she'd marry him in the end. Possibly he was just annoyed because she wasn't there to see him being helpful.

Carey was his usual blithe, unconcerned self. 'I rooted about in the biscuit tins and came up with these,' he said. 'Isn't it after reminding me of midnight feasts in the dorm.'

'Oh? Which school were you at?' Ilkton asked, his tone unpleasant. The way he phrased the question suggested only a very few schools were worth mentioning.

'None you'd ever have heard of,' Carey told him with an easy laugh.

'I thought not.'

Warming her hands on her mug of cocoa, Daisy hoped she wasn't going to have to listen to their sniping at each other for the rest of the evening. With luck, Ilkton would stop provoking trouble when Myra returned. Not that Carey's good temper showed any sign of crumbling, thank goodness.

Sybil took a mug over to Roger Knox. As she reached

him, he hung up the receiver and stood up. They came back together to the fireside, both smiling.

'You found someone,' said Daisy.

'Dr Harris. He took some persuading. He's on the elderly side so I can't blame him for not liking to turn out at night, even though he says it's clear down below. Then I had to ring my house keeper. Thanks for the cocoa, Simon.'

A few minutes later, Myra returned. 'You're all fixed up, Dr Knox. The room next to Mrs Fletcher's. Any cocoa left, Simon?'

'Nothing but the dregs.'

'Bother. I'll go and make some more for Aunt Ruby and me. She popped in to see if Uncle Humphrey needs anything.'

'I'll come and help,' said Neil Carey. Ilkton glared at him but didn't offer to go with them.

They were heading towards the back of the hall when Ruby came in from the east wing. She looked ghastly.

'Roger!' she cried. 'Humphrey's not breathing and I can't feel a pulse. He won't wake up. Come quickly!'

CHAPTER 12

Everyone stared blankly at Ruby Birtwhistle, except the doctor. He sprang to his feet, saying, 'I'm sure he's just very deeply asleep, but of course I'll check at once.' He strode out, Ruby trotting to keep up.

Just before she turned the corner, she looked back. 'Simon?'

'Coming, Mother.'

A tense silence enveloped those left behind. Daisy met Sybil's eyes and saw there a reflection of her own horror. Could it be that Sybil's suspicions were justified?

Myra broke the silence. 'Poor Uncle Humphrey,' she wailed. 'To think that he was feeling so full of beans just today!' She burst into tears and sobbed noisily, with abandon, like a small child.

Carey, on one side of her on the sofa, felt in his pockets, shrugged. On the other side, Ilkton whipped out a large, spotless linen handkerchief and pressed it into her hand.

Daisy had an almost irresistible urge to suggest a soothing cup of tea, but on top of the cocoa they had just drunk, it probably wasn't such a good notion.

Sybil got up and crossed to the sofa, saying, 'Excuse me, gentlemen.' When they rose and moved away, she sat down beside Myra and took her hands. 'Darling, it's not certain he's . . . gone. It's possible Ruby made a mistake, or

Roger will find a way to revive your uncle. He's a very good doctor.'

'I know he is, but …' Myra buried her face in Sybil's shoulder.

While Sybil murmured soothingly in Myra's ear, Ilkton and Carey came over to Daisy. Carey took a seat. Ilkton stood on the hearth rug, vacated by Scurry, who had doubtless gone with Norman.

'We ought to leave,' said Ilkton, shifting uneasily from foot to foot. 'Mrs Birtwhistle won't want guests underfoot at a time like this.'

'Fog,' Carey reminded him.

'Damn the fog! I beg your pardon, Mrs Fletcher, but it's an awkward situation.'

'I'm sure Mrs Birtwhistle wouldn't expect you to leave tonight, even without the fog, and no matter what's happened.'

He started to pace, head turned to keep an eye on the pair on the sofa. 'I'd like to take Myra out of it, drive her up to town.'

'You can't do that,' said Carey, startled and disapproving. 'She's family. She can't leave now.'

Daisy nodded agreement, her opinion of him going up a notch, and of Ilkton down a notch.

'She's not going to be much support to anyone. The poor child needs to be supported, and no one here's going to have time for her.'

'I shall. I can't see Mrs Birtwhistle throwing me out.' Carey lounged back in his chair, gazing up at his would-be rival. 'You can leave in the morning, fog willing. I'm staying.'

'So am I,' said Daisy. 'At least until I'm sure I can't help. Myra will decide for herself, but I don't think she'll want to desert her family.'

'Certainly not. Hasn't she more spunk than you give her credit for, Ilkton.'

Ilkton's lips tightened. Daisy was afraid he was ripe to escalate the sniping into open hostilities, but after a moment, he sat down without speaking. His fingers beat a tattoo on his expensively clad knee.

'She's had a nasty shock,' Daisy pointed out. Though it made her feel ancient, she went on, 'The young tend to see people close to them as immortal. She'll be all right.'

Neither of the men responded, and Daisy was quite glad not to have to talk. Myra's sobs had subsided to sniffs. She and Sybil talked quietly, their words for the most part indistinguishable. Daisy wondered if her casual words about no one in the household paying much attention to the girl had borne fruit already.

The only other sound was an occasional crackle or hiss from the fire. Ilkton went back to the hearth and stood leaning with one arm on the mantel, head bowed, staring into the flickering flames.

Approaching footsteps sounded loud. Everyone turned to look. Simon came in. His face was very pale, set in an expression of disbelief.

With a wordless cry, Myra jumped up and ran to him. 'Oh, Simon!' She clutched him.

Somewhat to Daisy's surprise, he put his arms round her and hugged her. He seemed unable to speak.

'Brandy!' said Carey.

'I'll get it.' Ilkton went towards the sideboard, twin of the one in the dining room, where the drinks were kept.

'No! No, I don't want it. I'm all right.' Simon came to the fire, his arm still round Myra's shoulders. After what seemed like a long pause, he said in a strange voice, 'Father's dead. And Knox won't give a certificate.'

'A certificate?' Myra sounded frightened. 'What does that mean?'

No one seemed inclined to tell her, so Daisy explained. 'When someone dies, a doctor has to issue a certificate listing the cause of death. If he's not sure, he won't sign it.'

'But Uncle Humphrey was ill.'

'Not of anything that could have killed him,' said Simon, achieving a normal tone with a heroic effort. 'At least, that's what Dr Knox thinks. He says he never did achieve a satisfactory diagnosis of what ailed Father.'

'It might have been a heart attack or a stroke,' Sybil suggested, almost hopefully. 'He wasn't a young man.'

'That's what he said. But he can't tell from a superficial examination, and he wants to be certain.'

'Does that mean they'll . . .' Myra's horrified voice trailed off.

'Yes,' her cousin told her savagely. 'They'll cut—'

'Simon!' Sybil cut him off.

'Sorry.' He passed his hand over his face. 'I'm just about done in. I'll take that brandy after all, Ilkton.'

Ilkton seemed no longer eager to oblige. 'What about Mrs Birtwhistle?' he asked, frowning.

'Poor Aunt Ruby!'

'Knox is taking care of her,' said Simon, flopping into a chair as Carey went to fetch the brandy. 'She's pretty shattered, of course. I think he's taken her up to her room.'

'I must go and help her,' Myra declared, and whisked out.

Sybil looked at Daisy. 'Do you think I ought—'

'Let Myra do it. Feeling useful will help her, I expect. Ruby will send her away if she doesn't want her.'

'Heavens, I've just thought: what about Lorna and Norman?'

'*I'm* not telling them!' Simon took a gulp of the brandy

Carey put in his hand. 'Thanks, Neil. I can't see any need to wake Uncle Norman and Aunt Lorna. They'll find out soon enough. And won't they be happy!'

'Simon!' Sybil protested.

'Well, they will. They've always wished he hadn't come back from America alive. Not that they'll have anything to gloat about. I suppose Mother or I will inherit his share of the farm. I could live happily without ever seeing the place again.'

Daisy began to fidget. She knew what the next move should be, but she didn't want to be the first to mention the police.

'Would you like me to tell them?' Sybil offered – very nobly, Daisy felt. 'Lorna and Norman, I mean. He's their brother, after all.'

'No need,' Simon insisted, slurring a bit now, after finishing off the brandy with a third gulp. On top of the shock of his father's death, it was enough to befuddle a stronger head than his. 'Why spoil their sleep? They're always complaining about how hard they work. Leave 'em to get their rest while they can.'

'I suppose it won't hurt to wait till the morning.'

'No. And it won't hurt to wait till morning to call in Dr Harris and the coppers. They can't get here in this damn fog anyway.'

'The coppers!' Carey exclaimed.

'Didn't I tell you? Dr Knox sent me to ring the police. Standard procedure when the cause of death is uncertain. We're going to have bloody coppers crawling all over the house tomorrow. Won't that make Uncle Norman and Aunt Lorna happy!'

'All the same,' Sybil advised, 'you'd better ring them up right away.'

'Why the hell should I?'

'You're not thinking clearly, Simon. Which is very understandable in the circumstances, but not at all helpful. The last thing we want to do is antagonise the police before they even begin "crawling all over the house". Can't you see, if there's something the least bit fishy about your father's death, they're going to start with the assumption one of us here at Eyrie Farm must be involved?'

CHAPTER 13

'Mrs Sutherby's right,' said Neil Carey. 'The sooner you notify the police the better.'

'I can't see that it makes much difference.' Ilkton was uneasy. Naturally he hadn't expected his pursuit of Myra to lead him into such troubled waters. 'There's nothing fishy about it. It was surely a heart attack or a stroke.'

'We can't be sure. Ring up *now*, Simon.' Sybil looked to Daisy, who nodded confirmation, hoping it looked like mere agreement.

She managed not to say anything about obstructing the police in the course of their duties, which would be liable to give away an unseemly familiarity with police procedure. The less the local force knew about her connection with Scotland Yard, the better. They were apt to be very touchy at the slightest hint that the Yard might find an excuse to trespass on their territory.

And Alec's boss, Superintendent Crane, was apt to be very touchy at the slightest hint that Daisy had got herself involved yet again in anything remotely criminal.

Roger Knox came in. 'Did you get through already, Simon? Is Harris coming?'

'I haven't tried yet,' Simon said sulkily.

Taking in the empty brandy glass at a glance, the doctor

laid a hand on his shoulder. 'No, I'm sorry, it was too much to ask. You're in shock. Now I've settled your mother – and Myra is looking after her surprisingly competently, I must say – I'll do it myself.'

'Roger . . .' Sybil hesitated. 'I suppose you can't tell us any more about . . . what's happened?'

'The less said the better, I think,' he said gently, 'until the police get here.'

'But that won't be till the morning!'

'I'll try to persuade them to get a move on.'

'The fog . . .'

'Haven't you looked out of a window recently? The fog is clearing. I shouldn't be surprised if we have rain before morning. There's nothing to stop them coming tonight – other than indolence. I must get another doctor here quickly, though. Simon— No. Carey, do you know how to deal with an oil lantern? Would you mind lighting the one in the porch?'

'Sure and I'll do it this minute, Doctor.'

'Thank you. Excuse me.' He went to the telephone.

Carey crossed to the front door. Beside it, on a small table stood an unlit lantern. 'This is it, I take it?'

'That's the one,' Sybil told him. She went over to help. 'There's a pole in a bracket on the wall, just behind the edge of the curtain— Yes, that's it, for lifting the lantern to its hook outside. Have you got matches?'

'In my pocket. Here.' Carey handed her a matchbox to hold while he opened the lantern.

Daisy tried to ignore them and listen to the doctor. The Matlock operator must have answered promptly, because a moment later Knox asked for the police station.

'Sorry,' said Sybil, 'I don't have much to do with the house-keeping. Simon, where's the lamp-oil kept?'

'Huh?'

'The lantern's low on oil.' Carey came over, carrying it. 'Be a good chap and show me where to refill it.'

Simon levered himself out of his chair and the two men went through to the back regions. Sybil left the matches on the table by the door and sat down again with Daisy and Ilkton.

Meanwhile, Knox had been speaking in a low voice and Daisy, to her annoyance, had missed what he was saying.

Ilkton, silent for some time, now said, 'I'm afraid you've lost your employment, Mrs Sutherby.' He didn't sound very interested.

'Eventually, yes, but I'll finish what I'm working on now. And I expect Mrs Birtwhistle will need help dealing with Humphrey's papers. I can't worry about that now. Poor Ruby! I must admit, Myra seems to have turned up trumps. I wouldn't have thought she had it in her.'

'Everyone here underestimates Myra. I've noticed it. She may be what they call a "bright young thing" in town, but she's not one of these brittle, shallow girls who care for nothing and nobody. Unlike most, she's very well-mannered and sweet-tempered . . .'

Daisy tuned out his catalogue of Myra's virtues like an unwanted wireless station, straining her ears to pick up Roger Knox's words. He was still talking too quietly, until he said with irritated emphasis, '*I* am the local police surgeon, Sergeant. I want a second opinion.'

Then he lowered his voice again. Ilkton was still boring on about Myra, with Sybil throwing in an occasional absent-minded comment as if to keep him talking so that she could think about other matters.

Daisy tossed in an innocuous remark to help keep the pot boiling. Just as her attention returned to the doctor, he said loudly, 'Yes, Scotland Yard, dammit, man! A detective chief inspector. So if you're calling in your inspector from Derby, you'd better . . .' Once again he lowered his voice.

Daisy fixed an accusing glare on Sybil. After swearing not to reveal Alec's profession to a soul, she had told her Roger! Her apologetic look showed she, too, had heard what he said.

They couldn't have it out in Ilkton's presence. At least he seemed to be winding down at last.

'So, obviously, she's much too sensitive to have to deal with cloddish policemen. As neither of us had anything to do with whatever happened to Birtwhistle, which in any case I'm certain must have been a heart attack, the best thing I can do is take her away.'

'You can't do that,' Daisy reiterated Carey's assertion.

'The fog has lifted, Knox said so. We could leave immediately.'

'If Myra's so sensitive,' said Sybil stringently, 'and please note I'm not denying it, she wouldn't dream of abandoning her aunt at such a moment. Besides, the police are bound to want to speak to both of you. You can hardly expect the rest of us to keep your presence here a secret! I can't believe you want to have them chasing after you, like a pair of felons!'

'The press would probably get hold of the story, too,' said Daisy. 'You can't have thought. You don't want to start married life with a scandal round your necks. And quite apart from the police, they'd have a field-day with the two of you going off together in the middle of the night, as if you were eloping.'

'I suppose so.' Ilkton managed to sound both disconcerted and annoyed. He summoned up a smile. 'Nothing but the best for Myra. I'm concerned only for her comfort.'

He greeted the return of Simon and Carey with relief. 'You managed all right, did you?'

'Weren't we after making a bit of a mess of it,' Carey admitted cheerfully, 'but we cleared up as best we could. Now to tackle hanging it up.'

Simon slumped into a chair. He leant forward, elbows on knees, his head in his hands. Carey gave him a pat on the back with the hand that wasn't holding the lantern, and went on towards the front door.

Ilkton muttered something about making sure he didn't make another mess and went after him.

'Escaping from us,' said Daisy. Simon was on the far side of the fireplace, so as long as she and Sybil kept their voices down, they could talk without his hearing. Not that he appeared to be in a state to take in anything he heard. 'The conceit of that man!'

'Don't you think it's rather sweet, the way he wants to protect Myra?'

'I suppose so, but he seems to think he's a superior being, above being troubled by a murder investigation like the rest of us.'

'Don't say that, Daisy! Not about Ilkton's conceit, I mean *murder*. It can't be! Roger's just being careful, because he's not absolutely sure—'

'*Very* careful, if he's going to the lengths of invoking Scotland Yard.'

'I'm sorry. I shouldn't have mentioned it. I didn't mean to, it just slipped out. It was when I was trying to decide whether to talk to him about my suspicions. I thought he'd be more likely to take me seriously if he knew I'd invited the wife of a Scotland Yard detective to visit. But he didn't seem particularly interested, and then you persuaded me not to alert him.'

'As I recall, you persuaded yourself. Never mind, it's no use crying over spilt milk when the cat's out of the bag, to coin a proverb. My guess is, Roger had his own suspicions about the cause of Humphrey's illness and didn't want to worry you by making a thing of it. Not knowing you were already wondering, he'd assume it was sheer chance my husband's being a . . .' Daisy glanced at Simon. He was surely blind and deaf to the world, or he would have reacted by now to what she and Sybil had already said. She decided on caution all the same. 'Alec being what he is.'

'You're hoping to keep it from the others, still?'

Daisy sighed. 'Probably impossible, but yes. I'd rather they didn't start giving me peculiar looks.'

The looks Roger received – when he finished on the telephone at last and came over to the fire – were accusing. 'My apologies to both of you,' he said wearily. 'I'll explain later,' he added, as Ilkton and Carey came in from the porch and Simon raised his head.

'What about Aunt Lorna and Uncle Norman? With the coppers about to invade shouldn't you wake them up and tell them?'

'Don't you think that's your responsibility?'

In the pause while Simon absorbed the import of this question, Carey said to Ilkton, 'Time for us to fade away?'

'Definitely.'

And fade away they did, in the direction of the dining room, with a stop en route at the sideboard for a bottle, two glasses and a couple of packs of cards.

Simon sat up straight. 'I'll tell Uncle Norman, but I'm not waking Aunt Lorna. Myra's the one who should do that.'

'Myra's with your mother,' Sybil reminded him. 'I'll go, if you like. Even though I'm not family, at least I'm female, and I get on with Lorna as well as anyone does.'

'Which is to say, not very well,' said Simon. 'But you are practically family, and I'd be very grateful if you'd tell her about . . . Father. Oh well, here goes!'

He went off to climb the west staircase as if it were a mountain.

As Sybil reluctantly came to her feet, Daisy said, 'Darling, would you like me to go up with you? I won't cross the threshold. I'll just wait outside her room, ready to hold your hand afterwards if you need it.'

'Would you, Daisy?'

'Miss Birtwhistle's bound to be upset,' Roger said with a touch of impatience, 'but she doesn't bite. I'm going to see how Ruby's doing.'

They all went up the east stairs. Roger turned right towards Ruby's room at the front end of the wing. Sybil and Daisy turned left. Lorna's room was in the part of the newer wing that shared a wall with the old house, right at the back. Sybil knocked on the door.

There was no response.

'Are you sure she went to bed?' Daisy whispered. 'Perhaps she and Norman are carousing somewhere together.'

'In the estate office? I can't see them carousing, but drowning their sorrows— No, I can't imagine it! They both always go to bed early and get up early. It's part of their martyr act, really. Admittedly, farmers do keep early hours, but Lorna insists on making breakfast for everyone, every day, though she and Ruby share most of the cooking.' She knocked again, more loudly.

'What is it?' came Lorna's sleepy, grumpy voice. 'Who's there?'

'It's Sybil. I must speak to you.'

'I was asleep. Can't it wait till morning?'

'I'm sorry, it's urgent.'

They heard a thump, followed by a shuffling noise. A couple more minutes passed before the door opened about four inches. Lorna peered through the gap, holding up a candle. If she had worn her hair in a fringe, it would have been in imminent danger, but the tightly pulled back bun had been replaced by a lank plait falling over her shoulder. She had on a brown flannel dressing gown and the same carpet slippers in which she slopped around the house during the day.

'Well, what's so urgent?' she snapped.

'I'm afraid I have bad news, Miss Birtwhistle. Perhaps you'd better sit down.'

'Don't be ridiculous. What's happened that I have to be wakened for in the middle of the night, with all the work that's to be done tomorrow? All the extra people may not make any difference to you, but—'

'Miss Birtwhistle, your brother—'

'Norman? Something's happened to Norman?'

'No. It's Humphrey. He died earlier this evening.'

'Humphrey!' Her sallow face paled still further and the candle drooped in her shaking hand.

Taking the candle from her, Sybil passed it to Daisy. She pushed open the door, took Lorna's arm and led the woman to a straight chair beside the iron bedstead, the only seat in the room.

Lorna sat down as if her knees simply gave way. 'Humphrey?' she quavered. 'He wasn't really ill!'

'I'm sorry to bring such bad news.'

'He wasn't all that ill!'

Daisy set the candlestick on the mantelpiece, noting the empty grate. The cold, sparsely furnished bedroom was more evidence of Lorna's determination to see herself as a martyr. Though it was a good-sized room, with two big sash windows, the only other objects in it were a big wardrobe and a bedside table. No looking-glass, unless there was one inside the wardrobe. Perhaps Lorna felt no need to look at herself.

She was pulling herself together. 'I suppose it was a heart attack. He wasn't a young man. I don't see why you couldn't have waited till morning to tell me. There'll be even more work than usual.'

'It may have been a heart attack,' Sybil agreed. 'Dr Knox can't tell for sure. He wasn't treating Humphrey for a heart ailment, so he's not willing to sign the certificate without a second opinion. That means the police had to be notified. We thought you'd want to know before they arrive.'

'The police . . .' Lorna's voice faded beneath the enormity of the thought.

'Daisy, do you think you can wrest the brandy from—'

'I won't drink spirits!' Indignation revived her. 'And what the police want to come poking their long noses into respectable folks's affairs that's none of their business, I'm sure I don't know. Humphrey must have had a heart attack, that's all there is to it. I can't see the police have any need to talk to me.'

'Perhaps they won't want to,' Sybil said soothingly. 'It's up to you whether you dress and come down or not. I just thought – Simon thought – you ought to know right away.'

'Why didn't Simon come himself?'

'He's telling Norman.'

'He could have sent that useless Myra, that's at least one of the family.'

'Myra's with Ruby.'

It was just as well Myra had come up to scratch, Daisy thought. So far Lorna had not, apparently, spared a thought for her bereaved sister-in-law.

'I dare say everyone's expecting me to go down and rush about making tea and sandwiches.'

'I really can't see any need for sandwiches,' said Sybil, beginning to lose her sympathetic, reassuring tone. 'I was going to make tea myself. Would you like someone to bring you a cup?'

'I'm perfectly capable of making it myself,' Lorna snapped. 'I might as well come down now. I'll never get back to sleep.'

'And if you did, the police might come and wake you again anyway. They might even wonder at your sleeping in the circumstances!'

With this waspish remark, Sybil whisked out of the room. Daisy trotted after her, closing the door behind her.

'Oh, that bloody, bloody woman!' Sybil said, and burst into tears.

'Darling!' Daisy put her arm round Sybil's shoulders. 'Don't take it to heart. You know she's nasty to everyone.'

'It's not that. How can she be so . . . so blasé about her brother's death, and not even care for what Ruby is suffering?'

'It was a terrific shock to her. You could see that. People do react oddly to that kind of news, as if they haven't assimilated it properly. Especially as it was a double shock, hearing about the police, too. Not everyone is as accustomed as I am to having them hanging about the place.'

Sybil summoned up a watery smile. 'No. And I want very much to find out what excuse Roger has for mentioning your august connections. Let's go down and corner him.'

'Are you sure you don't want to lie down for a bit? It's been a very long day.'

'Oh, Daisy, you must be exhausted. I'm so sorry this happened while you were staying.'

'It's my karma. My Indian friend Sakari told me so. Come

on, let's go and tackle Roger. He'd better have a good explanation ready!'

They went downstairs. Roger was standing on the hearth, staring down into the glowing coals as Ilkton had earlier. He looked even wearier than Daisy felt. He looked round at the sound of their footsteps.

'Here comes Nemesis, times two.' He added a couple of lumps of coal to the fire. 'It's going to be a long night, I'm afraid.'

'It's already been a long night. How is Ruby?' Sybil asked as they all sat down.

'As well as can be expected,' the doctor said wryly. 'I told her I'd requested a second opinion. She approved. She's as anxious as I am to know for certain what Humphrey died of. And when I explained I'd had to notify the police – well, she didn't like the idea but she understands that it's a legal requirement.'

'And when you told her you had called in Scotland Yard?'

'Sybil, I haven't "called in Scotland Yard". As I understand it, only the chief constable can do that.'

'True,' Daisy agreed. 'And I can't think of any good reason for him to want them involved in this.'

'I mentioned to the local man, Sergeant Ridd, that Mrs Fletcher, a guest at Eyrie Farm, is the wife of a detective officer at the Yard, for which breach of confidence I repeat my apology. I can only say that I thought it justified in the circumstances. What's more, I hope and expect that he'll pass the information on to his superiors in Derby, and that they'll decide they don't want the responsibility of having to treat Mrs Fletcher as a suspect, however unlikely.'

'Roger, Daisy has no conceivable motive! So why—'

'Because if Humphrey was – helped to his death, someone in this house was involved. If it comes to a serious police investigation, frankly I don't trust the local people to do a thorough job. I'm afraid they'll pick on the most likely person and look no further. And let's face it, it's not beyond the bounds of possibility that they could pick either you or me. Unlike Mrs Fletcher, we both have easily conceivable motives.'

CHAPTER 14

The criminals of England had unaccountably allowed Alec an entire uninterrupted weekend with Daisy and the twins. Evil-doers continued to snooze after she departed on Monday morning to visit her school friend. Since this provided Alec with no excuse not to tackle the paperwork piling up on his desk, he would just as soon they weren't quite so forbearing.

By five o'clock on Tuesday evening, he had read, initialled, or signed absolutely everything that could be read, initialled, or signed, and DS Tring, his right-hand man, had forwarded or filed everything that could be forwarded or filed. Tom Tring was, if possible, even less fond of paperwork than Alec.

'I wouldn't say no to a nice Bond Street smash-and-grab,' he said wistfully as he shrugged into a plaid overcoat the size of a tent. 'Otherwise, you know they're just going to come up with another load of bumf to keep us busy.'

'Or meetings. We haven't had a lecture from the Assistant Commissioner for a couple of weeks. At least your wife is there to be pleased to have you home on time for once. With Daisy out of town, I can't even take her to a show to make up for all the times I've spoilt her plans.'

'That's a pity, that is, Mrs Fletcher being away just now. Might as well have a smash-and-grab as not.'

Alec laughed. 'Don't say that in the Super's hearing.'

'Not bloody likely! See you tomorrow then, Chief. My love to my godson and Miss Miranda.'

He went out, walking with the light tread so unexpected in so large a man. A weekend off and two days of paperwork, however boring, had done Tring good, Alec thought. Long hours of activity and late nights took it out of him these days, though he'd be the last to admit it. He was still three or four years from retirement. Alec knew he dreaded finishing his career in a desk job.

He was still a valuable member of Alec's team. His expertise in questioning witnesses couldn't be matched by young Ernie Piper, or even DS Mackinnon, and he intimidated with his sheer bulk those recalcitrant members of society who needed intimidating.

Alec stuck his fountain pen in his pocket, folded his *Daily Chronicle* – for once he'd had time to read more than the headlines – and went to the window. The river and, beyond it, the glass roof of Waterloo Station gleamed in the westering sun. By the time he reached Hampstead, it would be a bit late to go for a walk on the Heath with Oliver and Miranda, but Nurse Gilpin might allow him to take them out into the Constable Circle garden for a quarter of an hour. They loved to dabble their hands in the fountain and the excitement engendered by throwing a penny into the water was out of all proportion. Alec collected his Burberry and his hat from the rack and departed homeward.

Alec was halfway up the stairs to bed when the telephone rang. He was tempted not to answer it, but if he didn't, one of the servants would. They were accustomed to urgent calls at ungodly hours. Besides, it might be Daisy.

With a sigh, he went back down to the hall and lifted the receiver.

'Fletcher, what the deuce makes your wife think she can call in the Yard when she's not happy with the local bobbies?'

Alec couldn't believe his ears, especially as Superintendent Crane's bellow had set the receiver vibrating in his hand. 'I beg your pardon, sir?'

'You heard me. Doesn't like the manners of the Derbyshire police, I'm told.'

'Sir, I'm certain Daisy doesn't believe any such thing. She knows perfectly well what the protocol is. There must be some misunderstanding.'

'Is she or is she not in Derbyshire?'

'Yes, sir. She's visiting an old school friend.'

'There you are, then,' said the Super, unfairly though more quietly. 'I don't know what's going on and I'm damned if I want to know, but you'd better get up there pronto and sort it out. You haven't anything else on your plate at present, have you?'

'There's always plenty on my plate, sir, though nothing desperately urgent just now, but—'

'Catch the earliest possible express. Wire the county HQ in Derby and they'll meet you at the station. You can send for your men tomorrow if you need them. Don't splutter at me. Apparently your wife needs your help. Get a move on, man!'

Crane hung up, cutting off Alec's fourth or fifth ineffective, 'But—'

He stood for a moment with the receiver in his hand, trying to work out whether the Super was furious with Daisy or concerned for her. Both, he decided. It behoved him to feel likewise, which was not difficult.

Frowning, he went into their shared office to look up trains for Derby. Bradshaw informed him that a mail train left St Pancras at midnight. He looked at his watch. Time enough to make it, if he didn't dally.

He wrote notes for Mrs Dobson, the house keeper, and Nurse Gilpin and took them out to the hall table, where Elsie, the parlourmaid, would see them first thing in the morning. He phoned in a cable to the Derbyshire police giving them his time of arrival. The early hour would not improve his popularity with that undoubtedly disgruntled force, but the Super's instructions had been precise. Though Crane was not in general an unreasonable man, he did expect explicit instructions to be obeyed.

Except by Daisy. All hope of that he had given up long since.

Nonetheless, Alec was quite sure Daisy had no illusions about her right or her ability to call in the Yard at her convenience.

What sort of a mess had she got herself into now?

He thought of ringing up the Yard and speaking to whoever had taken the request from Derbyshire. Crane, he was certain, had either received a garbled message or not passed on all he'd been told. But time was passing. He hurried upstairs, peeked into the nursery to blow the sleeping twins a farewell kiss, and retrieved from the wardrobe in his and Daisy's bedroom the suitcase that was kept packed for emergencies.

He'd have to wait till he reached Derby to find out what was really going on.

It was past midnight when the police reached Eyrie Farm. The hammering at the door startled everyone in the hall out of the silent, somnolent state they had drifted into while waiting. Daisy had actually dozed off for a few minutes.

Rudely awakened, she thought for a moment the noise was Alec's alarm clock. She detested that alarm clock, but it was definitely preferable to the present reality.

'Here they are,' said Simon. He got up. The knocker sounded again, impatiently, as he went to the door. He flung aside the curtain and opened it.

'Derbyshire police, Detective Inspector Worrall. We've had a report—'

'I know. I'm Simon Birtwhistle.' His voice was slightly unsteady as he continued, 'My father died unexpectedly and Dr Knox said he was required to report it.'

'That's right, sir.'

'So you'd better come in and talk to him.'

'Just a moment, sir. The county police doctor followed us up, and . . . Ah, here he comes now.'

The sound of a car door slamming reached those inside. 'Coming, Inspector, coming!' said a very North Country voice. 'Couldn't find my dashed bag in the dark.'

DI Worrall moved aside. The man who stepped past him into the house looked not much older than Simon, in spite of the dignity lent by the black medical bag he carried. He must have been several years older to have qualified as a doctor, though. His slight figure was respectably clad in a dark suit, in contrast to the inappropriate crimson velvet jacket Simon hadn't got round to changing out of.

'Dr Jordan,' Worrall introduced him, coming in after him, followed by a single uniformed constable. 'This is Mr Birtwhistle, Doctor, the son of the deceased.'

'How do you do, Mr Birtwhistle. My condolences on your loss. Now, where's . . . Ah, there you are, Dr Knox.'

'Glad to see you, Jordan. I hope we can sort this out in

short order.' They shook hands and, without further ado, went off briskly towards Humphrey's bedroom, the detective and the constable at their heels.

'Inspector,' Daisy called after them, 'are you going to want to talk to everyone tonight?'

Worrall turned back. 'No, no, I suggest you all go to bed. There'll be nothing done until morning, Mrs . . . Birtwhistle, is it?'

'I'm Mrs Fletcher.'

'Ah!' Worrall managed to pack just as much significance into the single syllable as Tom Tring, who was an expert. 'It'll be your husband that's coming up from the Yard, then.'

'Oh, *damn*!' said Daisy, her worst fears realised – well, almost the worst. 'I'll wait up and have a word with you after . . .' She gestured in the direction the doctors had taken.

'Right you are, madam,' the inspector said genially.

At least he didn't seem to be offended by the interference from London, but Daisy was furious with Roger Knox. Surely for once she might have got away with involvement in a police investigation without Alec finding out about it!

She noticed that Lorna was staring at her with more than usual disapproval. 'Really, Mrs Fletcher, your language is not what I care for!'

'Sorry, Miss Birtwhistle. It slipped out.' Amazing, Daisy thought, that the woman could care about such a triviality with her brother lying mysteriously dead and the police in the house. Perhaps it was what Sakari, that inveterate taker of classes and attender of lectures, would call 'displacement'. If Daisy remembered Sakari's explanation correctly, it meant something to do with shifting uncomfortable emotions from the appropriate object to a lesser target, as a way of reducing the discomfort.

Lorna headed for the stairs.

Myra was decidedly wan after staying with Ruby for ages. Returning to the hall half an hour ago, she had told them her aunt wanted to be alone. 'I'll go up, too,' she said now, 'if you don't mind, Mrs Fletcher.'

'Of course not,' Daisy assured her. 'You look all in. Sleep well.'

Sybil gave Myra a hug. 'Sleep well. You've earned sweet dreams.'

'Oh, I couldn't! Poor Uncle Humphrey!' Tears welled in her eyes.

Ilkton handed her another handkerchief. He and Carey followed her to the stairs, a pace behind.

'I hope they're not going to make nuisances of themselves,' said Daisy.

They both apparently realised at the same moment that they couldn't very well accompany Myra any farther, her room being in the east wing, theirs in the west. They returned to the fireplace.

'I'm turning in, if you'll excuse me, ladies,' said Ilkton. 'Good-night.' He went on to the west stairs.

'Want company, old chap?' Carey asked Simon.

Simon had been standing looking a bit disconsolate since the doctors and police had walked past him with scarcely a word. He shook his head. 'Thanks, but I think I'll just make sure Mother's all right, then head for bed. Myra's been a brick, hasn't she?'

'Sure and didn't Ilkton tell you, repeatedly, you didn't appreciate her properly. 'Night, everyone.'

According to Simon, Norman had absorbed the news of his brother's demise, muttered that he had to get up at six, turned over and gone back to sleep, so Daisy and Sybil were left at the fireside.

'Waiting for Roger?' asked Daisy.

'And keeping you company, if you insist on staying up to talk to that policeman. As the fog has cleared, Roger probably will want to go home for what little is left of the night.'

'Yes, running from my righteous wrath. I can't believe they've got Alec coming up here! We don't even know if there really is something unnatural about Humphrey's death. Perhaps Dr Jordan will take one look and diagnose a stroke.'

'I hope so. I do hope so. But if it were so simple, Roger would have known.'

'I wonder whether Alec will be angrier if he's been dragged up here for nothing or if I really have stumbled into another murder.'

'You'll never know,' Sybil pointed out, 'because it can only be one or the other.'

'True.' Daisy sighed. 'One way or another, he's going to be livid. And he'll say it's all my fault. And so will Superintendent Crane.'

'You can blame it on me. Not to mention on Roger. I should never have told him about Alec, let alone have asked you in the first place to try to find out whether my fears had any basis in reality.'

'Which, apparently, they did. And it looks to me as if Roger suspected the same, or he surely would have assumed that Humphrey simply had a heart attack in his sleep.'

'So you think it was . . .'

'I think it was an overdose, whether accidental or purposeful, of some drug someone had been dosing him with for years.'

'That must be why Roger said I'm an obvious suspect,' Sybil said unhappily. 'Humphrey's illness has made a bigger improvement in my life than anyone else's.'

CHAPTER 15

'Right you are, Dr Knox,' said Dr Jordan cheerfully, returning to the hall, 'I'll get those samples analysed tonight. Worrall, you'll send the body to me in the morning, for autopsy.'

'That I will, Doctor.'

'I'll be off, then.' Jordan noticed Daisy and Sybil as they stood up. 'Sorry, shouldn't have mentioned such things in the presence of ladies. Good-night!' He strode out to his car.

'Roger!' said Sybil.

'Inspector!' said Daisy.

'Looks like we've been ambushed, Doctor. What can I do for you, Mrs Fletcher?'

Worrall was remarkably perky for the time of night. Daisy guessed that, being on night duty, he had slept during the day, unlike everyone else. Now that she got a good look at him, he was about as average as a man can be: middling brown hair, slightly thinning; a face no one would pick out in a crowd; perhaps an inch taller than police height requirements; a figure a trifle thickened at the waist but unremarkable, as were his dark-grey suit and grey-and-cream striped tie.

She invited him to sit down, while Sybil and Roger drew a little apart.

'I can't tell you anything about . . . the doctors' findings,' the inspector said cautiously.

'Of course not. Though it's obvious Dr Jordan agrees with Roger – Dr Knox – that something is rotten in the state of Denmark.'

'Denmark?'

'Sorry! I have a bad habit of indiscriminate quotation. They agree that the cause of Mr Birtwhistle's death is not obvious and straightforward. Lucky for you, really, since you seem to have brought my husband rushing to Derbyshire already.'

DI Worrall shook his head. 'Not my doing, madam. You'll be aware, I expect, it takes more than a mere inspector's request to set things moving in that direction.'

'Yes, I know. I meant *you* as in the Derbyshire police force.'

'Ah. So I reported Dr Knox's call to my superintendent, as was my bounden duty. I'll tell you this much, he wasn't happy about it, having just gone to bed. Told me it was for the chief constable to make a decision. As if he didn't know the Colonel can't be got hold of – up in Scotland shooting some bird or other, unless it's deer he's after. Any road, his deputy, Mr Oakenshawe, doesn't want to take responsibility for whatever happens whilst he's gone. Specially a murder enquiry.'

'You rang up Mr Oakenshawe? What did he say?'

'He was right glad of an excuse to have the CID take charge.'

'The excuse being my presence, I assume.'

'That's right, madam,' agreed Worrall, straightfaced.

'I suppose I'm glad to have obliged him! I hope you don't mind having it taken out of your hands?'

'Well, now, we've yet to see if there's anything to be taken. All very vague and airy-fairy it is, so far, if you ask me. But so be there is a case to investigate, I'd just as soon have the help, to tell the truth. Most of the homicides we get in these parts, it doesn't take two minutes to find out who's to blame.'

'Did Mr Oakenshawe make you ring up the Yard?' Daisy asked.

Worrall grinned. 'Tried to, but I wasn't having any. They won't take any notice of a request from me, I told him like I told you. Next thing I know, just as I was leaving to come here, having notified Dr Jordan he was needed – next thing was a wire from Detective Chief Inspector Fletcher with the time of his train. Quick off the mark, those blokes.'

'Oh *blast*! Oakenshawe must have talked to the duty officer, and he rang Mr Crane, and Crane rang Alec and told him to come and get me out of trouble. It'll be all over the Yard,' Daisy said gloomily.

'Like that is it?' Worrall sounded sympathetic.

'I just wish Dr Knox hadn't taken it into his head to mention Alec to you. Then you could have solved your own murder—'

'If so be it is a murder,' the inspector reminded her, 'which isn't by any means a sure thing.'

'If it isn't, and Alec's annoyed about being called out for nothing, I'll make sure he understands it's not your fault.'

'I'd take it kindly, madam.'

'Roger and Oakenshawe can jolly well shoulder the blame,' Daisy said firmly. And Alec should jolly well give her some of the credit for Inspector Worrall's complaisance!

'Perhaps you wouldn't mind, madam, just giving me the names of everyone in the house, so's I have something to show the chief inspector come morning? Always supposing there should be anything here to interest him, other than your good self.'

'Certainly.'

He took out his notebook, then searched his pockets and produced a propelling pencil. 'Starting with the family of the deceased, if you'd be so kind.'

'Lorna – Miss Birtwhistle – and Norman are his brother and sister. Norman is also unmarried. I gather the place belongs . . . belonged to the three of them, though whether in equal shares I can't say. Eyrie Farm, that is, and as there are two tenant farms I suppose one might refer to it as "the estate". Norman runs the farms. Miss Birtwhistle shares house keeping duties with Humphrey's wife.'

'Ah, yes, the wife.'

'Ruby. She's American. Or was. She's been here since the Nineties. But that's beside the point. You asked for their names.'

'You just tell me in your own way, madam. It'll help me keep them straight, like, knowing a bit about them.'

'All right. There's Simon, Humphrey and Ruby's son and only child. Not long down from university – one of the red-bricks, not Oxbridge. And Myra Olney is not long out of school. She's some sort of cousin but she grew up here.' Daisy frowned. 'Actually, I don't know how long Eyrie Farm has been her home.'

'How remiss of you.'

Daisy looked at Worrall in surprise. To her relief, he had a twinkle in his eye. It boded well for his working relationship with Alec, she hoped. 'You're teasing! I've only been here since yesterday afternoon. No, the day before, now.'

'In that case, I'd say you've picked up a remarkable amount of information. Any more family?'

'No, that's the lot.'

'Servants?'

'Two farm girls who come in by the day. All I know about them is their given names, Betty and Etta.'

'Very confusing.'

'That's what Myra said. I think Norman has some help on the home farm, but I don't know anything at all about him or them. I don't think they ever come into the house.'

'We'll count them out for the present. Who does that leave?' He looked at Sybil and Roger, completely absorbed in each other. 'Who's Dr Knox's sweetheart?'

'They're not sweethearts. Not really. That's Sybil Sutherby. She's . . . She was Humphrey Birtwhistle's secretary. I was at school with her and she invited me to come and stay at Eyrie Farm.'

The inspector raised his eyebrows. 'The secretary invites her own guests?'

'Well . . . It's a bit more complicated than that.'

'Indeed!'

'No, she wasn't Humphrey's mistress!'

'Now, now, did I suggest such a thing?'

'Nor the doctor's. I could tell you were thinking it. I can't see any need to go into details of her position here unless you find out something suspicious about his death. She's a widow, and she has a young daughter who's away at school during the week.'

'Let's hope everything's cleared up before the child comes home,' Worrall said piously. 'Anyone else?'

'There are two more guests in the house. Neil Carey – he's a friend of Simon's, a few years older. And he flirts with Miss Olney, which won't surprise you when you meet her. The other is older still, in his thirties I'd guess. Walter Ilkton. He made Miss Olney's acquaintance on a tennis court and hopes to marry her.'

'Ah.' He pondered for a moment. 'That's the lot, then?'

Daisy nodded, then remembered: 'No, Mr Ilkton brought a manservant. I don't know his name.' She was taken by surprise by an enormous yawn. 'I do beg your pardon!'

'Think nothing of it. I must say it's not the effect a copper usually has on witnesses.' He closed his notebook. 'I'm much obliged, Mrs Fletcher, and I won't keep you any longer. Doctor, are you leaving now?'

'What's that? Oh, no, I'm staying the night. I was going to anyway, because of the fog earlier, so there's a bed made up. I want to have another look in on Mrs Birtwhistle.'

'Right you are, sir. I'd like a word with you before you retire.'

Accepting their dismissal, Daisy and Sybil said goodnight and went together up the west stairs. On the landing, Sybil stopped and looked down at the two men.

'What were you talking about? Did he tell you anything?'

'Not a thing. What about Roger? Did he tell you what Dr Jordan had to say?'

'Only that he agreed further investigation was warranted. It was a relief in a way, after he'd brought the police in. And Scotland Yard. Daisy, I'm really sorry about that. I hope Alec won't be terribly angry with you.'

'Don't worry about it. He's resigned to my getting mixed up in police business. Almost. Besides, I've been buttering up Inspector Worrall and I'm pretty sure he's not going to get shirty about Alec taking over. Local police are often resentful and uncooperative.'

'You sound like a real expert! I suppose I didn't actually believe half of what I heard about your exploits.'

'Darling, I sincerely hope you haven't heard about at least half of my "exploits"! If I were a real expert, perhaps I'd have worked out what was going on here and put a stop to it before Humphrey died.'

Sybil patted her shoulder. 'You had only one day, even if it felt like a century. It will probably turn out to have been a heart attack. Good-night. Sleep well.'

''Night. You too.'

Daisy didn't expect to sleep well with so much on her mind. As she climbed into bed, she was trying to decide whether to admit to Alec that she had come to Eyrie Farm specifically to delve into her friend's suspicions of serious wrong-doing in the household. Sybil would probably tell him. Daisy could have asked her not to mention it. However, Alec was almost certain to guess she was concealing something, not a good idea in a police enquiry.

So she had better confess right away, Daisy decided reluctantly. Unless, with any luck, it turned out that Humphrey's death was natural and Alec had rushed all the way to Derbyshire for nothing. Holding on to that hope, she fell asleep.

CHAPTER 16

Alec reached Derby in the early hours of Wednesday morning. A uniformed constable was waiting, as promised, to escort him to the headquarters of the county police. Having snoozed on the train, Alec was somewhat refreshed, and the crisp night air completed his revival. During the few minutes' walk through the silent town, he made an attempt to discover the reason for his despatch to Derbyshire. All he could extract from the man was that Detective Inspector Worrall was in charge.

He would have liked to ask whether the inspector was greatly put out at having the Yard brought in, but even if the constable happened to know, it wouldn't be at all proper to ask him.

'Is the inspector at the station, or still at the scene?'

'He's back, sir. Came in a few minutes before I left to meet you.' On the one hand, Alec thought, no time wasted waiting about; on the other, no time to feel out amongst DI Worrall's colleagues whether he was indifferent, disgruntled, or furious. He'd just have to tread with caution.

On reaching the station, he was invited to step straight up to the inspector's office. Following the constable up the stairs, he was struck by a sudden wave of fear for Daisy.

What was her involvement in whatever was going on? Was she a suspect? Could she even be in danger?

He clung to a slender hope that Superintendent Crane had misunderstood the situation, that at worst Daisy was mixed up in the business only peripherally.

His guide opened a door and announced him: 'Sir, Detective Chief Inspector Fletcher of New Scotland Yard.'

'Come in, come in, Chief Inspector, and set yourself down.' The man behind the desk half-rose and waved him to a chair. A neat, unobtrusively dressed man with an undistinguished face, he smiled, but his eyes were wary. 'You'll be wondering what's going on, I don't doubt.'

'How right you are!'

'I admit, I'm not sure yet myself. We didn't expect you so soon.'

So the urgency was the Super's notion. Any hint of Daisy's presence at the scene of a police investigation was liable to overthrow his usual sang-froid.

'No?' Alec said noncommittally.

'I'd best explain. It was Dr Knox rang up our chap in Matlock, saying he had an unexplained death on his hands, so to speak. Being as how he's the local police surgeon, the sergeant was bound to sit up and take notice. He reported to me, and . . . well, he told me the doctor said one of the sus – one of the people on the premises was the wife of a top CID man. Namely, yourself, sir.'

'Namely, myself.' Alec sighed. 'Of course you had no choice but to pass the information up to your superior. And he decided to alert your chief constable.'

'His deputy, sir. Mr Oakenshawe. The colonel's off somewhere inaccessible in Scotland shooting at inoffensive birdies.'

'Is he, indeed! I begin to see the light. Am I right in

assuming Mr Oakenshawe has even less police experience than the CC himself?'

'Far be it from me to contradict a superior officer.'

'So he didn't want the responsibility for a murder investigation— I suppose it is murder we're talking about?'

'That remains to be seen, sir. Our county medico agrees with Dr Knox that the cause of death is not clear. He's doing the autopsy later this morning, but in the meantime he's running some tests. Very up in the latest techniques, he is. He said they wouldn't take too long, so I'm waiting for the results.'

Alec sighed. 'All right, since I'm here, you'd better put me in the picture. All I know about the friend Daisy – my wife – is visiting is that she lives on a farm and is secretary to a literary man. Who else is on the scene?'

'As to that, Mrs Fletcher was very helpful, very helpful indeed. A very nice lady, if you don't mind me saying so.'

'I might have known she wouldn't be content with standing by, minding her own business.' He ought to be resigned by now. At least she seemed to have managed to get on the right side of DI Worrall. 'Let's hear it.'

He listened without comment as DI Worrall read from his notebook. By certain turns of phrase he could tell that the inspector was quoting Daisy directly.

She had provided a succinct overview of the household that would be useful if there was in fact anything to investigate. Alec noted – and wondered whether Worrall had noted – her protectiveness towards Sybil Sutherby. Inevitably, in every case she meddled in, Daisy took a suspect or two under her wing and refused to believe ill of them. Inevitably, in this case, her ewe-lamb was the woman she had been at school with. Usually, but by no means always, those she chose to defend turned out to be innocent.

By no means always. Moreover, their innocence was sometimes distinctly ambiguous. Daisy and the Law did not always see eye to eye on the subject of Justice.

As yet there was no case, Alec reminded himself.

Worrall pushed a sheet of paper across his desk. 'I've made a list for you, just in case. And I've booked you a hotel room, in case you want to try to catch a couple of hours of shut-eye. Or longer, if Dr Jordan's tests come back negative.'

'Thanks, but I'll wait with you for the results, if I won't be disturbing you.'

'Nothing pressing. I'll tell you what, I'd like to hear the inside story on the Epping Forest murders.'

In Alec's estimation, the tracking down of the man who had been dubbed by the press 'The Epping Executioner' had not been one of his great successes. But the story had some interesting points, so he obliged. Worrall was gratifyingly interested, especially in the team-work necessary to deal with the complicated case.

'That's where us provincials can't match you at the Yard,' he said. 'We just haven't got the manpower or the facilities.'

'It involved several different counties. We'd have had to be called in anyway. I can't see that my presence is necessary here, however.'

'That's yet to be seen, sir. If there's anything in it, I won't say no to a helping hand from—' The telephone bell cut him short. He lifted the receiver. 'Worrall. Yes, put him through.' Covering the mouthpiece with his hand, he said to Alec, 'Dr Jordan.'

'Good,' said Alec, suppressing a yawn.

'Yes, Doctor, please go ahead . . . Chloral hydrate? Would you mind spelling that, sir? . . . Thank you. It's a poison? . . . Oh, a sedative. How much . . . ? . . . Yes, yes, quite, a matter of the proportion in the blood. . . Yes, I understand. So you're sure it killed the victim? . . . Ah . . . Yes, I see, enough to kill him but . . .' Worrall listened intently for a minute. 'Right, Doctor. You'll do the postmortem examination first thing . . . Yes, sleep well. Thank you for ringing up.' The inspector hung up.

'Chloral?'

'As full as he can hold. Not just a few drops from a phial, at least several teaspoons. It's normally dispensed in a dark glass bottle like cough medicine, too big to be easily concealed. Isn't that the stuff that's sometimes used for doping race horses?'

'So I understand, though I've only been peripherally involved in any of those cases. It's not an uncommon sedative for insomnia or agitation in humans, though. The victim could have taken an accidental overdose, or even intentional. We'll have to see if it had been prescribed for him before we jump to any conclusions.'

'Yes, of course. Besides, Dr Jordan wouldn't swear the stuff was the actual cause of death or just a prox – proximate, I think was the word.'

'Proximate cause? That just means he won't commit himself until he's cut up the corpse. Doctors never will. Incidentally, I'm surprised a country doctor would be aware of the test for chloral. It's a fairly new development, I believe.'

'As to that, sir, Dr Jordan is the county pathologist as well as the county police surgeon. Keen as mustard, and he likes to keep up with that sort of thing. Prefers dead bodies to live ones, he told me once.'

Alec laughed. 'Still, I wonder what suggested to him that he should test for it.'

'As to that, sir, it was likely something Dr Knox told him. They were talking medical language, throwing Latin about if you know what I mean, and I didn't even try to follow it. I didn't ask for a translation. Dr Jordan'd've told me if there was anything I needed to know right away.'

'I expect you're right. What I didn't gather from my wife's chat with you, is whether Dr Knox was at the farm last night solely to visit Mrs Sutherby, sweetheart or not, or was he there in his medical capacity?'

'He was Mr Birtwhistle's doctor.'

'But not, apparently, treating him for anything that he considered might prove fatal.'

'No, he told me that much in plain English. But he didn't think it was proper to talk about his health history till he knew more about what killed him.'

'Reasonable.'

'I couldn't very well insist, seeing I didn't know but what his death was perfectly natural.'

'Quite right. I can't see that you could have done anything more last night. You didn't even have any real justification for leaving an officer on the premises.'

'That was my feeling, sir.'

'Right, I'm going to sleep on it for a couple of hours, but I think we'd better get out to the farm early, rather than wait for the autopsy results, if that suits you?'

'I'll get everything sorted. And I'll have someone take you to the hotel now.'

'Thanks,' said Alec, profoundly grateful for Worrall's cooperative spirit – and wondering how much of it was owed to the inspector's having taken a fancy to Daisy.

From the bridge, the farm house looked like a haven of peace, nestled in its green bowl in the sunshine. The peace was illusory. At best, a man had taken an accidental overdose of a medicine. At worst, someone had deliberately administered a dangerous drug with intent to kill.

Were the household mourning their loss, or had Birtwhistle's death come as a relief to some? What sort of man had he been? Knowing the victim, in Alec's experience, was the first step towards finding out why he had died.

And Daisy, presumably, had known the victim.

Hesitantly he asked Worrall, 'Would you think it unreasonable of me to talk to my wife first? About Birtwhistle's death, that is, not personal matters. Not that I necessarily consider her an impartial witness – in fact, I'm very sure she's not. But I can allow for her biases, and she is a good observer. On the whole.'

'Seeing I relied on her for most of what I know, I can't hardly object, sir! Would you be wanting me to take notes, or should I have a go at the doctor? Find out what he was treating the deceased for.'

'Won't he have gone home?'

The inspector explained that Dr Knox had announced his intention of staying the night at the farm, because of his concern for Mrs Birtwhistle.

'Hmm. No, unless the doctor's in a rush to get to his surgery or another patient, I think we'd best tackle him after we see what Daisy can add to what she's already told you. I'll be glad to have you take notes.'

Worrall's knocking on the front door was answered by a young woman in an orange-flowered overall with her hair tied up in a purple-flowered scarf, wielding a broom.

'You'll be the police, I dare say,' she greeted them with an air of satisfaction on her round, rosy face. 'Didn't I tell Etta, poor Mr Birtwhistle were 'orribly done to death in his bed, mark my words, weltering in his own blood.'

Alec let the local man take the lead.

'I'll thank you not to be spreading such nonsense, miss,' he said severely. He took out his notebook. 'I'm Detective Inspector Worrall, and you'll be . . . ?'

'Miss Hendred, to you,' said the maid.

'Given name?' the inspector enquired, unimpressed.

'Betty. Elizabeth, properly speaking, but no one ever calls me—'

'Thank you, Miss Hendred. I expect Detective Chief Inspector Fletcher will want to talk to you later, but for the present, be a good girl and inform the master or mistress of the house—'

'Now isn't that just the trouble? Who is the master, I'd like to know? Mr Humphrey it was, him being the older brother, but now he's gone is it Mr Norman or Mr Simon? I can't think of either of 'em as "the master", try as I may. Mr Norman never opens his mouth, saving to eat, and Mr Simon – well, he's only a lad yet. As for my mistress, that'd still be Mrs Humphrey, and nobody can make me say otherwise. If Miss Lorna thinks she can lord it—'

'Betty!' The shocked voice came from the rear of the murky hall, into which little of the sunlight outside penetrated through the small windows in thick walls. Alec made out another figure in an overall, plain dark blue, presumably another maid. 'If Miss Lorna hears you!' she added.

'What's she going to do? She'll never find anyone else fool enough to—'

'Miss Hendred, *if* you please,' Worrall interrupted. 'The chief inspector is anxious to speak to Mrs Fletcher. At once. I don't care how you get hold of her, but do it *now*.'

Offended, Betty Hendred drew herself up and put her hands on her hips. 'Well, really, I must say!'

Alec wished he had Tom Tring with him. Tom, though devoted to his almost equally massive wife, had a way with servants and with female servants in particular. He would have had the girl eating out of his hand, rushing to do his bidding. Talkative servants were often a fruitful source of information.

Meanwhile, the second maid squeaked in alarm, 'Oh, sir, Mrs Fletcher's still at breakfast. I'll tell her you're here to talk to her.' She scuttled out.

'I s'pose you'd best come in,' Betty snapped.

'Miss Hendred,' Alec said mildly, 'is Dr Knox also at breakfast?'

'Him! No, he's not. At least he had the decency to get up early for his surgery in town.' Turning her back, she moved away from them and went on with her sweeping.

Worrall grimaced as he stood aside to let Alec enter. 'Sorry, sir,' he said in a low voice. 'She set my back up with her gabbling, but I should have handled it better.'

A sharp retort sprang to Alec's lips but he swallowed it. A cooperative local detective was more important than an uncooperative servant. 'Pity the doctor left already,' he said. 'I wonder who *is* the master here now.'

'Mrs Fletcher said the two brothers and the sister were joint owners.'

'She wasn't sure of it.'

'Maybe she's found out a bit more by now. Good morning, Mrs Fletcher,' he went on as she came into the hall, followed by a stocky woman whose reddish, puffy eyes Alec discerned through the gloom.

'Good morning, Inspector.' Daisy's smile wavered. 'Alec, darling, I'm so glad you're here!'

CHAPTER 17

Daisy was so flooded with relief at the sight of Alec that she momentarily forgot all the reasons she had hoped he wouldn't come. She had just enough presence of mind not to alarm the inspector by flinging her arms about the chief inspector's neck.

'Darling, I'm so happy to see you. How are the twins?'

'You've only been away two days, love. They're blooming.'

'Good. When something like this happens, one starts imagining . . .' She had awakened earlier to a fresh sense of shock at Humphrey Birtwhistle's dying so unexpectedly. It seemed not to have sunk in properly the night before. She had made his acquaintance just two days ago, but she had liked him, enjoyed his dry wit and admired his fortitude in trying circumstances. Worse still, though she knew it was irrational, she felt guilty. Sybil had invited her to Eyrie Farm to find out whether someone was deliberately harming him, and she had failed to prevent his death.

But what did Alec's arrival mean? Even if Superintendent Crane had made him head for Derby, at the chief constable's request, surely he wouldn't have bothered to come all the way to the farm if Humphrey's death had been proved natural?

'Has Dr Jordan found out—?'

'Not here, Daisy. Is there somewhere we can go to be private?'

'Humphrey's study, I should think. Sybil's the one to ask. That part of the house is none of Lorna's business, and Ruby hasn't put in an appearance yet.' Turning, she saw her friend lingering at the back of the hall, called her forward and introduced Alec to her.

'I'm sorry we're meeting in such unhappy circumstances, Mrs Sutherby.'

'Does it mean . . . Was Humphrey . . . ?'

'I'm afraid we haven't a final answer yet. We were wondering— Daisy suggested we might use the late Mr Birtwhistle's study for a private discussion, if it won't inconvenience you.'

'As long as you won't mind that I'll be . . . typing in the next room. Though it's not really for me to say. Ruby – Mrs Birtwhistle – hasn't come down, but Simon, their son, might want to look through his father's papers. Though I can't think why he should. He's never taken the slightest interest in Humphrey's work. Besides, it's much too soon after . . .'

'In any case, we can't allow it. We have enough information to justify limiting access to Humphrey Birtwhistle's rooms for the present.'

'I locked 'em last night,' said the inspector, clinking keys in his pocket.

Sybil gasped. 'There *was* something wrong about it! What—?'

'Not now, please, Mrs Sutherby.' Alec nodded in warning towards Betty, who was dusting the mantelpiece with assiduous care. 'We'll talk to you later, when we have a better idea of what we're talking about.'

'When Daisy has told you all about us.'

'I hardly think she can know all about you after one day.'

'Perhaps not, but I'm not the only one who's found her easy to confide in.'

Alec raised his eyebrows at Daisy, who did her best to look as if she hadn't the foggiest idea what Sybil meant. Presumably she was talking about Myra. No one else had confided in her as far as she could remember. Except for Simon, and he had talked about Myra's admirers, not himself.

All the same, she did know enough about the household to be useful to Alec, if only to give him a foundation to build on.

They all went through to the east wing. Sybil went into her office and closed the door. DI Worrall took a ring with a couple of labelled keys from his trouser pocket, unlocked the door of Humphrey's study and stood back. Alec ushered Daisy in and the men followed.

'That door connects with Sybil's room, obviously,' said Daisy.

'Locked?' Alec asked Worrall.

'Yes, sir, though the keys to these three rooms are the same. They weren't usually kept locked. I've got two, but I dare say there are others floating about. For that matter, they're just ordinary household keys and it wouldn't surprise me if they worked for every door in the house.'

'Very likely. And that door?'

'The bedroom of the deceased.'

'Where he died? I'll take a look later. He and his wife had separate bedrooms? Suppose we start there, Daisy. Inspector, you take the desk.'

As in Sybil's office, a couple of easy chairs flanked the fireplace. The grate, however, was empty of all but ashes. The coal scuttle was empty of all but coal-dust and a few splinters from kindling.

'It's freezing in here,' said Daisy, shivering as she buttoned her cardigan and folded her arms across her chest.

'Ring the bell,' Alec said impatiently. 'We'll get a fire built in here.' He turned the two armchairs to face the desk.

Daisy pulled the bell-rope by the mantel, but she said, 'I doubt if it'll bring anyone running. There's just the two girls, and they're busy about the house, not in the kitchen waiting for the bell to ring.'

'Then you'll just have to put up with it, love. It won't be for long.'

'That's what you think.' She wrinkled her nose at him. 'When you've finished interrogating me, I'll send one of them to light a fire before you call in your next victim, otherwise you and Mr Worrall will turn into icicles before you're through.'

Worrall beamed at her. 'That would be kindly done, Mrs Fletcher.'

'Separate bedrooms,' Alec said firmly as they all sat down and the inspector took out his notebook. 'They weren't on good terms, Mr and Mrs Birtwhistle?'

'That has nothing to do with it. Humphrey was a writer. You knew that much?'

'Only because you told me, before you came, that your friend was secretary to an author.'

'Oh, yes. Well, apparently he sometimes used to stay up till all hours writing. Many years ago they made that room into a bedroom, so he needn't disturb Ruby in the middle of the night. Then, about three years ago, he fell desperately ill.'

'Aha.'

'There's no *aha* about it. He had bronchitis and developed a severe case of pneumonia. As I'm liable to do, freezing in here.'

'Daisy . . .'

'Sir, I happened to notice a woollen shawl in the chest-of-drawers in the bedroom next door when I was looking about a bit last night.'

'Yes, please.'

'Oh, all right!'

Half a minute later, Daisy draped about her shoulders a large, warm, but plain shawl, suitable for a male invalid, very likely knitted by Ruby. It was a pleasant shade of blue, more or less matching the colour of her eyes, she thought, those eyes that Alec frequently described as 'misleadingly guileless'. Perhaps it might make him take a more lenient view of her coming revelation. Or it might remind him of the 'misleading' part and make him less forgiving.

'Pneumonia,' he prompted, not visibly affected. So far.

'Obviously it was easier to care for him downstairs. He was very ill, and afterwards very run down. I don't know if he ever really moved back upstairs—'

'Something you don't know!' Alec said in a marvelling tone.

'Darling, don't be beastly. There's lots I don't know.'

'Sorry.' He directed his apologetic glance at Worrall, rather than Daisy.

She forgave him. After all, he had resisted reproaching her the moment he saw her, for her involvement in yet another suspicious death, which had no doubt brought down the Super's wrath upon his innocent head.

She went on quickly, 'Humphrey seems never to have recovered. At least, as far as I've gathered, his chest wasn't permanently affected, but ever since his illness he's been weak and lethargic and abnormally sleepy. Dr Knox couldn't see any reason for it – well, it's for him to tell you.'

'Come on, Daisy,' said Alec, 'out with it. What was Mrs Sutherby worried about?'

'She had an awful feeling someone could be dosing him regularly with sedatives.'

Both Alec and Worrall sat up straighter and looked at each other – evidence enough to convince Daisy that Humphrey had probably died of an overdose of a sedative.

'Who?' asked Worrall, pencil poised.

'She had only the vaguest of suspicions – some, I'm quite certain, unwarranted. I don't think it would be fair to tell you. It would just be a mixture of hearsay and rumour. Not even rumour; one person's surmise as told to me.'

'And why,' Alec demanded, 'did Mrs Sutherby tell you?'

Daisy had realised she would have to confess, but that didn't make it any easier. 'Well, actually, as a matter of fact, you see, she sort of wanted my advice. She didn't explain till after I got here that she was afraid Humphrey was being poisoned. She just said she had a feeling something unpleasant was "going on", so I couldn't possibly guess it might be something criminal, could I? In fact, when Lucy said I'd saved a couple of friends from the hangman, Sybil specifically denied that it was anything on those lines.'

'Lucy! Don't tell me she's mixed up in this, too!'

'Not at all. We just happened to be having lunch together when Sybil asked me to investigate. Not investigate,' Daisy corrected herself hurriedly as Alec's face grew still more thunderous, 'just to come and stay and . . . Well, what she really wanted was for me to tell her she was imagining things. And I did.'

'But she wasn't,' put in Worrall, who appeared to be enjoying himself. 'Or so it would seem. And in the end—'

'Let's not jump to conclusions, Inspector.' Alec aimed his formidable frown at the inspector for a change, but only for a moment. 'All right, Daisy, we'll postpone the question of why Mrs Sutherby brought you into the picture. Humphrey Birtwhistle has been ill for three years?'

'He has occasional good days. Comparatively good. He has a burst of energy, but it runs out quickly. That's what happened yesterday and the day before.'

'Has his health been improving, or deteriorating?'

'Darling, I've only been here a couple of days! But it sounds to me as if he's been getting weaker. Less because of whatever's wrong with him, or being done to him, than because he spends so much time lying down that his muscles have gradually atrophied. That's hearsay, too. I mean, I've seen how weak he is. The deterioration is hearsay.'

'He's weak and pretty much bedridden,' said Worrall, 'yet he's managed to go on writing his books?'

'You'll have to ask Sybil – Mrs Sutherby – about that. Unless, of course, this is a murder enquiry. I'm aware that any information may be pertinent in a murder enquiry.'

Alec and Worrall exchanged glances again.

'We're not sure yet,' Alec said resignedly. 'It may be. Your answer may help us to decide whether it was murder or not.'

Daisy hesitated. Others were in the secret, she reminded herself: Ruby and Simon, almost certainly Lorna and Norman, not to mention Roger Knox. 'If it turns out not to be murder, or not to be relevant . . . Never mind, I know you can't promise anything.'

'I won't write it down,' offered the inspector. 'That way, it needn't go into my report unless—'

'That's kind of you, Mr Worrall.' Daisy sighed. 'Come to think of it, quite possibly it really doesn't matter any longer who knows, now that Humphrey's dead.'

'In that case,' Alec pointed out stringently, 'it's extremely likely to be relevant to his death! Come on, Daisy, what is this terrible secret?'

'Humphrey hasn't . . . hadn't actually written a book since he fell ill. At least, if I understood correctly, he's thought up the plots. Sybil has done all the actual writing.'

'I don't know the lingo,' said Worrall, 'but isn't the plot the same as the story? And isn't that what a secretary's for, to write everything down?'

Daisy did her best to explain the division of labour. Worrall was clearly unconvinced that Sybil's part in the business was far beyond the merely secretarial. Alec understood, of course. Perhaps Scotland Yard's being called in was a blessing after all – in disguise, as far as Daisy was concerned, but it was just as well to have someone in charge who had a firm grasp of the issues.

'It sounds like a useful collaboration,' he said, 'one benefiting both sides. Assuming Sybil's increased role was recognised in financial terms?'

'Oh yes. She was happy with the increase in her salary. You see, the books started bringing in more money. They had much better sales once Sybil took over the writing.'

'So she felt she was fairly compensated for her contribution, as far as money was concerned? What about recognition of her talent?'

'Impossible. Publicly, at any rate. Readers want books written by . . . uh, under Humphrey's pen name, and they don't care who wrote them. I dare say most of them don't even realise it's a pen name. On the other hand, Humphrey signs the contracts with the publisher. There's no knowing how they might react if they found out they were written by a woman.'

'Shouldn't think they'd care,' Worrall commented, 'as long as the sales were up.'

'That's my feeling,' Daisy conceded, 'but I presume the Birtwhistles didn't want to risk killing the goose that was laying the golden eggs. Sybil certainly didn't. She relied on Humphrey for the plots. She— Someone's knocking on the door.'

'Who's there?' Alec called irritably.

The response was an indistinguishable mumble. He jumped up and went to fling the door open. Etta, the maid in dark blue, stood there looking scared half out of her wits.

'Well? What is it?'

'Please sir, I'm sorry, sir, I'm sure, but Miss Lorna said to come and tell you Dr Jordan's on the telephone.'

'Thank you, Miss . . . ?'

She stared at him blankly.

'Your name?'

'Please, sir, it's Etta.'

'Thank you, Etta. I don't bite, you know.'

'Oh no, sir, I never thought . . .'

He gave up. 'Would you be so kind as to light a fire in here?'

'Oh, yes, sir, of course, sir.'

'Thank you,' said Alec as she scurried away. He turned to Worrall. 'Dr Jordan already. Keen as mustard is right. You'd better take the call. He doesn't know me from Adam.'

'The only phone's in the front hall,' Daisy advised the inspector. 'And I was warned that the operator is liable to listen in.'

'Thanks, Mrs Fletcher. I'll have a stern word with her concerning unauthorised dissemination of police business.' He went out, closing the door.

Daisy decided it was past time to give Alec a proper welcome. She went to give him a kiss. It lasted an agreeable length of time, then she laid her head on his chest with a sigh. He kept his arms around her, warming her. She could hear his heart beat.

'*Ker-thump, ker-thump*.'

'I beg your pardon?'

'Your heart. It sounds very strong and dependable. Determined. Alec, I know I shouldn't have come without telling you.'

'If you'd told me, you wouldn't have come.'

For once she let him enjoy the delusion that he could have stopped her. 'I really am very glad you're here. I can't believe Humphrey was murdered, though. It must have been a mistake. Someone really was dosing him regularly and accidentally gave him too much.'

'Whether by accident or on purpose, the coroner would almost certainly advise his jury to bring it in as murder, because the drug wasn't being administered by a doctor as part of a course of treatment. At least, could Dr Knox—?'

'No. Absolutely not. He was extremely concerned about being unable to diagnose Humphrey's condition. He would never have prescribed a sedative when he was already dopy all the time.'

'For Mrs Sutherby's sake? So that she could continue to write the books and reap the rewards?'

'Darling, it was his doing that the police were called in at all, remember. He could have just signed the death certificate. Humphrey would have been buried and that would have been the end of it.'

'Unless he was afraid someone might question it. He told Worrall he had Birtwhistle taking nux vomica, a dangerous drug. Presumably Mrs Birtwhistle, at least, knew that. There was always the possibility she'd question whether the doctor had set the dosage too high, high enough to kill him.'

'I suppose so,' Daisy said doubtfully. 'Though—'

The door opened. Once more, Etta stood there with her

mouth open, this time apparently aghast at the sight of the Fletchers' chaste marital embrace. She bore a coal scuttle, which she almost dropped. Of course, she very likely didn't know they were married.

'I was so cold,' Daisy explained with a smile, stepping away from Alec. He, too, stepped back hurriedly, smoothing his hair, though it was the crisp kind that never looked ruffled. 'My husband was trying to keep me warm till you get a fire going. Come in, do.'

Daisy's mother, the dowager viscountess, would have been horrified to hear her daughter condescending to explain her actions to a house maid, or even simply to notice her presence. Alec's mother, the bank manager's widow, would have been horrified that they had indulged in such behaviour where a servant might come upon them. Both would have been appalled that Alec took the heavy scuttle from Etta and carried it to the fireplace.

Daisy suspected he was trying to put the girl at her ease in case he had to question her later.

In the quiet while Etta built the fire, the sound of Sybil's typewriter next door was faintly audible. Alec went over to the desk, where Worrall had left his notebook, and looked through it.

'Can you read it?' Daisy asked softly.

'Oh yes. He doesn't use shorthand. It means his notes are somewhat sketchy. I suspect he relies a good deal on his memory.'

'I bet you wish Ernie Piper was here.' DC Piper was an excellent shorthand writer, with a supply of well-sharpened pencils always at the ready and a memory to match. 'I'll take notes if you like.'

'I'm hoping Dr Jordan's report will mean no interviews and I can go straight back to town.'

'In that case, I think I'll leave with you. If you coppers have no reason to make us stay, the family won't want guests at a time like this. We can drive back together.'

Alec grinned at her. 'Now there's a pleasant prospect! Let's keep our fingers crossed.'

DI Worrall returned shortly thereafter. The omens did not look good. He was obviously bursting with news, and that could only mean Humphrey Birtwhistle had not died a natural death.

CHAPTER 18

Barely concealing his impatience, Detective Inspector Worrall watched Etta light the fire and sweep up the dust. The moment she rose from her knees, he thanked her punctiliously – with a glance at Alec – then escorted her and her dustpan to the door and shut it firmly behind her.

Turning, he announced, 'Birtwhistle died of chloral hydrate poisoning. No question about it, Dr Jordan says. A certain amount of alcohol in his system, but not excessive. He definitely didn't have a heart attack or a stroke, and there were no symptoms of nux vomica poisoning.'

'Did Jordan say how fast he would have reacted to a large dose?'

'Normally within half an hour, but you know how doctors are – they always hedge things about. Some react slower, some quicker. Whichever, he'd have gone to sleep, drifted gradually into a coma and then just stopped breathing.'

'So the first thing we need to know now is whether Dr Knox prescribed chloral.'

'I rang up Dr Knox, sir. His house keeper says he had very few patients this morning and he's on his way back here. Should be here shortly.'

'Excellent.'

Worrall looked gratified. 'Then I rang HQ to report.

You're not going to believe this, sir. Leastways, you haven't mentioned it: seems a couple more blokes from the Yard just turned up to join you.'

'Tom and Ernie!' Daisy guessed.

'DS Tring and DC Piper.'

'Alec, why on earth did you bring them all this way when you didn't even know there was anything to investigate?'

'I didn't,' Alec said grimly. 'The Super told me I could send for them if I found I needed them. He must have changed his mind and sent them helter-skelter after me.'

'But why?'

'When he rang me up at home, he sounded worried about you. I assume he considered three of us would be better able to protect you than one.'

'But Mr Crane loathes me! I always thought he rather hoped I'd be the next victim of murder, or else get arrested for it. He must be suffering from softening of the brain.'

Noticing Worrall's amused interest in this interchange, Alec said repressively, 'Nonsense.'

'Not to worry,' Worrall said. 'Probably just our Mr Oakenshawe on the fidgets. He's the deputy chief constable, Mrs Fletcher, and hardly dare blink in case the Colonel damns his eyes— Beg pardon! Tells him off for it when he comes back from the Highlands. I wouldn't put it past him to have rung up your Mr Crane again and asked for more men.'

'Not *my* Mr Crane,' said Daisy. 'But I'm glad Tom Tring and Piper are on their way.'

'They've been put on the train to Matlock. One of our chaps there is going to bring them up here. In the meantime, Superintendent Aves – the Matlock super – will have a man go round all the chemists in Matlock, asking about recent prescriptions for chloral.'

'Thank you,' Alec said with a sigh. 'You've got things well under way. Depending on what Dr Knox has to tell us, we may well need more men. In the meantime, Daisy, would you add a bit more detail to your picture of the household? Tell us about Mrs Birtwhistle.'

'You know she's American? By birth, at least. She may be a naturalised citizen. She and Humphrey met when he was in America. They married and he brought her back here to his childhood home, in the mid-Nineties, I think. She was devoted to him, I'd swear to it.'

'Hmm.' Alec looked sceptical. 'Their son? Simon, isn't it? How did he get on with his father?'

'Not particularly well, but I'd say it was just typical father-son conflict. He's a would-be intellectual and he despised Humphrey's books.'

'Oh? Why was that?'

'I suppose you have to know, but it's something else that really mustn't come out in public if it doesn't absolutely have to. Humphrey wrote Wild West novels.'

'I like a good cowboy story meself,' Worrall admitted, 'but I don't recall any written by a Birtwhistle. Oh, that's right. You said he used a pen name.'

'Eli Hawke.'

'Hawke! Tells a good tale, he does. Or she does, should I say? Seeing it's Mrs Sutherby writes 'em.'

'They collaborated.'

'Just fancy! Never met an author before in my life, and here I've got two I like, one dead and one alive and kicking. So to speak.'

Not exactly felicitously phrased, Daisy thought but didn't say. 'Simon fancies a literary life,' she continued, 'which so far equates pretty much to a life of leisure. The extra money Sybil's increased earnings has brought in helped to support him. In fact, she suspected he might be dosing his father to keep him in the background.'

'Aha!'

'But he was only a schoolboy when Humphrey fell ill. I told her I couldn't believe he was sophisticated enough to think up such a complicated plot, far less carry it out.'

'I dunno,' said Worrall, 'I've known a few pretty nasty schoolboys, and crafty with it.'

'In fact, now I come to think of it, he's been away at university, so it was impossible.'

'That's a point,' the inspector conceded, 'far as the long-term sedation goes, but it doesn't mean he wasn't the one poisoned Mr Birtwhistle in the end.'

'Thus, as I said before, killing the goose that laid the golden eggs. With his father dead, if Sybil managed to continue writing and selling the books, she'd have had no reason to give the Birtwhistles any of the proceeds.'

'For the use of the pen name,' Alec suggested, 'but you're right, it would be a chancy business.'

Worrall wasn't going to let Simon go so easily. 'Inheritance,' he said darkly.

'I don't know anything about that.'

'Never mind, we'll find out.'

'Who else did Mrs Sutherby suspect?' asked Alec.

'Myra. For much the same reason as Simon. I told you she's some sort of cousin?'

'Of Birtwhistle? That is to say, not on the American side.'

'Of the Birtwhistles. Though she didn't benefit so directly from the increased royalties, as she has a trust fund, she tends to go through her income gadding about, well before the quarter. She's in the habit of coming back to the farm till her next payment is due, so she has been taking advantage of their willingness to support her somewhat lengthy visits. Or so I gather. On the other hand, she can't have been more than fourteen or fifteen when Humphrey fell ill, and, frankly, she hasn't the brains to have worked out about Sybil taking over the writing, or how it affected her, or what she might do about it.'

'Bit thick, eh?'

'That's one way of putting it, Inspector. Light-minded would be more accurate. As far as Sybil was concerned, part of the reason she was troubled was that she likes both Simon and Myra.'

'And Mrs Birtwhistle?' Alec queried.

'She likes her and had no suspicions of her.'

'Ah,' said Worrall, 'that's worth noting that is, considering.'

Alec moved on. 'Humphrey Birtwhistle's brother and sister? Norman and Lorna?'

'Did Sybil like them? No, she did not. It's hard to imagine anyone liking them. Did she suspect them? She didn't say so.'

'I take it you don't much care for them, either. Why not?'

'Bad-tempered, discourteous, grudging and grudge-holding. Enough?'

'Enough to be going on with. Are you aware of any specific grudge?'

'Neither of them has yet got over Humphrey coming home, thirty years ago, to claim his inheritance. They'd settled in cosily together after their father died. Humphrey had run away ten years earlier to America. He told me he wasn't much of a letter writer. He led a fairly wild life in the Wild West.'

'Ah,' said the inspector. 'That'd explain the books.'

'That's right. Meanwhile, Norman and Lorna had no reason to suppose he was still alive, let alone that he'd ever come home to demand his share. It must have been a shock, but still to be muttering about it after three decades . . . !'

'Ah,' said Worrall again. Daisy tried to imagine him and Tom meeting and *ah*-ing at each other. Tom would win as far as the expressive content of his favourite monosyllable was concerned, she decided. 'All the same,' the inspector went on, 'it don't make sense for them to decide after all this time to do away with him. I can't see they'd gain much from it, him with a wife and son.'

Alec said a trifle irritably, 'I hope we're not going to have to wait for lawyers to produce wills and bankers to produce accounts. Daisy, you say Sybil didn't suspect either Norman or Lorna of doping their brother, but can you think of any motive for either?'

'Darling, don't tell me you're asking for wild speculation?' she teased. He frowned again. 'Oh, all right. Let's see. The trouble is, I know practically nothing about how the household finances were allotted, and neither does Sybil. Norman provides much, if not most, of the food, from the farms, which he's in charge of. Ruby and Lorna apparently share the house keeping duties that aren't performed by Betta and Etty. I mean, Etta and Betty, who just come in by the day. No, I really haven't the foggiest about expenses or inheritances. Ruby's probably the person to ask, though talking about finances when her husband just died . . . Rather you than me.'

'That's why women aren't police detectives,' said Worrall pompously. Alec wouldn't have dared. Not with Daisy listening.

However, a glance from Alec averted the tart comment hovering on her tongue. 'No more family?' he said. 'I doubt Etty and . . . the two maids are involved, though I'll keep them under consideration, of course, and they'll have to be questioned about anything they may have seen or heard.'

'They're not here in the evenings. I don't know what time they go home, but there are no servants helping at dinner.'

'So, the other guests. Presumably they can't be involved in the long-term nastiness.'

'No,' Daisy said decisively. 'They're both here because of Myra, and she's not long out of school.'

'Both after the same girl,' said the inspector, 'sounds to me as if they're more likely to murder each other than anyone else.'

'Did Birtwhistle forbid the banns, Daisy?'

'As far as I can make out, the only person who controls her actions in any degree is the lawyer who's her trustee. She told me all he cares about is that she doesn't overspend her quarterly allowance, poor girl.'

'Poor girl!' Worrall exclaimed.

'No one has really cared what she does with herself since she left school. I feel sorry for her.'

Alec wanted clarification: 'No one, including Humphrey Birtwhistle, was or is likely to put a rub in her way if she decides to marry either – what's their names?– Carey or Ilkton?'

'Neil Carey and Walter Ilkton. I'd be surprised if there wasn't a general feeling of relief that she's off their hands.'

'No apparent motive there, then. Now, what about Mrs Sutherby and Dr Knox? You told Mr Worrall last night that they're "not really" sweethearts. What exactly did you mean by that, Daisy?'

'They're friends. I believe he comes to Eyrie Farm somewhat more often than his patient's condition warrants, mostly to see her, though he's welcomed by the Birtwhistles. I can't see that Sybil and Roger's precise relationship has anything whatsoever to do with your investigation, even if I knew. After all, Sybil asked me to . . . um . . .' She had to avoid the word *investigate*, which would set Alec off again. '. . . to advise her, and Dr Knox refused a death certificate. And he got you involved, Alec, by telling them about my august connection with the Yard. Neither makes any sense if they planned to do away with Humphrey.'

'We've already discussed Knox's possible reasoning about calling us in. Doubtless it hasn't occurred to you that Mrs Sutherby could have involved you as a blind, that she may consider the rumours of your detecting abilities as a joke.'

'Certainly not!' Daisy said indignantly. 'Any more than Roger considers the Yard's detecting abilities a joke! Sybil was very much in earnest.'

'How well do you know her? I don't recall your ever mentioning her before you told me about this visit.'

'Not very well,' she was forced to admit. 'She was a year ahead of me at school, and you know what a gap a single year can be at that age. In fact, I'd just about forgotten her existence since she left school, until she wrote to say she was going to be in town a couple of weeks ago and then lunched with Lucy and me.'

'Just like that, out of the blue?' said Worrall. 'Sounds odd to me. I can't see why they'd be working together. Seems to me their motives clash. What I think – this is just a theory, mind! – is either Mrs Sutherby decided she could manage without the deceased and wanted all the proceeds for herself; or the doctor decided she'd never marry him as long as she was making her living with this writing business, but with the deceased out of the way, she'd have to take him.'

Alec nodded. 'Either would make sense. Sorry, Daisy. They have to stay on the list. Never mind, they have plenty of company.'

Daisy knew better than to argue. No one was ever stricken from Alec's lists of suspects until he had solid evidence of innocence or, alternatively, solid evidence of someone else's guilt. Myra and Simon were undoubtedly still on it, along with Lorna and Norman, and probably Ruby, too, however certain Daisy was that she would never have harmed her husband.

Unfortunately, in the past Alec had occasionally been proved correct about people Daisy could have sworn wouldn't hurt a fly.

CHAPTER 19

'Daisy, could you give us your impressions of how everyone took the news of Birtwhistle's death? How they looked, what they said and so on? It's not evidence but it might help to point us in the right direction.'

Daisy thought back to last night. The one thing she could recall clearly was Ruby's stark-white face when she rushed into the hall and reported that Humphrey was not breathing.

'I'm not sure. It's all blurred. As far as I was concerned, it wasn't just an elderly man dying quietly in his own bed, it was a horrible shock because of Sybil's suspicions.' She hesitated.

'I think I heard a car.' DI Worrall went out to the passage and across to the window. 'Yes, that's Dr Knox just pulled up,' he said, returning. 'I'll go and fetch him here, shall I, Mr Fletcher?'

'If you wouldn't mind. I'd rather he didn't talk to anyone else first.'

'Just what I was thinking,' said Worrall, pleased, and went out.

'Last night?' Alec prompted Daisy.

'Roger – Dr Knox – went off immediately with Ruby. He said something reassuring . . .'

'Start with that. Try to remember his exact words, and that may lead you to the rest. You have your notebook on you?'

'Always. One never knows when an idea will strike.'

'Good. Write it all down as it comes to you. Just stay where you are and concentrate, and do for pity's sake try not to interrupt.'

'You're not making me leave?'

'I don't want you talking to the others before I do.'

'But last night, and at breakfast . . . Though no one was talking much at breakfast. Lorna cooked it, just as usual, as if nothing had happened, and—'

'Just write it all down, would you, love? And while you're about it, try to remember where everyone was earlier in the evening, and what they were doing. I want to get my thoughts in order before I see the doctor.'

'Sorry.' Reluctantly, Daisy tried to concentrate on Ruby's entrance into the hall with her alarming announcement and plea for Roger's help.

Simon had gone with them, hadn't he? And Myra had burst into tears, she was sure of that. She scribbled a few notes as bits and pieces came back to her. Then DI Worrall ushered in Roger Knox, diverting her attention entirely from last night to the present.

She did her best to look as if she was still scouring her memory for details of last night, head down, pencil poised. Surely Alec didn't believe she wouldn't listen? He knew her better! Perhaps – dared she hope? – he actually wanted her to listen so that he could ask for her impressions later. He ought to have realised by now how helpful she could be, although doubtless he'd continue to describe it as meddling.

From the corner of her eye she saw Alec shake hands with Roger, a good sign as he always tried to avoid it with his major suspects. Roger, his eyes on the police officers, didn't appear to notice Daisy's presence off to one side.

'Thank you for coming up here, Doctor.'

'I wouldn't have left this morning,' Roger said dryly, 'if it wasn't that Dr Harris, though he agreed to act as my locum, wasn't at all happy about it. I thought I'd better spare him the morning surgery. I would have come back anyway, to see Mrs Birtwhistle, but I was sure you'd have a few questions for me, as Humphrey's medical attendant.'

'We do.'

'I assume you want to know whether I ever prescribed chloral hydrate for him. The answer is, certainly not. He was in need of stimulants, not sedatives.'

'What medicines was he taking?'

'Castor oil. Inactivity inhibits the normal motion—'

'Quite. Anything else?'

'Aspirin, to be taken as needed. He had the occasional rheumatic pains common at his age. And nux vomica, which I was reluctant to prescribe, but having already tried all the safer stimulants . . . However, Ruby – Mrs Birtwhistle – told me he didn't take it last night because he was in good form and he wanted a drink or two. Nux vomica and alcohol taken together often cause some discomfort.'

'I took all the medicine bottles and pill boxes last night, sir. They've gone for analysis.'

Alec nodded approval. 'What about mixing chloral and alcohol, Doctor?'

'Both depressants. The alcohol would enhance the effects of the chloral. What's more, as chloral is bitter-tasting, the particular drink that Humphrey favoured would tend to conceal the taste. He almost always drank pink gin, that is, gin and bitters.'

After a moment's thoughtful silence, Alec said, 'Suggesting that the drug was introduced into his drink.'

'Such would be my assumption.'

'Thank you, this gives us a place to start. Presumably the

glass has been washed, but we'll test the bottles.' He nodded to Worrall, who went out. 'Who poured the drinks?'

Roger hesitated. 'I can't believe—'

'Doctor, anyone who dined here last night can tell me. You just happen to be the first person I'm asking. Let me assure you, we're not going to jump to the conclusion that the poisoner must be the person who mixed the pink gins. I would guess it was probably young Birtwhistle, Simon, rather than his father or uncle?'

'Well, yes, usually.'

'Did he also hand them about?'

'I didn't get here till after dinner, and I wasn't paying much attention, but no, I'm pretty sure he didn't.'

'Who did?' Alec asked patiently.

'Come to think of it, it was one of Myra's admirers who handed me my whisky. Ilkton or young Carey, I don't recall which. You know about them, I take it?'

'We have a list of everyone who was here.'

'I've told you I wasn't here for dinner. If it was similar to the night before, Ilkton and Carey were vying to demonstrate their helpfulness all evening. The maids go home well before dinner, you see, so the family pitches in, though not in general their guests. As for after dinner last night, I couldn't say who took Humphrey his glass, not even whether it was one of those two, I'm afraid.'

Nor could Daisy remember. She had sat next to Humphrey at dinner, as she had the night before, and near him afterwards, before the card game started. Simon had poured drinks again, before, at, and after dinner, but who had delivered them she had no notion.

'Who else might it have been?'

'Myra was trying – successfully in the end – to persuade everyone to play Happy Families. A restful change after

Racing Demon the night before. Ilkton obviously would have preferred bridge or whist, but inevitably succumbed to her wiles. Miss Birtwhistle and Norman had gone off by then. Heaven alone knows how they spend their evenings.'

'Humphrey was drinking a pink gin cocktail when you arrived after dinner, though?'

'That's what it looked like.'

'Who was sitting nearest to him at that time?'

'His wife, and . . . yours? Mrs Fletcher.'

'My wife,' Alec acknowledged. 'If you have any doubts of my impartiality—'

'No, no. It was I who felt the local police ought to be made aware of Mrs Fletcher's . . . connections. I admit I hoped it would bring you here. While I've no reason to believe Inspector Worrall is not a capable detective, I was afraid there might be complications in the case beyond his competence.'

'Such as?'

'Such as the possibility that Humphrey's chronic debility was the result of taking a sedative drug, administered with or without his knowledge.'

'With! Why on earth . . . ?'

'This is what you may understand, whereas I very much doubt whether your colleague would. As long as Humphrey was ill, he didn't have to acknowledge, to himself or anyone else, that Sybil runs rings round him when it comes to writing ability. As long as he was too ill to sit at his desk and pen the words and sentences himself, he could keep on thinking of her as his secretary. He had an incentive not to recover.'

'I see what you mean. You're aware of the snag, of course. At least, I assume he wasn't fit enough to pop into Matlock, see a different doctor and buy his own prescription?'

'No. Not the slightest possibility.'

'So one way or another, someone else was involved, whether at his bidding or not.'

'You're right,' Roger said slowly. 'I hadn't really thought it through – tried to avoid thinking about it, as if that would make it go away. Which makes nonsense of the whole picture. The only person he would have trusted was Ruby, and it's inconceivable that she would agree to assist him in ruining his own health.'

Alec made no comment on this assertion. 'Accepting for the moment the hypothesis that someone was drugging him, were the symptoms consistent with long-term use of chloral?'

Roger frowned. 'No. Though there's nothing hard and fast about it, I would have expected—'

'No need to elaborate at this point, thank you. What drug had you in mind? If you went so far as to wonder.'

'Potassium bromide is the obvious choice. No doctor would hesitate to prescribe a low dose for a patient who claimed to have insomnia. He'd have no means of knowing whether such a claim was true or not. He'd probably advise against taking it regularly for long periods, which could account for Humphrey's good spells. But if the supposed patient showed no untoward symptoms and the doctor wasn't meticulous about checking dates, he might well go on renewing the prescription endlessly.'

'You, I take it, have not prescribed potassium bromide for anyone in the household?'

'Certainly not!' Roger bristled.

'I had to ask.'

'What's more, had anyone asked for bromide, or any sedative, in the past – oh, say eighteen months, I should have been on my guard.'

'Eighteen months.'

'A year is not an undue period for recovery from severe pneumonia, especially as Humphrey is – was – no spring chicken. Though the lungs may clear, the general weakness is hard to throw off. It wasn't until he started to show no further signs of improvement that I began to wonder what was wrong, and then to worry about my inability to diagnose the problem.'

'Did you call in a colleague for a second opinion?'

'Humphrey refused to see anyone else. By that point, I suspect, he was coming to grips with the fact that the books written by Sybil – Mrs Sutherby – were selling better than his own. He was in no mood to be fussed over.'

At this point, Worrall returned in triumph, bearing two bottles, one with an outsize label. He carried them carefully by the necks, each wrapped in a napkin to preserve fingerprints. 'Got 'em, sir. The only bottle of Angostura bitters in the house, and the only opened bottle of gin, and none emptied and thrown out last night.' He set them on the desk and retrieved his notebook.

Daisy gladly stopped taking notes in her idiosyncratic version of Pitman's shorthand, as she had been since he left, just in case they were needed.

'It's unlikely you'll find anything in the gin,' said Roger. 'Humphrey wasn't the only person drinking it. He may have been the only one to take bitters, but it'd be a bit of a risk doping the bottle.'

'It's a long shot, Doctor,' Worrall agreed, 'but we've got to test 'em any road. Most likely the stuff was put in his glass, don't you think, sir?'

'Most likely. Was his after-dinner drink his first of the evening, Doctor?'

'I doubt it. One before dinner, I expect, and another with his meal. He didn't care for wine. He was braving my disapproval, I may say. He always did when he was feeling his oats, though he did avoid alcohol while taking the nux vomica.'

The second pink gin had been at Humphrey's place when they went into the dining room, Daisy recalled. She was itching to say so, but managed to hold her tongue. Or, on second thoughts, was that the previous evening?

'I don't suppose you know who was sitting next to him at dinner?' Alec asked.

Roger grinned. 'No, but probably your wife, Chief Inspector. Humphrey took a fancy to her. Ruby always took the other end of the table, so Sybil was probably on his other side. But if you think Sybil—'

'I don't as yet think anything. Let's get back to the question of prescriptions. Have you any other patients in the household?'

'Mrs Birtwhistle, though she's very healthy and rarely consults me. The children – Simon and Myra – I used to see occasionally before they went away to school. If they've had need of medical attention since, it's been at their schools. The same goes for Monica, Mrs Sutherby's little girl.'

'And Mrs Sutherby?'

'Once or twice, a few years ago, not for anything significant. If she wanted to consult me now, I'd have to advise her to find another doctor.'

'Why is that?'

'The British Medical Association frowns on close relationships between doctors and their patients.'

'You have a close relationship with Mrs Sutherby?'

'Not at present, but I live in hope. I know the inspector was watching us talking last night, and I've little doubt that he drew his own conclusions and reported to you. Besides, we've nothing to hide.'

Alec nodded noncommittally. 'Miss Birtwhistle and Mr Norman?'

'I've never dealt with them professionally. It may be that they go to someone else, but they're of a class and generation that rarely seeks medical attention until in extremis.'

'Any further questions, Inspector?'

'You'll have covered a lot while I was gone after the bottles, sir. I'll wait and see what you've got.'

'Right-oh. Thank you, Doctor, you've been very helpful, and that will be all for the present. I may need your views on Birtwhistle's relations with the rest of the household, but I know you're a busy man, you're free to go back to your rounds. Please don't leave the Matlock district without informing us of your whereabouts. And I'd appreciate your not talking to anyone about the case.'

'I'm going to look in on Ruby. May I tell her ... it's murder?'

'Please do. Better from you than from a stranger. Nothing beyond the fact, though.'

'And I'd like a word with Sybil.'

'By all means. Same caveat.'

They all listened to the typewriter rattling away in the next room.

'You'll be able to tell exactly how long I'm talking to her,' Roger said ruefully.

Alec smiled. 'Yes, and we wouldn't want you to disturb her labours for too long.'

'Point taken. I'll see you later, no doubt. I'll be out on my rounds after I leave here, but my house keeper will know roughly where I am if you need me.'

'Thank you.'

Roger stood up. Turning towards the connecting door, he had his back to Daisy. She wasn't sure whether he had noticed her or not. He hadn't greeted her, but a man in the midst of a police interrogation might be excused from observance of such courtesies.

As he stepped towards the door, Worrall said, 'It's locked, Doctor. Just to keep people out of these rooms, not to confine Mrs Sutherby! Here, I'll get it for you.'

He opened the door, relocking it after Roger passed through. 'Quite alarmed he looked for a moment,' he observed softly to Alec. 'You don't suppose he suspects his ladyfriend?'

'No, but he's undoubtedly aware that we suspect her. How long do you suppose it'll be before my men and yours arrive? We need to send the bottles for analysis, and to search the house.'

'What for, sir? They've had plenty of time overnight to get rid of any evidence, before we even knew for sure it wasn't a natural death.'

'Time, but sense and forethought? People do stupid things under stress, and still more often omit to do the common-sense things.'

'Ah.' Worrall looked at his watch. 'They'll be here in an hour or less, I shouldn't wonder.'

Alec thought for a moment. 'Now that I'm pretty certain it's a case of murder, not accidental ingestion, I'm going to ask you to gather everyone together in the hall and keep them there until we've done a thorough search. That includes the maids. I don't want them running about emptying wastepaper baskets. Mrs Birtwhistle, too, unless Dr Knox insists on her staying in bed. And we'll have to have them turn out their pockets, I'm afraid, and the ladies' handbags. Better not warn them about that till we're ready to do it.'

'Er, were you going to tell me what Dr Knox had to say, sir?'

'It might as well wait until the others arrive.' Alec looked at Daisy for the first time in half an hour. 'That will give my wife time to write up her notes.'

'How do you know—? Oh, all right. I didn't bring my portable, though. You'll have to make do with longhand.'

'I expect Mrs Sutherby would let you use her machine, as I'll be asking her to step in here to answer a few questions.'

'Alec! But I wanted to—'

'I dare say, but you will be in there typing and she will be in here talking. I shouldn't worry, I expect she'll give you a verbatim report later.'

Daisy wanted to call him a beast, but – though she wouldn't have hesitated in front of Tom and Ernie – that wasn't proper language to use to a detective chief inspector in front of an officer from another force.

Worrall gave her a sympathetic grin as he went to unlock the door again. Opening it, he said, 'Mrs Sutherby, the chief inspector would like a word with you, in here, if you please.'

He stood aside, and Daisy went through. Sybil was standing up behind her desk, pale and a little flustered. She wore round-lensed eyeglasses with light-grey celluloid frames. For some reason they made her look much younger and defenceless.

The door to the passage was just closing – behind Roger, Daisy assumed.

'Sybil, may I borrow your typewriter while you're otherwise occupied? Oh dear, I hadn't thought. I'm afraid it'll muck up your carbons.' Reinserting into the roller a stack of three sheets of typing paper interleaved with two sheets of carbon paper was too rarely successful to be bothered with.

'I just started a new page. I can easily copy it over.' She took off her glasses, folded them and set them on the desk. 'Wh-what does he want?'

'Just to ask a few questions. He's not going to browbeat you, I promise.'

'Roger said Humphrey was . . . was murdered.'

'It certainly looks like it.' And Daisy could not conceive of any reason for Roger to invent a story that led inexorably to such a devastating conclusion.

CHAPTER 20

Mrs Sutherby came in looking cold and frightened. Alec moved over to the fireplace.

'Come and sit here, Mrs Sutherby.' He picked up the blue shawl Daisy had left behind. 'Put this round you. The room had no fire and it's just beginning to warm up.'

Obediently she took the shawl and, with shaking hands, draped it about her shoulders. She dropped into a chair as if her legs would barely hold her. 'I'm not really cold, I'm . . .'

'Afraid.' Alec sat down in the second armchair. 'Murder is frightening. It's not something even we in the police ever get used to, the deliberate taking of a human life. But I don't think the thought of murder – the idea of it – is really what you're afraid of, is it?'

'A murderer . . . in the house . . .'

'That's not it, either.' He tried to sound gentle yet determined. She'd been widowed young, he recalled Daisy telling him. At this moment she looked fragile, despite her sturdy figure, but she must be tougher than she looked to have built a new life for herself and her daughter. 'I'm not an ogre, you know.'

She managed to smile. 'That's more or less what Daisy said. You don't believe Roger – Dr Knox – killed Humphrey, do you?'

'I think it highly unlikely.'

'He wouldn't. He's the kindest of men. He'd never harm anyone, even if he weren't a doctor.'

'I'm interested to hear why you think I might suspect him, what motive you would ascribe to him. It might help me to understand the motive of the actual culprit.'

'I can't see how.' She blushed. 'It's private and personal.'

'Mrs Sutherby, in a murder investigation, even the most personal matters cannot remain private. Very often, in what you might call a domestic murder, relationships are all-important.'

'Didn't Daisy tell you?'

'No. How she interprets your dealings with Dr Knox is of little use to me compared with your own words.' To say nothing of the fact that Daisy had refused to talk about the couple.

'And Roger?'

'Dr Knox preserved a gentlemanly reticence on the subject.'

'He would.' Another smile, not forced this time: she was relaxing a bit. 'I suppose it's up to me, then. Will you have to tell Inspector Worrall?'

'Only if it seems likely to be useful. And it won't be made public unless it turns out to be material evidence, in my view a remote possibility.'

Her colour deepened and she looked down at her hands, clasped in her lap. 'Roger wants to marry me. I'm very fond of him, but . . . You see, I've been supporting myself and my daughter for a good many years now, doing work I enjoy, for the most part making my own decisions, not even having to deal with the dull business of keeping house. I'm used to being independent, and I can't easily give that up.'

'Very understandable. But, with your employer gone . . . ?'

'Did Daisy tell you about . . . the books?'

'That you've been writing them since Birtwhistle fell ill, yes.'

'It's not that simple. We've worked together. The stories are still Humphrey's. I don't know whether I could write a book without his ideas to start from, and if I could, under my own name, it might be years before I made a living at it. If it was just me . . . But I have to consider Monica. I'd have to try for an ordinary secretarial job, which wouldn't pay nearly enough for her to go to a private school. We'd be pinching and scraping to get by.'

'So Dr Knox might reasonably expect that Birtwhistle's death would make his offer of marriage and a comfortable home wellnigh irresistible.'

'Yes. But even if he were the kind of man who might commit murder – and of an old friend – it's not as if we're madly in love.'

Her last statement was unconvincing, as if she herself were not convinced by it. Alec wanted to tell her not to confuse 'madly in love' and 'deeply in love'. She had probably been madly in love with her husband. She must have been very young, and she hadn't been granted time for their love to deepen – or to dissipate.

The same was true of Daisy and her fiancé, also killed in the War. Much as he hated to admit it to himself, Alec still felt a twinge of jealousy on the rare occasions when the thought of the man Daisy had once been engaged to crossed his mind.

Alec had no way of comparing their experience with his own. He had been madly in love with Joan, his first wife, but they had had years together with their love growing stronger. Losing her to the post-War influenza pandemic had been agony.

And that was a train of thought not to be encouraged.

His daughter and his work had pulled him through. The same was very likely true of Sybil Sutherby, making it that much more difficult to give up her job voluntarily.

The job had vanished with Birtwhistle's death. On the face of it, she had every reason to want him alive.

'Have I helped?'

'A little.' This sort of case almost always started off with a process of elimination. While Sybil and Knox could not be dropped from his list, they had moved to the bottom, always to be desired when it came to those whom Daisy had taken under her wing. 'Tell me about Humphrey Birtwhistle. I have no real sense of what sort of man he was.'

'He was always kind and polite to me, generous, too. And kind to Monica, or I couldn't have stayed in the first place. Not that he's terribly interested in children – there are very few in his books. I don't know what sort of father he was when Simon and Myra were small children. Myra was five or six, I think, when the Birtwhistles took her in. I've just picked up bits of family history here and there, I'm afraid, apart from Humphrey's salad days, of course.'

'I'm more interested in his recent interactions with Simon and Miss Olney.'

'He didn't take much notice of Myra. I'm afraid no one did, except her endless string of beaux. Daisy pointed it out, and I feel guilty about neglecting her, poor girl, especially as she's always been very sweet with Monica.'

'Did Myra ever appear to resent the general neglect?'

'Not at all. She's a good-natured girl, happy-go-lucky. She's away a lot of the time, visiting friends. She seems to have an endless supply. She comes here when she runs out of money before the end of the quarter. I always assumed that was the only reason she visited, but I gather she told Daisy something about depending on us – or rather, on the Birtwhistles – for a respectable family background.'

'Which will hardly be enhanced by a murder in the family.'

'Very much the reverse. Besides, she couldn't possibly have been giving Humphrey daily doses of some drug or other. She's elsewhere most of the time. The same applies to Simon. He was away at university during term-time.'

'It would certainly appear that neither could be responsible for the long-term poisoning, if any.'

'I don't know why I ever thought it could be them!'

'It's hard to see clearly through one's fears. What about Simon and his father since he's been home?'

'Not good. About a year ago, Simon started to grow too big for his boots, fancying himself as a member of the literary avant garde. He announced that he despised Humphrey's books and, what's more, had no intention of becoming a sheep farmer, thus offending both his father and his uncle. But it's just a stage he's going through, I'm sure.'

Alec remembered that stage. His father, a bank manager, had strongly opposed his going into the police. Alec had followed his own road, and rarely regretted it, but there had been a degree of estrangement for a while. 'Very likely,' he said.

'Doesn't every child start out believing his parents know everything? Then he discovers they're not omniscient after all, and then he reaches an age where he deludes himself that he's the one who knows everything.'

'A new seven ages of man?'

'I've only got as far as three, though I dare say I could develop it further if I made the effort. What I'm attempting to say is that at his age it's normal, if not universal, for father and son to be at odds. Simon's trying to prove himself, and as he hasn't got much to show, he's set about it by belittling others. My brother was just the same.'

'You have a brother?' Alec wasn't sure why he was surprised. He'd taken for granted that Sybil lacked a family to help her in her widowhood.

'I do. He's a clergyman, working his way up through the cathedral hierarchy in Norwich. He's always struggled with a feeling that he ought to be supporting me, a desire for an unpaid house keeper and a strong disinclination to introduce a child into his household. We exchange birthday and Christmas cards. But that's beside the point. Humphrey himself was about the same age as Simon is now when he ran away to America, as Daisy pointed out to him.'

Alec laughed. 'Daisy would.'

'Humphrey liked her. He pretty much ignored our other guests. Ilkton and Carey, I mean. He was good at ignoring people. I suppose he had to learn the art when he came home from America with his bride to a less than rapturous welcome from his brother and sister.'

'Ah yes, Norman and Lorna Birtwhistle. Tell me about them.'

'I hardly know them,' she said awkwardly. 'You may think that's not possible after living in the same house for years, but they've always managed to ignore me, the way Humphrey ignored them. When I first came to Eyrie Farm, I had to be very firm with Miss Birtwhistle about not helping with the house keeping. I was employed as a secretary, not a maid or a kitchen skivvy. She didn't take it kindly and she's scarcely spared me a word since. You'll have to talk to them. I wish you luck; they're both of them taciturn in the extreme.'

'All right. That leaves Mrs Birtwhistle. Daisy told me you like her.'

'So anything I say in her favour is liable to be biased?'

'It's something I have to take into account. As with everything Daisy tells me, too. Ruby Birtwhistle, please.'

'She's been invariably kind to me. I've never seen any signs of strife between her and Humphrey, and she cared for him in his illness with unfailing patience. As you're going to take anything I say with a pinch of salt, I'll stop there.'

'For now,' Alec said with a smile.

She was a different woman from the terrified creature who had crept into his lair. Sometimes he wondered whether it would be easier to use the tactics of those police officers who worked by intimidating witnesses and suspects, rather than trying to set them at ease. He always decided in the end that the old proverb was right: honey catches more flies – though Daisy claimed he could, with a single glance, freeze an evil-doer to the marrow of his bones.

He asked Sybil for a description of people's movements on the previous evening, but for the most part she was unable to add to what Daisy and Knox had told him. She and Daisy had indeed sat on either side of Birtwhistle at dinner, as Knox had surmised, but they had been talking and she hadn't paid attention to who brought the drinks, as one doesn't notice a waiter in a restaurant. One new fact emerged: Ruby had helped her husband to bed.

'When she came back, I heard her tell Roger that Humphrey had suddenly become sleepy and rather dizzy. Roger went to see him.'

Daisy would doubtless have got round to that if they hadn't been interrupted by the doctor's arrival, and Knox likewise if the question of bottles had not diverted their course. There was definitely something to be said for being alone with one's witness in a quiet room at a police station.

Having a spare constable to guard the door and run errands would be a major improvement. Alec frowned, wondering where the troops had got to.

Sybil Sutherby looked at him questioningly.

'I'm expecting some colleagues,' he explained. 'DS Tring and DC Piper—'

'DS? DC?'

'Sorry. Detective Sergeant and Detective Constable. My men from Scotland Yard. Daisy knows them well. And at least one local officer will be coming up from Matlock.'

Some of her new ease evaporated. 'We're going to have police "crawling all over the house", as Simon so charmingly put it?'

'I dare say there will be a certain amount of crawling involved,' Alec admitted.

'I don't want my daughter to come home to a swarm of coppers – I hope that's not an offensive term?'

'Not at all. We use it ourselves.'

'Will you be finished by the weekend?'

'I have no idea, can't promise anything.'

'I'd better write to Monica's headmistress and ask if she can stay at school, or go home with a friend. Oh hell! as my cowboys are wont to say. If ever I'm tempted to commit murder, I'll remind myself just how inconvenient the consequences are for innocent and guilty alike!'

'Rather more so for the guilty, I hope. But you're right. The deliberate taking of a life always has reams of unintended, unforeseen, unimagined consequences and often disrupts the lives of those who have little connection with either the victim or the villain.'

'I can't claim that distance. After years working closely with Humphrey, I . . .' She bit her lip but couldn't stop the tears flowing.

Alec passed her a handkerchief. Expecting a tearful interview with Ruby Birtwhistle, he hoped he had brought an adequate supply.

CHAPTER 21

Daisy was a trifle indignant that Detective Inspector Worrall insisted on her joining everyone else in the main hall. His wink did not mollify her. Not that she really wanted to be anywhere else.

'Everyone' did not include Sybil, who was being interrogated by Alec at that very moment; Ruby had not come down yet – Roger Knox was said to be with her; and Norman Birtwhistle had gone off somewhere on the farm, as usual. So everyone, besides Daisy, was Simon, Lorna, Myra, Ilkton and Carey, gathered by a blazing fire, with Betty and Etta huddled whispering as far as they could get from the rest. Ilkton's servant stood near the maids, against the wall, hands folded in front of him, looking supercilious.

'There'll be no lunch for anyone,' Lorna said ominously, 'if I'm not allowed in the kitchen.'

'I'm sorry, madam,' Worrall said cheerfully, 'but the chief inspector said everyone in here till our reinforcements arrive.'

Lorna pursed her lips but said no more.

'Reinforcements?' Simon laughed, rather wildly. 'What did I say? A copper in every corner! Peering under the beds, digging through the flour canister, hiding behind the arras.'

'Exactly, sir.' The inspector beamed. His sharp eyes flitted from face to face. 'You've got the idea down pat. Raking through the ashes, opening every drawer. Shouldn't be surprised if you read detective stories.'

'Pah!' said Simon.

Neil laughed. 'I'm afraid he regards that as an insult, Inspector. Though Poe has artistic merit, old chap, you must give him that.'

Whether or not it was Neil's intention, he diverted his friend from outrage at the police presence to an argument about Edgar Allan Poe. He himself seemed as chipper as ever, taking the rough with the smooth, aided by an ever-ready quip.

Daisy's gaze followed the inspector's from face to face, lingering to analyse what she saw.

Simon, she thought, had not yet altogether come to grips with the fact of his father's death, let alone his having been murdered. There was no telling how the mercurial young man would react when it finally sank in.

Lorna's usual combination of sullenness and aggression was overlaid with disquiet. To one so limited in her outlook, so bound to 'the trivial round, the common task', the present upheaval must seem overwhelming. If she weren't so phlegmatic by nature, she'd probably be in hysterics.

Myra's beautiful, artfully rouged mouth had a tragic droop, and her mascaraed eyes were red-rimmed. She was painting her fingernails carmine. Daisy guessed that the familiar action took her mind off the distressing circumstances surrounding her. She was wearing a tailored forest-green tweed costume, probably her church clothes – needed at some of the houses she visited – and the most sober she possessed.

Walter Ilkton hovered over her with his usual proprietary

air. Nonetheless, the glance he cast at DI Worrall was unmistakably edgy. Here he was, a man of the world, not only compelled to hobnob with the minions of the law but to do so in a milieu not his own where his superiority was not obvious! At home, the police would be more clearly distinguishable as his inferiors. Perhaps, though, Daisy thought, he considered it preferable to suffer the indignity out of sight of his peers.

Ruby came in, followed by Roger Knox. Hollow-eyed and hollow-cheeked, she looked as if she hadn't slept a wink all night.

'Aunt Ruby!' Myra jumped up, spilling nail varnish down her skirt. 'Oh, *blast*! It'll never come out. Aunt Ruby, are you all right? Come and sit down.' She was about to hug her aunt, then looked ruefully down her front and took her arm instead.

Ruby sank bonelessly onto a sofa. Simon tucked a cushion behind her and sat down beside her, taking her hand.

'Mother, you shouldn't have come down. Do go away, Myra, that stuff stinks to high heaven. It's going to make everyone sick.'

'I'll go and change, but I haven't got anything else that isn't a bit on the bright side.'

Ruby reached up to squeeze her hand. 'It's all right, my dear. The colour of your clothes is the least of our worries.'

Myra stooped to kiss her cheek. Straightening, graceful as ever, she said, 'It does smell rather foul. Oh, but the inspector doesn't want us to leave the room.'

Worrall's nose twitched as the smell reached him. 'Mrs Fletcher, would you mind escorting Miss Olney?'

Everyone looked at Daisy, that sidelong, wary glance she had become accustomed to, though not quite reconciled to, since marrying a detective. In spite of it, she would have preferred to stay in the hall, watching and listening, but she couldn't deny that it made more sense for Worrall to remain and her to go with Myra.

Myra was apparently immune to the others' misgivings. As she and Daisy went up the stairs, she said, 'Mrs Fletcher, what am I going to do about this skirt? Do you know how to get out the stain?'

'Oh dear, I don't. If it was just a little dab, you could use remover, or petrol perhaps. But I don't think it'd be healthy to use the amount you'd need for that streak, breathing all those fumes.'

'I've got a wonderful dry-cleaner in London, but I'm afraid by the time I get it there, it'll be too late.'

The conversation continued on the same lines while Myra changed into an emerald-green woollen frock. She donned the dark green jacket over it, 'To tone it down a bit. Poor Aunt Ruby! Isn't it too awful for her?'

'Dreadful,' Daisy agreed as they returned towards the stairs. 'And for Simon, too.'

'Simon? Oh. Yes, I suppose so. I must try to be kinder to him, but he can be such a pain in the neck.'

'I know what you mean. Be patient. I don't think he's yet quite made up his mind who he wants to be.'

Myra looked baffled. The concept obviously meant nothing to her: she had never suffered any doubts about who she was, or what she wanted to do. In her way, she was as sure of herself as Walter Ilkton. Daisy couldn't see the pair as a happily married couple. Walter would expect her to conform; Myra would go her own sweet way, quite likely not even noticing his efforts.

The hall was so quiet that their footsteps on the stairs sounded loud. Even the maids had fallen silent. The effect was more of lethargy than of tension, as if everyone had already said everything there could possibly be to say, at least in the presence of the police.

Worrall, slightly apart from the group about the fire, was inconspicuous, unthreatening, but unmistakably present.

Ilkton came across to meet Myra and Daisy.

'My skirt's a dead loss, darling,' Myra told him mournfully. She looked up at him through her darkened eyelashes. 'Unless your man could do something with petrol . . . ?'

Ilkton looked startled. Doubtless his mind had been on worse calamities than Myra's spoilt clothes.

'The inspector wouldn't let him go,' Daisy reminded her.

Myra's eyes rounded. 'Does the . . . Does Mr Fletcher think Walter's servant killed Uncle Humphrey?'

'Highly unlikely, but he has to apply the same rules to everyone.'

'Oh yes, that's only fair.'

'Daisy!' Sybil came in behind them, from the passage beneath the stairs. 'Alec said to tell you he needs you. But just a jiffy—' She went on towards the fireplace. 'Ruby, Mr Fletcher wants to talk to you, in a couple of minutes, and he's wondering whether it would distress you to go to Humphrey's study, whether you'd rather see him in a different room.'

Ruby shook her head. 'No. It doesn't really make any difference. He's gone.' She dabbed at her eyes with a hankie.

Myra sat down beside her and patted her arm.

Sybil nodded to Daisy, who dashed off to find out what Alec wanted. She was fairly sure he needed her to take notes for him, as DI Worrall was employed in watching all the suspects. She was also fairly sure he'd be annoyed about it. His instinct – not to mention his training – was always to keep her as far away from his investigations as possible, but he wasn't very successful at it. One way or another, once she was involved, she stayed involved.

And however much he'd like to deny it, she was more often than not a help to him.

He was sitting at the desk, frowning at the notes she had typed for him and given to Worrall to pass on.

'You didn't remember much about last night,' he greeted her.

'Darling, I was taking notes on your interrogation of Roger, which you have in front of you. Do you want me to start thinking about it again?'

'What the doctor said didn't jog your memory?'

''Fraid not. It's all mixed up in my mind with the evening before.'

'And getting more mixed up as time passes, I'm sure. Perhaps Mrs Birtwhistle will remember more clearly.'

'She'll be here any moment. Sybil said you wanted her in a couple of minutes. I assume you want me to take notes again?'

He pulled a wry face. 'Yes, please, love. I can't wait till reinforcements arrive, and I can't risk one of that lot suddenly recalling some vital bit of evidence he failed to destroy. They had all night as it is. Even after I arrived, we hadn't any authority until we knew for sure there had been dirty work at the crossroads. Sit at the desk, will you? Mrs Birtwhistle will be more comfortable by the fire.'

'I'm glad you're thinking of her comfort. She's pretty fragile.'

Hearing footsteps in the passage, Daisy said no more. She sat down at the desk.

Ruby came in. Introducing himself, Alec steered her to an armchair and took his seat opposite. He offered his condolences. He had to do it quite often, usually to people he didn't know and more than likely suspected, for the unnatural deaths of people he didn't know. Daisy admired the way he always managed to sound sincere. In fact, he really was sincere. No policeman she'd ever met was reconciled to the seemingly inevitable occurrence of murder.

Gently Alec led Ruby through the previous evening. If anything, she remembered less detail than Daisy and Sybil about people's movements. She had been happy about Humphrey's unusual vigour and good spirits – 'He very much enjoyed talking to Mrs Fletcher,' she said apologetically, with a glance at Daisy – and she hadn't noticed much of anything else.

'Your son poured the drinks?'

'He usually does. But he wouldn't – he *wouldn't* harm his father. They had their disagreements, but it's not as if Humphrey threatened to throw him out of the house, or cut him off without a dime, or anything like that. Simon has a comfortable home. He has as much leisure as he can possibly want for writing, if he ever decides to get down to it seriously, and time to find out whether he can make a go of it. He had no serious quarrel with Humphrey and he has nothing to gain by his death.'

'He doesn't gain by Mr Birtwhistle's will? It'll be public eventually, but it might help us to know right away how he left things.'

'He told me all about it when he had it drawn up. It's complicated by provisions of his father's will though. I'll have to explain that.'

'Go ahead.'

'It was one of those ridiculously complicated Victorian wills. The estate was left to the three siblings, half to Humphrey as the eldest son, one third to Norman, and one sixth to Lorna, the only daughter. Humphrey would have it he was just being ornery – that's an American word meaning—'

'I know it.' Alec smiled. 'No need to explain.'

Returning his smile, Ruby began to relax a little. 'The

lawyer had some complicated explanation of the old man's reasons, the details of which escape me, except that if Lorna married her share was to go to Humphrey, to keep the farm in the family. There was a proviso that if Humphrey hadn't turned up within two years of his father's death, the property would revert to two thirds to Norman, one third to Lorna, though again she'd lose it if she married.'

Daisy was indignant. No wonder Lorna was such a wet blanket. Her father had ensured her a home for life, but materially reduced her chance of finding a husband. She would have had more say in running the place, though, if Humphrey hadn't come home, and brought his bride. It wasn't surprising she had resented his return, but to hold a grudge for three decades and then decide to do away with him seemed beyond the bounds of likelihood.

Ruby continued, 'I haven't read Humphrey's will, but he told me he left his share of the farms to Simon, and you can bet your bottom dollar that Norman's going to expect him to pull his weight if he wants to live here. No more relying on daddy's royalties. Any money that continues to come in from the books goes half to me, half to Sybil. Humphrey's life insurance and savings come to me. I don't know how much that will be. Certainly no fortune. I doubt it will be enough to support my son in idleness.'

'You don't sound dismayed at the prospect.'

'Where I was brought up, in the West, everyone worked. There was plenty to do on the ranch for both men and women. My father paid for me to go to college back East, but then I found myself a job, and believe me, teaching in a one-room school house was no picnic. Here in England, you're used to people with money not lifting a finger, and I've heard it's like that some places in the States. Simon's not in that position. With his share of the farm, he won't starve, but he's going to have to make his own way if he wants any more than that.'

Alec summed up. 'So neither of you is materially better off. I assume your husband made his most recent will fairly recently.'

'Yes, but how did you . . . Oh. You're right, he wasn't quite so generous to Sybil in the previous will.' Ruby sighed. 'I don't know what we'd have done without her. I hope she'll marry Roger and have just as much success writing her own books.'

That would be perfect, Daisy thought. She wrote down the bit about Sybil being indispensable but not Ruby's hope for her future, which she didn't consider to be any business of the police.

Returning to the sequence of events on the previous evening, Alec had Ruby start again at the beginning, but no further information emerged. What with Simon, Myra and Lorna all helping to serve, 'and Myra's young men were very good-natured about lending a hand, too,' she had no idea who had brought Humphrey his drinks.

'Who was seated next to you, Mrs Birtwhistle?'

'I was at the end of the table, opposite Humphrey, with Mr Ilkton and Mr Carey on either side. In spite of their helping, they never left me alone. One or the other was always there for me to talk to. Very mannerly, if only to impress Myra.'

'Are they both regular visitors?'

'This is Neil's third or fourth visit. He's really a friend of Simon's, not Myra's. I think this is the first time they've been here at the same time. Mr Ilkton's been once before, calling on Myra on his way to see his uncle at the Hydro in Matlock. You'll think me very slow, Mr Fletcher, but after three decades in this country, I still feel an obligation to invite callers to stay the night, as we used to in the West, where the next homestead might be a day's travel or more. So each time he turned up, I offered Mr Ilkton shelter for the night, and . . . well, he's rather taken advantage to stay for several days. He's very taken with Myra. Captivated, even.'

'So the visit to the uncle is just an excuse?'

'Oh, I believe he exists. A cousin, actually, I think he said. Mr Ilkton spent an hour visiting him at Smedley's Hydro yesterday, when we all went to Matlock. Whether, if Myra were not in the neighbourhood, he would be quite so assiduous in his attentions to an ancient relative who, I understand, is wandering in his mind, it's not for me to judge.'

In Daisy's view, something else Ruby hadn't lost over the years was a touch of the tart schoolmistress. When it emerged, she tended to sound more American. However, the Northern English influence became more pronounced when Alec asked how Humphrey had got on with his brother and sister.

'He had as little to do with them as possible. They made it plain when he first brought me here, in 1897, that the prodigal brother and his bride were not welcome. He had a bit of a nest egg, and they had no objection to his spending it on putting in running water! Humphrey was already eager to write about his experiences in the "Wild West". He had no interest in interfering with the way Norman ran the farms. Over the years, he's pretty much left me to work out a fair financial modus vivendi with Norman and Lorna.'

'They didn't quarrel? At least, not openly?'

'Norman's the silent type. He'll drop an occasional snide remark, but Humphrey never had the slightest difficulty in ignoring him. Lorna— Well, to tell the truth, Lorna complains so constantly, about everything under the sun, that after a while one ceases to hear her. I wouldn't expect people who vent their grievances gradually and continually like that to build up enough steam to suddenly . . . But *someone* killed Humphrey.' Ruby's calm dissolved in fresh tears. 'I can't believe it. I just can't believe it.'

Alec passed her one of his large linen handkerchiefs to replace the sodden scrap she had screwed up in her fingers. Daisy wondered with a silent sigh how many he would hand out during the course of this case. She always packed half a dozen in his travelling bag. Sometimes he came home with none at all, an expense Scotland Yard didn't reimburse.

Not that she begrudged a grieving widow a handkerchief in time of need.

Whatever Alec thought, Daisy was convinced that Ruby genuinely mourned her husband. She wouldn't have murdered him. What she might conceivably have done was obtain chloral for him. Suppose he had tired of his half-life lived in the shadow of constant lassitude. Suppose he had decided to end it at a moment when he felt well, before he slipped down again into lethargy.

Would Ruby have helped him to commit suicide?

CHAPTER 22

Alec sent Daisy to escort Ruby Birtwhistle back to the entrance hall. 'I'll see Mr Carey next, Daisy. Come back with him, please.'

He usually followed the path of trying to knock the least likely suspects off his list before he tackled the more likely. In this case, with Daisy able to give him only the vaguest outline of this odd household, and Mrs Sutherby not much more help, he had turned to Mrs Birtwhistle in spite of her position at the top of the list.

Husbands and wives were always prime suspects in a murder investigation.

While Daisy was gone, Alec sat at the desk and went over the case against Ruby Birtwhistle. She had more than one motive for wishing to be rid of Humphrey: his savings and a life insurance payment beckoned to her; perhaps she was fed up with nursing an invalid who seemed unlikely ever to recover; perhaps the possibility of leaving her unpleasant in-laws was irresistible. As for opportunity, she had sat with him after dinner, when the dose was probably administered, and she had accompanied him to his room when he retired; he was accustomed to her help with his medicaments.

Means was going to be the key to the case, Alec decided. Chloral hydrate was not something one happened to have sitting about the house. The murderer had to have obtained a prescription from a doctor and bought the stuff from a registered chemist. Somewhere were records waiting to be found.

Mrs Birtwhistle had said they 'all' went into Matlock the day before. Probably she had used the word loosely. Alec made a note to himself to find out exactly who had comprised the party.

A Matlock officer was calling on all the local chemists, according to DI Worrall. How many could there be, even in a spa town crammed with invalids? With any luck they'd soon have irrefutable evidence of who had bought the stuff. It wouldn't be absolute proof that the same person had poured the fatal dose, but the purchaser was going to have a lot of explaining to do.

Frowning, Alec recalled Dr Knox's concern that someone might have been drugging Birtwhistle with potassium bromide. Though Knox hadn't prescribed it for anyone in the house, some other doctor in Matlock might have. The chap who was checking the chemists ought to be asking about that, too.

Alec wrote a note to Worrall, requesting that he telephone the Matlock station and put them on to it.

Daisy returned, with a Black Irishman in tow. 'Neil Carey, Detective Chief Inspector Fletcher.'

Carey's bright blue eyes sparkled with mischief. 'How do you do, Detective Chief Inspector. Is it your charming wife, now, who'll be taking down my every word? Not quite according to Hoyle, is it?'

'In a moment, Mr Carey. Daisy, would you take this to Worrall, please?' He gave her the note.

'A secret order for your execution, Mrs Fletcher. You know too much. Beware!'

Daisy laughed. 'Don't be silly, Neil. Alec, you mustn't take anything he says too seriously.' She went out.

'I take murder seriously, Mr Fletcher,' Carey said soberly, 'and I assume Birtwhistle was murdered, or you wouldn't be here. How can I help?'

'For a start, tell me who went to Matlock yesterday.'

'Everyone except Humphrey and Norman Birtwhistle. Oh, and Mrs Sutherby. She stayed at home to get on with her typing. I gather Norman took some sort of livestock to market in Derby.'

Damn! Alec hoped they wouldn't have to check all the chemists in a city the size of Derby, let alone along Norman's route. It was too early in the investigation to set such an immense job in train. From what Alec had heard so far, Norman hadn't had much opportunity to dose Humphrey, though he could have been in league with his sister.

Alec returned his thoughts to the young man lounging in the chair on the other side of the desk. 'Would you mind explaining what brought you to Eyrie Farm?'

'Not at all. I met Simon Birtwhistle in Leeds – he was a student there – and we became friends. He invited me to stay. Being a bit of a rolling stone, I never turn down an invitation.'

A rolling Blarney stone, Alec thought. 'Leeds doesn't have a large Irish community, does it? What took you there?'

'There's a fair few, but it's to meet Bonamy Dobrée I went. I happened to hear he was giving a talk at the university, before going off to teach in Egypt, of all places! You won't have heard of him, I expect. I'm by way of being a playwright, you see, and isn't it himself wrote a grand book on Restoration Comedy.'

'Quite a gathering of writers here.'

Carey grinned disarmingly. 'And would-be writers. You're not interested in the travails of the unpublished, though.'

''Fraid not. I'm interested, first, in who did what in Matlock.'

'I rode my motorbike up to Smedley's Hydro to meet Mrs Fletcher, Miss Olney, Simon, and Ilkton, who'd gone in his car.'

'Mrs and Miss Birtwhistle didn't go with you?'

'No, Ilkton let them off in the town square to do their shopping. Ilkton had to visit a relative at Smedley's. Myra – Miss Olney – wanted Mrs Fletcher to admire the view. Ilkton went off to do his duty by his aged relative. The rest of us walked about a bit, then they walked and I rode down into the town. Myra and Mrs Fletcher looked round the market, and then Myra got bored and talked me into taking her on the motorbike up to Riber Castle. We arrived back here in time for lunch. The others had already come back in Ilkton's car.'

'So any of the party could have visited a chemist's shop without your knowing.'

'Anyone other than Myra. During the time I wasn't with her, I believe she was with Mrs Fletcher.'

'What's that?' Daisy returned. 'Someone taking my name in vain?'

Carey explained, and Daisy confirmed she and Myra had stayed together until he turned up and the girl went off with him. 'Simon had deserted us in favour of a pint,' she said.

'He wasn't with you?' Alec asked sharply. 'Why didn't you tell me—?'

'You didn't ask me about yesterday morning, only the evening.'

'True. How long were you apart?'

'Less than half an hour, I'd say.'

Time enough to fill a prescription, though hardly time to consult a doctor. But he could have done that previously. The same applied to all the family. 'Do you know whether Mrs Birtwhistle and Miss Birtwhistle stayed together?'

'No,' said Daisy and Carey simultaneously.

Daisy elaborated. 'No, they didn't. They're not on that sort of terms. Later, after the market, I met Ruby and we went for coffee— Oh! She was coming out of a chemist's. That's what all this is about, isn't it?'

Alec nodded. 'Do you recall the name of the chemist?'

'Gosh, no, but it was right by the bridge. Darling, there could be a million things she was buying! I'm always popping into a chemist for something or other.'

'I realise that. No one's going to be arrested on the strength of a visit to a chemist. Mr Carey, do you mind if my wife records the rest of this interview? I'm short-handed at present, but this interview can wait till my men arrive, if you prefer.'

Carey grinned. 'It's only pulling your leg I was. I've not the least objection.'

'Let's get on with this, then. I want your recollections of yesterday evening, from the moment you first saw Humphrey Birtwhistle in the hall.'

Carey had taken Birtwhistle his first pink gin, mixed by Simon, but neither the cocktail he had with dinner nor the third and last. He had no idea who did. At dinner he'd been either talking to Mrs Birtwhistle and Myra, or getting up to help pass drinks and plates, not watching what anyone else was doing. After dinner, he'd helped Myra find the Happy Families cards and then joined in the game.

Though Alec managed to squeeze a few more precise details from him, nothing of interest emerged. He had been at Eyrie Farm for five days, each much like the last except for particular events that stood out – Daisy's arrival, Birtwhistle's emergence from seclusion, the visit to Matlock. The rest blurred together in his memory. It wasn't surprising, but it was irritating.

Alec was about to dismiss him with a request to rack his memory, when a rap on the door preceded the appearance of the maid Betty on the threshold. She announced belligerently, 'That inspector said to tell you there's a bunch more coppers come. One of 'em's about the size of a hephelant.'

'Tom!' said Daisy.

'And what my dad's going to say about all these carryings-on, casting inspersions on good girls like me and Etta— Well, it don't bear thinking of!'

'If you haven't done anything wrong,' said Alec, 'you've nothing to worry about.'

'You don't know my dad.'

'That will be all, thank you.'

Pouting, Betty departed.

'Does your hephelant step on witnesses to make them squeal?' said Carey, grinning. 'I can't wait to meet him.'

'Come on then, I'll introduce you.'

Daisy was already on her way. They followed her along the passage and through the door into the hall.

The hall seemed to have shrunk. Tom – Detective Sergeant Tring – always looked particularly large in his tan-and-yellow check suit, the wearing of which meant he considered the inhabitants of a farm not to qualify as 'nobs'. Two of the men with him, in uniform, were equally tall and broad-shouldered, if less bulky. DC Ernie Piper, who barely met the height regulations, was inconspicuous in his blue serge.

To others, they must seem an intimidating group, standing just inside the front door. DI Worrall was talking to them.

By the fire, Ruby Birtwhistle seemed unconscious of the invasion of her home. She sat, head bent, twisting Alec's handkerchief between her fingers. Sybil Sutherby and Dr Knox stood to one side. They appeared to have been talking together and were now watching the invasion with more interest than alarm. Sybil had apparently given up trying to write in the face of constant interruptions and distractions.

A dowdy middle-aged woman, sitting bolt upright, wore a stony face, but her eyes moved restlessly from group to group, person to person. Miss Lorna Birtwhistle, Alec assumed. The pretty girl sitting beside Mrs Birtwhistle must be Myra Olney. She was looking about with a lively interest.

Near her, a man of about Alec's age, perhaps a little younger, stood with his hand on the back of her chair. His immaculate tweeds proclaimed the townee dressed for the country. He looked rather as if he was trying to pretend he was somewhere else, while preserving an air of superiority: Walter Ilkton, tied to this unsuitable place by his passion for Myra. The other man, dark-suited, had to be young Simon Birtwhistle. He was obviously bursting with indignation that might explode at any moment in words he'd probably come to regret.

Which could prove instructive, even illuminating.

Piper was the first in the room to spot Alec. He discreetly drew Worrall's attention to the chief inspector's arrival. Meanwhile, Carey moved swiftly across to the fireside group, put a calming hand on Simon's arm and started talking to him in a low voice. Worrall came over to Alec. The remaining four policemen followed him. Two pairs of uniform boots thudded on the stone floor. Tom, despite his size and approach to retirement age, walked almost as lightly as Ernie.

Tom and Ernie punctiliously – and with pleasure – greeted Daisy before getting down to business. Ernie Piper no longer regarded her as infallible, as he once had, but he still considered her an asset to any investigation. Tom, who had been Alec's sergeant for aeons, was their son's godfather and a mildly sceptical admirer of hers.

Worrall observed their obvious friendliness with tolerant amusement. He introduced the uniformed men to Alec. 'Constables Harwell and Bagshaw, sir. What's next?'

'Pockets. We're looking for a bottle.'

'Darling, you don't expect me to do the ladies'!'

'No. We're going to go through yours, as a good example for the others.' He raised his voice. 'Your attention please, ladies and gentlemen.' As if he didn't already have it. 'I'm afraid I have to ask you to turn out your pockets. All of you.'

'What the hell?' Simon Birtwhistle burst out.

'Simon!' said his mother sharply. 'That will do.'

'Daisy, would you mind?'

Daisy was wearing a warm skirt, with a thick cardigan over her blouse. She took off the cardigan and handed it to Worrall. She stuck her hands in the skirt pockets and took out a handkerchief, which she fluttered like a conjurer to show nothing was hidden inside, then she pulled the pockets inside out.

Sibyl was quick to copy her. As Alec had hoped, her example persuaded the others to comply, however unwillingly. The two maids even giggled as they handed their overalls to one of the constables. Alec suspected him of winking at them. He thanked heaven that the girls were decently clad underneath!

No bottle of any description was found. It was too much to hope for, but they had had to check.

'Thank you. And now, I'm afraid, I must request that you all stay in this room while the house is searched.'

Again there were grumbles. 'What for?' demanded Simon Birtwhistle.

'I'm afraid I can't tell you that. We'll be as quick as we can, I assure you. And in the meantime, I'll be interviewing those of you I haven't yet talked to.' Alec turned away and gathered his men – and Daisy – about him at the east end of the hall.

'You'll stay and keep an eye on them, Harwell. Inspector, I'd like you to take charge of the search. DS Tring and PC Bagshaw will assist. You'd better start with the bedrooms. My wife can show you which bedroom is whose, I hope.' From the corner of his eye he saw Daisy perk up. 'You know the lay-out, Daisy?'

'I think so. I'm pretty certain.'

'Can you get to all of their rooms without returning through the hall?'

'I think so. The house is a bit complicated because of the wings having been added. I'm not familiar with the old part.'

'Do your best. I want you to start with Mrs Birtwhistle's, Simon Birtwhistle's and Lorna Birtwhistle's. DC Piper will take notes for me. All right? Any difficulties?'

'No, sir, we'll get right on to it.'

CHAPTER 23

Alec hadn't enough men to cover everything, so he'd made a quick decision that he'd have to trust the two maids, who had no space of their own in the house, to guard the west wing. While Daisy led her detachment through the door to the east wing, he sent Piper to explain to the farm girls that if anyone tried to enter a room, one of them must come and tell him.

He went over to the fireplace. 'Those of you whom I haven't already met have no doubt gathered that I'm Detective Chief Inspector Fletcher. I'm in charge of this investigation, which – in case you're still wondering – I will here and now officially confirm is a murder investigation.'

The blunt statement was effective in shutting up Simon Birtwhistle, who had been about to burst into intemperate speech, in spite of his friend's restraining hand.

'Poor Uncle Humphrey!' the girl exclaimed.

'How can you possibly be sure?' asked the well-dressed man.

'Mr Ilkton, is it? I'm afraid I can't discuss that, sir. But it does make it imperative that everyone should give us every assistance with our enquiries.'

'Of course, of course.'

'So let's get on with it. I'll have a few words with you next.'

'Me? You're aware that I'm just a guest here, not one of the family?'

Alec had already turned away.

Behind him, Piper said firmly, 'This way, if you please, sir.'

Opening the door to the east wing, Alec looked to his right, where the new stairway led directly up from Humphrey's sickroom to Ruby's bedroom above. Constable Bagshaw's boots were just disappearing up the flight. Though the search could not be kept secret, Alec didn't want attention drawn to it. He appreciated Daisy's not having led the way up the stairs in the hall, in full view.

Ilkton and Piper followed Alec across the passage to Humphrey's office. Alec sat down behind the desk. Taking a seat opposite, Ilkton offered a chased silver cigarette case.

'I suppose we can smoke in here,' he said. 'They don't have a smoking room, and with an invalid in the house, one doesn't care to—'

'Better not. I have ladies to interview still.'

'Miss Olney won't mind. She's a thoroughly agreeable young lady, never makes a fuss.'

'But Miss Birtwhistle might.'

'Oh, yes, bound to. I'd forgotten about her. She's very forgettable. Could be any old farm wife, or even a house keeper.'

'You'll excuse me if I say you're a bit out of your usual milieu, Mr Ilkton.'

'Rather. I was a bit stunned when I first found out what Miss Olney's home and family in Derbyshire consisted of, but she's worth my putting up with them until we're married. We met at Stansted House.'

Alec raised his eyebrows questioningly.

'The Bessboroughs' place,' Ilkton elucidated.

'Miss Olney flies high.'

'She went to a good school and met the right sort of people, and she has a gift for making friends. All the fellows are at least half in love with her, of course, but the girls like her, too. She'll be a very acceptable wife for someone in my position, once she's cut her ties with these poor relations. Distant relations, fortunately.'

Alec wasn't sufficiently interested in him to ask exactly what his exalted 'position' was. 'I haven't yet the pleasure of Miss Olney's acquaintance. I'll be asking her shortly the same questions I have to ask you now.'

Ilkton frowned. 'She's very young. She shouldn't be interrogated on her own.'

'If she's uncomfortable, she can choose someone to be with her. We're not going to bully her. Now, may we get down to business? I'd like your view, as an outside observer, of how the members of this household got on with each other.'

'Oh, is that all? I can't say I've really noticed. One couldn't miss a certain amount of friction between young Simon and his father. Nothing out of the ordinary. I remember considering my own father a hopeless old fogy when I was about that age. Though it could have been a symptom of a more serious disagreement, I suppose.'

'You wouldn't rate it as a quarrel?'

'Not what I observed. I can't speak for what may have gone on before I came, or out of my hearing.'

'Naturally. Anything else?'

'Nothing that comes to mind. I must say, Mrs Birtwhistle seems to have been an exemplary wife, constantly concerned for her husband's comfort and well-being. I say, how can you chaps really be sure he was . . . murdered? There must be some mistake. He was an invalid, ill and elderly. Isn't it far more likely his heart simply gave out?'

'We're sure, believe me, Mr Ilkton. If you have no further insights about the family . . . ?' He paused. 'Then we'll move on to yesterday. You went with several others to Matlock.'

'I drove them. Even in my Packard we'd have been cramped if my man had chauffeured, though the Irishman rode his motorcycle – an invention of the devil, I'm inclined to think. If you want to know what they all did in Matlock, I can't help you. I went straight to Smedley's Hydro, where I paid a call on a relative who resides there. He's on the verge of senility, I'm afraid.' His mouth twitched. He raised a hand to cover it. Was he anxious lest Alec should suppose his family was prone to senility? 'But what can one expect of anyone who lives into the nineties? A grand old boy!'

'After your visit, you joined the others in the town?'

His mouth pursed in a near pout. 'When I returned to the town centre, Myra had already gone off with the Irishman on some expedition. The rest were ready to leave.'

Alec decided it was pointless to ask whether any of them seemed unusually agitated. Ilkton, self-absorbed to the nth degree, would have been far too put out by Myra Olney's defection to notice.

'All right, what about yesterday evening? You were helping to pass round drinks, I understand.'

'Myra – Miss Olney – was expected to help, so what else could I do? It's really most unsuitable . . . The sooner I can get her away from here, the better.'

'I'm afraid I can't let anyone leave for the present, sir. Getting back to last night, please tell me what you recall of everyone's movements from the moment Humphrey Birtwhistle arrived in the hall.'

Ilkton remembered no more than Alec had already heard from others. His inability to give a straightforward, detailed account flustered him. Perhaps it damaged his view of himself as a superior being. Grimacing, he apologised.

'It's a pity, but it can't be helped,' said Alec. 'People always have difficulty with the specifics when it's a question of one among several similar occurrences. Sometimes an emotional shock makes associated memories indelible, but as often as not it blurs or even erases them.'

'Emotional shock?'

'The murder of your host . . .'

'I hardly knew the man. I don't suppose we'd exchanged more than a dozen words. It was a great shock to Miss Olney, however. She was fond of the old man. So it's iniquitous to make her stay in this house—'

'I'm sorry, I can only repeat that you are *all* going to have to stay here, within easy reach, until I no longer require your presence.'

Alec half expected him to threaten to ring up his lawyer, but he just said sulkily, 'I suppose you know your own business best.'

Alec stood up. 'Thank you for your cooperation, Mr Ilkton. I hope you'll put your mind to trying to remember more about yesterday evening – though sometimes memories crop up when your mind is elsewhere. Don't hesitate to ask to see me if anything occurs to you. I'd like you to rejoin the others in the hall now. Piper, I'll see Miss Olney next. Make sure you find out whether she wants someone to come with her.'

Ilkton stood up, hesitated, then went out. Behind his back, Piper pulled a face before following him.

A true gentleman is never above his company. If that was a quotation, Alec couldn't pin it down. Ilkton, with his proud good looks, reminded him of Darcy in *Pride and Prejudice*, in love with a woman he considered beneath his station. In this case, instead of a sister's elopement, an uncle's murder had further muddied the waters. Perhaps, like Darcy, he would learn from love to be less censorious.

Alec was eager to meet Myra Olney, though she didn't sound in the least like Lizzie Bennet. Rather more, in fact, like Lydia . . .

She came in with a cheerful smile, ushered by a grinning Piper.

'Mr Fletcher!' She held out her hand and they shook. 'Or should I call you Chief Inspector? I simply adore Mrs Fletcher. She's not a bit like Sybil. Though I'm very fond of Sybil, too. She's practically family, after all, and she has the sweetest little girl. Mrs Fletcher said you have a young daughter?'

'Yes. She's thirteen, a bit older than Mrs Sutherby's, I understand.'

'I'd love to meet her. And twins as well?'

'Miranda and Oliver. They're still toddlers.'

'They sound absolutely adorable. I don't suppose I could come and meet them when I'm in London?' Myra asked wistfully.

'Why don't you talk to Daisy about it?' he suggested, conscious that Piper's grin had changed to a smirk. 'We'd better get down to business.'

'Poor Uncle Humphrey!' Her beautiful eyes – Alec couldn't decide whether they were green or blue – filled with tears. He felt for a handkerchief, but he'd run out. Fortunately the tears didn't spill. 'Sometimes I can almost forget for a few minutes. He was always so kind to me, taking me in when Aunt Lorna didn't want to at all. I can't believe anyone at Eyrie Farm would do anything so horrible!'

Myra's version of the outing to Matlock was mostly concerned with the girl they had met at the Hydro – quite pretty but rather dim – and the necklace she had helped Daisy choose for Belinda, at the market.

'Then I got rather bored,' she confessed. 'I mean, a market's not fun for very long if you haven't any money to spend, is it? So I talked Neil into leaving early. Aunt Ruby had agreed that I could go home on his motorbike. He said I'd be stiff and sore afterwards, but I'm not, not a bit. I often go riding when I visit friends in the country. I think that must be it, don't you?'

'Very likely. You left Matlock early, you were saying?'

'Only a tiny bit early, and took the long way round. Walter was a bit peeved, but I *didn't* go off without a word, I told Simon where we were going.'

It was none of Alec's business, but he couldn't resist: 'Are you going to marry Mr Ilkton?'

'Goodness, no!' She giggled. 'I'm not going to marry anyone for simply ages. Years and years. Not till I'm twenty-one, at *least*. I told Walter, but some people just refuse to believe you're serious when it doesn't suit them.' She sounded as if she had considerable experience, as she quite likely did.

'Very true. Was Simon with you the whole time until you and Mr Carey left?'

'No, he went to a pub to drink beer. It was knowing the Hydro is TT, you see. It made him thirsty.'

'I see.' Alec managed to keep a straight face. 'And your aunts, did you see either of them after dropping them off in the town square?'

'Not till lunchtime. Neil and I were home in time for lunch. I promised Simon. He didn't want Aunt Ruby to worry. It's a bit of a bore, in a way, having someone worrying about you, but it's sort of nice, too, if you know what I mean. I don't mind helping in the house, either, whatever

Aunt Lorna says, as long as they don't expect me to cook. And they're not likely to ask me, after last time!' Again came that infectious giggle.

Alec refrained from enquiring about the domestic disaster. 'Tell me about the evening,' he said. 'You were helping then?'

'Yes, I gave Aunt Lorna a hand in the kitchen. She does breakfast and Aunt Ruby does lunch, and they take turns, week by week, with dinner. I just help with dishing up and carrying stuff to the dining room. Oh, and washing up after. But Neil and even Walter have been jolly good sports about carrying in the trays. They've even helped with the washing up.'

'So you spent some time in the kitchen, and you were in and out of the hall and dining room?'

'Exactly.' She beamed at his ready comprehension.

'You don't help with drinks, though?'

'Hardly ever. If I'm at home and Simon's not, as often as not we don't have cocktails or wine. Uncle Norman sometimes drinks beer. Last night, Simon was in charge, and I think I saw Neil and Walter helping when they weren't helping me. And Aunt Lorna.'

'Did you happen to notice who served your uncle's drinks?'

Her eyes grew round. 'No. Is that how he was killed? How mean! He enjoyed his pink gin so much, and he was hardly ever well enough to have it.'

A novel view of murder! Alec asked a few more questions, with little hope of anything new emerging. She told him, in considerably more detail than he wanted, about coercing Ilkton into playing Happy Families.

'He only plays bridge, really, but he couldn't not, not without looking like a rotten sport. He couldn't play for toffee. I suppose he couldn't be bothered to put his mind to a children's game. He was hopeless at Racing Demon, too.'

Alec sincerely hoped Myra would not marry Ilkton. He didn't think she'd suit him at all.

On the other hand, he was clearly crazy about her. Perhaps he wouldn't find fault with her silly chatter when artless spontaneity aged to stupid tactlessness, à la Mrs Bennet. They might rub on together well enough.

After all many people, including Alec's mother, Daisy's mother and Lucy, her best friend, had prophesied disaster for his own marriage.

He thanked Myra and sent her out. She paused in the doorway, looked back and said with a dazzling smile, 'Aren't you coming, Mr Piper?'

'He'll be along in a minute or two,' Alec told her. 'I'm sure I can trust you to go straight back to the hall.'

'Of course,' she said indignantly. With one of her lightning changes of mood, she then confessed, 'This is quite the most exciting thing that ever happened to me!' And changed again to a disconsolate: 'If only it wasn't for poor old Uncle Humphrey!'

With that, she took herself off. Piper, apparently mesmerised, watched her go.

'Don't tell me she's struck you all of a heap,' said Alec, with some asperity.

'She's quite a . . .' Piper, unusually, was lost for words. He shook his head. 'Sorry, Chief. Who'd you want to see next?'

'Norman Birtwhistle, but I suppose he's still out on the farm.'

'D'you want me to go and look for him?'

'No, he'll have to wait. He usually comes in for lunch, I gather.'

'That leaves Miss Birtwhistle and Simon Birtwhistle. You reckon they're our best bet, one or t'other?'

'I do indeed, Ernie, I do indeed, unless I've very much misread Mrs Birtwhistle.' He yawned enormously. 'Beg your pardon! I got very little sleep last night. Yes, Simon's top of my list, so let's see if we can eliminate Lorna before I tackle him.'

CHAPTER 24

Daisy had led her three policemen up the extra staircase put in for Humphrey's convenience. It took them up towards the front of the house to a landing just outside Ruby's bedroom.

Feeling like a traitor to her kind hostess, Daisy opened the door and stood back. 'Mrs Birtwhistle's room.'

Worrall went in and stood looking about him. Tom stood on the threshold, blocking Daisy's view, for a minute, then joined him. Daisy and the uniformed constable stayed at the door, awaiting instructions. The room, its walls white, was well-lit by windows in two walls. Summer-sky blue curtains matched the bedspread. The furniture was Arts-and-Crafts of the plainer sort, double bed, night tables, chest-of-drawers, wardrobe and a couple of straight chairs. A blue-and-beige rug covered part of the wood floor, picking up the colours of a couple of paintings of New Mexico scenery hanging on the walls.

'Mrs Fletcher,' said Worrall, 'what's through there?' He gestured at a door in the north wall.

'Mrs Birtwhistle's sitting room. I think it used to be a dressing room.'

He went over, opened the door and glanced in. 'A desk,' he observed. 'Well, you're the great Scotland Yard expert, Mr Tring. How would you go about the search?'

'Ah,' Tom ruminated. 'It's not a question of fingerprints at present, not till we find something that needs checking. Mr Fletcher would likely say divide up the task so's we're each of us responsible for a part of it.'

'Do you want to take the desk?'

'Not me! I'm no great shakes at paperwork.'

'All right, I'll do that. Wardrobe, chest-of-drawers and bedside drawers for you. Mrs Fletcher, would you mind keeping an eye on the corridor and letting me know if anyone tries to get into any of the rooms?'

'Isn't the constable in the hall supposed to keep everyone together?'

'Yes, but there's only one of him and quite a few of them. If someone claims to need to . . . er . . . visit the cloakroom and tries to sneak up—'

'Oh, of course. I'll stand guard.'

'Thank you. Bagshaw,' he said to the constable, 'all the usual places in here. Then come through to the other room.'

'It's a medicine bottle we're looking for, sir?'

'That's right.'

'Inspector,' said Daisy, 'I've just thought. You're looking for a typical brown glass medicine bottle, right? But mightn't the chloral have been transferred to some other container before it was brought to the farm?'

'You've got a point there, Mrs Fletcher. Any small bottle that has no obvious purpose, I suppose. Even if it's been washed out, the cork or stopper might still have traces of chloral.'

Daisy watched the swift but meticulous search, with an occasional glance along the passage, though she was sure she'd hear if anyone came up.

PC Bagshaw stripped the bed, including taking pillow-cases off the pillows, swept his hand under the mattress from both sides and made it up again with a speed and neatness that any house maid might do well to emulate. He lay full length on the floor to peer under the bed, climbed on a chair to look on top of the wardrobe and pulled the chest away from the wall in case anything had been slipped down the back. Then he rolled up the rug. He tested the end of every plank with his foot, presumably to make sure none were loose enough to make a hiding place. He took a sheet of newspaper from his pocket and emptied the waste-paper basket onto it, poked through the ashes in the fireplace and even looked behind the pictures.

Meanwhile, Tom went through every pocket of every garment in the wardrobe, pushing aside the hangers to check behind them, even pulling the two drawers at the bottom all the way out to look into the cavity. Daisy was particularly impressed by the care he took to return everything to as near its original state as possible. He gave the bedside tables the same treatment, and flipped through the three books on top of one of them.

If anything were hidden anywhere in the room, they would find it, Daisy reckoned. What 'it' might be, other than the bottle that had held the chloral, she wasn't certain. No one could hide a bottle between the pages of a book or behind a painting.

'I'm about done, Sergeant,' said Bagshaw. 'Need any help?'

'No, thanks,' said Tom. 'You can go next door.' He turned to the chest-of-drawers, now back against the wall.

In the top left drawer, beneath a pile of undies, he found a bulging manilla envelope.

'Not Ruby!' Daisy exclaimed, shocked.

Tom opened the unsealed envelope and took out a thick wad of papers. He shook his head benignly. 'Fivers. Must have a couple of hundred quid here. You wouldn't believe how many women keep a cache of cash or jewellery in their *lang-jerry* drawer.' Tom had a notable vocabulary, but French pronunciation was beyond him. 'I hope you don't, Mrs Fletcher. It's the first place a burglar looks.'

'So Alec told me.'

A twitch of Tom's moustache gave away his grin. 'You used to.'

'Just a few pounds, for emergencies. No one ever found it. But then, we never had a burglary.'

'And I hope you never do.' He tucked the notes back into the envelope and returned it to the bottom of the drawer.

As he started to fold Ruby's plain cotton undies, Daisy offered, 'Would you like me to do that?'

'You're s'posed to be watching the hallway, Mrs Fletcher.'

'Oh, yes.' Daisy turned and stared along the hall. 'I have been, honestly.'

'I'll tell you what, I'll put one of these chairs out there for you to sit on while we do the rest of the rooms.'

'Thank you,' she said meekly.

'If you want to leave before we're done, just let DI Worrall know. That Bagshaw can take care of it. Not but what he's a fair hand at a search,' Tom conceded, setting down a bentwood chair facing the length of the corridor. Returning to work, he closed the door behind him.

Daisy could hear the sounds of Tom finishing off the chest-of-drawers and going through to Ruby's sitting room, from which came voices and the clomp of Bagshaw's boots. After a couple of minutes, the door to the corridor opened and Tom and Bagshaw came out.

'Enough stuff in that desk to keep the inspector busy for a while yet,' Tom said to Daisy. 'Whose is the next room?'

'Simon's, I'm pretty sure. The victim's son.'

'Ah,' said Tom.

'He's a budding author, so you may find a lot of papers in there.'

'Ah,' said Tom with a note of gloom.

He and Bagshaw disappeared into the room. Daisy sat on her chair, which grew harder and harder as she grew more and more bored with watching an empty passage. The only movement was a couple of crows flapping past the nearest window and a pigeon strutting on the bit of roof within her view.

She was tempted to tell Worrall she was ready to abandon her post. However, in the past she had been forbidden to take part in enough investigations to appreciate being given a task at least potentially useful. Admittedly, the prohibitions had rarely had much effect on her subsequent involvement. Still, it was nice to be asked.

What would she do if someone did come up? Simon might turn tail if warned that the police were in his room. If not, he could go in and try arguing with Tom Tring. Myra, Daisy thought she could deal with. But if Lorna appeared . . . Well, Lorna was not the sort of person one would choose to try to dissuade from a course of action she had set her mind on.

The other constable was watching them, she reminded herself. And if Lorna did escape him, Daisy could always call for help.

In fact, Worrall had instructed her to inform him, not to deal with an intrusion herself. No doubt he'd be annoyed if she sent Simon or Myra back downstairs with a flea in his or her ear. She would have liked to be able to tell Alec she'd been really helpful, but come to think of it, Worrall might well want to question an interloper on the spot.

The only person who appeared was Worrall himself, coming out of Ruby's sitting room.

'The others are still next door, in Simon's room,' she told him.

'No one . . . ?'

'Not a soul.'

He thanked her and joined the others. A few minutes later they all came out. If they had found anything incriminating, they hid it well.

'The next is Myra's,' Daisy said.

The monotony continued. No one came up Humphrey's stairs. No one came through the door from the hall stairs. The chair turned into an instrument of torture. Daisy decided Worrall wouldn't mind if she strolled back and forth for a while.

Myra's room didn't take them very long. Daisy was halfway along the passage when they came out.

'Just marching up and down on sentry-duty,' she explained. 'The end room is Lorna's. Miss Birtwhistle.'

'And the three doors in the opposite wall?' Worrall asked.

'They open into the old house. If it's the same lay-out as the west wing, the one at the end is the bathroom, then the lav, and this one is Sybil's – Mrs Sutherby's – bedroom and sitting room. They used to be the nurseries and before that, before the wings were built, the main bedrooms.'

'Miss Birtwhistle's first,' the inspector decided.

Daisy couldn't help herself – she followed them and glanced through the doorway as they trooped in. She had seen Lorna's bedroom only in the middle of the night, by candlelight. By daylight, it looked just as drab but the plain iron bedstead had a spring mattress and a thick eiderdown.

Tom glanced back at her. The door closed as she hastily resumed her patrol.

When she returned to that end of the corridor, she noticed that the door was slightly ajar. The latch must not have caught. She could hear their voices. Stopping where she couldn't possibly be seen, she listened.

'She's been burning paper in the grate, Mr Worrall,' said Bagshaw.

'Anything identifiable?'

'Naw. It'd crumble if you touched it.'

'What about the w.p.b.?'

'Just getting to it.'

Daisy heard the rustle of paper as he spread out his sheet of newspaper and dumped the contents of the waste-paper basket. 'Tangles of grey hair cleaned from a hairbrush, bits of paper ... Here, look at this! A torn-up receipt from Asbury's.'

'Asbury's?' Tom asked.

'The chemist's,' the constable told him. 'Right by the bridge in Matlock it is.'

Daisy pushed the door open another few inches, enough to watch as Bagshaw sorted out eight scraps of paper from the other odds and ends. Worrall took them from him and pieced them together on the bed.

'Yesterday's date all right. But it's not for chloral. Chloral is dispensed as a liquid.'

Tom, peering over his shoulder, rumbled, 'What's it for?'

'"Miss Birtwhistle, the powders, one at bedtime as needed,"' Worrall read, then, energized, 'Could be bromide. Come on, fellows, we've got to find the stuff. Sergeant, check the bathroom, would you?'

Daisy hastily backed away. Tom came out, saw her and raised his eyebrows. Since his forehead reached all the way to the nape of his neck, it was rather like a couple of hairy caterpillars shuffling sideways up an egg.

'Just patrolling.'

'But you heard.'

'Well, yes. It rather looks as if Sybil was right.'

'Sybil? I haven't heard a lot of the story yet, remember.' As he spoke, he crossed the passage and went into the bathroom.

Daisy followed and leant on the doorpost, watching him turn out the contents of a small, white-painted cabinet. 'She wouldn't hide anything in here. Several people use this bathroom. Sybil is Mrs Sutherby, my friend. Humphrey's . . . secretary.'

'Mistress?' Tom asked bluntly.

'Heavens no! It's just complicated.'

'The Chief'll explain if I need to know. Nothing in here.' He straightened and looked round for other possible hiding places.

'You know Humphrey Birtwhistle had been ill for years? Never properly recovered from pneumonia? Sybil was afraid someone was drugging him with some sedative.'

'Sleeping powders, such as potassium bromide. It doesn't look good for Miss Birtwhistle, but let's not jump to conclusions. I'll take this waste-basket across and let Bagshaw deal with it.'

'May I come?'

'No. But you can lurk and I won't give you away.'

Daisy stretched up on tiptoes to kiss his cheek.

Standing outside the door of Lorna's bedroom, she listened to mutterings of, 'Nothing here,' and tried to think what the discovery of the chemist's receipt meant.

As Tom said, they mustn't jump to conclusions. Perhaps Lorna had trouble sleeping and took a bromide now and then 'as needed'. In that case, they should be easily available, in the drawer of her bedside table, or at least in her chest-of-drawers. Perhaps the prescription was for some quite different medicine. But why should she hide the powders if they were for her own legitimate use? Sybil hadn't discussed her fears with any of the household, let alone Lorna, so she couldn't know there was a suspicion of Humphrey having been drugged for years.

On the other hand, supposing her responsible for that, why get a new prescription when she was about to finish off her victim with a different drug?

'Those papers in the fireplace . . .' said DI Worrall. 'Could they have been papers – those little envelopes – of bromide?'

'Better look for yourself, sir.'

'Hmm.'

After a moment's silence, Tom said, 'Don't think so, but that's just the top layer. At a guess, they're pages from the *Illustrated London News* – I noticed a few were torn out. Should we check what's underneath?'

'Yes, go ahead.'

A poker clinked against the iron grate.

'Ah!' said Tom. 'Half a mo, I've got a torch in my pocket.'

Daisy was irresistibly drawn to the doorway. The three men were crouching by the fireplace.

'Well I'll be damned!' the inspector exclaimed. 'What d'you make of this, Mr Tring?'

'She tried to destroy the medicine by burning the packages. When it wouldn't burn – it looks as if it half melted – she burnt more paper on top of the mess to conceal it.' Tom raised his voice slightly. 'Would she have cleaned out her own grate, Mrs Fletcher?'

Abashed, Daisy stepped into the room. 'Last night, when Sybil and I came to tell her that her brother was dead, she didn't have a fire at all. Assuming she never did, or seldom, the maids probably wouldn't come in here to do it without being given a specific order. My guess is she'd have felt pretty safe until she had time to deal with it.'

Worrall stood up. 'She must have realised we'd search.'

'I expect so, though I'd be very surprised if she had any idea how thorough modern detectives are. She doesn't seem to read widely.' Daisy pointed at the small table by the bed, which held only a prayer book on top of the diminished *Illustrated London News*. 'They don't get a daily newspaper. That magazine is not noted for detailed descriptions of police methods. And she's pretty isolated up here on the farm. She wouldn't have had much, if any, contact with the police. I could be wrong, but I didn't get the impression she has friends in Matlock, just went down for shopping and so forth.'

'And picking up prescriptions,' Worrall said grimly. 'Bagshaw, collect a good sample of that mess in a clean envelope. It'll have to be analysed. Assuming it's bromide, Mr Tring, as the doctor suggested, or even some other sedative, what do you think it means?'

'Ah, meaning! I leave that sort of thing to the Chief. Young Piper's getting to be a fair hand at theorising, too, I must admit.'

If Daisy theorised, Alec called it guesswork, but it came to the same thing. She hadn't actually worked out a theory yet, though, so she held her tongue.

CHAPTER 25

'Darling, could I have a quick word with you?'

Alec frowned. Daisy did her best to look as if she had something frightfully important to tell him. Which she did.

Worrall had decided Daisy's appearance in the hall would cause less disturbance, less curiosity, than his own or DS Tring's. He didn't know who was being questioned at present by the chief inspector and, short of bursting into Humphrey's office, the only way to tell was to see who was missing from the hall. If Lorna were there, she might take fright at his arrival. If she were not, that would mean she was in the middle of an interview and might take fright if the inspector asked to speak privately to her interrogator.

Daisy had managed to count heads from the doorway under the stairs, so she didn't need to actually enter the hall. She suspected Roger Knox had spotted her, but no one else. Lorna was missing.

She softly closed the door and stood thinking for a moment. Lorna was with Alec and Piper. With any luck, she would assume Daisy had some personal reason for interrupting, but if Alec had the same idea, he might refuse to cooperate. Sadly, no brilliant ploys came to mind. She crossed the passage, knocked on the door and opened it without waiting for a response.

'What is it, Daisy?' Alec asked irritably.

Lorna sat stolidly in front of the desk, not turning her head to look at the intruder, so Daisy risked a wink and an urgent jerk of the head towards the door.

'It won't take a moment, honestly.'

'Excuse me, Miss Birtwhistle.' Alec kept his impatient expression pasted to his face until the door closed behind him. Then it changed to eagerness. 'They've found something?'

Daisy explained about the prescription receipt, dated the previous day, in Lorna's waste-paper basket and the apparent burnt remains of potassium bromide powders in her grate. 'They couldn't find any sign elsewhere of the powders she bought. If she takes it herself, why try to hide it?'

'She could have been afraid it would draw suspicion to her. She doesn't – or shouldn't – know that chloral was used, unless she administered it. And in that case, why get bromide as well?'

Daisy was crestfallen. 'It doesn't really mean anything, then.'

'That's not what I said. It doesn't prove anything, but it suggests a great deal.'

'I wonder why she didn't burn the receipt.'

'Probably threw it away automatically when she came in after shopping, and forgot about it.'

'I suppose so. It was torn up and mixed with other rubbish. So what next?'

'We'll have to send the stuff from the fireplace to an analyst, to make sure it actually is bromide, or whatever potassium bromide turns into when it burns. Or some similar drug. We'll have to go to the chemist and get the name of the doctor who wrote the prescription, and interview him. We'll have to—'

'Shouldn't you get back to her now, though, darling? Or she'll start wondering.'

'Let her wonder. She won't wonder for long. I'm taking her into the Matlock station. She has some serious questions to answer. So far, I haven't got much more than "yes," "no," and "I can't remember" out of her. She's not exactly communicative.'

'To be fair, one couldn't call her communicative at the best of times.'

'If she hasn't a good explanation to give us, she's in a lot of trouble. Tom and Worrall are continuing to look for a chloral bottle, I hope?'

'Yes. Worrall and PC Bagshaw seem to be pretty thorough searchers. Not as good as Tom, that goes without saying.'

Alec grinned. 'Of course. Let me think.' After a moment's consideration, he went on, 'First of all, I'll have to consult Worrall. For one thing, if they don't find that bottle in the house, we're going to need a lot more men to search outside.'

'What if she and her brother are in league together? Norman could have taken the bottle with him and tossed it in a ditch or buried it somewhere. I don't know how big the farm is, but I shouldn't think you'd ever find it.'

With a groan, Alec admitted, 'You're probably right. Would you say they're on such terms that they might have conspired?'

'To tell the truth, I haven't a clue. I've never seen them talking to each other. For all I know they dislike each other as much as they disliked Humphrey.'

'Which wouldn't, however, prevent their conspiring to do away with him. Now, Worrall.'

'Will you go up to see him, or shall I fetch him?'

'Would you mind, love? I'd rather not leave Ernie alone

with Miss Birtwhistle when he hasn't heard the latest news.'

'You'll have to start paying me a salary soon.'

'Don't hold your breath. And Daisy, don't take this as licence to meddle.'

She ignored this with what she hoped was an air of injured innocence. She never meddled. She couldn't help it if she got involved in his cases from time to time. This one wouldn't even be his if it hadn't been for Superintendent Crane's meddling.

'Tell Worrall to knock and come in.' Alec returned to Humphrey's office.

Daisy wished she could listen to what he said to Lorna about the chemist's receipt. She trudged back upstairs, where the men had moved on to Sybil's rooms.

'If you find the bottle in there,' Daisy said from the doorway, 'it's because someone else put it there.'

'We'll bear that possibility in mind,' said Worrall with a touch of sarcasm.

'But we haven't found anything yet,' Tom reassured her. 'What's the chief going to do next?'

'Miss Birtwhistle was with him. He wants to take her in to Matlock, to the station, but he'd like to consult you first, Inspector. Just knock and go in, he said.'

Worrall left. Daisy stepped into the room. It was Sybil's sitting room and served also as Monica's playroom when she was at home. Both Tom and Bagshaw were going through the three overstuffed bookcases against the wall facing the windows, taking every book out, shaking it and checking behind. As well as a selection of modern novels and histories, all the children's classics were there: *Wind in the Willows, Alice, Black Beauty, Heidi, The Water-Babies, Five Children and It, A Child's Garden of Verses, The Secret*

Garden . . . Daisy recognised most from her youth, a few later ones from Belinda's bookshelves at home. An ottoman in a corner probably held toys and games.

'Shall I help?' she asked Tom.

As expected, he rejected her offer. The room was her friend's, after all.

'What's through there?' he asked, gesturing at the door opposite the one she had entered by.

'Sybil's and her daughter's bedrooms, I suppose. Once the night nursery and the nurserymaid's bedroom, perhaps. I haven't seen them.'

'So you don't know whether there's a door at the end to the west wing?'

'I'm pretty sure there is. When I went to bed last night – this morning – Sybil came with me up the west stairs in the hall. There's another staircase at the north end of the wing, for Norman's convenience, I assume. His bedroom is above his estate office.'

'This is an exceedingly complicated house,' Tom said severely. 'I've been in great mansions that were simpler to find your way about.'

'Fairacres, my family's home, is complicated if you're not familiar with it. It's all the alterations and additions over the years. The original farm house must have been quite simple.'

'What's the other side of this wall?' He knocked on the wall behind the bookcases.

'At a guess, a warren of small rooms. The original house must have had rooms for children, and the Victorian house for servants. A sewing room, perhaps. That sort of thing. Now that they haven't any live-in servants, they may be full of lumber. Old furniture, superannuated curtains, all kinds of junk, you know.'

Tom and Bagshaw groaned in unison.

'If we did find a bottle,' said Bagshaw gloomily, 'we couldn't tell who put it there.'

'Unless it has fingerprints,' Daisy pointed out.

'Too many crooks these days read detective stories,' said Tom, 'or at least hear about others being caught because they left their dabs at the scene of the crime.'

'Lorna isn't a crook in that sense,' said Daisy, 'and not much of a reader, either. I doubt she would think to wipe them off, if she did it.'

Tom's eyebrows crawled up his forehead. 'You don't believe it was her?'

'Well, I'm quite prepared to believe she's been drugging poor Humphrey for years, a mixture of spite and wanting the increased flow of money to continue . . .'

The men looked at her blankly.

Tom asked, 'Wasn't Mr Birtwhistle an author, bringing in money for his books? How did drugging him increase—?'

'Haven't you heard the whole story? I'd better let Alec or Mr Worrall explain. The question is, why did Lorna bother to acquire a new supply of bromide if she intended to kill her brother with chloral?'

'Could be she wasn't sure she'd be able to nerve herself to do it. If you ask me, there's a lot more murders planned than ever get carried out.'

'That makes sense. Sort of. Do you think a doctor would give her prescriptions for both chloral and bromide, though?'

'Two different doctors,' Tom suggested. 'Or maybe she got the chloral a while ago and only just decided to use it.'

'The receipt we found is only for powders,' PC Bagshaw put in. 'She must have gone to two different chemists, too, if she got both yesterday.'

'We weren't in Matlock long enough yesterday for her

to visit two doctors and two chemists' shops. She did some other shopping, too. Her basket was quite full.'

'Ah.' Tom paused for reflection. 'Been hoarding it then, likely. Maybe waiting till there were plenty of people about to confuse things, to increase the number of suspects.'

'Not just the number. With so many people moving about, passing food and drink and so on, no one can remember who did what when or where.'

'Not even you?'

'It was so similar to Monday evening, my first here, I get the two confused.'

'Sounds like a right muddle! The Chief'll sort it out, though. You know how it is, one person remembers one little detail, and that leads to another, and soon the whole lot's disentangling. What you said just now, Miss Birtwhistle's basket being full of shopping and her not likely to get the bromide if she was planning to use chloral to do away with the old man, either of those could be a loose end that'll start things rolling. Or have you already told the Chief?'

'No, I haven't had the chance.'

'You'd better go and tell him.'

Daisy wasn't so sure. About the basket, perhaps, though he'd probably be annoyed that she hadn't mentioned it before. But once she embarked on theoretical matters, either he'd already considered the possibilities himself or he'd accuse her of indulging in wild speculation. *And* meddling.

All the same, she might as well go down and see if she could at least mention the basket without interrupting an interview. It just might provide a way to insinuate herself back into the heart of the investigation from which the arrival of the reinforcements had dislodged her.

CHAPTER 26

When Daisy reached the bottom of the stairs, Alec and Worrall were just going into Humphrey's office. Worrall glanced back and saw her. He nodded, followed Alec, and closed the door firmly.

'Blast,' said Daisy. She didn't like any of the choices left to her. She could press her ear to the door and try to hear what was going on, but she was much too well-brought-up to descend to such unambiguous eavesdropping. She could lurk waiting for them to come out – and be found lurking when they came out. Or she could resign herself to being excluded, return to the hall, and be peppered with questions by the others, questions she either couldn't or shouldn't answer.

She was willing to brave the questions if Sybil needed her hand held, but she had Roger to support her. Even Tom wouldn't appreciate Daisy's returning upstairs to disturb his search.

The only useful action she could come up with was to go to the west wing and relieve the maids of watching for Norman. If she told them to go and make lunch for everyone – sandwiches would do – they were not likely to argue that the police had told them to stay there. She was trying to work out whether there was a way to get there without being seen in the hall or intruding on Tom's search, when Ernie Piper came out of Humphrey's office.

'Mrs Fletcher!' He, at least, looked pleased to see her.

'I was thinking of lunch.'

'Can't say the thought hadn't crossed my mind. But the Chief sent me to fetch you, so if you were going to actually do something about it, it'll have to wait.'

'What does he want?' Daisy asked, a trifle suspiciously.

Grinning, Piper shrugged. 'I expect he'll tell you.'

Half expecting to be asked to make lunch herself, or at least to provide coffee, Daisy went in. Lorna glowered at her, as sour-faced as ever. Any fears or regrets the woman felt were subordinate to her permanent sense of injury. Worrall was obviously torn by conflicting feelings, as if he wasn't sure he approved of the course of action Alec had proposed. Alec stood behind the desk, looking tired and irritable.

He would soon catch his second wind, though, given a cup of coffee. Daisy's resistance to the menial task melted.

'Coffee?' she said brightly.

'Good idea!' said Alec, perking up. 'Inspector, ask – no, tell the maids to make coffee for everyone. And make that telephone call, would you? I know it's awkward but do your best not to be overheard.'

'Right you are, sir.' Worrall went out.

'Daisy, I'm afraid I need your help again. We'll go through to Mrs Sutherby's office. Piper, stay with Miss Birtwhistle. She is not to leave.'

Piper solemnly acknowledged the order, and Daisy and Alec went through the connecting door.

Daisy waited to hear the click of the latch as Alec closed the door, before she asked, 'What's up, darling?'

'I told you I was going to take Miss Birtwhistle to Matlock?

But I don't want to leave before I've talked to the last two, Simon and Norman. Worrall's bringing Simon here, then going to the west wing to lie in wait for Norman. The search mustn't be interrupted, nor can that lot in the hall be left to their own devices, so will you take notes again?'

'I'll be happy to.' Daisy tried not to sound too enthusiastic. She was back in the game.

Alec sighed. 'If I hear a word from you,' he threatened, 'I'll manage somehow to dispense with your services.'

'Quiet as a mouse.'

'No squeaking.'

Daisy laughed. 'No squeaking. I'll sit over there by the fire and disappear into the woodwork.'

Alec moved Sybil's typewriter to one side of the desk so that he'd have a clear view of his suspect.

A couple of minutes later, Worrall ushered in Simon. No longer the carefree dilettante youth, he was haggard, now older than his age.

'Mr Fletcher,' he burst out desperately, 'can't you let my mother go to bed? She's in a bad way!'

Alec looked at Worrall, who had stayed on the threshold.

'The lady's not holding up well.'

'Tell her she's free to go to her room. If she needs assistance, Miss Olney or Mrs Sutherby may go with her.'

'Thank you!' said Simon, as Worrall departed. Gratitude quickly changed to belligerence. 'Well, have you found out yet who poisoned my father?'

Sitting down behind the desk, Alec gestured him to the chair in front. 'Not yet,' he said mildly.

'But you suspect my aunt.'

'What gave you that idea?'

'It's obvious. Everyone else returned to the hall before you called in the next person.'

'We have no evidence that your aunt was responsible for the death of your father.'

Simon took a moment to digest this cautious statement. 'But she did something. What—?'

'I'm afraid I can't discuss the matter. Tell me about your father. Often, understanding the victim suggests the motive for his death, and that, of course, leads to the person who caused it.'

'Hasn't everyone else already said all there is to say?'

'I have their views. I want yours.'

'Well, he was all right, I suppose. I mean, he was pretty much like any father. He sent me to a decent school, and to university, though it was Leeds, not Oxford or Cambridge. Not bad, really, considering my great-grandparents were just small-holders. And he never interfered too much. We got on perfectly well until just recently.' He fell silent.

'What changed?'

'He was ill. One has to make allowances. I didn't spend much time at home while I was up at Leeds. Then . . . I dare say I made myself fairly obnoxious,' Simon admitted, shamefaced. 'Father didn't have a university education. It's not his fault he wasn't an intellectual. Yet he did quite nicely with his writing even before Sybil took over most of it. I didn't have to rely on scholarships or anything; he paid all my fees. If I'd only known . . .' He buried his face in his hands.

Alec regarded him with scant sympathy, though not with disbelief. 'We all say things we regret. Did you have any particular quarrel with your father last night?'

'No. Oh no, nothing like that. I made some remark about . . . about his books being rubbish, and he hit back with my general incompetence. I suppose I'll have to find some sort of job now,' he added despondently.

'Why so?'

'It's that or work with Uncle Norman on the farm. I can't very well live here without contributing either money, as Father did, or labour. And I'll be damned if I'm going to be a farm labourer. Father didn't give me my education so that I could do the work he escaped by running away.'

It was a pity, Daisy thought sadly, that it had taken Humphrey's death to make his son appreciate him. She was pretty sure he was sincere, and certain that a major quarrel last night would have had any number of observers.

Alec's line of questioning moved on to the events of the previous evening.

Simon's recall was better than Daisy's and the others she had heard. In his position as acting host, he had paid attention to what people were doing. He had poured Humphrey's first gin and bitters.

'Not just a swirl of the Angostura,' he said. 'Father liked four or five dashes of the stuff. He used to say his taste-buds were ruined by the muck he drank in the Wild West. Carey took it to him. When dinner was ready, he wanted another pink gin with his meal. The rest of us drank wine, except Uncle Norman, who stuck to beer, and Aunt Lorna, who had water as usual.'

'So neither your aunt nor your uncle was particularly familiar with the contents of the drinks cupboard, or the mixing of cocktails?'

'No. I don't suppose either ever mixed a cocktail in his – or her – life. Someone brought me Father's glass – Ilkton it was – and I filled it with the usual and carried it through to his place at the table. I can't see how anyone could have introduced poison unobserved!'

'Your father had a third drink, after dinner?'

Simon frowned. 'I don't know. I wasn't watching how

much of the second he drank at table. If he was drinking after dinner, it could have been the remains of the second.'

'You didn't notice whether he was drinking?'

'No. What with clearing the table, washing up, helping Myra find the Happy Families cards, setting up the card tables and then playing the stupid game, I didn't even notice when he went to bed. If he had a fresh drink, someone else got it for him.'

'What about other people's movements?'

'Let's see. Mother and Father stayed at the table after dinner, talking to Mrs Fletcher and Sybil. Uncle Norman stayed for coffee, then disappeared in his usual companionable way, to the estate office or his bedroom, I assume. Aunt Lorna was in the kitchen for a while, making tea and organising the rest of us.'

'The rest of you: that's you, Miss Olney, Mr Ilkton and Mr Carey?'

'Yes. Ten people at dinner use an awful lot of dishes, so we were going back and forth. Carey helped because he's a good pal, and Ilkton, with his nose in the air, to impress Myra.'

'And the four of you – five with Miss Birtwhistle – didn't drink tea or coffee? Or had it in the kitchen?'

'No, sorry, I've confused you. We cleared the table, went back to the dining room for coffee, then Carey and I washed up. Myra and I take turns when we're both at home, and Carey offered to dry for me. It doesn't take long when there are two. When we finished, we went to the hall. That was when Myra asked me to find the cards.'

'Who, besides Miss Olney, was in the hall when you reached it?'

'Everyone. Except Uncle Norman, as I said, and Aunt Lorna had buzzed off by that time, too.'

While Daisy couldn't fault his account, nor could she confirm large parts of it. There had been a great deal of confusing to-ing and fro-ing, and she hadn't been paying close attention. Unless Simon's story combined usefully with one of those she had missed, she didn't think it was much help.

Any of those clearing the table could have popped into the hall without being missed. The door between the hall and the west wing passageway was kept closed against draughts. It would take only a minute or two to pour the fatal drink and place it by Humphrey's favoured seat. No one else was at all likely to drink the pink mixture.

Either Lorna or Norman could have done it after coffee, when they left the dining room. Apart from Simon and Neil, together in the kitchen, the others had stayed at the table talking for several minutes before moving to the hall.

Ruby, Sybil and the doctor seemed to be out of the picture, however, a great relief.

Alec had finished with Simon. 'For the moment,' he warned. 'I'll be talking to you again. Come in!' he called in answer to a brisk *rat-a-tat* on the door.

Betty stalked in with a tray. 'That inspector said you'd be wanting coffee. Three cups is what he said, so that's what I brung.' Glancing round the room, she spotted Daisy. 'Oh, I didn't see you there, madam.' She set down the tray on the desk, precariously balanced on Sybil's manuscript.

'Thank you. Mr Simon is just leaving.'

'I'll take my cup with me.' Simon stood up and leant with both fists on the desk. 'Find whoever did it, won't you, Mr Fletcher? No matter who it is!'

'Don't worry,' said Alec, 'we'll find him. Or her. Return straight to the hall, please.'

With a sharp nod to Alec, and a gentler one in Daisy's direction, Simon went out. He looked much restored by his interrogation. Was he happy to feel he'd been able to help the investigation? Or relieved to feel he'd got away with spinning a tissue of lies?

The door closed behind Betty. Daisy heard no click of the latch. Alec went over and opened it. 'You needn't wait, Miss Hendred. We'll deliver the tray to the kitchen.'

An offended sniff reached Daisy's ears, and the sound of receding footsteps. Alec pushed the door shut gently but made sure the latch caught.

'What do you think?' He brought the tray to the fireplace and sank into the chair opposite Daisy.

'I think Miss Betty Hendred was hoping to do a bit of eavesdropping.'

'About Simon's story,' he said impatiently.

'It seemed to me he was telling the truth, and nothing but the truth, and as much of the whole truth as he knew, or could remember. You didn't ask him if he saw anything in Matlock, or about Lorna's and Norman's attitude to his father.'

'No. I may well get back to that with him, but with any luck being taken to the police station will encourage Lorna to be a little more forthcoming.'

'Has she given you an explanation of the prescription?'

'She hasn't given me anything but complaints. If she was willing to offer a reasonable explanation, I might not have to take her down to Matlock. As it is, I can only draw the worst conclusion.'

'What I can't see, darling, is why she wanted the bromides if she intended to kill her brother.'

'Perhaps she was afraid a guilty conscience would keep her awake,' said Alec with somewhat ghoulish humour. 'I can't begin to guess unless she'll talk. But even if all we can prove is that she's been administering a sedative to Humphrey for several years, that's "causing bodily harm" and will put her away for a while. That would be something, though I'd rather find evidence that she administered the chloral, of course, or find out who did. Doctors, chemists, the analyst – I've got a lot to do.' He swigged down the remains of his coffee, crammed a last gingersnap into his mouth and stood up.

'You're not going to wait for Norman?'

'No, I'll have to leave him to Worrall. So would you please type up your notes pronto and give them to him.'

'All right. But you move the typewriter back into place for me.'

Alec obliged, and with a sigh Daisy sat down at the desk. It was a pity that taking notes invariably led to having to type them.

CHAPTER 27

If Lorna voiced any objection to being carted off to Matlock police station, Daisy didn't hear it over the rattle of the typewriter's keys and the *ding* of the bell. She had nearly finished – Was that word *repress* or *depress*? No, *impress*, if she looked at the sense rather than just rattling along – when Worrall came in.

'Just a moment, Mr Worrall.' She finished the last sentence, rolled the page out, removed the carbon papers, squared the three sheets with the others and presented the second copy to him, saving the top copy for Alec. 'Alec's interviews. I haven't proofread—'

'As long as I can read 'em. Thank you, Mrs Fletcher. Now, I've never worked with Scotland Yard before, and it's a rare pleasure watching how the chief inspector goes about things. And seeing he trusts you to take notes on his interviews, I'm going to ask if you'd be so good as to do the same for me. DS Tring and Bagshaw are still searching, and my other chap needs to be in the hall – not that he or Bagshaw is much hand at taking notes any road.'

'Have they moved on to the west wing? Oh, will they search my room?'

''Fraid so. Someone could've hidden something in there. Sergeant Tring'll be doing it.'

'That's all right then, I don't so much mind Tom rummaging about in my things.'

'He's doing the west wing. Bagshaw's taken on the back of the main house, the kitchens and rooms above.'

'Good luck to him!'

'Seeing they didn't find anything in Mrs Sutherby's rooms, I've let the doctor go off to do his rounds, as the chief inspector advised.'

'I'm sure his patients will be grateful.' Daisy was torn between going to talk to Sybil and her opportunity to stay involved in the investigation. Actually, the decision wasn't difficult: 'I'll do your note taking, Inspector.'

'It's very good of you. I'll just read this through and then I'll fetch Ilkton's servant, unless Norman Birtwhistle has turned up.'

'I'd almost forgotten the servant. I still don't know his name. Do you?'

'MacGillivray. Archibald MacGillivray.'

'Heavens, what a mouthful! I'll fetch him for you, him or Norman.'

'Oh no, Mrs Fletcher, that would never do. We'll go back to Mr Humphrey's office and you sit yourself down comfortable by the fire.'

'Comfortable and inconspicuous?' she suggested.

'That's the ticket. You've had plenty of practice, I see!'

Sitting at Humphrey's desk, he read quickly, underlining bits in pencil and making notes in the margins. Daisy tried to review mentally everything she had heard. She couldn't put it together to make a coherent story pointing at Lorna or anyone else as the poisoner. She had missed too much, she decided. Somewhere in the missing parts was the answer.

But she had a feeling she had failed to spot the significance of something she did know, or omitted to put two facts together. She hoped Alec would be more percipient.

Worrall emerged from his reading with a frown. 'Very neat, Mrs Fletcher, very complete, only reports never quite give you the feel of a person. What's your opinion of young Simon?'

'I thought he was sincere.'

'And what he said of people's movements last night?'

'It doesn't contradict anything I remember. He didn't try to make it seem he had no opportunity, either.'

'Ah, but he's a clever one, isn't he?'

'He certainly likes to think so. You mean, he might have worked out that you'd be suspicious if he'd given himself an alibi?'

'And there'd always be the chance that someone else would contradict it.'

'But, you know, though he had time to go to a chemist's shop when he said he was at a pub, I can't see that he could possibly have managed to see a doctor to get a prescription in the time available after we all came down from the Hydro.'

'He could have visited a doctor earlier. In Leeds, even. Could have had it filled there and waited to use it till there were plenty of people in the house. It'd've looked pretty funny if his father'd been done in just after he came home from the university. Lor', if we have to check all the chemists in Leeds . . . !'

'Let's hope it won't come to that.'

'The chief inspector seems certain Miss Birtwhistle is involved.'

'It doesn't look good for her. Only for the bromide, though.'

'Two poisoners in one household's stretching it a bit!'

'Not if it's Lorna and Norman. Perhaps he found out what she was doing and decided to take it one step further. Perhaps he even hoped she'd get the blame.'

'I don't recall you saying they disliked each other.'

'No, it's just a possibility. They could equally well be in league. I really have no idea how they feel about each other.'

The inspector sighed. 'Something else that needs finding out. And people wonder why we have to interview them more than once! First time round, we don't properly know what questions we ought to be asking. But I'll tell you this, Mrs Fletcher, if it all comes down to trying to find a medicine bottle on the farm, we're sunk.'

He went out gloomily. Daisy seized her chance to appropriate the last biscuit on the plate. She would have liked more coffee, but it had been brought in cups, not a pot.

She wondered whether to take the tray to the kitchen, as Alec had promised Betty, or would Worrall return and find her missing? Before she decided, Etta crept in.

'Good, you've come for the tray.'

The maid let out a startled squeak. 'Oh, madam, I didn't know you was still here.'

'I'm just waiting for the inspector.'

Etta cast a frightened glance at the door.

'He doesn't bite, you know. But if you'll answer a question for me, then he won't have to ask you.'

'Oh, madam! I'll try, madam.'

'It's very simple,' Daisy reassured her. 'How do Miss Lorna and Mr Norman get on with each other?'

'I'm sure I can't say, madam.'

'Come along, Etta, you must have noticed whether they're friendly or not.'

'Oh, madam, it's not my place to talk about . . .'

'I suppose you're right.' Daisy heaved a sigh. 'You ought to be telling the police, not me.'

'Oh no, madam, I didn't mean . . . The truth is, they don't hardly say a word to each other at all. Unless maybe evenings, when me and Betty go home. What've they got to talk about, after all? He don't care 'bout house keeping and she don't care 'bout farming.'

Depressing, Daisy thought, but no doubt true.

'Any road, Mr Norman's out all day most days, 'cepting dinnertime – what you'd call lunch, madam. And when Mr Simon and Miss Myra's not here, nor Miss Monica that's such a chatterbox you wouldn't believe! – mostly it's Mrs Humphrey and Mrs Sutherby that talks, not Miss Lorna.'

Daisy sighed again, a genuine sigh this time. She had hoped for something worth reporting to Alec, whether sightings of Lorna and Norman with their heads together in a corner or the pair of them quarrelling noisily. Apparently, two less likely conspirators would be hard to find.

'Thank you, Etta,' she said. 'Are you and Betty preparing lunch? Or dinner?'

'Yes, madam. The inspector said to make lots and lots of samwidges because Mrs Humphrey's not fit and Miss Lorna . . . He said the man from Scotland Yard's tooken her away.'

'That's right.'

'Oh, madam!' But Etta's mind was on the fearful responsibility of preparing lunch without supervision. 'Betty's worried the bread'll run out afore we've made enough for everyone.'

'Baked potatoes in their jackets?' Daisy suggested. 'Or scones or something like that?'

'Oh, yes, madam, thank you. There's lots of 'taties and Betty makes ever such good scones. Even Mrs Humphrey says so.'

'There you are then. You'd better go and get on with it.'

Etta bobbed a curtsy and scuttled out with the tray.

Out in the passage, cups rattled, Etta squeaked and Worrall said, 'Careful, young woman!'

The inspector came in, followed by Ilkton's servant, the small sandy man in black who rejoiced in the imposing name of Archibald MacGillivray. Or perhaps he hated it. His face was as bland and impassive as was proper to a gentleman's gentleman. When Worrall sat down behind the desk and waved him to a seat, he chose to remain standing, hands folded in front of him.

Worrall asked for his name, occupation and address for the record. Without a trace of a Scots accent, he gave two addresses, one of which Daisy recognized as a very superior and expensive block of flats in Mayfair, the other a country house in Lincolnshire. Ilkton's background was such that he must move in the same elevated sphere as Lucy and Gerald. He might even be an acquaintance of theirs. Daisy wondered whether the Bincombes' paths had ever crossed Myra's when that young lady was living in her other world.

'How long have you worked for Mr Ilkton?' the inspector asked.

'Six months. And it probably won't be much longer. This is the second time Mr Ilkton has come to visit this *farm*.' He pronounced the word with distaste. 'And I don't mind telling you, it's not what I'm used to. Even without this . . . this *murder*.'

'Very unfortunate,' Worrall agreed. 'I'm hoping you'll be able to help us clear it up, so that you'll be able to leave the farm. They say the onlooker sees most of the game, so I expect you've a very good notion what's been going on in the household. Give me a bird's-eye view, so to speak, of the people involved.'

'I fear that is quite impossible,' MacGillivray said stiffly. 'There being no house keeper's room – indeed, no staff worth speaking of – I've kept myself to myself. Apart from taking care of Mr Ilkton's clothes, and polishing his motor car, which is not something I'd normally demean myself with, but lacking a chauffeur in the house, and no nearby service facilities, I've taken it upon myself to keep up its appearance as best I can.'

'I'm sure Mr Ilkton appreciates your care.'

'Him! He doesn't even notice. Eyes for nothing but that young woman, and if he's going to marry a girl from a farm— Well, I assure you, I can get a good position elsewhere at any time without scarcely lifting a finger.'

'So, as you were saying, Mr MacGillivray, you've kept yourself to yourself, but a noticing person such as a gentleman's gentleman must be has surely formed his own opinions of the family—'

'Indeed, I have not! The doings of farmers can be of no interest to one who has had the opportunity to observe the aristocracy in most of the best houses in the kingdom. Here, I have even been forced to take my meals on a tray in my room, since the family is constantly in and out of the kitchen.'

'Very shocking,' Worrall commiserated, almost ready to give up. 'But you've observed the young . . . person Mr Ilkton intends to make his bride.'

'In and out of the kitchen! Helping to serve at meals! I have observed Miss Olney in other company, admittedly. Pretty enough manners, I dare say, but no breeding. Thoroughly unsuitable.' He sniffed. 'With proper training, she might make a passable lady's maid.'

The inspector stroked his face to conceal a smile. Daisy was amused at the notion of the volatile Myra as a lady's maid, but also angry on her behalf. She was a nice girl who was making the best of her opportunities, performing a skilful balancing act between two worlds. True, she was not a suitable wife for Ilkton: she deserved better than that conceited snob.

'Thank you for your time, Mr MacGillivray,' said Worrall, despairing of extracting anything useful. 'I'll let you go back to your room.'

The manservant departed at a dignified pace.

'As snooty as his master,' Daisy observed.

'Dead useless. I hope the chief inspector's getting on faster than I am!'

CHAPTER 28

On arriving at Matlock police station, Alec had deposited Miss Birtwhistle, sullen and silent as ever, in a typically dingy and depressing interview room, with a cup of muddy coffee and a constable standing at the door.

The mass of charred material from her grate was rushed off to the analyst in Derby.

Awaiting Alec in a minimally more congenial office was the young constable sent to call at every chemist's shop in Matlock and its associated villages, Matlock Green, Matlock Bridge, Matlock Bank and Matlock Bath, not to mention Matlock Dale and Dimple. Still red-faced and puffing from his strenuous bicycle-ride, PC Phipps stood stiffly at attention as Alec and Piper entered.

Alec sat down at the desk. Ernie Piper took a seat nearby. 'Go ahead, Officer,' Alec invited.

Phipps turned slowly through the pages of his notebook, found his place, and started reading in a monotone.

'"In accordance with instructions, I proceeded to—"'

'No, no,' Alec said, trying to conceal his impatience. One couldn't expect a country constable to equal the quick wits of a Scotland Yard detective constable, or even an ordinary uniformed bobby of the Metropolitan Police. 'I don't need every word. Can you pick out the relevant parts for me?'

Phipps blenched. 'I'll try, sir. Umm ...' He turned a couple more pages, seeking inspiration. 'What it boils down to, really, sir, is four of 'em filled prescriptions for chloral yesterday, but none of 'em was for any one of the names I was told. They was all personally known to the chemists, sir.'

'Damn!'

'Then I was sent back to Asbury's, sir, down by the bridge, about the bromide. Sergeant Cappendell said to find out the doctor who prescribed the stuff to Miss Birtwhistle. We got more doctors hereabouts than most towns this size,' Phipps confided, 'acos of the sick people coming to stay at the hydros. The smaller ones don't employ their own medical men. Mr Asbury said it was Dr Harris wrote the prescription.'

'Harris.' The name rang a bell.

'Dr Knox's locum last night, sir,' Piper reminded him. It was the sort of detail Piper always had at his fingertips, like sharp pencils.

Sometimes Alec wondered whether he relied too often on Ernie's memory, his own atrophying from lack of use. 'We'll have to see Dr Harris,' he said. 'Piper, see if you can set up an appointment, will you? Or at least discover where we're likely to find him at this hour.'

'Happen he'll be at home, sir,' put in PC Phipps. 'Getting on a bit, he is, and don't do more home visits than he has to these days.' He tilted his hand in a significant gesture: Dr Harris was a tippler.

Alec nodded to Piper, who went out, there being no telephone in the room. 'Anything else that struck you, Officer?'

'Well, sir, Mr Asbury did mention that he'd warned Miss Birtwhistle about taking the stuff all the time.' He consulted his notebook. '"Long-term use," is what he said.'

'He didn't say how long Miss Birtwhistle has been taking it?'

'No, sir.' Phipps crimsoned. 'I didn't think to ask, sir. I can go back . . .'

'That's all right. We'll get on to it.' Thanking him, Alec dismissed him to go and write up his report, in which, no doubt, he would 'proceed according to instructions.'

Things looked black for Lorna Birtwhistle on the bromide front. However, the fatal dose of chloral was far more important, and the lack of information about its origin was exceedingly frustrating. Two possibilities remained: someone had obtained it some time ago and awaited an opportunity to use it; or Norman Birtwhistle had got hold of it on his journey to Derby. In either case, the likelihood was that it had been prescribed by a Matlock doctor.

He should have asked Phipps just how many doctors and chemists dwelt in the Matlocks. It looked as if it might be necessary to visit all the former and revisit all the latter, checking past records.

Piper returned. 'Dr Harris is at home, Chief. He takes a nap after lunch, his wife said, so we'd best go right away. But Miss Birtwhistle—'

'Let her stew in her own juice for a while. She can be thinking about how she's going to explain why she tried to destroy the bromide.'

Superintendent Aves delayed them for a few minutes. He was hoping to have his decision to ask the deputy CC to call in the Yard justified by their rapid progress in solving the case.

He was not very happy to hear that they had been 'sidetracked', as he put it, by the issue of Humphrey Birtwhistle's long illness.

'When there's a murderer at large,' he pointed out, his

moustache bristling, 'I'm not going to be able to fob off the press with an arrest for grievous bodily harm, if that's what it amounts to. The fellow from the *Derby Telegraph* is already hounding me.'

'I don't know about that, sir,' said Alec. 'It seems to me, if you put it to him right, he can make a good story of a woman deliberately dosing her brother to keep him in poor health, for years. Not that we're at the point where you can say much more than that someone is helping us with our enquiries.'

Aves grunted. 'We don't want too good a story, come to that, or we'll have the London papers round our necks. I can't think how it got about, how the *Telegraph* obtained the news,' he added crossly. Alec raised his eyebrows. 'Oh, I know,' Aves went on even more crossly, 'a small town, everyone knows everyone else's business. Police coming and going, making enquiries. The fellow even knows chloral was used.'

'Between the switchboard girls and the chemists' shops, it was bound to come out. With luck, it may help us to have that information in the paper. Someone somewhere must know where the damn stuff came from.'

The superintendent brightened. 'I should confirm the chloral, then?'

'Yes, by all means, sir.'

'It's something to give him, at any rate. Better not go out through the front lobby. He's lying in wait and you don't want him getting his hooks into you.'

'Thank you, sir. I'll just have a word with your inspector – Kennedy, is it? And then we'll sneak out the back way.'

Inspector Kennedy, stout, round-faced, his moustache slightly bushier than his super's but no rival to Tom Tring's, absorbed with gratification the Scotland Yard man's praise of his constable's thoroughness and ability to summarise. He was less pleased to hear that the same ground might have to be covered again.

''Fraid so,' said Alec, 'unless Dr Harris has and is willing to give us the information we need.'

'But checking back records! How far back? Days? Weeks? Months?'

'Good question. I don't know how long the stuff remains effective after dispensing, but I presume any chemist can tell us.'

'My men do have a lot of country to patrol, Chief Inspector. Wild goose chases . . .'

Piper cleared his throat.

'I'll put DC Piper here on it,' said Alec. 'It's the sort of detail work he's best at.'

Somewhat mollified, Kennedy offered, 'Phipps can show him on a map the best route to cover all the chemists' shops.'

'Thank you. Piper, you'd better come with me to see Dr Harris first, in case his records have to be gone through. We must get going. We don't want to interrupt his lunch.'

Leaving by the back door, they made their way to Dr Harris's house and surgery on Dimple Road, near the bottom of the hill, fortunately.

Ernie looked up the hill, gazed round at the lie of the land – rising in all directions from the river, and said, 'I hope I'm not going to have to cycle from chemist's to chemist's! I'm out of practice.'

'Out of shape. It's too easy to hop on a bus or take the tube in town.'

'A sight quicker.' Ernie rapped on the doctor's green front door with the brass staff-and-serpent knocker.

A parlourmaid in white cap and apron opened the door. 'Ooh, you'll be the detectives from Scotland Yard? Doctor's waiting for you. Please to come this way.'

Alec and Piper exchanged a look. Small town – everyone knew everyone else's business.

She ushered them into a small waiting room. A miscellany of well-worn chairs lined two walls, all unoccupied as surgery hours were over. Cane-bottomed, rush-bottomed, Windsor, no two matched. They looked as if they had been picked up here and there second-hand and had a hard life since.

The maid went straight to an open door on their left and announced dramatically, 'It's the detectives, sir. From Scotland Yard.' 'Yes, yes,' said a testy voice, 'show them in.'

Dr Harris was a small man with a grey Edwardian beard and moustache. He peered at his visitors over half-glasses, then stood up behind a knee-hole desk littered with papers held down by a stethoscope, an otoscope and a box of tongue-depressors.

'Detective Chief Inspector Fletcher, sir.' Alec offered his warrant card.

The doctor waved it away with a 'Yes, yes, they rang up from the police station. What can I do for you?'

He sat down, and Alec took that as an invitation to seat himself on one of the two elderly mismatched chairs opposite him. A good thing he hadn't sent Tom, he thought. The chair might not have survived. Ernie Piper remained on his feet, his back to one of the bookcases stuffed with ancient medical tomes. Another held dusty box files, squeezed in in such a way as to make extracting any particular one a major exercise. Loose papers jammed the space between each row of files and the shelf above. A chaise longue covered with faded American cloth presumably served as the examination couch.

'Doctor, we have evidence that yesterday you prescribed a sedative, specifically potassium bromide, to Miss Lorna Birtwhistle.'

'Yes, yes, she has trouble sleeping. Not uncommon in females of a certain age. Miss Birtwhistle has been taking it for a couple of years now without any ill effects. Yesterday I merely renewed her prescription.'

'A couple of years? Can you give me a precise date when she started . . . taking the stuff?'

Harris looked helplessly at the surface of his desk, then round the room. 'Well, no, as it happens I can't at present lay my hands on the information. Miss Birtwhistle has been my patient for many years, you know, and one can't be expected to keep notes forever. I do remember that when she asked for it, she reminded me that she had taken it for a short period some thirty years ago. It was trouble with her nerves at that time, I recollect. A brother believed to be dead unexpectedly returned . . .' He waved his hands. 'Something of the sort.'

So Lorna had got the idea of sedating Humphrey from her own long-ago experience with bromide. 'Have you ever prescribed any other sedative for Miss Birtwhistle, Doctor?'

'No, no, certainly not.' He glanced at the window. 'The sun's over the yardarm, I see. May I offer you . . . ?'

'No, thank you, sir.'

'You'll excuse me if I pour myself a drop. I usually have a little something at this hour.' He took a flask from a bottom drawer and poured an amber liquid into the cap with a liver-spotted hand that shook slightly. Age, or earlier libations, rather than nerves, Alec diagnosed.

'You haven't, for instance, prescribed chloral hydrate for Miss Birtwhistle?'

'Certainly not. It's most inadvisable to mix sedatives.'

'Or for anyone else in the household?'

'She's the only Birtwhistle who's a patient of mine. I could hardly fail to note such a name.'

'How about Olney? Or Sutherby?'

Harris shook his head, uncertainly. 'No, no, if the address was . . . was Eagle Farm, I would have made the connection. No,' he said with sudden vigour, 'I'm afraid that is all I can tell you, Mr . . . Inspector.'

Alec thanked him, and they left.

'*Not* a good witness,' Piper said disapprovingly as they turned towards the police station. 'I bet I could find Miss Birtwhistle's records in all that mess. If he kept any.'

'I expect you could, Ernie, but not without going through a lot of other people's confidential medical records. It's questionable whether we could get a warrant, even if we had more reason to suspect the woman of the chloral poisoning as well.'

'You don't, Chief?'

'I'm inclined not to. The bromide had the rationale of a mixture of spite and the money motive, making her life easier by increasing the household income. By killing him, she'd lose the financial benefit.'

'It's going to be hard to prove she wasn't taking the stuff herself, isn't it. That she was feeding it to the old man.'

DC Ernest Piper, as well as his excellent memory for detail, had the ability to see the big picture, to extrapolate, and to develop tenable theories. He was due to take his sergeant's exams soon. Alec fully expected to see him continue to climb the promotion ladder thereafter.

'It won't be easy,' he agreed. 'But we have means, and opportunity— Someone said she usually makes breakfast—'

'Miss Olney, Chief.'

'Yes, and Daisy, too, before you arrived. Early morning is when he must have been taking it, to keep him dopy during the day. And Lorna's got a motive, always useful in persuading a jury, though we don't have to prove it. Add her effort to destroy the powders a few hours after obtaining them, and we can already put together a pretty convincing circumstantial case.'

'She'll say when he died she was afraid someone might've given him an overdose of the same stuff. I s'pose she knew the police had been called in?'

'You haven't had a chance to read all the reports yet, have you? They're extremely spotty as yet. But Daisy did say in her written report that she and Mrs Sutherby woke Lorna to tell her her brother was dead and the police were on their way. Daisy happened to notice that the grate was empty at that time. I should think Lorna did the burning as soon as they left her.'

'That's why you don't think she did the chloral as well?'

'That's part of it, yes. Well, here we are. You to the chemists' now, and I to see what I can get out of Miss Lorna Birtwhistle.'

'Sure you don't need me to take notes, Chief?' Piper said hopefully.

'I would *like* to have you to take notes, but it's more important to find the source of that chloral. I know you can do it if anyone can. If Matlock doesn't have a competent shorthand writer on hand, I'll just have to manage without.'

Matlock, not having its own detective division, did not have its own shorthand writer. Superintendent Aves, cock-a-hoop over what he perceived as a victorious encounter with the press, offered to send for one from Derby.

'How long would it take, sir?'

'Shouldn't be more than an hour or so. It depends whether he's on duty, and which train he catches. You can have a bite to eat in the meantime.'

'Derby has a couple of girl stenographers, too,' Inspector

Kennedy put in. 'Maybe one of them would be better, seeing the suspect is female.'

'Women don't belong in the police,' said Aves dogmatically.

'Mr Kennedy has a point.' Alec tried to be diplomatic. 'I must admit, in this particular case, I should be happier with another female present. Circumstances are such that I'm going to have to try to get a confession out of Miss Birtwhistle. Both the press and defence lawyers have been known to allege intimidation if a lone woman is confronted by two men.'

'All right,' sighed the superintendent, 'have it your way. See if one of the girls can be sent over here quickly, Kennedy.'

'Sir.' Kennedy saluted.

'Mr Kennedy,' Alec said as the inspector turned to leave the room, 'would you arrange something to eat for Miss Birtwhistle, please? Keeping her waiting is one thing, especially as with luck the pathologist will ring with results before I see her. But we don't want her complaining of being starved.'

Alec certainly wasn't starved. Aves took him to the Crown, where he was evidently well known, and treated him to an excellent lunch. They were about to embark on cheese and biscuits when PC Phipps came in with a message that Alec was wanted urgently on the telephone.

Excusing himself, he hurried back to the police station. Dr Jordan was on the line from Derby.

'You'll be getting my written report by the end of the day, Chief Inspector, and you already know that Birtwhistle died, unmistakably, of an overdose of chloral hydrate. But I thought you'd want to know that, after I was informed about the possibility of the overuse of potassium bromide, I went back to my notes. I found slight but definite indications of bromism. Let me just add, nothing I found postmortem would have been sufficiently apparent on normal examination to have aroused more than vague suspicion in Dr Knox.'

'Thank you, Doctor. Did you receive the substance I sent you?'

'Yes, I was just coming to that. The test is simple and quick. It's potassium bromide, as you expected.'

Alec was pleased: much better to face Miss Birtwhistle with fact in place of assumptions.

One thing remained to be done before he tackled her. While he was out, Worrall had rung up and left a message asking to speak to him. Wondering what had been going on 'meanwhile, back at the ranch,' Alec asked the operator to connect him to Eyrie Farm.

CHAPTER 29

After DI Worrall had dismissed MacGillivray, Daisy asked whether he wanted her notes of the interview typed. As far as she could see, the gentleman's gentleman had contributed absolutely nothing to the investigation.

'Don't trouble yourself, Mrs Fletcher. He didn't say anything worth tuppence. I scribbled down a couple of points to mention to the Chief Inspector later and that'll do.'

'What's next?'

'I'm off to the west wing to see how the search is going and whether Mr Norman's come in yet. If not, I'll tell Mrs Sutherby she can have her office back, for the present at least, and you're welcome to go and join everyone in the hall. You won't tell 'em anything you shouldn't, I'm sure.'

'Of course not,' Daisy said indignantly, then felt a twinge of guilt as she recalled one or two occasions when she had told people things she shouldn't; always for an excellent reason, naturally.

She wasn't at all sure whether she wanted to join the others, especially if Sybil wasn't going to be there. How would they feel about her working with the police? On the other hand, the innocent should be grateful for her assistance in finding the guilty. It was possible that she'd be able to guess which was which and thus point Alec in the right direction.

Simon? Ruby? Myra? They all seemed so unlikely and Daisy refused to consider Sybil or Roger Knox. It must have been Lorna, or Norman, or the two together . . .

And Norman was still a complete enigma. She hoped Worrall would return with him in tow, but it was Sybil who came in.

'Daisy, the inspector asked me to tell you that Norman hasn't appeared yet, but they've finished searching the house and they're not keeping everyone together any longer. He said I could come and get on with my writing, though I shan't get much done before lunch anyway. Is it true that Lorna's been arrested?'

'Sorry, I can't say. I promised Worrall; not to mention that Alec would have my blood if I spoke a word out of place.'

'We saw her going off in the police car with your husband.'

'As they always write in the papers, she's "helping the police with their enquiries". That's all I can tell you, so please don't ask me.'

'Oh, very well, I won't, but the others are bound to.'

'I shan't give them any information, either. I've a good mind to retreat to my room and lock the door.'

'Don't do that!'

Daisy laughed. 'I didn't mean it. I'm much too hungry for lunch.'

'If you really want to escape,' Sybil said anxiously, 'and I wouldn't blame you, surely there wouldn't be any objection now to your driving down to Matlock.'

'I'm not going to desert you.'

'I'm so sorry your visit has turned out so horribly.' She was near tears.

'It *was* to investigate a sinister mystery that you invited me. I have only myself to blame for accepting.'

'Yes, but I never dreamt—'

'Exactly. You couldn't anticipate someone going off the rails and doing in your employer while I was here. I know you were fond of him, Sybil, but do buck up. Ruby's in no state to hold things together. Lorna's been carted off to the police station. Neither Myra nor Simon is capable of keeping the household on an even keel.'

'Daisy, I can't run the household! I've never had to learn how.'

'You'll have to when you marry Roger.'

'He has a house keeper.'

'So do I, but even the best house keeper needs guidance to make everything run smoothly. You are going to marry him, then.'

'Yes. Independence does rather lose its lustre when one loses one's job. I do love him, and I know he'll be a good husband and father, it's just . . .'

Though Daisy had expected Sybil's answer, it gave her a twinge of unease. Alec might see it as reinforcing Roger Knox's motive for doing in Humphrey. She told herself not to be silly, Alec had more or less dismissed the doctor as a suspect.

More or less: he hadn't crossed him off his list.

'It's just,' she finished Sybil's sentence, 'that getting married feels like changing from a person into an appendage. The doctor's wife. Believe me, I understand. You'll just have to keep writing. It's bound to come out, at least in publishing circles, that you were responsible for the great success of "Eli Hawke", so you already have a good footing.'

'I suppose so.' Sybil sounded doubtful. 'But that's not going to help me to take the place of Ruby and Lorna right now, with both of them out of the picture.'

'I wouldn't expect you to; that's not what I meant. It's

more that Simon and Myra need you to be a good example, an example of steadiness. Perhaps just getting on with the book you have to finish would be the best way. I don't know. But wait till after lunch. It's ages since Betty and Etta were asked to make sandwiches. Let's go and see what they're up to.'

Entering the hall, they found only Simon and Neil Carey. Carey, lounging by the fire, apparently quite happy doing nothing, stood up and lounged against the mantelpiece. Simon was staring moodily out of one of the small front windows. He turned at the sound of footsteps.

'It's going to rain.' He came towards them. 'Mrs Fletcher, what's going on? All I can get out of the coppers is that Aunt Lorna is helping the police with their enquiries. A fat lot that tells me.'

'I'm afraid I can't tell you any more.'

'Has she been arrested?'

'Simon, don't pester. Daisy is bound by an oath of secrecy. Where's Myra?'

'She went up to Mother, to see if she wants something to eat. She's becoming positively filial.' His words were flippant but his tone was anxious.

'Sarcasm does not become you, boyo,' his friend admonished him lazily.

'I didn't mean it that way. She's being very good with mother, a regular brick. Behaving better than I am, I dare say. I still just can't quite take it in, Father's being . . .' His voice cracked.

Daisy hastily distracted him: 'Where's Mr Ilkton?'

'Dogging Myra's footsteps.' Neil grinned.

Restored by scorn, Simon said, 'It's nauseating, the way he moons about after her. He was a little more discreet about it while Father . . . But now, he hardly lets her out of his sight.'

'I hope he hasn't followed her into Ruby's room!' Sybil exclaimed.

'I'm sure he wouldn't,' Daisy said soothingly.

'He offered to fetch a tray from the kitchen for Mother if she doesn't want to come down.'

Neil snorted. 'Sure and it's himself had never seen the inside of a kitchen before he came here. What a man will stoop to for love!' He held up his hand as Simon started to speak. 'Hush! I feel a play coming on.'

'Not about us? Neil, you can't do that.'

'An artist takes his material where he finds it.'

Daisy and Sybil left them arguing and made for the kitchen to see what the maids had done about lunch. The room was wonderfully warm from the coal-fired range. They found on the table a tray piled with sandwiches, great doorsteps consisting of thick slabs of bread, roughly buttered, with a slice of either cheese or cold meat slapped between. Nearby was a piece of paper held down by a ladle.

Over Sybil's shoulder, Daisy read the painstaking printing: 'Are Tom brung a missige from Mam us got to go home. Acos of Perlees. So us went.' 'Went' was crossed out, with 'going' substituted.

'Bother!' said Sybil. 'Just when we really need them. I suppose Norman must have told the Hendreds. Oh dear, I'm sure Ruby won't be able to manage one of those monstrous objects.' She waved at the sandwiches.

'I will, even if I have to take the top slice off to get it in my mouth.' Daisy sniffed. 'I can't smell potatoes baking. They must have left before they put them in the oven.'

'At least they scrubbed them. There's a bowlful here in the sink. They'll do for dinner.'

'Where's the larder? Perhaps there's some soup left from yesterday's lunch that would be better for Ruby.'

'I'll look.' Sybil opened a door and disappeared within. Her voice echoed back, 'Yes, there's quite a bit of the leek soup left. Let's heat up all of it.'

Daisy decided to take the top slices of bread off several sandwiches, remove the crusts, cut them into triangles and serve them with the soup. They were busying themselves about these tasks when Myra came in, Ilkton on her heels.

'Mrs Fletcher, Sybil, you're not supposed to do kitchen work! Where are Betta and Etty?'

'They went home. Mrs Hendred doesn't care for police in the house.'

'Nor do I,' Ilkton muttered.

'Nor do any of us,' Sybil said sharply, 'considering the cause.'

'But they'll go away now, because Aunt Lorna's been arrested,' Myra said cheerfully. She sniffed at the pot Sybil was stirring. 'Is that soup? That's just the thing for Aunt Ruby. I'm sure I'll be able to persuade her to eat a bit. She can't face sandwiches.' Taking a second look at the sandwiches, she giggled. 'Especially if those are them. No wonder the aunts don't let the girls do much in the kitchen.'

DI Worrall arrived next. 'I thought I'd find the maids in here,' he said, frowning.

Daisy explained their departure.

'I haven't said anyone was free to leave! They're from one of the tenant farms, aren't they? I was hoping they might have some idea where Norman Birtwhistle can be found.'

'Hasn't he come in yet?' Daisy asked.

'I bet I can explain that,' said Myra. 'Sometimes, if he's at one of the farms in the middle of the day, they invite him to eat with them.'

'I hope that's all it is,' Worrall said ominously, 'and he hasn't done a bunk. I'm going to have to ring the station and talk to the chief inspector, see what he wants me to do. Unless he tells me to chase off after Mr Norman, me and my men would appreciate a couple of those sandwiches there.'

'I don't mind taking soup up to Aunt Ruby,' said Myra, glancing round the kitchen, 'even though Walter's not here to carry up the tray for me. But I'm not setting the table in the dining room just for sandwiches and soup. Why don't we all eat right here, policemen and all?'

'Suits me,' Worrall grunted and went out.

'If you're hoping to get any information out of them,' Daisy said dryly, 'you'll be out of luck. The other way round is more likely.'

'Oh, no, I don't need any more information since they arrested Aunt Lorna, and I haven't got any to give them, either. Is the soup hot yet, Sybil? I'll just lay a tray. What should I take Aunt Ruby to drink, do you think? I wonder where the tray-cloths are? Should I go and pick a flower? A tray always looks nicer with a flower on it.'

Tray-cloths were found, tea decided on – 'The universal panegyric,' said Myra with satisfaction just as Simon, Carey and Ilkton came in.

'Where did you learn such a long word?' Carey teased her.

'I must have heard it somewhere, darling. Would you be awfully kind and go out to pick a flower for Aunt Ruby's tray?'

'Your wish is my command, my sweet.' He took the scissors she offered.

Ilkton looked as if he was about to dispute Carey's right to pick flowers for Myra, even if their ultimate destination was her aunt, but a glance at the window showed teeming rain, so he thought better of it.

'Are you sure you don't mean "panacea", Myra?' Simon asked sarcastically.

'I don't think so. Isn't that a kind of Italian ham? I'm sure I had some once at that restaurant in Soho.'

'You're the only one of the family who dines in Soho.'

Myra pursed her lips in thought. 'Perhaps it's "paregoric" I meant. I'm sure paregoric is something you drink.'

Sybil, Simon and Daisy burst out laughing. Ilkton again appeared about to take offence on Myra's behalf, then thought better of it as she, obviously unoffended, went on making the tea. Daisy, regarding her plateful of neat triangles of bread and butter, decided she had beheaded enough sandwiches.

Carey brought in a yellow rosebud, unmarred by Monday night's frost. Myra departed, with Ilkton following her, carrying Ruby's tray. He looked remarkably like a butler, as Carey pointed out. 'Don't say it in his hearing,' Sybil begged. 'If his nose gets any higher, I swear I'll hit him on it.'

'What's that, Mrs Sutherby?' Worrall came back in.

'Just Walter Ilkton being his insufferable self,' Simon explained.

'Not, to be fair, that he actually *does* anything insufferable,' said Carey, 'or even, on the whole, *says* anything. It's his nose that gives offence.'

The inspector grinned. 'I know exactly what you mean, sir, but I hope Mrs Sutherby won't carry out her threat or I'll be compelled to take official notice.'

'Of course not, Mr Worrall. I work off my aggressive impulses in fictional gunfights on Main Street and ambushes in hidden gulches.'

'Did you get through to my husband, Mr Worrall?'

'No, Mrs Fletcher. Seems Superintendent Aves bore him off for lunch somewhere. I left a message.'

'Then you can sit down with a clear conscience and have some soup and a sandwich,' said Sybil.

'And your chaps,' Simon added, 'or isn't it proper for a mere constable to sit down with an inspector?'

'Tom – DS Tring – will certainly join us,' Daisy said firmly.

'I need one man to watch for Mr Norman Birtwhistle and one to listen for the telephone bell.'

'Simon, why don't you take each of the constables a sandwich,' Sybil suggested, 'and invite Mr Tring. We'll need more chairs.'

Carey offered to fetch a couple of chairs from the dining room. The two young men went out. Ilkton returned to say Myra was staying with Mrs Birtwhistle to make sure she ate her soup. Sybil sent him back with soup and a sandwich for Myra.

'You seem to me to be managing the house keeping very adequately,' Daisy congratulated her.

'Well, someone has to take charge,' she said with considerable exasperation, 'or nothing would get done. But I simply must get on with writing this afternoon.'

'Myra and I between us will do something about dinner, though I don't suppose her cooking skills are any improvement on mine.'

'Bless you, Daisy!'

Soon the odd collection of people were sitting round the kitchen table, tackling the monstrous sandwiches and inadequate supply of soup with varying degrees of aplomb. Conversation languished in the presence of the police, except between Daisy and Tom, who had a source of mutual interest in the twins' progress. The case was, of course, another mutual interest, but one not to be discussed in present company.

They were all munching and sipping when the constable from the hall came in. Worrall started to rise.

'Sorry, sir, not for you. Dr Knox on the telephone for Mrs Sutherby.'

Sybil jumped up. Catching Worrall's eye, she said, 'Don't worry, Inspector, I'll keep it short.'

'If you please, Mrs Sutherby.'

She was back in three or four minutes. 'Roger just wanted to say he's been very busy catching up with the patients he missed, but he'll come up as soon as he can to see Mrs Birtwhistle. Your man listened to everything I said, Mr Worrall.'

'Nothing but yeses and nos, I'll be bound.'

Sybil smiled at him. 'Mostly. But I thought you wouldn't mind if I told him Norman hadn't turned up yet, and he was able to shed light on the question. Today is Michaelmas—'

'Quarter Day!' Simon exclaimed. 'Of course, he must have gone to the farms to pick up the rent. Uncle Norman always does a bit of an inspection on rent day. He's usually invited to take a bite with one of the farmers, though I can't imagine he adds much to the social ambiance. He hasn't scarpered, Inspector.'

'That remains to be seen, sir, but I must say it's a load off my mind to know he has a good reason for stopping away.'

'You suspect he was in league with my aunt?'

'All I know is, he's the only person who was in this house last night who hasn't been interviewed yet by me or the chief inspector. Suspicions or no suspicions – and I'm not saying either way, mind – we've got to talk to him.'

'Well put, Inspector,' Carey applauded. 'May I quote you?'

'If it's in a play you mean, sir, as long as you don't mention my name in something that's liable to be banned by the Lord Chamberlain. I dare say I'm as articulate as the average Constable Plod you see on the stage.'

Carey laughed. 'So you've heard about my last little

effort. Touché! I do believe I shall put an articulate detective inspector in my next play.'

Simon scowled at him, and Daisy remembered their argument about the ethics of Carey writing a play about the troubles at Eyrie Farm.

Worrall and Tom Tring, accustomed to periods when they had to eat fast or not at all, chewed their way through their sandwiches before anyone else.

'If you'll excuse me, ladies and gents,' said the inspector, 'I'm going to try again to get hold of Mr Fletcher. Sergeant, I'll trouble you to come with me.'

The two detectives went out. In the kitchen, there was a perceptible sense of relaxation, but still no one had much to say, not even Neil Carey.

Daisy was quite glad when, a few minutes later, Tom stuck his head round the door. 'Mrs Fletcher, DI Worrall would like a word with you, please. When you've finished eating, of course.'

Intrigued, Daisy willingly abandoned the remains of her doorstep. On her way to the door, she felt the gaze of four pairs of eyes on her back.

CHAPTER 30

When Alec at last had a chance to return Worrall's telephone call and the operator connected him to Eyrie Farm, the voice answering was not that of a police constable. 'Daisy?'.

'Darling, at last. I've been waiting by the phone for you to ring.'

'Sorry, love, it's DI Worrall I want to talk to. He left a message—'

'Yes, but he's gone to find Norman, with Tom and the bobbies. He asked me to let you know.'

One could never tell how provincial detectives would react to Daisy. Alec was resigned – almost – to everything from outright hostility to her being regarded as his deputy and a sort of unofficial member of the force, as seemed to be the present situation.

'He left a message for me. What did he want?'

'To ask whether you wanted him to go and look for Norman. He didn't come in for lunch—'

'Don't tell me Worrall's gone tramping about in the rain hoping to come across him! I thought he had more sense. Norman could be halfway to—'

'Darling, do listen instead of interrupting. The inspector is pretty certain of where to find Norman. It's Quarter Day, you see.' She started on a lengthy rigmarole about rent and the maids going home. Dr Knox came into it somewhere, though Alec couldn't quite understand his role in the affair.

Once again he interrupted. 'Yes, all right, I get the idea. The inspector couldn't get hold of me, so he made his own decision. I take it the house search didn't turn up anything else.'

'No, nothing. He wanted to tell you that, too. And to know what Lorna's said.'

'I wouldn't relay that to him through you, Daisy, even if I'd had a chance to interview her. Which I haven't. I'm just on my way now.'

'What have you been doing? Besides having lunch with the superintendent.'

'Finding the doctor who wrote the prescription for bromide, and interviewing him. Avoiding the press.'

'Oh dear, have they turned up already?'

'Only the Derby paper. I'm hoping it's not a sufficiently spectacular crime to interest Fleet Street, but local reporting might be useful. I must go. Tell Worrall I'll be in touch later.'

'All right, darling. Are you coming back to the farm this evening? If not sooner?'

'It depends entirely on circumstances. Probably. Even if Lorna confesses to the murder, there'll be a lot of questions still unanswered and we'll need evidence to support her confession.'

'I'll see you later, then. Good luck with Lorna.'

Alec rang off. The stenographer sent up from Derby was waiting for him, a plain, stoutish young woman in glasses, a grey costume and sensible shoes. She had a canvas satchel slung over her shoulder.

'I sent for you for two reasons, Miss Stott,' he explained as they walked to the room where he'd left Lorna under guard. 'First, of course, I want a verbatim record of the interview.

But also, I want a woman present. I have absolutely no sense of the character of Miss Birtwhistle. I don't know whether she's liable to burst into tears, or fits of screaming, or floods of obscenity. I hope you can cope with whatever happens.'

'Certainly, sir. Officially I'm just a secretary, but I do a bit of everything that's needed.'

'Excellent. From what I've seen of Miss Birtwhistle, she may simply remain silent.'

'In which case, I'll have had a wasted journey,' Miss Stott observed dryly, 'which is no skin off my nose.'

He grinned at her. 'That's the spirit.'

They entered the interview room. The constable on duty, standing at ease beside the door, came to attention and saluted. Lorna was sitting bolt-upright at the table, but Alec had the impression that she had straightened from a slump at the sound of the door opening. Though she didn't turn her head to look at him, her eyes slewed in his direction.

'Good afternoon, Miss Birtwhistle.' No response. 'I trust they've been taking care of you, something to eat and a cup of tea?' No response. Alec raised his eyebrows at the constable.

'Yes, sir, lunch was provided, but she didn't touch it.'

'Ah well, you can lead a horse to water and all that. But perhaps you could find a more comfortable chair for the lady?'

'I'm perfectly comfortable,' Lorna snapped. 'Unlike some people, I've never coddled myself.'

Alec hid his satisfaction. What she said was irrelevant. What mattered was that she had spoken. Now she would find it very much more difficult to keep her mouth closed. All the same, Judges' Rules prevailed, and the required caution might be enough to shut her up again. He sat down opposite her.

'Miss Birtwhistle, I must advise you that you are not

obliged to speak, but if you choose to do so, everything you say will be taken down in writing and may be used in a court of law. If you wish for the advice of a solicitor—'

'Solicitor!' She flung herself to her feet and, leaning on the table with both fists, shrieked in his face, 'I didn't kill him! I've done nothing wrong.'

Alec remained silent.

'That incompetent ninny who's too busy chasing the Sutherby woman to take proper care of my brother . . . If no one else could see it, I could. What he needed was rest, so I made sure he got it. Taking bromides to help you sleep never hurt anyone. I took it myself thirty years ago, when he turned up again like a rotten apple.'

Alec's swift glance at Miss Stott showed her pencil racing over the paper.

Without prompting, Lorna's rant continued – and it was a rant, not the ravings of a maniac. After her perfunctory attempt to justify her actions, which she had probably thought up since being brought in, she let her hatred of Humphrey flow. While he was gadding about the world, she and Norman had worked their fingers to the bone on the farm and taking care of their ailing but despotic and penny-pinching father. At last the old man died. At last they enjoyed the fruits of their labours.

And hardly a year later, Humphrey turned up demanding his share. Not only had he never lifted a finger to keep the place going, he had no intention of helping with the dirty work now he was home.

He'd brought with him a foreign bride who talked a funny kind of English nobody could understand. They had produced a son as useless as his father, with la-di-dah airs, who refused to have anything to do with the farm though he expected it to support him and his equally useless friends.

'The best thing Humphrey ever did was fall ill!' Lorna showed no sign of running out of steam. 'Mrs Sutherby's better at turning out that drivel than he is himself. She brings in a lot more money, even after allowing for the ridiculous salary they pay her. Two maids, no more doing laundry and scrubbing floors! It was plain common sense to make sure he stayed out of the way. And that's all I did. I didn't kill him. The last dose of bromide I gave him was on Sunday morning. I ran out of the stuff and had to get another prescription. It was good for him to rest.'

'Dr Harris wrote the prescription?'

'He's always been our family's doctor, since long before Dr Knox came to Matlock. I wouldn't go to anyone else.'

'So he's been writing regular bromide prescriptions for you, for the past two years?'

'Isn't that what I said? It was him that gave it to me in the first place, back when Humphrey came home and I couldn't sleep. I told him I was having the old trouble again.'

'The old trouble' had been a combination of bile and choler, Alec assumed, though she wouldn't have admitted that to the doctor. Harris had probably put down the new trouble to the change of life and a man of his generation, even a medical man, wouldn't have probed any further.

'Let me get this straight, Miss Birtwhistle. For the past two years, or thereabouts, Dr Harris has been writing regular prescriptions for potassium bromide to treat your ailments, not for Humphrey Birtwhistle?'

'Of course he wrote them for me,' Lorna said scornfully. 'Humphrey wasn't his patient. If I'd told him I was giving the powders to Humphrey, he wouldn't have let me have any more.'

'Why did you try to burn the medicine?'

'Isn't it obvious? When Humphrey died, I was afraid I'd

be blamed, even though all I did was give him a harmless sleeping powder.'

Alec had heard all he needed, and he had no desire to listen to a repeat of her self-justification. 'That will do for now, Miss Birtwhistle.' He couldn't bring himself to thank her. 'I'm just going to have a word with the superintendent. I'll be back in a few minutes.'

He beckoned to Miss Stott to follow him, nodded to the constable to stay, and went out, followed by a cry of, 'I didn't kill him!'

Miss Stott closed the door. 'Did she, sir?'

'I don't think so. I doubt she'll go down for worse than aggravated assault. I've got to discuss the proper charge with Superintendent Aves. Will you get that typed for me right away, please?'

'Right away, sir. It shouldn't take more than ten or fifteen minutes.'

Aves listened gloomily to Alec's account of the interview and agreed with his conclusion. 'I don't need to ask a man of your credentials whether she was properly cautioned. Harris is a bloody incompetent fool,' he went on forcefully. 'He ought to retire. This means we still have a murderer running loose. Where do we go from here? Any ideas?'

'DI Worrall may get something useful out of the brother. Or even better, my man may find a recent prescription for chloral at one of the chemists'. He should be back soon.'

Miss Stott brought in three copies of the verbatim report. Aves quickly read through it. 'Just as you said, Mr Fletcher. The silly woman condemns herself out of her own mouth.'

'It left an unpleasant taste in mine. She's taciturn as a rule, I gather, and it was as if once the floodgate opened, she couldn't stop herself.'

'It sometimes takes 'em that way. Shall I have my Inspector Kennedy deal with the arrest, or would you prefer to handle it yourself?'

'I'd much sooner he did. Thank you. Strictly speaking, it's none of my business. I was sent to investigate the murder.' Actually, to keep Daisy out of trouble, but he wasn't about to admit that. 'This part is all yours, though I'll write up a summary of the supporting evidence while I wait for DC Piper.'

Miss Stott, who had lingered unobtrusively, offered, 'If you'd like to dictate it, sir, I'll type it before I go back to Derby.'

'Wonderful woman!' said Alec.

Miss Stott blushed. 'If you have more reports to be typed, I could stay the rest of the day, I expect. I'm sure they can spare me.'

'My wife typed a couple.' He turned to Aves. 'I hope you don't mind, sir. Daisy knows shorthand,' – *sort of* – 'so she can be quite helpful. We had rather a lot of interviews to cope with and not much manpower.'

The superintendent grinned. 'Yes, I had a word with Mr Crane on the subject of Mrs Fletcher's inclination to "assist the police",' he said, to Alec's dismay. 'Don't worry, I shan't breathe a word.'

'Thank you, sir.' Not that it would make the slightest difference. Crane would be convinced of Daisy's meddling, whatever he was told.

The stenographer looked disappointed. She was in no hurry to return to Derby.

Anxious not to lose her services, Alec said, 'I do have some notes in need of typing, and DI Worrall must have a lot, too . . .'

'Of course, sir.'

'Make sure I get copies of everything as soon as possible, Fletcher. Oh, by the way, Mr Crane is expecting to hear from you today.'

'No doubt,' Alec muttered.

In due course, Ernie Piper returned, steaming from the combination of bicycling up hill and down dale and the rain that was now falling lightly but persistently.

'Not a thing, Chief. I went back through all their prescription books for three months. Several listings for chloral, but the chemists concerned swore they were well-known customers having no connection with Eyrie Farm.'

Alec sighed. 'You realise what this means?'

'I can see three possibilities, Chief.'

'That's one more than I can.' He rubbed his eyes. 'No sleep last night. Go ahead, Ernie.'

'Could be someone planned this more than three months ago.'

'Yes. We'll have to find out how long the stuff stays potent after it's dispensed.'

'I asked. It's all right indefinitely if it's stored properly. Could be was got hold of somewhere else.'

'I suppose we'll have to have every chemist on the road to Derby and in the city called on. The county people aren't going to like that a bit.'

'It's not only Norman Birtwhistle had the chance, Chief. Simon and Miss Olney have both been away. And didn't I hear that Mrs Sutherby was in London?'

'You did. Seeing "Eli Hawke's" publisher and lunching with Daisy and Lady Gerald. Damnation!'

'It's a tall order,' Piper agreed. 'And then there's the doctor. Dr Knox, I mean, not Dr Harris. He wouldn't need a prescription to get hold of the stuff, would he? He likely keeps some in his surgery in case it's needed when all the chemists' are closed. None of 'em would think twice about supplying it to him.'

'I'd rather dropped Knox from the picture,' Alec admitted. 'He had the means. He was there in the house, and no doubt Humphrey would have swallowed anything he offered. On the other hand, his motive is thin. But before we start a major operation hunting down prescriptions for chloral over half the country, we'll take a good hard look at it.'

'You mean Mrs Sutherby losing her job, Chief, and having to marry him? Love's all very well, but maybe he's got a financial motive we don't know about. Maybe Mr Birtwhistle remembered him in his will. Maybe his practice isn't doing too well— There's plenty of competition in the town.'

'Mrs Birtwhistle told me that Mrs Sutherby will continue to receive half of all royalties coming in from the books. I haven't the slightest idea how much that might amount to, but if she marries him . . .'

CHAPTER 31

When Daisy returned to the kitchen after talking to Alec, only Simon and Neil Carey were there. They were still seated at the table, regarding the dirty dishes with disillusioned eyes.

'Don't get up,' said Daisy as they started to rise. She sat down, but they continued to stand.

'We'd better get on with it,' said Carey, sighing. 'We promised Mrs Sutherby we'd wash up.' He started clearing the table.

'She had to go and get on with her work.'

'Myra's not come down yet?'

'No,' Simon told her. 'We've been waiting, but you can bet she'll appear with the tray just as we finish and hang up the tea-towels.'

'But at least, as she's not here, Ilkton's taken himself off,' Daisy pointed out.

'He might have stayed to help!'

'I'd as soon have his room as his company,' said Carey. 'Twitchy as a . . . Well, twitchy.'

'Censored?' Daisy enquired.

'How did you guess?' Carey gave her a wide smile. 'But seriously, I'd never have believed he was sufficiently devoted to the girl to stay in a situation that manifestly makes him horribly uncomfortable.'

'Too many adverbs,' Simon advised him.

'I'm talking, me boyo, not writing a literary masterpiece. Too many police, for his liking. The nobs don't like hobnobbing with coppers.'

'Unless he's afraid he'll be the next victim,' Daisy suggested.

'That's another possibility,' Carey agreed.

'If he stays much longer, he may be, in which case your husband can arrest me, Mrs Fletcher. But not for Father's murder. Do you know what's going on with Aunt Lorna?'

'I just spoke to Alec on the telephone, but he hadn't interviewed Miss Birtwhistle yet,' Daisy said as an alternative to her usual plea that she wasn't allowed to pass on information.

'I know she never forgave Father for coming home, but I can't believe . . . I can't believe any of it. I can't believe I won't wake up from this nightmare!' Falling silent, Simon sought refuge in the prosaic business of washing up. He turned on the taps and water whooshed into the washing-up bowl as Carey piled the last plates beside the sink.

Watching the men clearing the dishes took Daisy's thoughts back to the previous evening. Was it really only last night that Ruby had come into the hall, cried out that Humphrey was not breathing, and begged Roger Knox to come quickly? Alec and Worrall and their men had accomplished an awful lot in such a short time.

Such a short time— If she tried again, surely she could summon up more accurate details of who was where when. She had been interrupted earlier, when Alec asked her to write down her recollections. Though she had typed her notes for him, along with those of the interviews she had attended, she still had the original shorthand squiggles in her notebook. She took it out and read through it.

The main difference between Monday and Tuesday nights – apart from the horrible ending of the latter – was that Roger had come to dinner on Monday but not until after dinner on Tuesday. Perhaps if she concentrated on that she could sort out the muddle in her mind.

She scribbled down a couple of thoughts, followed by heavy question marks. The trouble now was that her own memories were contaminated by what the others had told Alec and Worrall in her presence, though they had all been about as vague as she felt. Suppose she concentrated on the characters of those concerned. If everyone claimed not to know who had poured the fatal drink, someone had been lying.

What it all came down to was who was the most convincing liar?

To consider that question, one didn't have to confine oneself to the events of any particular period of time. Daisy set herself to thinking back over all her interactions with everyone at Eyrie Farm.

Simon's voice interrupted her thoughts. 'What are you writing, Mrs Fletcher?' Simon's voice . . . Something Simon had said . . . The fleeting hint of a memory slipped away as he went on, 'You wouldn't write about us, for a scandal sheet?'

'Certainly not!' said Daisy, outraged. 'That's not at all my sort of thing. I write travel articles for respectable magazines.'

'Are you going to write about Matlock?' Neil Carey asked, adding the soup plate he'd just dried to the stack on the table.

'Possibly. I'm not sure I have enough material. But what I was actually doing is trying to make sense of the situation. Sometimes it helps just to write down everything—'

'Simon?' Myra came in, looking as haggard as a very pretty eighteen-year-old girl can look. 'Simon, Aunt Ruby can't seem to stop crying. I don't know what to do. Will you go to her?'

Simon blenched but said manfully, 'Of course.'

Relieved, Myra set down the tray. 'I'll finish the washing up.'

Simon dried his hands. As he strode out, Daisy said, 'Myra, it looks as if you and I are going to be responsible for dinner. I hope your cookery skills are better than mine.'

Myra swung round. 'Me? I can't cook! I've helped the aunts, but I wouldn't know where to begin preparing a whole dinner.'

They both turned to Carey. He backed away, both hands raised. 'Not me! But there's a bowl of scrubbed 'taties over there to start you off.'

'Oh yes, the ones the girls scrubbed but never put in the oven. I can bake potatoes.' Daisy gave the big cast-iron stove a doubtful look. 'In a gas oven.'

'How different can it be?' Carey hastily finished drying the dishes and took himself off.

'The first thing to do,' said Myra, displaying an unexpected practical streak, 'is look in the larder and see what we have to work with.'

The larder was more of a full-fledged pantry. It was at least four times the size of the Fletchers' at home in Hampstead, where the butcher, baker and milkman delivered daily and the shops were five minutes' walk. On the north side of the house, with thick stone walls and a tiny window on either side for ventilation, it was decidedly chilly after the warm kitchen. The shelves and bins and meat safe were well-stocked with supplies from both the farm and the Matlock shops.

Daisy and Myra sat at the kitchen table with cups of coffee, discussing what to do with what they had found.

To make things more difficult, they had no idea how many people they would have to feed.

'Surely not the police,' said Myra, 'now that they've arrested Aunt Lorna. They've all gone away. Unless your husband's staying?'

'They haven't left, they've just gone to find your uncle.' Daisy was trying to explain why the police had to conduct another series of interviews, while not revealing anything she ought not, when Simon came back.

He slumped onto a chair. 'Mother's a little calmer. I rang up Knox anyway. He said the chief inspector is there, at his surgery, poking about – sorry, Mrs Fletcher, but those are the doctor's words – and asking more questions. Knox promised to come right away, even if he has to drive and answer questions at the same time. What's going on? I thought it was all over bar the trial.'

'I've just been explaining to Myra, it's more complicated than that. They have to make sure they've collected every scrap of evidence, as well as getting official signed statements from everyone. They'll be interviewing all of us again.'

'I won't have them pestering Mother!'

'They won't insist on talking to her if Roger says she's not up to it.'

'Do go away, Simon,' said Myra. 'Mrs Fletcher and I have to make dinner and neither of us has a clue, and if the police are going to keep interrupting us— Unless you'd like to peel the potatoes?'

To Daisy's relief, he departed in haste. Though her explanation of the return of the detectives was true as far as it went, she was not at all happy to hear Alec had been 'poking about' in Roger's surgery. She had hoped he and Sybil were well out of the picture by now. Had Lorna somehow implicated him? And if so, was she telling the truth?

Myra sighed heavily. 'I wish I was in London!' She spread her hands and pouted at her varnished fingernails. 'Peeling potatoes will ruin my hands.'

'We'll bake them, as intended. If they come out burnt or half raw, people will just have to make do without. I wonder whether they should go in the slow oven now or in the hot oven later? When I lived in Chelsea, we used to set the dial at Mark 6 and cook them for about three quarters of an hour.'

'The range doesn't have a dial,' Myra pointed out unnecessarily.

This and other domestic conundrums still occupied them when Walter Ilkton wandered in. Considering the circumstances, he looked indecently cheerful.

With a polite nod to Daisy, he said, 'Myra, I wondered where you had got to. Now that your . . . hmm . . . Now that an arrest has been made, I expect you're as anxious to get back to town as I am. It's a bit late to leave today, but I thought we might take a run up to Buxton and have dinner at the Old Hall Hotel.'

'I'd love to!' Myra glanced at Daisy's raised eyebrows and added hurriedly, 'But sorry, it's not on. I can't leave Mrs Fletcher alone to make dinner for everyone else, can I? Are you any good at peeling potatoes?'

His jaw dropped. 'You're not serious. I wouldn't know where to begin. I could have my man give it a try, but it's not what he's used to. It's all I can do to persuade him to polish the car. He'd probably give notice.'

'Oh, no, that would never do.' Myra sounded shocked, and since she was incapable of irony, in Daisy's opinion, doubtless she was shocked. 'I know you'd be lost without him. Never mind, he'd probably make a mess of it, and we can manage that quite well ourselves.'

'You shouldn't be doing such chores. When we're married, you need never see the inside of a kitchen again. Surely the maids would be willing to come back now that the police have left? They won't want to lose their wages.'

'It's probably too late. What's the time?'

Daisy looked at her wristwatch. 'Nearly four. Heavens, I didn't realise how time was passing.'

'Betty and Etta always go home at four. They have to take care of chickens and cows and things at home. Besides, the police haven't gone away. Mrs Fletcher says they want to talk to us again.'

'What?' Now Ilkton was shocked. 'Why?'

'Just tying up loose ends,' Daisy said vaguely. 'But they won't want anyone to leave just yet. Myra, we've got to decide what we're going to cook and actually start making preparations. There's tea to think about, too.'

'I'll drive into Matlock and buy a tin of biscuits for you,' Ilkton offered, 'or a cake from the bakery.'

'If you don't mind, sir—' Tom Tring had come in with the silent tread so unexpected in so large a man '—I believe Chief Inspector Fletcher would prefer everyone to remain on the premises until he's finished.'

'That's all right, darling,' Myra said to Walter. 'Aunt Ruby enjoys baking so there's always something. Why don't you go and explore the tins in the larder?'

'Mrs Fletcher, DI Worrall would like a word with you, if you please.'

As Tom and Daisy went out, Myra called after them in dismay, 'Don't be gone too long! I can't cope without you.'

'I'll be as quick as I can. Tom, did you find Norman?'

'Yes, and he seems to be out of the picture, at least as far as the trip to Derby is concerned. One of the farm lads went with him – he's teaching him to drive – and he swears they didn't stop for "nowt", except petrol and at the Derby butcher's when they got there. They even took bread and cheese rather than pay for a bite to eat. They were together the whole time. A right old penny-pincher, he called Mr Norman Birtwhistle, and sour-tongued, but fair with it.'

Daisy laughed. 'I take it he was interviewed separately!'

'Oh yes, Mr Worrall's got his head screwed on right. He had me have another go at the sisters, too, the girls who are in service here. I asked them had they ever seen anyone giving medicine to Mr Humphrey, and . . . But I'd better let him tell you if he chooses to.'

They had reached Humphrey's office, where the inspector awaited, with Bagshaw and the other constable.

Daisy got her word in first. 'Mr Worrall, what did the maids tell Mr Tring? When you asked about seeing anyone giving Humphrey medicine?'

Worrall frowned at Tom, but told her, 'DS Tring had them eating out of his hand. It was Miss Hendred this and Miss Etta that, till they really cottoned on to him.'

'Ah,' said Tom, his eyes twinkling at Daisy.

'The cheeky one, Betty, said she'd never noticed anything like that, but the other remembered one morning when they arrived a few minutes early.' Worrall gestured to Tom to finish the story.

'Seems Miss Birtwhistle was just about to take her brother his breakfast tray. She put something in his tea and stirred it before she realised the maids had come into the kitchen. Betty says it was probably sugar, but Etta claims there was a sugar-bowl on the tray, so why would Miss Birtwhistle sweeten his tea for him?'

'Not proof,' said the inspector, 'but another scrap of evidence if it's needed. Do you know what Mr Fletcher's got out of her?'

'No, when I spoke to him, he hadn't interviewed her yet. But I gather he's on his way here now, with Dr Knox.'

'Ah,' said the inspector with satisfaction. 'Then I won't keep you, thank you, Mrs Fletcher.'

Blast! thought Daisy, making her way back to the kitchen. If she had just managed to withhold that information a bit longer, she might have learnt more. On the other hand, Worrall probably didn't know much more than she did, unless he had read the reports of the interviews they had both missed.

She should have tried to keep him talking until Alec arrived, and then hidden in a corner to listen while they brought each other up to date.

CHAPTER 32

During Daisy's absence from the kitchen, Myra had retrieved a large vegetable marrow from the larder and put it on the draining board. She was contemplating it with an apprehensive air.

'It won't take much washing,' she explained, 'and it's easy to cut up, and I know Aunt Ruby just puts it in a big pan with some butter and salt and pepper, but I don't know how long to cook it.'

'If it's done too soon, we'll put it in the warming oven to stay hot. But shouldn't it be peeled?'

'Oh yes, I forgot. But I've done that before. If it's cut in slices first, it's not difficult.' She looked wistfully at her fingernails.

'Did Walter desert you?'

'Yes. He said he didn't know anything about cookery and we'd do better with him out of our way. Which is true. Even Simon isn't quite as useless. Besides, I hardly know anything about cookery, either. Are we going to have the ham hot or cold?'

'Cold,' Daisy said. 'And your uncle Norman can carve it.'

'Did Uncle Norman ever come home for lunch?'

'No, apparently today is Quarter Day, Michaelmas, and he went off collecting rents from the other farms.'

'Is it?' Myra said, surprised. 'I didn't realise. I'd lost track of the date.'

'So had I. Now do concentrate on dinner. Cold ham, that's easy—'

'Doesn't it have to be boiled first?'

'Does it?'

'It certainly does.' Ruby's voice made them both jump. 'It's salted not smoked. Mrs Fletcher, it's very kind of you to be willing to help Myra, but I shouldn't dream of expecting a guest to do the cooking.'

'Aunt Ruby! Are you feeling better?'

'Not exactly.' She smiled wryly. Her eyes were red and puffy, her face drawn, but her squared shoulders expressed determination. 'Life must go on and people must eat.'

Myra ran to her and hugged her. 'Aunt Ruby,' she whispered just loud enough for Daisy to hear, 'I'll still be able to visit you, won't I?'

'Of course, my dear.' Her arms encircled the girl. 'Always.'

Daisy slipped away. In the hall, she met Simon.

'Mrs Fletcher, have you seen Mother? I went up to her room and she's not there.'

'In the kitchen.'

'She's supposed to be in bed!'

'Well, she's rallied round. Why don't you go and help? You can lift and carry, if nothing else.'

'Oh, I can chop and stir with the best, as long as someone's looking over my shoulder. I'm not utterly useless, you know, in spite of the impression you may have been given. I don't mind lending a hand in the kitchen. It's sheep on the hoof I can't stomach.' Over his shoulder as he went off, he delivered a parting shot: 'Father couldn't stomach the brutes, either.'

Daisy decided to go up to her room and fetch *Halfbreed*

Hero. The shenanigans in the Wild West would take her mind off the shenanigans at Eyrie Farm for a while – at least until Alec arrived. Which should be any minute, come to think of it, if he'd started out soon after Simon had reported calling in Roger Knox.

By the time she realised this, she was at the top of the stairs, so she went to powder her nose and tidy her hair. She took the book back down with her just in case Alec for once succeeded in shutting her out of his deliberations.

She was upstairs only briefly, but when she went down, Carey and Ilkton were in the hall, apparently in the middle of an angry dispute about Myra.

'No bloody bog-trotting Irish sponger can expect to understand a delicate, sensitive girl—'

'*Raiméis!* What bilge! Your trouble is, you don't even try to understand her. You've stuck her up on that clichéd pedestal, and if she's fool enough to marry you, the little idiot will regret it all her—'

'She's going to marry me. She needs to be taken care of. There's not a chance in hell that she'd give a moocher like you a second glance. If you can't keep your jealousy under control—'

'Jealousy!' Carey burst out laughing.

Ilkton gave him a look of utmost disdain and stalked away, unfortunately to the stairs, where he met Daisy coming down. 'Insufferable!' he exclaimed, standing aside to let her pass and then stamping upwards.

Carey grinned at Daisy. 'It's not myself is jealous,' he observed. 'Sorry you heard his disgraceful language.'

They both turned as the front door opened, admitting a gust of damp air, Dr Knox – black bag in hand – Alec, Ernie Piper and, unexpectedly, a young woman wearing glasses, who carried a canvas satchel.

Knox looked grim. 'Daisy, Ruby's in her room, I take it?'

'As a matter of fact, she's in the kitchen, making dinner. And I shouldn't stop her, if I were you, Roger,' she advised his back as he strode towards the back of the hall. 'It takes her mind off . . .'

He was gone.

Alec also looked fairly grim. 'Daisy, where's Worrall?'

'Last I saw of him, he was in Humphrey's office.'

'Thanks. Oh, this is Miss Stott,' he added with a wave at the bespectacled young woman. 'From Derby. My wife, Miss Stott.'

He turned towards the east wing. Miss Stott and Ernie Piper each gave Daisy a friendly wave and followed.

Daisy thought she could guess what was in the satchel: typed reports. Alec had somehow acquired a stenographer, and her own services would not be needed. She sighed.

'Do you ever feel as if you didn't exist?' Carey asked plaintively. 'I'm going to put a character in my next play, a meek, inoffensive little man who's always on the stage but whom no one ever notices, far less speaks to.'

'Inoffensive, I dare say, would depend on the circumstances,' Daisy retorted, 'but no one could ever call you meek.'

'I might become meek if constantly ignored. From time to time he'll make a feeble effort to accost someone but they'll just brush past him. Yes, all the other characters will be Very Important People, and he'll represent Everyman. No, the Man in the Street. Mr Smith? No, too obvious. Excuse me, Mrs Fletcher, I must go and make a few notes.'

Daisy settled by the fire with *Halfbreed Hero*. She had read half a chapter and the unfortunate hero was about to be thrown out of a saloon – he probably wished no one ever noticed him – when Ernie Piper came to summon her to join the police confab.

'What's going on, Ernie?'

'Well, I don't suppose the chief'll mind if I tell you Miss Lorna Birtwhistle's been arrested. Couldn't stop talking once she started, blaming the victim, like some of them do. Just aggravated assault, though, not for murder, more's the pity.'

'And now Alec suspects Dr Knox of the murder?'

'I'd better let him tell you about that, if he wants to, Mrs Fletcher.'

They entered Humphrey's office. It seemed full to bursting with large men, most of them damp. Miss Stott sat quietly to one side on a straight chair, a shorthand notebook in her hand, her satchel limply empty at her feet. The desk was covered with reports, both originals and carbon copies. With both Miss Stott and Piper available, Daisy was sure she would have no role in the coming interviews.

She opened on the offensive. 'Why do you suspect Roger, darling? I thought you'd more or less decided he was out of it.'

'More or less. Less, as it turns out. We haven't been able to tie anyone to a prescription for chloral hydrate, but he keeps a supply in his surgery and always carries some with him in his little black bag, in case of need. He was here at the relevant time.'

'He was the one who declared that Humphrey's death wasn't natural.' Daisy at last recognised her role: she was playing devil's advocate, for the benefit of Alec's team. 'No one would have asked questions if Roger had just written out a certificate. Everyone knew Humphrey was ailing. And the last I heard, you hadn't come up with a serious motive. Yes, he wants to marry Sybil; yes, she'll probably marry him now she's lost her job, though I do think she would have anyway. But though I do believe he truly loves her, it's not as if he's absolutely besotted with her, as Ilkton is with Myra.'

'We did wonder if there might be a financial incentive for the marriage. Mrs Sutherby will continue to receive royalties—'

'And he'll be taking on a stepdaughter, with associated expenses, including private school fees.'

'True. In any case, he freely showed us his financial documents. He inherited his house, freehold, and it's a comfortable one. He's a panel doctor with a lot of panel patients, but enough well-off private patients, too. His bank balance is healthy and he has investments that appear to be sound. No sign of gambling problems – half-a-crown each way on the Derby is about his limit, he says.'

'He sounds like a wonderful match. I shall tell Sybil she has my blessing. So you think a doctor who saved his patient, his friend, from death by pneumonia and has tried for two years to pep him up, would suddenly turn about and kill him?'

'The pepping-up failed,' Alec pointed out. 'Had it succeeded, presumably Humphrey would have taken over the writing again, leaving Mrs Sutherby out in the cold.'

'She'd still have had a job, the same as before he was ill. No, I just plain don't believe he did it.'

'I'm inclined to agree. His reporting his suspicion of the death is a big stumbling block. But if not Dr Knox, then who? You've spent a bit more time with them, now. You've seen how they've reacted to the situation. Haven't you noticed any anomalous emotions or behaviour?'

'Well, yes, but all positive. You've bagged Lorna. Ruby and Norman have acted just as I would have expected, and Sybil, too, of course. On the other hand, Simon and Myra have come through with flying colours, both much more sensitive and sensible than I would have dreamt possible.'

'That's not much help.'

'I can't help it, darling. I'm just reporting what I've observed. There is something niggling at the back of my mind, though, that I can't quite get into focus—'

'Great Scott, Daisy, not now! Inspector, any questions?'

'Mrs Fletcher, have Simon and Miss Olney talked at all about their futures? Miss Olney about getting married or Simon about his great writing career?'

'Myra's not going to marry Ilkton. She made that plain before her uncle's death and she hasn't changed her mind since. Simon assumes he'll have to get a job. They've both been very worried about Ruby – Mrs Birtwhistle.'

'Who, the chief inspector says, is now cooking dinner?'

'And a jolly good job, too! With Lorna gone, there's no one else competent to do it. At least, I don't know about Sybil's cooking skills but I'm dubious. Myra and I were about to make a tremendous mess of it when Ruby came galloping to the rescue like the U.S. Cavalry in a Western film. Only she didn't gallop, of course. She's looking fearfully unwell. I suppose growing up in the Wild West, one just has to get over things and get on with what needs doing.'

'Very likely,' Worrall agreed solemnly. 'And Mrs Sutherby, seeing she's been writing about the Wild West for years, she's absorbed a bit of that . . . Now, what's the word I want?'

'Ethos?' Tom suggested. His vocabulary never ceased to astonish.

'I dare say, Sergeant. Mrs Sutherby went back to her typing.'

'"Like a well-conducted person,"' said Daisy, '"went on cutting bread and butter."'

'Ah, that'll be from a poem, Mr Worrall,' Tom advised the startled inspector. 'A great one for quoting poems is Mrs Fletcher.'

'In the most inappropriate circumstances,' Alec said impatiently.

'Yes, Sybil went back to her typing,' Daisy confirmed, and in a moment of silence they could hear the typewriter rattling away in the next room. 'I have some experience of publishers, and I assure you they can be extremely exigeant. Eli Hawke's are baying for the next book. Not to mention his readers.'

'Any more questions?' Alec looked at Worrall and, when he shook his head, round the others.

'Just one little thing, Chief,' said Piper. Blushing to the roots of his hair, he asked, 'Mrs Fletcher, Simon Birtwhistle and Neil Carey – they're not . . . um . . . You know?'

'I haven't seen the slightest sign of it. They're just friends, drawn together by intellectual iconoclasm. Actual in Neil's case, if his stories are true; would-be as far as Simon's concerned.'

'All right, thank you, Daisy. I hate to disturb Mrs Sutherby, but we're going to need to use her room, as well as this . . .'

'She usually stops at five, for tea. It must be about that now. Yes, a couple of minutes past.'

'Any hope of a pot of tea for us?'

'I'll see what I can do, darling.'

As she left the room, Daisy heard Ernie say, '"Iconoclasm," Sarge?' Closing the door, she didn't wait to find out whether it was part of Tom's vocabulary.

Sybil came out of her office.

'How is it going?' Daisy asked.

'Well; surprisingly in the circs. I didn't expect to be able to concentrate. But all I want now is a cuppa.'

'So do a roomful of police. Let's go and make it if no one else has.'

CHAPTER 33

Tea was not the social and sociable occasion Daisy had experienced her first evening at Eyrie Farm. Neither Ilkton nor Carey turned up, perhaps dissociating themselves from the family's troubles, unless Carey was simply in the throes of creation. Simon reluctantly took a tray to the police and didn't reappear. Myra brought tea to Daisy and Sybil in the hall, then went back to the kitchen. PC Bagshaw tramped through and out to the west wing.

Roger Knox, bringing his own cup of tea, joined Sybil and Daisy. 'I followed your advice about letting Ruby get on with the supper preparations,' he said to Daisy. 'But I'm trying to persuade her to eat quietly in her sitting room and then go straight to bed. I'll give her a bromide.' He grimaced. 'The stuff has a bad reputation here just now, but it's exactly what she needs.'

Bagshaw tramped back, escorting a disgruntled Norman carrying a cup and saucer – he must have been taking his tea in the estate office. The dog was missing from the hearth rug, Daisy noted. It usually followed Norman about when he was in the house, possibly the only living creature to want his company.

Roger jumped up. 'Is Mr Fletcher interviewing people again, Officer? If so, I must insist that he sees Mrs Birtwhistle first, in my presence. Otherwise he's going to have to wait till the morning.'

'You'd best just come along now and speak to the chief inspector yourself, sir,' Bagshaw said stolidly.

The three men disappeared into the east wing.

Sybil gulped the last of her tea. 'I can't stand this. I need a breath of fresh air. Coming, Daisy?'

'It's raining.'

'I don't think so. It had stopped when I last looked out of the window. Anyway, I don't care. Just a quick turn round the garden before it gets too dark.'

'Shall we take Scurry?'

'Where is he? Oh, I bet he followed Norman and they shut the door on him.' She went to the west door and opened it. The dog, patiently waiting, padded through.

Daisy's coat was upstairs but there were plenty of umbrellas and old mackintoshes in the cloakroom, and several pairs of Wellingtons. She picked out a mac that wouldn't drag on the ground and a pair of boots that more or less fitted, and they went out.

The rain had ceased. The clouds were being torn into scraps by a chilly wind from the east, where the evening star shone bright in the darkening sky.

'Brrr.' Daisy hugged the coat about her. 'Frost tonight, I should think, at least up here in the hills.'

'Yes, and after the rain the road will be icy. I must tell Roger to be extra careful when he drives home.'

Despite the chill, the brisk walk twice round the garden – Scurry made it round once – was the high point of the evening. Daisy spent much of it in the hall, reading *Halfbreed Hero*, while people passed back and forth on their way to being questioned. Ruby didn't appear at dinner, and Roger had already left for his evening surgery. Myra and

Daisy did their best to keep up a bit of chit-chat but the others matched Norman's taciturnity. The gift of the gab seemed to have deserted even Neil Carey, who sat silent with a faraway look in his eye, though his lips moved occasionally as if he were trying out a phrase for his next opus.

Before she retired, Ruby, typically hospitable, had offered to feed the police. They chose to dine at their desks. Daisy gathered that Alec and Piper were using Humphrey's office; Worrall and Miss Stott, Sybil's. Ruby had also invited Alec to stay the night, and he had accepted. The others left for Matlock shortly before nine. Everyone went to bed early.

Infuriatingly, Alec refused to tell Daisy anything. 'We're getting nowhere fast,' he said. 'Unless we get a lucky break soon, I might as well get back to the Yard and leave the case to Worrall. My desk was clear when I left, but you can bet it's already piled high again.'

'If you go, I'm coming with you, darling. I'll even let you drive. After all, the part of the puzzle I came to help Sybil with has been solved. We could get an early start in the morning and—'

'No, I'll have to stay at least long enough to discuss everything with Worrall and report to his superior in Derby, and to Aves, the local super, and to their deputy CC, not to mention Crane.'

'At least Mr Crane-fly-in-the-ointment should be glad to know I'm leaving the scene of the crime.'

Alec produced the obligatory groan at her pun. 'All very well, but he expects me to solve crimes I'm sent to solve, not to leave it to the locals.'

'You can worry about it tomorrow. Come to bed.'

What nobody had remembered to worry about was breakfast. Next morning at a few minutes after half past eight, as the Fletchers went downstairs, it suddenly dawned on Daisy: 'Oh dear, no Lorna, no breakfast?'

Alec sniffed the air. 'I can't smell bacon. Or even toast.'

'Ruby's probably sleeping in, because of the bromide Roger gave her. Perhaps I'd better go and see if Myra's having trouble in the kitchen. You go to the dining room and see whether Simon's there. If so, send him to help.'

But Daisy found Simon in the kitchen. He was standing at the open larder door, staring in in a helpless sort of way.

At the sound of her footsteps, he turned, saying, 'I've put the kettle on, but— Oh, good morning, Mrs Fletcher. I thought it was Myra. Or Mother.'

'Good morning. I was rather expecting to find Myra here.'

'I suppose she's still in bed, the lazy . . . Well, never mind that. I can manage coffee and toast. If people want bacon and sausages and eggs and such— '

Alec came in. 'Simon's not— Ah, he's here already.'

Close behind him came Sybil. 'Myra's not down yet? I'll help.'

'Thanks, Sybil, but it's not your responsibility.' Simon looked harassed. 'Would you mind going to see if she's on her way? Tell her to hurry up, for heaven's sake!'

'All right.'

In the doorway, Sybil met Ilkton. He stood aside to let her pass, then stepped in, his usual smooth façade ruffled by an irritable look. 'What's going on? Fletcher, I presume you're not going to keep us all here forever? Miss Olney and I want to leave for London today, in time to arrive before nightfall.'

'I can't tell you till later whether that will be possible. In any case, the present hold-up can't be set at my door. Miss Olney hasn't yet put in an appearance, and breakfast is waiting on her assistance.'

'Myra didn't say anything about going to London with you, Ilkton,' Simon objected.

'You can't expect my future wife to stay here acting as your cook-maid forever. She doesn't need your permission to leave.'

'I must say, I think it would be indecent to talk her into dashing off, with the family in mourning. And Myra's part of this family, make no mistake about it, even if that school of hers put some high-falutin' ideas in her noddle. She jolly well owes the rest of us a bit of help when it's needed, and to do her justice, she knows it!'

'She—'

'Oh, stop it, both of you,' Daisy snapped, her stomach rumbling. 'Simon, why don't you start slicing bread for toast, and the rest can wait until Myra arrives. Ruby's probably still asleep. I'll make the coffee. We'll eat in here. There's no sense in carrying everything to the dining room.'

Sybil rushed in, out of breath. 'She's left!'

'Left?' Alec stiffened.

Ilkton gaped. 'Left!'

'What do you mean, left?' Simon pulled out a chair from the table and Sybil sank onto it. 'What's she been and gone and done now?' he asked with a sigh.

'She's stripped her bed and packed her bags and left them stacked by the door, labelled for her London address. There's a note, but it just says, "Please forward. Will write."'

'How can she have left?' said Ilkton, outraged. 'She has no car.'

'Where's Neil?' Daisy enquired. 'Has anyone seen him this morning?'

Everyone stared at her, then looked at one another. Heads shook.

'Simon,' Alec ordered, 'go and look in his room. Ilkton,

you know where he kept his motorcycle? See if it's gone. I'll be at the telephone.'

The men hurried out.

Elbows on the table, Sybil dropped her head in her hands and closed her eyes for a moment. 'I can't believe it!' She looked up at Daisy. 'At least, I can. It's typical of Myra, really, acting on impulse, and Carey likewise. But Alec believes she killed Humphrey, doesn't he? Because she went off without his permission?'

'I'm afraid so. That is, he doesn't exactly *believe* it – he'll have to have more evidence than her unexpected departure – but you must admit it looks suspicious.'

'Only if you don't know Myra. Goodness knows what sort of maggot she's got into what passes for her mind, but I'm sure she has a reason that appears perfectly sound to her.' She stood up.

Daisy laid a delaying hand on her arm. 'I know exactly what you mean. The trouble is, the same applies to her motive for murdering her uncle. Don't bite my head off!' she said hastily as Sybil glared at her. 'I'd be very surprised if she did. But you must admit that her apparent lack of a motive has no relevance, given the way she thinks.'

'*If* she thinks. I'm not sure the word can be applied to what happens inside her head.'

'Quite. What I meant to point out is, if you were to try to persuade Alec that her flight may well have nothing whatsoever to do with her guilt or innocence, it would be a two-edged sword.'

'I do see that. Let's go and see what's happening, though.'

They went into the hall. Alec was beating an impatient tattoo on the telephone table while he waited for the operator. He looked round, frowning, then turned towards the west staircase as Simon came dashing down.

'He's not there. And he's taken all his traps. He left a note but all it says is, "Thanks. Will be in touch."'

'Bloody fool,' Alec grunted. 'Yes, operator, I want the Matlock police station. Police priority call. Detective Chief Inspector Fletcher, Scotland Yard.'

'What are you going to do?' Simon demanded aggressively. 'Myra didn't kill Father, I'd take my oath on it. She hasn't got the brains.'

Alec ignored him. 'Yes, DI Worrall, or Superintendent Aves. Simon, what colour is the motorbike, and do you know the make?'

'Green Triumph. But—'

'Go and call Ilkton back. Something tells me he won't find it.' Simon scowled, but went sulkily to open the front door, admitting an icy draught. As he stepped out, an engine roared. A moment later, Ilkton's Packard flashed past.

'He's escaping!' Daisy exclaimed.

'He's going after her,' cried Sybil. She gave Daisy a questioning look. '"Escaping"?'

'Now what made me say that?' She held up her hand. 'Hold on a minute, let me think.'

'Worrall?' said Alec into the phone, and started giving instructions for an alert to be sent to all police forces along the route to London.

Simon came in, slamming the door behind him. 'What a fool. Myra's not going to marry him. Or Neil.'

The elusive thought clarified in Daisy's memory. 'Something Simon said. Simon, the first evening I was here, after dinner, you apologised for not having any liqueurs or good brandy. And you mentioned that you thought Walter Ilkton had brought his own.'

'And wasn't sharing. Why—? Yes, you're right, Mrs

Fletcher.' His eyes gleamed with excitement. 'I'm pretty sure he had a pocket flask.'

'Alec . . .' Daisy shrugged as Alec put his finger to his lips, shaking his head, listening intently to whatever Worrall was saying. She turned back to Simon. 'Come on, let's go and ask his valet. Do you know where to find him?'

'Somewhere in the old servants' quarters, the original farmhouse bedrooms. This way.'

'He might be in the kitchen by now,' suggested Sybil, tagging along, 'wondering where his breakfast is. But Daisy, the police searched the house for a bottle. They wouldn't have ignored a flask.'

'Ilkton wasn't really a serious suspect. If he hid it well—'

'In the car, I bet!' said Simon, bursting into the kitchen ahead of them. 'Locked in that toolbox. Hey, you, MacGilli-whatsit!'

The servant, like Simon before him, was at the larder door, peering in hopefully. He swung round, saying stiffly, 'MacGillivray, sir. I beg your pardon, sir, I was just—'

'Never mind that. Take what you want to eat. But tell me, did Mr Ilkton have a pocket flask?'

'Yes, sir.'

'Where is it?'

'I'm afraid I don't know, sir.'

'When did you last see it?' Daisy asked.

'I'm sorry, madam, I don't remember, but I do know it wasn't in any of his pockets when I dealt with his clothes on Tuesday evening.'

'And you didn't tell the police?'

'They didn't ask me, madam.'

Simon looked ready to explode. Daisy said quickly, 'You're probably right, Simon. He slipped out and locked it in the toolbox. Even if they searched the cars, they might not have bothered about asking for the key to it.'

'The master did go out to the car that evening, madam. He told me he'd put the rug over the bonnet, so I needn't.'

Sybil grasped Simon's sleeve and tugged. 'Let's go and tell the chief inspector.'

'If Ilkton gets away, I'm going to make sure this slimy little man pays for it!'

'Don't be silly. Come on, the sooner we tell him the better.'

'It may be irrelevant,' Daisy warned, as they hurried back to the hall.

Alec was still on the phone. 'Yes, the black Packard,' he was saying. 'He left just a couple of minutes ago. All right, get right on to it, and ring me back.' He hung up.

'Darling, we've discovered a clue. I remembered—'

'Ilkton had a pocket flask,' Simon interrupted. 'His man has confirmed it.'

'MacGillivray?' Alec said sharply. 'Let's hear it.'

Simon explained, giving due credit to Daisy for the initiating idea, discredit to MacGillivray for not informing the police, and credit to himself for the theory of the toolbox.

'It must have been Bagshaw who searched the Packard,' said Daisy. 'Tom would have found it.'

Alec grinned at her. 'If it's there. Hold on while I tell them to look for it.' He was put through immediately this time. The girl at the exchange must be on the lookout by now for police calls on this line. Alec left a message for Worrall rather than asking to speak to him. Hanging up, he turned to the waiting trio. 'I think you deserve to know what's happened this morning.'

'Just a minute,' said Sybil, 'here's Ruby.'

Simon rushed to support his mother, who stumbled into the hall swathed in a blue flannel dressing gown, her hair wild. She looked half asleep, and very shaky. In her hand was a sheet of paper.

'I heard a car. It woke me up.' She held the paper out to Alec. 'Mr Fletcher, I just found this, pushed under my door. I thought I ought to show you at once.'

CHAPTER 34

Alec took the note from Ruby. As he read, a sort of grim amusement grew on his face.

'Myra?' asked Sybil.

'How did you guess? What it boils down to is, she hadn't realised yesterday was Michaelmas, which is Quarter Day, when her allowance is due. When it was brought to her attention, she talked Carey into taking her up to town to call on her lawyer.'

'Typical!' said Daisy. 'Of both of them.'

'I could skin the pair of them, but it's hardly worth the effort. Not worth the effort to try to stop them on the way, either, when we can pick them up easily in town.' He strode over to the fireplace, where Simon had installed his mother in a chair by the empty grate. 'Mrs Birtwhistle, I hope you know the name of Miss Olney's solicitor?'

'Yes, of course.' She gave the name and address. 'Myra won't get into a lot of trouble, will she? She's just thoughtless and impulsive, truly.' Ruby was shivering convulsively.

Hardly surprising: Daisy was half frozen, too. She hugged herself.

Simon took off his coat and draped it about Ruby's shoulders. 'The girls should be here by now, if they're coming. I'll set them to lighting fires, or do it myself if they haven't turned up. Come to think of it, I might see if I can coerce that worm MacGillivray into doing it.' He headed for the kitchen.

'Hot water bottle!' Sybil called after him.

'We shan't be prosecuting Miss Olney just for leaving without notice,' Alec reassured Ruby, 'though she deserves a good talking to. Excuse me.' He returned to the telephone.

Sybil sat beside Ruby and chafed her hands. 'What on earth do you think happened this morning?' she said to Daisy. 'Apart from Myra and Carey decamping, I mean.'

'I just hope Alec won't decide not to tell us after all.'

Alec's phone call was short. He came back to the fireplace and said, 'Too much excitement before breakfast!'

'You haven't had breakfast yet?' Ruby started to get up. 'I'm so sorry. I'll—'

'No, you won't,' Sybil said firmly. 'You're going back to bed, and someone will bring you breakfast there. The only question is, do you want to stay and hear what Mr Fletcher has to say before you go.'

'Oh yes!'

Simon returned with a hot water bottle in one hand and a full coal-scuttle in the other. 'The kettle was just on the boil. Betty's making tea and toast and bacon and eggs. Etta's going to light the fire in your room first, Mother, then do this one. I'd suggest we all move to the kitchen, which is nice and warm, but I expect Mr Fletcher needs to be within hearing of the telephone. Are you going to reveal all, sir?'

'I can't promise all, but if you'll all promise to keep this under your hats . . .'

Everyone promised.

'Early this morning, a nurse from Smedley's Hydro went into the Matlock station. She'd heard – or read, I'm not clear about that – about our hunt for the source of the chloral.

It seems she's been worried since Tuesday evening about the disappearance of the contents of a bottle of chloral. The contents, note, not the bottle. It was prescribed by the Hydro's own doctor for an elderly resident, because he naps so much through the day that without it he was wakeful at night and constantly ringing his bell.'

'Ilkton's ancient uncle!' Daisy exclaimed. 'Or cousin or whatever he is.'

'So it would appear. There's a record of Walter Ilkton visiting him on Tuesday. The medicine is kept in a cupboard in his adjoining lavatory. When she went to give him his dose at bedtime on Tuesday, she found the bottle just about empty, though it had been nearly full the previous evening. The old man showed no symptoms of having taken even his usual dose.'

'Didn't she report it missing?' Simon demanded.

'Oh yes, she went to the doctor. He gave her another bottle and told her to keep mum.'

'Bad publicity for the Hydro,' said Sybil, 'if people knew dangerous medicines were going missing.'

Tears streamed down Ruby's face. 'But why? What had Humphrey ever done to him?'

'That's a matter for speculation until—' The ring of the bell called Alec back to the phone.

'Yes, why?' said Simon, as puzzled as he was angry. 'He knew Father couldn't forbid Myra's marrying.'

'I think I can guess.' Daisy turned to Sybil. 'More or less the same motive as the police imputed to Roger.'

'That I would marry . . .' She blushed. 'That Myra would marry Ilkton if Humphrey were dead?'

'Myra's had a safe haven here all these years. I think Ilkton reckoned that Lorna and Norman would not put up with her flitting in and out. Myra had refused time and time again to marry him, but she would be left rudderless and in desperate need of a home of her own.'

'Myra will always have a home with me,' Ruby said quietly.

'Of course, Mother.' Simon took her hand. 'She may be a little idiot, but she's our little idiot. He must be mad!'

'He's obsessed,' said Sybil, 'literally mad with love. Or rather infatuation. It's a useful trait in a novel, but I hope I never run into it again in real life.' She shuddered.

'Was it his car that woke me?' Ruby asked. 'Will they catch him?'

'Alec was on the telephone within a couple of minutes of his roaring off. I don't see how they can possibly miss—'

The door-knocker banged. Simon ran to the door and opened it. 'My God!' he exclaimed.

He stood aside and Roger Knox came in, supporting a sodden Ilkton, whose head was bleeding. As Simon helped get the half-conscious man to the sofa, Roger explained.

'I was coming up to see how Ruby is. The roads are extremely icy, so I was driving very carefully, but apparently this maniac wasn't. He skidded on the bridge and went into the brook.'

'Yes, bring a warrant,' Alec said into the phone. 'And drive carefully, it's icy.' He hung up and came over to join the others. 'Walter Ilkton, I have applied for a warrant for your arrest on a charge of murder. It is my duty to caution you . . .'

EPILOGUE

The maître d'hôtel at Maxim's was said never to forget a patron. He greeted Daisy: 'Mrs Fletcher, *enchanté de vous revoir*, madame. Lady Gerald Bincombe is not yet arrived but she has reserved a table on the balcony. You wish to ascend?'

Daisy ascended the elegant staircase. A menial showed her to a table overlooking the ground floor, and whisked away her tweed coat.

She took her list from her bag and read through it. The editor of the book on follies had asked Daisy and Lucy to do another on inns with odd names. Daisy had consulted Alec and Tom Tring, who travelled all over the country, and they had come up with some beauties: The Magnet and Dewdrop, for instance; the Tippling Philosopher; Rent Day; the Cat and Mutton; and the World Turned Upside Down; and just across the river, in Southwark, the Boot and Flogger.

Lucy didn't keep her waiting long. The maître d'hôtel himself escorted her ladyship upstairs and caught her fur coat when she let it slip from her shoulders, folding it carefully over his arm.

'May I recommend the *faisan aux champignons*, milady, madame,' he suggested. 'This is the first that has hanged long enough – to perfection! – because the season of the pheasant, it has begun only since ten days.'

'And I shall be sick of it long before the season's over. I'll have a prawn salad, thank you.'

Daisy decided on the pheasant, a rare treat for her.

'Have you found some good inn names?' she asked Lucy.

'A few. But who cares, darling. That can wait. This morning's post brought an invitation to Sybil Sutherby's wedding. I'm sure there must be some connection with the murder you got involved in when you went to stay with her. Tell all.'

'I've already told you most of it. And the papers reported the arrest of Walter Ilkton.'

'Of course. The younger sons of peers don't often get arrested for murdering popular authors.'

'We – at the farm – weren't aware that he was Lord Harrington's son. You know I don't keep up with that sort of thing. Not that it would have made any difference to Alec's arresting him.'

'Darling, I wouldn't dream of suggesting it might have. You didn't tell me about the doctor waiting in the wings to come to Sybil's rescue.'

'I'm pretty sure she'd have married him anyway. "Eli Hawke's" death just precipitated matters. Keep this under your hat – which is absolutely stunning, by the way—' Daisy paused to study the creation, a sort of shako with a ribbon round the non-existent brim, tied in a small bow in front, and a small plume of feathers drooping gracefully on one side at the top. *Stunning* was the word. If she turned up in something like it, her friends would faint, but if it caught on, every shop-girl would be wearing cheap versions in a month or two. 'Paris?'

'Naturally. The latest. What is it you want me to keep under it?'

'Dr Knox, Sybil's fiancé, was actually suspected of the murder for practically the same reason Ilkton committed it. By the way, did you manage to find out exactly what Myra Olney's up to, living it up with the nobs?'

'It wasn't difficult. So far, she's running with a perfectly respectable crowd, mostly the families of her school friends, as you said. But of course that leads to invitations from friends of friends, and some of them are somewhat less respectable, though she hasn't reached the level of the raffish set yet.'

'"Yet"?'

'*Yet*,' Lucy said firmly. 'She has no family capable of protecting her, nor even aware of the sort of people she's meeting. She's far too young and unsophisticated to cope for herself. And no, I am not going to take her under my wing.'

Daisy sighed. 'I'm going to have to introduce her to Melanie – my friend Mrs Germond, the banker's wife. I don't think you've met her. She's been very good with the girls from the Tower – you remember that business.'

'How could I forget, Mrs Sherlock Holmes? I'm glad you didn't get me mixed up in that one.'

'I never get you mixed up in any of them on purpose, darling. In fact, I don't get mixed up myself on purpose. Mel was very good about weaning Fay and Brenda from their addiction to uniforms and the unsuitable officers wearing them.'

'Preferable to Irish adventurers! What happened to Carey?'

'He dropped Myra at her lodgings and faded away. I haven't heard anything of him since.'

'Not surprising, as Myra has no money.'

'No, but nor did I.'

'A middle-class policeman,' Lucy grumbled.

'Don't talk rubbish, darling. You're long reconciled to my marrying Alec. At least Myra has looks. With any luck Melanie will manage to persuade her to be satisfied with middle-class jollifications, tennis club parties and genteel, chaperoned flirtations, till she finds herself a husband. It's far more her level of sophistication.'

'Not to mention her family background,' Lucy said dryly.

'Yes, but she really is a thoroughly nice girl, however scatty, or I shouldn't bother. She already came to call, in Hampstead, and she's dotty about the twins.'

'Ah, the passport to a mother's heart.'

'You wait! Speaking of family, I had a letter from Ruby Birtwhistle. The author's widow,' Daisy explained as Lucy looked blank. 'Myra's aunt by marriage. Or cousin or something. She's taken a house in Matlock Bank and she says Myra will always have a home there if she wants it. So that's a relief.'

'Isn't there a son?'

'Simon. Apparently, he's decided to take articles with the family solicitor. A bit of a change from wanting to be an avant-garde writer! He was impressed by his wicked aunt's trial, it seems.'

'Sybil's not going to give up her writing career, is she?' asked Lucy, suddenly militantly feminist. 'Just because she's getting married?'

'No. Calm down. She's not sure what she's going to write, though. She doesn't want to try to continue the Westerns without Humphrey.'

'I don't blame her. Good for her. Perhaps I'll go to the wedding after all.'

'Lucy, you must! It will be a very small do. She has no family at all except her little girl. Ruby and Simon and Myra will be there, but she needs our support.'

'All right, all right. We Old Scholars must stick together, and I'll haul Gerald along. As long as you promise there won't be another murder.'

'Darling,' said Daisy, 'you know very well, that's a promise I can't possibly make!'

NOTES

The Smedley's Hydropathic Establishment visitors' illustrated handbook for c. 1924 can be seen at http://www.wirksworth.org.uk/HYDRO.htm.

Card games played at Eyrie Farm

Racing Demon is a game of speed, and breaks all the rules of turn-taking and patience! Any number can join in: the more the merrier. Each player starts with a complete pack of cards (it's important that each pack has a different design or colour on the back) and deals a pile of thirteen face down except for the top card which is turned face up. This is called the 'Pile'. Four more cards are then dealt out in a line face up next to the Pile. The rest are kept in the hand.

At the word 'Go' the game starts: any player who has turned up an ace moves it into the middle and immediately replaces it from the top of their Pile, turning the next card in the Pile face up. Each player always has five cards face up: The top of the Pile, and a line of four. There is no turn taking: each player goes through their remaining cards as quickly as possible, one, two, or three at a time (one at a time is easier and quicker) building up the suits in the middle that have started with aces and all the time watching for opportunities to move a card from their face-up line onto one of the suits that are being built in the middle. Cards from the face-up line are always replaced with the top card of the Pile, and the next card in the Pile is turned up. The player who puts the final King onto a suit in the middle takes that pile and puts it to one side.

The winner is the first player to get rid of all their Pile – not the four face-up cards as well: when they play their final card, putting it onto one of the suits in the middle, they say 'Out' and play stops immediately.

Scoring is as follows: the winning player gets ten bonus points. Any player who has claimed a suit with a King gets two bonus points for each suit. All the suits claimed are now put back in the middle, face down, and the cards remaining in the middle are also turned over. Each player now collects all their own cards from the middle and counts them up, then subtracts, as penalty points, the number of cards they have remaining in their Pile (not the four face-up cards as well). A winning score is usually in the thirties; we usually play up to a hundred, which is probably four or five games and gives everyone a chance to go out.

[Thanks to Gillian, of http://www.grandparentscafe.com.]

Happy Families is similar to the well-known game, *Fish*, except that instead of ordinary playing cards, a special pack is used. Picture cards include Mr Bun the Baker, Mrs Bun the Baker's Wife, Master Bun the Baker's Son, Miss Bun the Baker's Daughter, and the families of Mr Soot the Sweep, Mr Bone the Butcher, etc. Instead of collecting all four Kings, for instance, players try to collect complete families.

The game was devised by John Jaques II, also credited with inventing tiddlywinks, ludo and snakes and ladders. It was first published before 1851. Cards following Jaques's original designs, with grotesque illustrations (possibly by Sir John Tenniel), are still being made.